For the Ones Who Are Forgotten

R. Collins

Samsara Fleet | Book Two

Books By Riley Collins

To learn more about Riley Collins, see an updated list of titles, and join his mailing list go to his webpage at https://www.rileycollins.info.

Samsara Fleet Series

Book One: For the Ones Who Remain
Book Two: For the Ones Who Are Forgotten
Book Three: For the Ones Who Rebel

Copyright © 2021 Riley Collins
All rights reserved.
ISBN: 1-7359029-3-4
ISBN-13: 978-1-7359029-3-7
Print Edition

Cover Art by: 17 Studio Book Design
Editing by: Garity Editing

For Bug, Booboo, Little Bear, and Lilypad.

Love, Dad

Chapter One

Six months had passed since they destroyed Earth. It had been two and a half years since Nicole had betrayed everything she cared for. She stared at the monitor on her desk, eyes unfocused, mind on the events leading up to where she was now—aboard a military ship, about to infiltrate an enemy-occupied colony.

Nicole was supposed to be reviewing the files on New America that she had collected, processing every bit of information she could get her hands on in case it might be useful in the future. She would do everything and anything in her power to get back at the creatures that had taken so much from her. However, all she could focus on right now was the golden starfish pendant she twirled in her hands, glimmers of light sparkling as she moved it back and forth.

It had been a gift from her sister Sylvie before Nicole left Earth. "So you will always think of me when you are traveling the stars," Sylvie had told her, face lit up in pride. Now, it was all Nicole had to remember her by.

Nicole had been the first person in her family to get out of the communes, the slums that covered much of the cities on the planet. She had it made as an attaché for the United Earth Government posted to the Kurz homeworld of Gorash. It was her first posting after graduating near the top of her class from the University of Lagos, one of the top diplomatic schools in the United Earth Government.

When Humanity had discovered that they were not alone in the galaxy, society and governments had fractured. Two competing factions formed—those that felt they should band together as a species and those that felt it was every nation for itself. It was a time of turmoil, but after several years, the former won, and the United Earth Government was born. As Humanity expanded through the galaxy, they colonized the planets of New America, Patagonia, Mariga, and Wudexingqiu—all of them under the sovereign rule of the UEG, with the Earth Defense Force as the military power protecting Humanity.

The colonies had developed their own identities, and chafed under the rule of the UEG, light-years away from them. However, they ultimately remained loyal, dependent on the order and protection provided by the EDF.

Before leaving Earth, Nicole had stopped by her family's room in the commune to say goodbye, knowing that she wouldn't see them for years. Now, closing her eyes, she could still picture the musty room with beds piled on top of one another and a small table in the corner where they ate every night. Her parents kept their room clean but were never able to expunge the musky odor that pervaded the communes. Her family had tried to cheer Nicole up, to let her know how proud they were, and it had worked—Nicole had left Earth content, feeling she was on her way to breaking the cycle of poverty that had affected the Bergerons for generations.

She held the pendant in front of her face. Where had Sylvie earned the money for it? She would never steal. And why had Sylvie picked a starfish? They'd never had the credits to go to the beach. They didn't even know how to swim. It was so like Sylvie—small and beautiful, a mystery. The pendant blurred as Nicole felt her eyes well with tears, remembering how it had all gone wrong on Gorash.

After a few years on the planet, Nicole had become disillusioned, realizing that she could never lift her family from poverty. The work she did was dull, and she didn't have the money or connections to maneuver into a better position within the diplomatic corps. Her career was at a dead end before it even started. Despite the public cries of equality and meritocracy within the UEG, there were still classes, and for someone like Nicole, who had born at the bottom, there was no chance of reaching higher.

She had been eating at a restaurant, alone, when a Nordlok approached her, sliding into the seat across from her, its fur-covered torso masking any sound. The genderless alien, which called itself Two, deftly struck up a conversation, talking about the native Kurz and the loneliness of living on an alien world. Then it listened quietly as she complained of her own loneliness and the futility of her job. Off the cuff, it offered to help—it worked for a company that always had need of information that she may have access to. If she would just provide it with a few bits of information, just trade routes and such, it could give her credits to help her family. Where was the harm? How could she refuse?

That conversation started a relationship that lasted for years and ended with Nicole barely escaping an assassination attempt.

When Nicole awoke several weeks later, she learned that a race called the Ukhel had destroyed the Earth. They had done the same to four other homeworlds—including Gorash—decisively crushing potential opposition in a series of genocidal attacks. Two had been working for them, an agent paid to gather information ahead of their attack on Gorash. The Ukhel had appeared in each of the systems and fired a weapon that caused the star go supernova.

In the months since, she had grappled with the extent of her responsibility for the attacks. When she was being honest with herself, she knew that it couldn't be that much. The information she'd provided was minor, almost all unclassified—but that did little to provide solace. Now, she had only one choice: to try to somehow make up for a little of the damage that she had caused.

A chime rang through the stateroom, announcing someone at the door and interrupting Nicole's introspection. She rubbed her fingers against her eyes, stuffed the pendant in her pocket, and instructed the computer to open the door so Chief Taisha Kanumba could come in.

"Nicole!" Taisha stopped and did a double take as she noticed Nicole's red eyes. "Not the best day, huh?"

"It's nothing." Nicole wiped her eyes again. When on duty as the ship's chief engineer, Taisha was the picture of stern professionalism. Off duty, she had a soft streak a mile wide. Now, her typically sweet face, bisected by a scar she had received months ago, was the picture of concern.

"Reliving the past does nothing to change it." Taisha took a seat on Nicole's bed. "That's what my dad always said."

"I know. I know."

Taisha leaned forward, an earnest look on her face. "Don't let them get into your head, they're morons."

Nicole was caught off guard. Clearly, people had been

talking about her. "What, who?"

Taisha shook her head. "Damn. Any chance you'll forget I said anything?"

"Tell me."

"Fine." The chief sighed. "Those two new Tac-I's have been talking." Tac-I's, short for Tactical Insertion Specialists, were the elite of the elite. Their role was to board other ships, repel enemy boarders, and act as the ground security in clandestine missions. A five-soldier squad was on board the ship they were traveling on, the *Oruc*. "It's nothing. They've just been saying things about you to some of the others. I told them to stow it."

Nicole felt a surge of anger and embarrassment. "Like what?"

"Just stories, most of them BS. You know soldiers, they have to do something when they're in transit."

The *Oruc* was en route to New America. When folding between systems, life on board a ship could be unbelievably boring—the quarters were tight, and there was little to do for the days or weeks it took to travel between systems.

"Thanks, I'll keep an eye out." Nicole felt a surge of gratitude for Taisha's friendship. It was one of the bright spots in her new life, after the Ukhel attack.

She noticed a small bracelet around the woman's wrist, colorful beads strung on a delicate cord—clearly handmade. "What's that?" Nicole asked, gesturing to the bracelet.

Taisha's umber face took on a rosy hue as her eyes darted down. "Just a little gift," she demurred.

Nicole felt herself smiling—Taisha could be so shy when

not on duty. "From a certain special admirer?" she asked in a faux falsetto. Nicole knew who it was from—during their last mission, Taisha and Jae-Ho Park, one of the ship's pilots, had become something of an item. They tried to keep it quiet, embarrassed, but everyone knew about it.

"Stop it!" Taisha replied in mock anger, slapping at Nicole's leg, the upturned corners of her mouth betraying her.

Nicole continued to pester her, enjoying Taisha's weak protests and the beaming smile that showed her proper feelings. She was thankful for the distraction. It allowed her to forget about her depression, at least temporarily. Her past, her mistakes, and the dangerous mission they were on would always be there, in the corner of her mind, but for a few minutes, she was pleased to think of something else.

"General Norman to the cockpit. We're beginning our staged approach." Brigadier General Kal Norman sat up in his chair, his mind slammed back to the present by Major Karl Garcia's voice over his stateroom's speakers. He'd been staring at the room's viewscreen, watching the stars flicker in and out as he reflected on the past six months.

Half a year ago, he'd been a retired EDF colonel, living off his pension and traveling from one backwater planet or station to another. The pension had been just enough to keep him full of booze and light recreational drugs—ideal for banishing the ghosts of the past. Between then and now, so much had happened, so quickly, that he hadn't even started to process it all. Often, he found himself sitting in his stateroom and reflecting on how his life had changed during their voyage to New America.

Kal thought back to ten years ago, when he heard the news that his family had died, the memory was still so vivid. He was sitting at his desk, reviewing the latest transit reports for the system. His aide interrupted him, telling him there was a priority visitor waiting to enter. Kal thought nothing of it—as the chief logistics officer in system, he was used to VIPs and senior officers showing up at his office with minor issues.

The official walked into Kal's office and seemed unsure what to do, her mouth somewhat open. She struggled as Kal waited for her to say something, knowing that whatever she had to say was going to be hard to hear. When she finally told him what had happened—that his family had died when their transport had collided with another ship—he could feel himself falling.

The fall had lasted a decade as he struggled to grapple with his entire life being ripped from him. Only when the rest of Humanity had fallen as well had Kal hit bottom and begun to rebuild his life.

"On my way," Kal replied as he stood up and adjusted his clothes, pulling down the front edge of his tunic to smooth out the wrinkled fabric over his dwindling midsection—he hadn't had a drink in the past six months. Kal gave the picture of his family a last look and tucked it into his pocket. Although he was now a brigadier general in Samsara Fleet, he still wore the loose tunic and cargo pants of an independent merchant captain.

After the Ukhel had destroyed Earth, crushed the EDF, and occupied the Human colonies, only a few soldiers and ships had remained. As the survivors found each other, they started the process of building a new force, dedicated to defeating the Ukhel and freeing Humanity. Kal wasn't sure where the name "Samsara" had come from, but he was told it was an ancient word and a promise to rebuild Humanity.

Kal exited his stateroom and walked the short distance to the cockpit. As the senior officer aboard the ship, his quarters were next to the cockpit, close enough that he could run there in an emergency. The other stateroom on the ship was across the corridor from his and belonged to their diplomat, Nicole Bergeron. The remaining cabins and crew bunks were on the lower deck of the ship.

The *Oruc* was a military corvette, almost fifty meters long, disguised as an average civilian merchant ship. When Kal had first seen the vessel, it had been identical to any other corvette in the fleet. Now it was one of a kind, its blocky and dated exterior hiding systems and weapons that no Human ship had ever carried before. The ship was designed to help them infiltrate heavily patrolled worlds to bring back information and conduct sabotage against the Ukhel occupiers.

"How's it goin', sir?" Captain Jae-Ho Park looked up from his console as he heard the cockpit door slide open. Seated next to him was Major Karl Garcia, the ship's commander and chief pilot. Behind them, facing a viewscreen on the bulkhead, was Chief Kanumba, the ship's chief engineer.

"You tell me," Kal responded. He sat down in his chair at

12

the back of the cockpit and studied the tactical map on the viewscreen in front of him.

"We're about a light-day out from New America," Garcia reported, turning his chair so he could focus on Kal. "Our scans show two Ukhel capital ships in orbit. Planet's surface doesn't look too bad, some scarring from orbital fire, but looks like the major cities are relatively undamaged."

"What about Caracas?" Kal asked. Caracas Station was the cargo port for New America, used by the large ships that were unable to enter the atmosphere and land on the planet. Transports and freighters would offload materials and passengers at the port, to be transferred onto small atmospheric ferries to the planet's surface.

"Can't tell much from this distance. It's in one piece at least." Garcia gave a shrug.

Kal remembered the last time he had seen Caracas Station. After fleeing from the invading Ukhel fleet in Kurz space, he'd flown there, and an old friend had coerced him back into the EDF. It was also where he had first set eyes on the *Oruc*. Unfortunately, the Ukhel had arrived soon after—Kal and the other soldiers on the *Oruc* had barely made it off the station alive.

"Let's move in," Kal said. Garcia activated the ship's fold drive, and the stars blinked and shifted position on the viewscreen. The fold drive created a wormhole in space and moved the ship through it, instantaneously changing its location by a fraction of a light-year. To a bystander, it would appear as if the ship had disappeared from one place, only to reappear in another instantly. Through chaining hundreds or thousands of these folds, ships could traverse the galaxy faster than the speed of light without violating the laws of physics.

The fold drive allowed ships to travel between systems faster than light, but there was no way to communicate at the same speed. Physics and the limitations of relativity meant that all forms of signal communication could only travel at, or below, the speed of light. To overcome this issue, a network of probes connected the inhabited planets of the galaxy—receiving, storing, and carrying news and messages between the planets. When the Ukhel had arrived, they had severed this network, plunging much of the galaxy into darkness. With the network gone and civilian traffic between planets brought to a standstill, information had become scarce, and almost always dated.

The discovery of the fold drive had revolutionized Humanity, allowing the species to travel outside of its home system and explore the galaxy. Development had taken decades to perfect, and had come at substantial cost. Prior to the development of the drive, Humans had crowded the earth and depleted its resources. There had been increasing pressure to grow beyond the borders of the Sol System. Earth's governments had first used unmanned probes to develop the fold drive, but found them to be ineffective and unreliable in their tests. They resorted to coercing prisoners and debtors to serve as passengers on experimental voyages, testing and perfecting the drive. Although the project had ultimately been successful, many of their unwilling test subjects had died or never returned, victims of science and progress.

The Ukhel were the offspring of one of these groups of unwilling explorers. They had returned, destroyed Earth, and done the same thing to many of Humanity's neighbors. They had attacked and conquered the Kurz, X'Ado, Qudoru, and Tounous, destroying their homeworlds then spreading across their colonies, subjugating them and forcing them to provide resources or face extinction. After they subdued each planet, the Ukhel left behind a small token force responsible for reporting any insurrection or failure to live up to the conditions of surrender. If there was any violation of the terms of surrender, they promised to destroy the entire system.

For the Human colonies, like New America, it was different. The Ukhel had conquered them but kept their ships in orbit. No one knew what they were doing on the Human planets since the Ukhel had set up blockades, preventing communication in or out. The intelligence officers in Samsara Fleet suspected they were building permanent bases, taking the planets as their own. The *Oruc's* mission to New America was to confirm what the Ukhel were doing there and to try to uncover their next steps.

Garcia recalibrated the fold drive and activated it, changing their position in space. There was no sensation of movement—the only clue that let Kal know what had happened was seeing the stars in the cockpit's main viewscreen shift slightly.

"Now half a light-day outside New America. Activating long-distance scanners." Kanumba didn't look away from her screen as she scanned New America. The sudden jump not only brought them closer to the planet, allowing their sensors to have a higher-resolution scan, but also brought them forward in time. The light and information coming from New America was now only twelve hours old rather than a day. During their staged approach, they would take several small folds closer to New America, each time getting more recent and higher-resolution scans. It was an effective technique for entering potentially hostile areas, allowing them to see the enemy's positions before the enemy could spot them.

Kanumba called out information as she saw the scan results on her monitor. "Still got two capital ships—they don't seem to have moved. Overall damage to the planet is relatively light. Looks like there are some signs of activity on Caracas Station, so safe to assume it's still functional."

Kal studied the results on the viewscreen in front of him. On it was a grainy image of New America with wire-frame boxes highlighting areas of interest. The ship's AI scanned for signs of activity, major damage, or anything that looked unexpected, and highlighted them for him.

New America was Humanity's first colony. The planners had divided the planet into large zones based on their function, each one millions of square kilometers in size. Their intention had been to allow a more efficient use of the planet's surface and require less movement within zones, making commerce more efficient and keeping loud and noxious industry away from homes. From a distance, the zones had clear borders, making the surface appear quilt-like. There were a few craters annotated on the map, scars from the Ukhel's orbital assault. Thankfully, the destruction was much less than Kal had feared—although the urban zones bore scattered craters from orbital fire the rest looked pristine.

At this range, he could also see the damage to Caracas Station. Parts hung off at odd angles, evidence of decompression and explosions. There was still some activity around the station, small ferry ships traveling to and from the planet's surface. He noticed that there were no large interstellar transports in the area, a sign that the station was still not receiving traffic from outside the system.

"What's this?" Kal highlighted a small cleared area within one of the urban zones on the planet. There was no debris or damage within the circular region; it was not a crater or a result of any weapon that Kal knew of. He could see hundreds of buildings under construction in the zone—a city within a city.

"Looks like the Ukhel are building something there," Park responded. "I would guess it is some sort of base camp for their soldiers."

"I hope the tech you rigged up works, Chief," Garcia said. "Those two capital ships'l make quick work of us."

Samsara Fleet's engineers had made several upgrades to the *Oruc* since their last mission. The fleet had destroyed a Ukhel capital ship, and the wreckage had already proven to be a treasure trove of information about the aliens and a host of new technologies. Much of it would take years to fully integrate into their ships and equipment, but there were a few devices and upgrades they were able to make immediately. The engineers had enhanced the ship's weapons, shields, and sensors to varying degrees. Also, they had developed two new devices for their mission—a cloak and a communications intercept. The cloak *should* prevent Ukhel scanners from being able to pinpoint their location and the communication intercept *should* allow them to intercept the Ukhel's ship-to-ship comms network.

"So do I. No promises, though—it's all untested," Kanumba replied.

Garcia sighed. "Not what I want to hear."

"Well, I'm staking my life on it working." Kanumba arched her eyebrow.

"I just don't want to stake mine." Garcia raised his hands in a pleading gesture.

"I don't think you've got a choice, sir," Park interjected. "Besides, if you fold in close enough, we should be able to reach the surface in one piece, even if they do notice us."

While the *Oruc* had been in transit to New America, Kal had convened a crew-wide meeting to go over their strategy when they arrived in system. They'd decided their best option to reach the planet's surface alive was to fold in as close as they could and dive into the exosphere before the Ukhel fleet could engage. Unfortunately, folding was still an imperfect science—they could only estimate the fold's endpoint within a hundred-thousand kilometers, meaning that there would likely still be some time for the Ukhel to spot and intercept them. Once in the atmosphere, it would be much harder for the Nasi to find them, since the ship would be concealed amid the general commercial traffic.

Their ultimate destination on New America was the largest

urban zone on the planet, the city of Tiradentes. Once in the planet's atmosphere, they could fly nap-of-the-earth, with the *Oruc* only meters from the planet's surface—their low altitude would also help to keep them off the Ukhel's sensors.

"Jae-Ho, you'd better line this up right." Kanumba had slipped by addressing Captain Park by his first name. Kal tried not to chuckle. He wondered if anyone else on the ship realized that their relationship was not just professional.

"Of course, Chief," Park said. Kal thought he saw a trace of a smile on the young officer's face as he turned his head to respond.

"Okay, get ready," Garcia instructed. He activated the ship-wide broadcast system and advised the personnel in the back to prepare for their fold into the system and descent onto the surface of New America. The maneuver would take the *Oruc* to the limit of its design specifications, so they were expecting a bumpy ride.

"And we're folding," Garcia said as he tapped on his console, activating the drive. The central viewscreen blinked, and New America loomed before them.

"Is the communication intercept on?" Kal asked.

"Roger, nothing so far," Kanumba replied. She had set it up to interface with her neural implant rather than piping it through the cockpit's speakers.

Neural implants were small biometric computers implanted into the brain. They were indispensable, and almost every sentient species in the galaxy had a version of them. The implant could directly interface with the host's thoughts and senses, merging almost seamlessly with their normal brain functions. It allowed the host to understand almost any known language by seamlessly transforming the experience of sight, sound, and smell. It could connect to other computers and systems, allowing the user to manipulate them with only a thought. Kal couldn't imagine what life would be like without the tiny device implanted in his brain, he depended on it for so much.

"Seems like the cloak is working as promised, so far," Kanumba said. "Beginning our descent into the exosphere now."

Garcia pushed the ship's thrust to maximum, hurtling them toward the planet. In the vastness of space, it was hard for Kal to gauge how fast they were traveling, despite knowing it was faster than he ever had gone, this close to a planet.

"Shit. They realized that something isn't right," Kanumba swore, hand cupped over her ear to block out the cockpit noise.

"What are they saying?" Kal asked. His hands tightened on the arms of his chair, knuckles going white.

"Right now they aren't sure if it's a technical malfunction or not," Kanumba said. "One of their ships is moving toward us to investigate."

Kal adjusted his monitor back to the tactical map, and sure enough, one of the Ukhel capital ships had broken its position in orbit and was moving toward the *Oruc*. It was roughly twice the size of a large EDF battleship, more than enough to make quick work of the *Oruc*. Ukhel ships looked almost biological, with irregular, bulbous shapes and nacelles dotting their surfaces. Their dark finish made them difficult to see in the darkness of space and gave them a sinister feel. Their irregular shapes and strange protrusions reminded Kal of rotting fruit, an apt comparison for the species that had laid waste to Humanity.

"We should be able to make the atmosphere before they know we're here," Garcia said. Kal felt he was being more hopeful than anything given the cloak was untested.

As it came closer, the Ukhel ship fired several salvos of their plasma cannon. The shots streaked wildly near the *Oruc*, none coming too close to the ship. It appeared the Ukhel only knew the relative vicinity of where they were and not their exact location.

"Abort?" Park asked. He had plotted several alternate headings on the shared tactical map if they wanted to cut off the landing. They could use the planet's gravity to slingshot back away while using its mass to block any attacks.

"No, don't," Kanumba said, listening to the Ukhel net. "They still don't know where we are. They're trying to pressure us into doing something reckless."

"Keep going," Kal agreed. The risk was about the same whether they went through with the landing or aborted from what he could tell. Humanity had almost lost in the first weeks of the war because of indecision—a mistake he didn't want to repeat. He watched the Ukhel ship getting closer to their position. Eventually, they would be within visual range, and the cloak would be useless. They just needed to reach the planet's atmosphere before that happened.

The seconds ticked by as the *Oruc* hurtled toward the

atmosphere of New America. Kanumba continued to listen to the communication intercept, stoically relaying the Ukhel's communications as they tried to track the ship down. The ship continued to get closer to their position, it was now only tens of thousands of kilometers away.

"They've got visual on us!" Kanumba cried out.

"Dammit!" Garcia swore. "Park, you take helm. I'll get ready to launch countermeasures." Park nodded and took over the flight controls using his monitor. "You're better at actually flying this thing anyway," Garcia added.

"They've launched missiles," Kanumba shouted to Park. "Looks like we've got at least ten of them."

"We should be okay. We'll hit the atmosphere before they get near." As Garcia was speaking, plasma bolts flew from the planet's surface, bracketing the ship. The Ukhel must have already set up ground-to-space defense systems—they were planning on staying for the long run.

"Dammit, they've got defense systems online." Kal began second guessing his decision to have them press forward. However, there was no going back now.

Park took evasive action, swinging their heading back and forth while still making quick progress toward New America's exosphere. Plasma bolts continued to streak around the *Oruc*, missing by what felt like a hair's breadth. Kal wanted to flinch every time he saw one of them pass near them.

Garcia launched several countermeasure drones, trying to throw off the oncoming Ukhel missiles. Each drone projected a holographic image of the *Oruc* and generated heat and emissions almost identical to the ship. They were state-of-the-art, upgraded with tech they had salvaged from the Ukhel.

Kal's hand flew out to steady himself on the bulkhead as the ship jolted, a plasma bolt directly striking their fore energy shield. He hoped that their upgraded shields would be enough to prevent major damage. He had seen the Ukhel's plasma cannons take down more heavily armored ships than theirs with only one or two hits.

"Looks like the shields held up. Some minor damage to our outside plating, but other than that, we're good." Kanumba reported.

"Entering the atmosphere," Park said. Kal could detect the hint of relief in his voice. As they descended, the *Oruc* began to rumble and shake, a low hum permeating through the hull. The friction of their rapid entry caused the external temperature to skyrocket on the monitor. For many ships, a maneuver like this would be fatal, but the *Oruc* should be able to survive, albeit with some damage.

As they flew farther into the planet's atmosphere, the Ukhel missiles behind them detonated one by one, either hitting one of the drone countermeasures or burning up in the atmosphere. Kal could feel the collective breath of the soldiers in the cockpit being released.

"Now's the hard part," Park said.

He reversed the ship's thrusters, and their speed rapidly dropped, throwing them against their restraints as the inertial dampeners were not able to completely compensate for the sudden deceleration.

The planet's surface opened up below them. A blanket of clouds covered the landscape, and the small, patchy zones they had seen from space now stretched to the horizon. Kal could make out distinct terrain features, like lakes and rivers, marring the perfect quilt he had seen from a distance. He noticed they were directly above one of the farming zones, neat rows of plants stretching almost as far as he could see. Roads crisscrossed the landscape, to allow automated drones to reach the crops for cultivation and harvesting.

As the ship's speed continued to drop, the planet's surface rushed toward them at an alarming speed. Just when Kal felt like he was sure they were going to crash into the ground, Park lifted the *Oruc's* nose and Kal was pressed into his seat by the sudden change in momentum, the pressure on his chest almost too great for him to breathe.

"Okay, we're leveling off and ready for nap-of-the-earth flight," Park reported, panting from the maneuver.

"What are the Ukhel saying?" Kal asked Kanumba.

"They lost visual. They think we're heading toward Xin Chengdu," the chief answered after what felt like an eternity. Xin Chengdu was another of the enormous megalopolises on the planet, far from Tiradentes. The Ukhel clearly hadn't been able to track their descent into the atmosphere.

Kal said a word of congratulations to the crew and let out a breath he hadn't realized he'd been holding in. Despite being found out, they had at least been able to make it past the blockade. Looking at the fields stretched before them, Kal wondered what they would find when they landed.

Chapter Two

When the cargo bay door opened, the air of New America struck Nicole like a wall. Warm and fragrant, it was a welcome change from the stale, recycled air inside the *Oruc*. They had put the ship down in the middle of a field, as far from the service roads as they could manage. Immediately after landing, Park and Kanumba had placed holographic projectors around the ship, creating a three-dimensional holo, that essentially rendered it invisible except at close range.

Nicole watched the Tac-I squad checking their battle suits before putting them on, their nervous expressions giving the lie to their jocular back-and-forth banter. She was always amazed—and a bit jealous—at their ability to laugh in the face of danger. She would have been curled up in a ball with fright. Sergeant First Class Asif Jones, their squad leader, walked down the line, inspecting each soldier's suit—checking propellant, ammunition, and the seals around each joint and seam.

Jones performed his role as squad leader with intense precision. When she had first met him, Nicole had thought he was too driven, to the point of being uncaring. Over time, she'd realized that beneath his façade, the sergeant cared deeply for his soldiers. He expressed his feelings through his actions rather than empty words or meaningless gestures.

Kal stood next to her in the ship's cargo bay, watching the squad prepare. He was silent, almost distant, though she knew that he was paying close attention to everything that was happening around them. Kal's quiet demeanor threw people off, but she knew him well enough to have a good idea of what was going on in his head. When on a mission, he was continually thinking about the next move, the next decision that he would have to make—it was one reason the soldiers on the *Oruc* trusted him.

The Tac-I squad's mission was to scout the area immediately around their ship. They had no idea what changes the Ukhel may have already wrought on New America and wanted to make sure that there were no surprises just around the corner.

Jones slapped Sergeant Ekon Kimathi's shoulder, a sign he had passed inspection. The young sergeant began circling around the remaining squad members' suits, triple-checking seals and equipment before Jones made his final inspection.

Ekon was Jones's team leader, a position he'd earned through his hard work and having survived for six months. Although he could be impulsive and hotheaded, Nicole knew that the young NCO had both Jones and Kal's trust—which spoke volumes. Ekon was the only Tac-I who hadn't been through their rigorous training course. They'd permitted him on the squad because he was one of the first Humans to face the Ukhel in combat, where he'd lost his legs.

"Kimathi, finish this up. I want to be off this ramp in three," Jones barked as he turned his attention to his own suit.

Battle suits were gray-armored exoskeletons that completely covered the wearer's body and head. Besides providing protection from kinetic and energy weapons, they gave the user increased strength, the ability to operate in a vacuum, a host of built-in small arms, and the ability to fly using their thrusters. Nicole had received some training on them and had used them a few times, though she would still classify herself as a novice. They were hard to handle—since they worked directly with the user's neural implant, one idle thought could cause you to lose control of the suit. It took weeks of dedicated training before they allowed soldiers to use them in any real-world scenario.

"Roger," Ekon responded, walking between the other three squad members in various states of readiness. He watched Private Linda Sakata get into her suit, stepping through its rear opening. Seams running down the back and along each arm and leg allowed her entry and then closed once she was in. As the seams fully knitted themselves together, they created a vacuum-tight seal.

Ekon reviewed Linda's readouts and inspected her suit, before slapping her shoulder and stepping to the next soldier. Private First Class Hasin Kondari was large, almost two meters tall, with a mop of brown hair and ruddy tan skin. He almost looked bored as he stepped into his suit, the back and limbs closing around his enormous frame.

Nicole hadn't talked to Kondari much on their journey to New America. His dead-eyed expression made her shiver whenever she tried to engage him in conversation. She would have bet money that he was one of the soldiers who had been talking about her to the others.

"Okay, Kondari, you're good to go." Ekon slapped the man's back and moved on to the last soldier.

Private Changying Pudari's slight demeanor and bubbly

personality hid a ferocious attitude. During the Tac-I squad's training sessions, Changying amazed Nicole with how she transformed into a vicious fighter almost instantly. Nicole had spoken with her a few times, mostly small talk. The young soldier didn't have Kondari's dead-eyed stare, but Nicole always got the impression Changying would rather be anywhere else than talking with her.

"Good to go." Ekon slapped her shoulder. The five squad members put on their helmets and walked down the ramp, their metallic boots clanging.

"Remember, do not make contact unless absolutely necessary, even if they seem like friendlies," Kal warned. "You'll be too close to the ship, and the Ukhel could trace you back here."

"Yessir," Jones said, his voice coming from the suit's external speaker. Nicole almost rolled her eyes, Kal had given the same warning at least three times since they landed. She had to admire Jones's discipline and restraint in not telling Kal to shove it.

"I think they've got it," Nicole whispered. She fought an urge to squeeze Kal's shoulder.

"I know, I know," Kal replied testily. He walked down the ramp and gave each soldier an encouraging slap on the back before they set off, walking through the shafts of wheat.

Nicole worried about what the team would find. The Ukhel had shown themselves to be merciless, destroying entire planets. There was nothing that she couldn't picture them doing if it suited their needs.

She walked with Kal to his stateroom to watch the squad's

progress through their video feeds. The Tac-I squad cautiously crept through the field, careful to avoid open areas or avenues. They soon arrived at one of the many farming depots, which also served as a small town for the few inhabitants in the area. It was used to store the harvest prior to being transported to the mills. There were several storage areas for fertilizer, and a drone-charging station in the depot as well.

The squad set up several observation posts around the town, watching for traffic going in and out. At each OP, the squad members unfolded a long-range microphone and high-resolution camera to track anything and everything going on in the area.

As they sat in the stateroom, Nicole couldn't help but study Kal out of the corner of her eye. He had become a bit of an enigma to her. When she first met him, she had been struck by the miasma of sadness surrounding him—the death of his family still weighed heavily on him, even a decade later. Once she had gotten to know the man, she had seen glimpses of what he must have been like before: carefree, and with a wry sense of humor that she adored. Whenever these small flashes of levity occurred, a period of sullen non-communication invariably followed them. He had become a puzzle to her. She felt like she was piecing it together, but knew she still had a long way to go.

The squad monitored the depot for several hours. Other than a few drones passing through to pick up or drop off supplies, it was quiet. Whatever the Ukhel were doing to the planet, it hadn't affected what was going on in the agricultural zones as far as they could tell.

❖

An hour after the crew returned, Kal sat at the head of a large rectangular table in the ship's galley. The *Oruc* was small enough that the galley also doubled as a conference room. Besides the central dining table, viewscreens lined two of the walls and a large food fabricator was centered on the other.

Major Garcia, Nicole, Ekon, and Sergeant Jones sat with him around the table. Jones had gone through the mission report from the agricultural depot, concluding that they hadn't been able to gain any significant intel. It appeared the Ukhel hadn't affected the farming in the area, and Kal guessed that they would find the same in the other agricultural zones.

This aligned with what they had seen on the non-Human colonies they had visited. The Ukhel appeared to take a hands-off approach, letting the locals run their planet as they saw fit. New America was different, though, since the Ukhel had kept their fleet in orbit and were clearly building *something* permanent on the planet's surface. He was eager for them to reach Tiradentes, to understand exactly how Ukhel were consolidating their hold on the planet.

"We need to be careful," Nicole warned, catching Kal with her gaze. "They're not stupid, they'll have tight security."

Jones snorted. "Sitting in a rice field with our thumbs up—"

"Wheat field," interrupted Garcia, a faint smile playing across his face. "We're sitting in a wheat field with our thumbs up our asses."

"Whatever, sir. We need to get movin' or else we're going to get found. What happens if they go to harvest this field and this ship is still in it?" Jones asked.

"I hear you," said Kal, "but we need to have a plan."

"Sir, Sergeant Kimathi is from New America—from Tiradentes, in fact." Jones gestured at Ekon. "He can be our guide, get us into the city and find us some place to lie low. We can blend in, see what's going on, and then play it from there."

"How do we even get into Tiradentes?" Nicole asked. "We can't just walk in with battle suits on. They have to be monitoring traffic in and out of the city."

"The thrusters in the suits will get us most of the way there," Jones responded. "Then we hole 'em up somewhere safe and walk the rest of the way."

"I know a place," Ekon offered. "When I was a kid, we used to sneak into the fields outside the city. The irrigation system has culverts that aren't monitored, where we can stow the suits."

Garcia studied the map thoughtfully. "You may not have enough fuel to get back. It would be close, at least."

Ekon marked the map using his neural implant, and a yellow dot appeared directly next to the border between the agricultural zone and Tiradentes. "Sir, we can make it. I've done some quick calculations—we can get there and back with about five percent of our fuel remaining." He paused.

31

"We gotta do something. Those bastards could be killing people."

"These culverts, can we enter the city through them as well?" Jones asked, studying the map. Kal knew what he was thinking; anything they could do to stay underground and out of sight helped their chances.

"Yeah, it leads into the city's primary water system," Ekon replied.

"You know your way down there?" Kal asked. Nicole had already reviewed all the information that they had on New America and confirmed they didn't have any detailed infrastructure plans.

"Mostly. I used to play down there. They also have signage that we can use." Ekon looked uncertain.

"Yes or no, Sergeant? Can you lead us into the city?" Jones looked up from the map to stare directly in Ekon's eyes.

"Yes, sergeant," Ekon confirmed, wiping the look of uncertainty from his face.

Kal regarded the map. It seemed like Ekon's plan was the best that they had—they couldn't stay in the field forever. He sighed. Once again, he faced a decision where there was no suitable answer. He knew Jones was right—they could discover the *Oruc* at any time, despite the holographic camouflage. He also knew Nicole was right, and they could very well be walking into a trap.

"Who knows what the Ukhel have changed, though?" Nicole said. "We very well could be walking into a trap."

They looked at each other across the table. Nicole was right, but there wasn't any choice. They had to get into the city.

"It's a risk we've got to take," Kal said. "I want everyone ready in an hour. Flight crew will stay here, and the rest of us will take the battle suits to the edge of Tiradentes and stow them."

Ekon and Jones smiled at Kal's orders. He appreciated their aggressiveness; they needed it for their line of work. But he would have to make sure the two of them didn't take it too far. This was a recon mission, not an attack.

"Ekon, any ideas where we can hole up once we're in?" Kal asked.

"Yessir, we can stay in my family's house. It's near the edge of the city, and we live in a pretty busy area. No one would notice a few extra people walking around."

"Not an option," Nicole hissed. "Aside from the fact that we don't know what's happened to your family, we would put them in immense danger by staying there."

"I'm sure—" Ekon started, his face getting red.

"Ms. Bergeron is right," Kal interrupted. "We need to find someplace else." His voice softened. "I know you must want to see your family, but you'll get to see them when we've liberated this planet."

Ekon's mouth twisted into a hard line as he took a moment to calm himself. "There's also some communes in that area of the city. They're just filled with squatters. We could hide there, and no one will even notice."

Kal nodded—it seemed like the best option that they had. He was familiar with stories of the communes on Earth; based on what he had heard, they would make the ideal place to hide out of sight. Their dark corridors, lack of police, and constantly revolving citizenry would make it simple to stay there unnoticed. He hadn't realized that there were communes on New America, though.

"What about communications?" asked Garcia.

"We can't risk talking over the net except in emergencies," Kal responded. "Suit-to-suit communications should be okay, but we have to assume that the Ukhel have compromised our long-distance encryption. Only contact us if there is an emergency. If you do communicate, you will need to immediately relocate as a precaution."

Their neural implants communicated directly to each other when they were close enough—usually less than a kilometer apart. For anything farther than that, they used the local net, which meant that anyone who had access might intercept their comms. Every planet and station had one or more networks citizens used for news, communications, and a host of other activities.

"Roger, what about if you're caught?" Garcia shrugged. "Don't mean to be negative, but you might not be able to reach us, and we can't stay in this field forever."

"Give us a week. If we're not back, leave without us," Kal instructed. This was not what he would have wanted, but leaving the *Oruc* sitting in the field indefinitely was not an option.

"Sergeant Jones, is your squad ready?" Kal asked. Jones nodded in the affirmative.

"Let's go," Kal stood up and walked out of the galley, with the rest of the crew on his heels. He felt a knot building in his stomach, knowing that he was about to put the lives of his soldiers in danger once again.

Chapter Three

As Jones had promised, the Tac-I squad was ready to go when Kal arrived at the cargo bay. It took about thirty minutes for him and Nicole to conduct pre-mission checks and get their battle suits on. The fleet's engineers had upgraded two of the suits on the *Oruc*, installing portable versions of the communication intercept and cloak devices from the ship. Kal took a few minutes to make sure he knew how to use them. Unfortunately, only Kal and Sergeant Jones had the upgrades—there hadn't been enough time to adjust the other suits.

Kal studied the landscape as he gently hovered a few centimeters above the ground, testing his thrusters. The wind blew through the shafts of wheat, creating swells and waves that caught rays of sunlight from overhead. Unbidden, his deceased family came to mind. He sent a silent wish that they were at peace, that they were as calm as the wind-caressed field.

Jones motioned for the group to move out, shattering his momentary sense of calm.

Ekon had added a marker on the shared tactical map that showed where they would stow their suits. The squad would travel in two separate formations, keeping close enough to ensure that they could communicate verbally, or through gestures if need be. Splitting up allowed each group to provide cover for the other and provided them some flexibility of maneuvering if they were to come under fire.

Kal and Jones would be the two element leads. Kal had

Private Linda Sakata, Changying Pudari, and Nicole with him, while Jones would lead Ekon and Private Kondari. They made good time as they traveled over the fields using their suits' thrusters, their boots occasionally brushing the tops of the grain stalks. Whenever they came across a town or depot, the two teams would change their direction to bypass it. Whenever they needed to cross any service road or aqueduct, the elements would cross one at a time, with the other providing cover from a hidden location.

As they traveled, the purplish silhouette of Tiradentes became more defined, growing larger on the horizon. What had been an indistinguishable blur became a mass of buildings, and Kal could make out the features of the individual structures. Although Tiradentes was considered one city, it was actually a large conurbation, a zone of multiple cities, each with their own center filled with commerce and large office towers. The disparate hubs made Tiradentes look like a mountain range from afar, with peaks and valleys showing where one city began and the other ended.

As they traveled, the fields became more sparse and downtrodden, the noise and pollution from the city affecting it despite laws and regulations. The sparse cover forced them to land and walk sometimes, not willing to take the chance of being spotted.

After about an hour, they arrived at Ekon's marker on the map. Jones gestured for Ekon to take lead, and the sergeant scrambled down an embankment at the side of the road. At the bottom of the ditch was a small irrigation canal with a trickle of clear water leading from the city and out into the fields.

The group walked along the canal, the depth keeping them invisible to any passerby. They finally arrived at a large culvert. As they entered, Kal turned on his suit's night vision, transforming the pitch-black tunnel into a green-hued daylight. The team continued to walk down the tunnel until there was only a pinprick of light from the entrance. The culvert was made of Ultracrete, the smooth, seamless sides making it appear as if it had been hewed directly from the bedrock underneath the city.

Ekon stopped, and the group lifted off their helmets. A dusty smell quickly filled Kal's nostrils. In the complete darkness, he turned to look back the way they had come and could barely make out the small portal of the tunnel's entrance. He stepped out of his suit, the rear opening up along the legs, arms, and back. Once he was completely out, Kal detached his communications intercept and used his neural implant to close and lock the suit, preventing anyone outside their group from using it. He could hear soft hisses and whirs as the rest of the group did the same thing.

Jones turned on his headlamp, forcing Kal to twist his head as the sudden light seared his eyes. He blinked a few times and slowly turned his head back, allowing them to adjust.

The seven of them stood in a circle, glancing around at each other. Jones's headlamp created a soft blue glow that cast shadows on the walls around them and seemed to envelop their small group in a halo of light. Despite the musty smell, the tunnels were immaculate, free of debris or any signs of pests or animals. Although New America had industrial and commercial zones, its agricultural system set it apart from the other Human colonies. Clean, efficient, and fertile, it had been the source of half of all food supplies for the former UEG. The industry was so vital, it didn't surprise Kal that the local government had kept the waterways well maintained.

"Ready to go?" Jones asked. The acoustics of the tunnel amplified his question and made his voice reverberate down the hallway. The sergeant surveyed the group, his headlamp making their silhouettes dance on the tunnel walls. No one said a word, instead nodding their heads slowly in agreement. "Sergeant Kimathi, lead the way."

Ekon turned on his headlamp and began to lead them down the tunnel. The group split back into their two elements, following Ekon as he navigated them through the tunnels and into the city's drainage system. Kal's team remained back ten meters and kept watch, looking for any signs of activity in the intersections and branches around them. He felt the darkness pressing in on him and turned his head, trying to see if he could hear any signs of activity. The only light came from Ekon's headlamp several meters in front of him.

As they progressed beneath Tiradentes, the water at their feet grew in volume—from a trickle under their boots' soles to a quickening stream that reached the knee. The square culvert where they had stored their suits had given way to a circular Ultracrete tunnel with regular forks and intersections. At each intersection, Ekon stopped to examine a small placard affixed to the wall, identifying what part of the city was above them, and then led them down one of the identical passages. It was quiet except for the gurgling sound of the water, which masked their footfalls.

Kal wondered what was going on in the city above them. What would they find when they finally emerged? What had Ukhel occupation done to the people? He looked for any sensors or recent modifications to the tunnel walls. It didn't look like the Ukhel had been down there.

After an hour, Ekon stopped at one intersection and announced, "We're here." Looking up, Kal saw that there was a chain dangling from the ceiling that was connect to a folded metal ladder above it.

"This ladder leads to one of the service buildings," Ekon said. "The commune is not far away—only a hundred meters." Kal could only imagine what was going on through Ekon's head as he prepared to return to the neighborhood he'd grown up in.

"Everyone, mask on," Jones barked out, pulling a facemask over his head. Kal and the rest of the team put their masks on as well—the black cloth baklava completely covered his head except for the thinner material over his eyes, which allowed him to see.

"What are you waiting for?" Jones asked Ekon, his voice edged with a nervous energy. "Pull it and let's go."

Ekon did as instructed, and the ladder unfolded smoothly and silently, the bottom dipping into the small stream at their feet but not touching the tunnel floor. Sergeant Jones pulled out the small sidearm he had strapped to his torso and climbed up the ladder, leading with his weapon. Ekon stood beneath him, his own weapon raised for cover. The other three soldiers had oriented themselves outward, covering the four tunnels that intersected at their location. Kal was impressed—they acted like they had practiced for this type of scenario countless times.

Kal and Nicole stood next to each other silently, peering into the murky shaft that Jones had disappeared into. Kal studied Nicole's profile, backlit by the glow of Ekon's headlamp—she had her head raised, staring into the dark shaft leading to the surface. Kal couldn't imagine the amount of strength the women possessed to take part in an undercover reconnaissance mission in enemy territory. He had over two decades of military experience and still sometimes felt like soiling himself.

After a minute, a loud metallic clang reverberated down the shaft, almost overpowering the expletive-laden shout that came with it; Jones clearly had an extensive vocabulary. Another minute went by until they could make him out as he slid down the ladder, clasping the sides with his hands and feet to control his descent, and landed in the middle of their group.

"We're clear up above. Kimathi, you stay down here until everyone else is up," the sergeant instructed. "Give me five minutes, then start sending them up. Start with the general and the diplomat."

He climbed back up the ladder without waiting for acknowledgment. After a few minutes, Ekon tapped Kal and Nicole on their shoulders and nodded toward the ladder. Kal climbed the ladder, keeping his cybernetic right arm pointed upward as he climbed. The mechanical limb was relatively new; he had lost his arm only weeks ago in a firefight against the Ukhel. Samsara Fleet doctors had replaced the arm with an advanced prosthesis that enhanced his strength. To everyone else, the prosthesis was indistinguishable from Kal's natural arm, but he still felt a sense of loss whenever he thought about it.

Kal felt like the ladder would never end. His left arm was growing tired, and he realized that he could save himself a lot of effort through using his mechanical arm to lift himself up and his left simply to steady himself. He wondered how Nicole could keep up with him, considering she didn't have the same advantage.

After an eternity, he reached the top of the shaft and swung his legs over the lip of the entrance. He was in a small storage room, with metal shelving affixed to three of the walls and a reinforced metal door was centered on the fourth. A square cover, clearly tossed to the side, sat in the corner next to the door.

Kal knelt, eyes trained on the door and the entrance he had just come in as he waited for the rest of the team to arrive.

❖

Nicole waited a minute for Kal to begin his ascent and then followed him up the ladder. She felt her arms and legs flag as she trudged up, thanking herself for the hours she had spent in the consulate gym and training with the Tac-I squad.

Finally, she pulled herself into a small storage room. Kal and Jones were on opposite corners, watching the door. Nicole took a position opposite them and waited for the rest of the team to arrive.

Once everyone had made it up the ladder, Jones and Ekon placed the cover back on the shaft. It looked to be incredibly heavy. Both soldiers grunted in relief as they finally sealed up the opening with a solid clunk.

"Okay . . . what's next?" Nicole asked, still slightly winded from climbing the ladder.

"Out the door and then left down the hallway. There's a silent alarm on the door to the outside, but as long as we move fast we'll be long gone before they can send anyone." Ekon smiled conspiratorially. "I used to sneak into these tunnels all the time as a kid and never got caught."

Nicole wondered about the young soldier's state of mind. His voice had an edge to it, one that she hadn't heard before. She knew it would have been strange if he wasn't nervous, but there was something in his behavior that made her question his judgment. Ekon was dedicated, but he also was prone to acting before he thought things through, not a good trait when conducting a mission on an enemy-occupied planet.

"You'd better hope that your streak doesn't end," Jones said.

"Don't worry so much—" Ekon stopped talking as he heard the low growl coming from beneath Jones's mask.

"You'd better not finish that statement, Sergeant." Jones drew out the last word for emphasis. "Let's go."

Nicole trained her kinetic pistol on the door. As an

attaché, she'd never received weapons training. After their first mission together, Sergeant Jones had let her train with the Tac-I squad. At this point, she could shoot the weapon but was still far from an expert on it—the gun still felt heavy and awkward in her hand.

Privates Sakata and Pudari moved to either side of the door and kept their weapons at the ready to cover Ekon. He slowly pressed down on the release latch, bracing his body against the door as it quietly swung outward into the hallway. A harsh, unnatural light streamed through the crack between the door and the frame, slicing through the dark of the storage room and causing Nicole to avert her eyes.

Ekon crept through the door, rifle raised. After a moment, he motioned for the team to follow, and one by one, they exited and staggered themselves on either side of the hallway. Jones, the last one out, closed the door quietly behind them, leaving no trace that they had been in the room.

They proceeded down the hallway until they reached a large metal door. It looked to be almost identical to the door to the storage room except for several wires that snaked from it to conduits lining the walls.

After quickly inspecting the door, Ekon turned around to face the rest of the group. "Doesn't look like they've changed the security system. Once we go through this door, we gotta move. They have cameras and sensors trained on it. As soon as we open it, the alarms will go off and they will send the local police after us. Keep up—we'll have to lose them in the streets to make sure we aren't followed."

Ekon shoved the exterior door open and immediately broke into a run. The rest of them followed, their neat formation breaking as they ran. Nicole barely had time to process the chaos of Tiradentes as she strained to keep up with the group. They were on a two-lane street with mid-size towers extending fifty to a hundred meters into the sky on either side. Over time, the locals had covered the original drab exterior of the Ultracrete buildings with bright paints and murals, adding color but still not completely obfuscating their utilitarian history. The streets were busy, with locals hustling on the sidewalks and transport pods flying above their heads.

Nicole looked for signs of the Ukhel occupiers. She couldn't see anything obviously out of place. The only real clue lay in the faces of the pedestrians they ran past. Their visages were grim, eyes cast down, not even looking up as she ran past them at full speed. Nicole had half expected to see checkpoints, manned by armored and armed Ukhel soldiers—but there was no trace of the occupiers at all.

Ekon slowed as they weaved through the crowds, trying not to cause a disruption. Abruptly, he plunged down a side alley, pulling off his mask without breaking stride. The rest of the team followed, stuffing their own masks into their pockets as their pace decreased from a jog to a quick walk. Ekon made several more turns up and down various alleys and side streets until Nicole had no idea where they were and how far they had traveled. Finally, they turned onto a street lined with multistory residential complexes. The buildings were identical, each one split into multiple homes with a small yard in front. Ekon walked casually, looking around the neighborhood as if he hadn't a care in the world. The rest of the group had slowly separated to avoid notice, now traveling in pairs or alone as they walked down the street.

The slower pace allowed Nicole to study their surroundings in more detail. She noticed small scars of scattered plasma fire pockmarking the faux-brick buildings around them. The marks were grouped together and ran in a straight line across the buildings' facades, signs that these were the marks of executions rather than combat. She couldn't see anything that looked like a commune around them, and the neighborhood looked too nice to have one close. These were not large estates, but they were nothing like the buildings she would have seen near her commune back on Earth.

Ekon's pace quickened almost imperceptibly; clearly, he'd seen what he was looking for. With a casual air, he turned down a pathway leading to one of the housing units. It looked the same as the others—three stories with a small yard and the dingy brick facade.

Without breaking stride, the young sergeant opened the front door and the rest followed quickly behind, eager to get off the street before anyone noted them.

The interior of the building had the warm chaos of a home with a family living in it. The Plasteel furnishings were humble but functional, matching the working-class feel of the neighborhood. To the right of the small entranceway was a living area with couches arranged in an L shape and children's artwork affixed to the walls. Nicole could see a dining area with a kitchen behind it in front of them with a circular faux wood table that had toys and knickknacks scattered across the top. Behind the table, the kitchen area had a food prep device, food fabricator, and refrigerator affixed against the wall.

Nicole studied the artwork that lined the entranceway. Clearly something was wrong, and she could feel rage and joy rising in her chest, battling each other, as she realized what it was.

Kal turned to Ekon, confusion and anger playing across his face. "Ekon, where are—"

A scream, quickly followed by the sound of something crashing on the tile floor, interrupted the general.

Nicole spun from her inspection of the art to see a middle-aged woman, hair tinged with gray, run to Ekon. She pulled the young soldier tight, clutching him to her as she buried her face in his neck. After a moment she released him, tears streaming down her cheeks.

"Honey, you came home!"

Chapter Four

"What the—"

There was a squeal as a young girl, perhaps twelve years old, ran into the room and clung onto Ekon before Sergeant Jones could finish. Moments later, a middle-aged man, about Kal's age, rushed into the room and wrapped his arms around the other three.

Kal wanted to smack something, perhaps himself—of course Ekon had lied. The young soldier hadn't been able to resist the opportunity to see his family again, even if it meant disobeying orders. Kal should have known that Ekon would do something like this.

The rest of the group stood silently, bashfully looking around the room, voyeurs in a touching family moment. Kal saw a smile play across Nicole's lips, which quickly ended when she saw him looking at her. Her smile released something in him, and Kal realized he was happy for Ekon and his family, happy they had this chance at a reunion.

Jones just stared at his second in command, wringing his hands, his face contorted in anger.

"Sergeant Kimathi, come with me, now!" Jones pointed to the living room.

Ekon wiped the smile from his face and reluctantly followed Jones to the other room. The rest of the family and their away team stood in the entranceway awkwardly, as if they'd suddenly noticed each other's presence. Ekon's mother and father looked cautiously around the room, studying the small group of soldiers that had materialized in their home.

"Mr. and Mrs. Kimathi, my name is Kal Norman. We're sorry for barging in on you." Kal proffered his hand to both parents. "We didn't realize that Ekon was taking us here. I fear that we may be putting you in danger."

Ekon's dad shook his head ruefully. "That sounds like Ekon, always acting before thinking. I'm sorry he did that, but hopefully you understand." The man had a thick New American accent, rolling his R's and blending the words together, as if he wanted to taste each one before letting it go.

"Well, I'm glad he did." Ekon's mother folded her arms defiantly. "We didn't know what happened to him—whether he was alive or dead."

"Jendayi . . ." Ekon's dad started.

"Don't Jendayi me, Zane. You know I'm right."

Zane closed his mouth, clearly unwilling to fight this battle.

"Who are all of you?" Ekon's younger sister stood slightly behind her mother, her wide brown eyes fixated on Kal. "Where did you come from? Is my brother in trouble? Why are you here?"

Kal put what he hoped was a pleasant smile on his face. "We're just friends of your brother. We came to New America to look around since we haven't heard anything since the Ukhel took over your planet."

"Who?" Zane cocked his head. After a moment, understanding dawned on his face. "You mean the Nasi— that's what they call themselves at least."

Kal needed a moment to register what the man had said.

He was shocked to realize that he hadn't even known their enemy's name. The Ukhel, the Nasi that is, had subjugated nearly all of Humanity, killed billions, and still six months later, they knew so little about them. The name Ukhel had come from Humans—they'd needed to call these invaders something. It was a stark reminder of just how in the dark they remained.

"Those bastards." Jendayi spat on the floor. "The Nasi ships arrived one day and bombarded the city, the whole planet. Our government lasted less than a day. They knew what had happened to Earth and all those other worlds. Figured better to surrender and fight another day than to have everyone die."

"The Nasi sent troops down to the planet's surface, met with our planetary government. To her credit, our governor refused to be part of their plans. Then, all of a sudden, she disappeared." Zane raised his hands, making air quotes.

"A couple of days later, a new video came onto the news net," Jendayi continued. "They finally found someone who would be their puppet: Choi." She turned her head and spat again.

"She had been the mayor of Xin Chengdu," Zane explained. "I guess she was the first person who would do what those bastards wanted."

A humbled Ekon walked back into the entrance area with Sergeant Jones behind him. The soldier trudged to his parents and gave them another, more reserved, hug. Jones caught Kal's eye and gestured toward the living room.

"Sir, we have to leave immediately," Jones said as soon as

they were out of earshot.

"Agreed, but where to? Does Ekon—Sergeant Kimathi—actually know of a place to hide out?" Kal asked.

"He wasn't completely lying. Kimathi confirmed there are communes near here, about half a kilometer away. They sound like the ideal place to set up operations." Jones shot a look toward the front hallway, his eyes boring holes in his second in command.

"I've been talking to the parents. Before we go, we need to ask them everything we can about what's happened here," Kal said. "We can't waste this opportunity to talk to locals. Then we get out and don't tell them where we're going."

"Yes, sir."

"What about Kimathi?" Kal asked. "Is he staying here?"

Sergeant Jones looked at him with disbelief. "What d'you mean? He's a non-commissioned officer in Samsara Fleet in the middle of a critical mission. He can't stay home."

"When we left Kapustin Station months ago, I told everyone they were volunteers and they could leave at any time—that hasn't changed. If Sergeant Kimathi wants to stay, I really don't want to have to go back on my promise." Kal said. Jones's cheekbones stood out on his angular face as he clenched his jaw.

The sergeant breathed in slowly before responding. "Sir, war changes things. You made that promise in good faith, but you let him go and you'll be risking Kimathi, his family, our mission, and the entire fleet."

Kal knew that Jones was right. He couldn't keep his promise. Not without breaking other promises he had made.

Not without risking everything. He knew it, but he'd wanted Jones to say it. Wanted the confirmation of what he knew to be true. Wordlessly, he nodded at the NCO.

"I'll talk with him." Jones turned and walked back to the front hall.

Kal waited a moment before following him back to rejoin the group. Ekon's sister hovered around her older sibling, her eyes still wide, trying to drink in the image of a brother she had thought she had lost.

"Mr. and Mrs. Kimathi, we can't stay long," Kal said. "But before we leave, I need to talk to you. We need to know everything that has happened here on New America."

Nicole, Kal, and Ekon's family sat around the small table in the center of their dining room. Sabah, Ekon's younger sister, brought some pastries from the kitchen area and sat down next to her brother. She remained glued to his side as the family quietly talk to themselves for a moment.

Nicole picked a pastry from the plate, wrapped it in a paper napkin, then placed it in her cargo pocket, not sure when she might find food again. Jones had ordered the Tac-I squad to take defensive positions throughout the house, placing them in positions to observe anyone approaching the building.

"Eek, you were fighting the Nasi in space?" Sabah asked. The child's wide-eyed expression contained a mixture of awe and curious innocence plain for all to see. Nicole felt a pain in her chest as an image of Sylvie and the starfish pendant flashed into her mind. She didn't know how Ekon wasn't bawling his eyes out at the sight of his family.

"Yeah, we fought them several times—on Caracas Station even. They got a few good ones in"—he gestured to his legs—"but we did as well." The young soldier had unconsciously puffed out his chest and put on a facade of casual indifference.

Ekon told his family everything that had happened to him in the past nine months, starting with relaying the after-graduation trip he had been on with his secondary school friends. He talked about how they had been at their final destination, slumming on a Kurz mining station, when they had met Kal and everything had gone wrong. His family sat captivated, listening as Ekon described their retreat from Caracas Station and how they had finally defeated a Nasi battleship—Sabah pumped her arm in the air at that part. Occasionally, Kal would interrupt the story, preventing Ekon from revealing key details about their mission or Samsara Fleet. Nicole knew all too well that any information might make them targets, and Kal clearly realized it as well.

After Ekon had finished, Kal put down his pastry and cleared his throat. "So, that brings us to now. You must understand why we're here. We need to know what's been going on, what the Nasi are doing here."

"We know so little about the Ukh— the Nasi," Nicole added. "Anything you can tell us will help."

"Of course," Zane said, the proud smile disappearing from his face. "We'll tell you everything we know." He sat up in his Plasteel chair before continuing. "The Nasi took over Caracas and then captured the planet. They installed Fulki Choi as the planetary governor. As soon as she was in power, she started to ferret out any of the so-called rebels from the government."

"Only the crap remains," Jendayi added. "The corrupt and the people motivated by money and power. Choi declared an emergency and had her cronies installed. Then they started rounding up people, anyone who they thought was a threat."

Nicole shuddered, sad to hear how quickly people could turn against each other. "Have there been people fighting back? Any sort of rebellion or resistance?" she asked.

"Some people tried to fight back at first, right after the Nasi appointed Choi," Zane said. "The Nasi killed them, and their families, and then razed their homes to the ground. That pretty much put an end to that. Now Choi has her Domestic State Patrol firmly in place. The Domespat is the muscle behind Choi's edicts—they ferret out anyone who doesn't agree with her. The people in the police who cared about justice and the law are gone. All that remains are her lapdogs, motivated by power, money, or sadism."

"But"—Jendayi held up a finger—"there are stories. A lot of young people have gone missing. We hear whispers that they're being rounded up by the Domespat. But I think there's more to it than that. I think they're in hiding." She turned to Ekon. "Your friend Li Wei, I saw him on the street— he had his head down and was walking real fast, but I saw him! When I called his name, he disappeared though, ran right down an alley. When I talked to his mother, she said that he never returned home from your trip."

"If he made it, then Sandra and Klarissa would have too." Ekon looked hopeful. The two women had been with Ekon and Li Wei when they had returned to New America with Kal.

"Maybe," Zane said doubtfully, "but we have no proof."

"With Choi controlling the populace, what are the Nasi doing?" Kal asked as he grabbed another pastry from the tray Sabah had brought. "We know they're building structures and defenses on the planet—we saw firsthand that they've set up ground to space cannons. It seems like they're here to stay."

"Oh yes, they're doing somethin' alright." Jendayi nodded. "They've been building these big bases on the planet—there's one here in Tiradentes. Not too many Humans get to go inside; they're real hush-hush about the whole thing. But anyone can see towers behind those vast walls they built. Weird, twisty-lookin' things."

"You said not too many get inside those bases. So some do?" Nicole asked.

"Yeah, they have some of us Humans in there to deliver goods, menial labor, that sort of thing," Zane replied. "It pays pretty well, actually. I wouldn't take the job, but some people just want money."

"Some people *need* the money, and it *does* pay a lot," Jendayi said. "Though some of these people just disappear from time to time. I bet if there is a resistance, they don't take too well to collaborators."

Nicole arched her eyebrow. "That does seem like a good sign that there's a resistance."

Jendayi nodded. "That's what I think."

"Maybe," Kal admitted, "or maybe it's just individuals acting on their own who don't like these collaborators. Or maybe it's the Nasi. If there is some sort of resistance, where would they be? How could we contact them?"

Ekon leaned forward. "Li Wei's mom. If he's involved, he'd tell her something. I know him, total momma's boy. I can talk with her, she only lives a few blocks away."

"That's the only thing I can think of too," Zane agreed after a pause. "She would be your best bet. She always did like Ekon—him and Li Wei were thick as thieves."

Nicole turned to look at Kal. He stared at the far wall, lost in thought. She wasn't sure what to think of Ekon's idea—if there was a resistance, then they had to make contact with them. They would have an intelligence network already established, and the information they could provide would incalculably better than anything the small away team could find. Also, a resistance could help them break the hold that the Nasi and their lackeys had on the planet. Samsara Fleet by itself may not be enough to liberate New America.

"Okay," Kal said. "Contact Li Wei's mother and see if you can find anything out. Get back here quickly—for your family's safety, we need to leave as soon as possible."

Ekon nodded and jumped up from the table. After giving his parents and tearful sister a hug, he ran out the front door.

"So," Nicole said, once Ekon had left, "what else can you tell us about the Nasi?"

❖

Nicole peppered the Kimathi family with a barrage of questions about the enemy. Some of them were obvious to Kal, while others seemed to come from out of nowhere. He knew Nicole well enough to know that nothing she asked was pointless; each question had a thought or hypothesis behind it. Kal would interject when appropriate, but let Nicole drive the conversation, trusting in her expertise in foreign cultures and diplomacy. He used his neural implant to transcribe and save the conversation for future review. The answers that the Kimathi family provided would be an enormous leap beyond anything Samsara Fleet had known before.

Zane and Jendayi often seemed frustrated by their inability to provide suitable answers to Nicole's questions. The Nasi were extremely secretive, preferring to work through their puppet government—which Choi had named the New American Empire—rather than directly interact with the people of New America. It made it impossible for the average citizen to know anything of their plans or intentions. From what Zane and Jendayi had heard, the Nasi were using the NAE to leech as many resources and materials as they could from the local populace. They added new taxes for almost every transaction and had doubled or even tripled the ones that were already in place. They had instituted strictly enforced quotas on raw materials and industrial production, funneling the output to the Nasi bases being built on the planet.

The bases themselves were an enigma. Tales ranged from the mundane, with them serving as homes and recreational areas, to the fantastical—inter-dimensional portals. The only thing that seemed certain was that the Nasi were establishing a permanent presence on New America.

The Nasi seemed to rely heavily on their new puppet state to keep order. The NAE had rewritten the planet's laws; instituting severe penalties for assemblies, anti-government sentiment, and other crimes against the government. The Domespat were brutal in the enforcement of these edicts— ignoring procedure, or Human decency as far as Kal could tell, to enforce them. Ironically, crime had flourished under the new regime, the new taxes created a significant black market, and many citizens were desperate to get basic supplies.

As they talked, Kal touched the Alliance chit in his pocket. The Alliance was a clandestine criminal organization with fronts on planets and stations across the galaxy. He knew that they dealt in smuggling and other non-violent crimes, but no one knew everything that the organization had a hand in. Everyone knew of the Alliance, but few knew anything about them, an arrangement that Kal suspected they had carefully orchestrated over the years. When he had been an independent merchant, he'd also been an occasional operative for them, taking a few contract jobs when he couldn't find legitimate work. As an operative, they gave him a chit that allowed him to find and access their fronts on any planet or station.

His connection to the Alliance had already proven valuable in their fight against the Nasi. They had provided intelligence and materials that had helped Samsara Fleet defeat the Nasi battleship. During a meeting with one of their representatives, Kal and Nicole had learned that the Alliance was willing to provide more aid in order to defeat the Nasi, which was targeting their organization. The difficulty was contacting them without the Nasi knowing.

An hour later, Ekon returned, a storage container in hand. He walked over to the table and opened it, revealing a freshly baked loaf of bread, tendrils of steam still rising from it.

"How'd it go?" Kal asked, eyeing the bread. The smell was intoxicating, especially since he had spent the last several months only eating food that had come from a food fabricator.

Ekon didn't say a word, instead plunging his hand into the bread. Kal had to stifle a gasp as he watched the bread destroyed. After a moment of feeling about, Ekon pulled a small piece of paper out and handed it to Kal. "Pretty sure Li Wei's house was under surveillance, but his mother gave me this. She put it in the bread in case they stopped me."

Everyone at the table froze except for Kal, who bolted out of his chair without looking at the paper. "Why do you say that?"

"Well, the first clue was that she whispered it to me as I was leaving," Ekon responded sardonically. "When I came in, she acted like I was our friend Toshi—talked about the weather, all while making this bread. She put something in it and gave it to me and then rushed me out the door. The last thing she told me was that she would let Li Wei know I stopped by if she saw him and that I should eat the bread today. I took the long way back, trying to lose anyone who might follow just in case."

"Did you see anyone?" Kal asked.

"Nope, no one. But I'm not exactly a spy, sir," Ekon replied.

Nicole stood up. "We need to get out of here."

Kal unfolded the piece of paper, brushing off the crumbs that clung to its sides—Li Wei's mother had written a pair of numbers, coordinates, on the paper along with a time. 1700. He handed it to Nicole so she could look.

"This must be for today," she observed. "Looks like we have a few hours until we need to be there."

"Agreed. We need to get out of here and find someplace safer to hide while we wait." Kal felt the itch of invisible eyes watching him. He knew that they may already be in the crosshairs of the Nasi or the Domespat. Kal turned to Ekon's family. "You need to get out of here too. Is there somewhere you can go?"

"We have friends." Zane looked grim. "We'll be able to find a place. Don't worry about us, just get out of here."

Kal turned to back to Ekon. Sabah was clinging to his side, and he pulled her close with his left arm. His hand had tightened around his sister's arm, clinging to her. "You know you can't stay, right?" he asked Ekon. "I told you, you were always free to go, that I won't make anyone stay who doesn't want to. I meant it, but I can't keep that promise."

Ekon looked at his family and made eye contact with his parents, his face a mixture of sorrow and yearning. Kal could see the emotions play across the young man's face. To be reunited with a family he thought he might have lost, only to be ripped from them again. Ekon's parents also looked torn—the son they had thought was dead had just returned, and now he had to leave them again. Kal felt like an interloper as he watched the unspoken dialogue between Ekon and his parents.

It was impossible to keep all your promises. Impossible to always do the right thing. When it came down to it, Kal had to sacrifice Ekon's family's happiness for the mission.

"We need to get ready. Take a moment, talk with your family." Kal gestured to Nicole, and they walked to the living room, joining Sergeant Jones.

"We've got to go," Kal said. "Sergeant Kimathi is saying goodbye to his family right now. We should be ready to go as soon as they're done."

Jones glanced solemnly at the adjoining dining area. "Roger, sir. We'll be ready in five." He walked upstairs to let the other squad members know of their imminent departure.

Nicole turned to Kal. "Where are we going to? We can't just head to those coordinates."

"The communes Ekon mentioned—they're apparently real. We can head there, then send out a few people to check out the coordinates before the time." Kal responded.

"What if it's a trap?" she asked.

"Doubtful. Why go through all that trouble? They could have just picked up Ekon at Li Wei's house and tortured information out of him." Kal had no doubt that the Nasi and Domespat would not hesitate to torture them for information. He also knew that they had little other option than to trust the coordinates.

"You're not giving Ekon the option to stay with his family?" Nicole asked.

"When I promised everyone that they could leave, I didn't mean like this." Kal knew Nicole's question was innocent. But he felt like she was grilling him. "I wish I could let him stay. But I can't risk it."

Kal looked around the living room. It reminded him of a time when he had a family—couch not quite square with the wall, some small stains on it, and probably dirt and crumbs between the cushions. The picture screens with the kids' artwork loaded hung crookedly on the wall, the images changing each minute to the next masterpiece. The home was perfect because of the imperfections. Every dirt smudge and stain gave it a certain presence and a history, making it something wonderful. He'd had that life before and had lost it; he didn't know if he would have been able to leave his family a second time like he was ordering Ekon to.

"Sir, we're ready when you are," Jones announced, flanked by the other three Tac-I soldiers.

"Okay, I'm going to check with Ekon," Kal responded. He brushed past the soldiers and into the kitchen.

Ekon sat huddled with his family, all of them sobbing. He waited until one of them tearfully looked up before speaking. "Ekon, we need to leave now. We'll be in the hallway. Mr. and Mrs. Kimathi, thank you for your hospitality. I wish you the best, and I hope that we haven't placed you or Sabah in any danger."

They all nodded glumly as Kal left the room, letting them say their final private goodbye. Nicole waited in the hallway entrance with the Tac-I squad. The squad had their weapons drawn, and Pudari knelt by the small window facing the front of the house, her eyes scanning the Kimathis' front yard.

"That's tough." Nicole shook her head sorrowfully as she read Kal's expression.

"Sometimes, it's a blessing to be alone," Kal replied. He didn't really believe his pat answer, but he had nothing else to say. The emotions of watching the family say goodbye reminded him too much of the loss he'd already had to face.

Nicole didn't reply. Instead, she studied the view through the front window, peering over Pudari's shoulder as she scanned the yard and street outside.

Less than a minute later, Ekon walked into the entranceway, eyes red. "Ready," he told Sergeant Jones.

Jones looked at him silently, then grasped his shoulder, giving it a small squeeze. It was the biggest show of compassion that Kal had ever seen from him. The sergeant turned to the rest of the group. "Okay, let's go. Kimathi's in the lead. Everyone else, follow behind. Keep eyes and ears open. Don't use your implants unless necessary."

The Tac-I squad holstered their weapons and walked out the door, with Ekon in the lead. Kal took a final wistful glance backward, then followed.

Chapter Five

The knock was faint, barely audible over the low-level hum that seemed to permeate the room. It was a signal, letting them know that the two soldiers who were about to walk through the door were friendlies. Sergeant Jones had told Nicole that if they didn't hear the knocks, or they were any more or less than two, then she should immediately open fire on anyone who entered.

It had been several hours since they'd left the Kimathis' home. They'd used a communication intercept they'd detached from their suit to listen in on the local net. Li Wei's mother had been right—the Domespat were looking for Ekon. They hadn't identified him, but had tagged him as the potential associate of a known insurgent and a person of interest. They had increased their patrols in the area around Ekon's and Li Wei's homes, a few hundred meters from the commune, looking for any clues where he went.

Kal had tried to use his Alliance chit to see if they there were any fronts near them. The device registered nothing, though—the Nasi must have found the front and cleared them out.

The dilapidated commune was the perfect place for them to avoid notice. It was made up of several blocks of enormous dormitories, gutted and rebuilt multiple times until they were a confusing nest of dark rooms and dead ends. Ekon had told the group they were the oldest buildings on the planet, used by the first settlers to New America. They had grown into disrepair until the homeless and the forgotten had moved in and made them their home. These inhabitants had transformed the interiors of the buildings, tearing down walls, building makeshift stairs and bridges, and turning the blocks upon blocks of buildings into a maze filled with small rooms, nooks, and cubbyholes. The negligence of the rest of society had allowed them to create a kingdom of their own out of the rubble they had found.

To Nicole, it felt like home—the small room they were in was about the size of the room she had grown up in with her family. She remembered the depressing, yet somewhat liberating feeling of being forgotten, of not having society care about you. The people of the commune were beneath the notice of the authorities, even the Domespat. As long as they kept their nose down and avoided scrutiny, they were free to live in the relative squalor of the decrepit buildings.

After an hour of walking the twisting corridors, the team had found a small room in the middle of the complex that suited their needs perfectly. It was at the end of a long, winding corridor and offered them the privacy they needed while also having a small ceiling vent that they could escape through in an emergency. The room was a simple Ultracrete box, streaked with dust and smelling of mildew. As soon as they had established their location, Jones had sent out Privates Sakata and Kondari to investigate the coordinates provided by Li Wei's mother.

Ekon crouched in the corner of the room across from Nicole, hands on his head, his mind clearly still with his family. The rest of the team left him alone, giving him time to reflect. They had already lost their families and were still processing their own grief—they could understand how difficult it must have been for Ekon to give up his family again in order to continue on with the mission. Nicole's eyes glanced from Ekon and paused on Sergeant Jones, his face stoic as he watched the door. She wondered what he had lost, if he had lost anything, since he never talked about a family or friends.

Sakata and Kondari walked back into the decrepit room, returning from their recon of what the team called the rendezvous site. It was a waste refinement plant at the edge of Tiradentes, close to where they had entered the city. The plant processed trash and waste from the city and either recycled it or broke it into component elements that could be safely used as fertilizer. Based on their recon, it seemed to be the ideal location to bring refugees or fugitives in and out of the city—its proximity to the agricultural zone allowed for quick escape, and the transports bringing materials to and from the facility would provide cover for anyone who needed to travel there.

"So what did you find?" Kal asked after the privates sat down on the floor.

"About what you would expect, sir. Just a normal waste plant," Sakata responded. "Mostly automated. There were a handful of workers in the area. There's concealment around the building, so you can get eyes on without being visible."

Kondari opened his water flask and took a deep gulp—it was summer and the heat was becoming oppressive. "There's nothing else there, sir. We looked around and couldn't find anything out of place. Seems safe enough to meet someone there though."

66

"Did you see anyone watching the area or hear anything on the intercept?" Jones asked, turning his body so he was facing the rest of the soldiers.

"No, Sergeant," Kondari shook his head. "Intercept was quiet, and I didn't see anyone or anything." He handed the device back to Kal. It was a small square that fit in the user's pocket and connected directly to their neural implant.

Ekon shifted himself forward and leaned in. "Sergeant, I should go out there. Li Wei knows me."

They had already decided that they couldn't risk everyone going to the rendezvous point. The plan was to have a small group make contact. Once they were in touch with the resistance, they would come back and get the rest of the group. Their assumption was the resistance had a safehouse, some place where they could get away from the Nasi and Domespat. Nicole guessed Kal didn't want their team to be split for any longer than they had to. Bad things happened that way.

"Yeah, you're also known by the Domespat too," Kondari scoffed, adding a "Sergeant" at the end when he saw Jones's steely glare.

"Private"—he emphasized the rank—"Kondari is right," Sergeant Jones agreed. "You should be the last person we send out there."

"Li Wei also knows me," Kal said. "I'll head out there. It's almost 1600, so I need to leave now to make it in time."

"Sir, you need someone else to go with you," Jones advised. "Take Kondari—he's been there before and could be useful in a tight situation."

"That's a good idea," agreed Nicole. "He also may see something you miss."

Kal nodded. "You ready to head back out, Kondari?"

"Yessir." The private slowly got up on his feet, his head almost touching the low ceiling.

"Let's go then."

Nicole watched as Kal stood up, stretching his legs. If she hadn't known him better, she would have thought he was almost eager to meet the resistance. But she could see the small tightening in his cheek, the way his eyes darted quickly as he stood up, that told her the truth.

Private Kondari led Kal through the warren of hallways that made up the communes. As they walked along the winding corridors, Kal could see hunched figures—sometimes moving, sometimes not—crouched in corners. Once or twice, drug dealers trying to make a sale would stop them, offering Rapturium on the cheap.

Finally, the two soldiers crawled out what must have originally been a window into a narrow alley. Overhead, the brilliant, sunlit sky had given way to a blanket of light clouds, with small panes of blue peeking out. Kal followed Kondari discreetly through the city, keeping his distance so it wouldn't be obvious that they were together. Around them, the streets seemed muted to Kal. The citizens seemed sullen, their eyes firmly on the ground in front of them. There was no chatter, no laughter, just the sounds of the city's traffic and machinery around them. The buildings abutting the street they were on cast shadows that covered Kal despite their relatively low height. It all felt dead, a corpse that was ready for burial.

DSP Echo, this is DSP Alpha. We've received word from citizens they saw the suspect with a group, entering the communes in the Mosaic District. The chatter from the communication intercept fed directly into Kal's neural implant. He kept his expression blank, nonplussed, despite the ominous news.

There was no going back for the team now. Kal tried to comfort himself by thinking of how difficult it would be for the Domespat to find anything in the commune. He imagined that half the inhabitants were on the run from the police—it was like trying to find a very specific needle in a pile of other needles.

Kal glanced ahead and saw a Domespat checkpoint ahead of them. There were no side streets to turn down, and turning around would invite the patrollers to stop and thoroughly search them, which was probably why they had placed the checkpoint there. A couple of barriers were stretched across the street with a parked a patrol transport behind them. Two patrollers were standing behind the barriers, their weapons slung on their backs and their eyes lazily glancing around at the people walking past. Kal swore under his breath as one of the patroller's made eye contact with him.

The man was Kal's height, with ruddy brown skin and an almost snide expression on his face. His uniform was black with a few dark green highlights and bulky exterior armor plating that made the officer seem enormously muscled. Kal assumed the effect was intentional.

"Hey, citizen!" The man held up his hand and looked at Kal like he had just pulled him from the bottom of his boot. "Where are you going?"

Kal froze—he hadn't even thought of a cover story. "Coming from my friend's house, officer," he replied, the words leaving his mouth before he had time to process them. It took every bit of his restraint not to look to see if Kondari had stopped to wait. Hopefully, the young private would be smart enough to keep walking and wait for Kal down the road or just meet him at the rendezvous point.

"Really?" The question had the sarcastic edge of someone who didn't trust the answers he was getting. In Kal's experience, people like that didn't trust others because they knew themselves to be untrustworthy.

He put on as genuine a smile as he could. "Yes."

"Hmmm . . ." The officer paused dramatically, his mouth turned in a frown. Kal kept the silly smile plastered on his face, doubting it was doing much to help. "Well, what's your name?"

"Asif Bergeron," Kal responded, concatenating the first two names that came into his head.

The officer continued to draw out the conversation, dramatically inhaling as if smelling a fragrant flower. "Well, Asif. You got some ID on you? Your implant isn't registered. We'll need to log you into the system." The man tapped a small wrist-mounted computer, showing that he had scanned Kal and come up blank.

Because they were used by species throughout the galaxy,

neural implants were anonymous. Although they communicated with the planetary network, the actual connection was the same for every person on the planet. When communicating with secure networks, like Samsara Fleet's, the implant would provide credentials so it could be authorized. Planetary nets were open for all though, so there was no way to isolate one person's implant from another.

At close distance, implants emitted unique electromagnetic waves due to the unique neural interface with their users. These "fingerprints" were sometimes registered at the planetary level. However, under the UEG, it had been against the law for planets to share implant registration data with each other to maintain some sense of personal freedom for their citizens.

Kal patted his pockets, pretending to feel for an ID chit. As his hand touched his breast pocket, he could feel the hard edges of his EDF retirement card, which provided his actual identity. He quickly moved on though, acting the part of a citizen who had lost his ID card. The last thing he needed was for them to know who he really was.

DSP Bravo team, Kal heard through his neural implant's connection to the communication intercept. He saw the officer stiffen, obviously listening to the transmission through his own implant. *We need you down at control point 39. Citizens are reporting looting in the vicinity.*

"Well?" The officer's eyes focused back on Kal. "Where is it?" The question dashed Kal's hopes of the officer leaving for the call.

Kal pulled his empty hands out of his pockets. "It must've

fallen out of my pocket at my friend's house. I can go get it."
He looked back the way he came.

"Not your day, Asif. Gonna need you to—" A Domespat patroller came running up, interrupting the officer.

"Gutierrez, let's go. We don't get there now, Sarge will kill us." He gave a sly smile. "You know he needs his cut. That district has some nice shops."

Officer Gutierrez seemed torn for a moment, looking at Kal. Finally, he exhaled and nodded to the other patroller.

"Move out, citizen. And get your implant registered as soon as possible." He dismissed Kal and turned to the Domespat transport. The vehicle was vaguely egg-shaped, with skids on either side supporting the weight. It was the same black color as the patrollers' uniforms and had clearly been modified, with additional armor plates attached and a large plasma machine gun affixed to the top.

As soon as the two patrollers got in the vehicle and it lifted off, Kal walked away, his pace a fraction slower than a run. As he walked toward the rendezvous point, he watched out of the corner of his eyes for Kondari. The private was tall enough that he should stick out in a crowd, but Kal couldn't see him anywhere. His only choice was to continue to make his way to the coordinates and hope that Kondari met him there.

❖

The waste-processing plant was in the middle of a paved lot, dotted with enormous stockpiles of refuse. Kal could see vines from the agricultural zone starting a few hundred meters behind the building, the rows spreading like fingers to the horizon. Plants like this one had a small crew to operate the machines and supervise the automated bots. A few of the workers were walking through the lot, sweeping loose pieces of trash and conducting maintenance on the attendant bots. Kal got the impression they were conducting final checks before leaving for the night.

He checked the time on his neural implant. 1645—fifteen minutes until the rendezvous time. Despite passing another Domespat checkpoint the rest of the walk to the refinery had been uneventful. Kal had yet to see Kondari again; he hoped the young soldier was somewhere close.

From his observation point, Kal scanned the foliage surrounding the lot, looking for the missing private. Large bushes about two meters high, composed of bundles of stiff, narrow leaves, surrounded the lot on three sides—perfect hiding places for anyone who wanted to remain unseen. A light breeze rippled across the branches, causing them to sway rhythmically. Occasionally he thought he saw movement in the bushes, only to realize it was caused by the wind.

One by one, the workers left the area, hopping into transportation pods and taking off. Soon the lot was completely empty—only the attendant bots remained, moving between the piles of refuse.

Kal checked his implant again. It was 1700. He knew he had to commit to some course of action, either walk away or try to make himself known. He pulled himself out of the bushes and ambled across the lot, toward the processing plant, trying to appear as if he had business inside. He felt the prickle of eyes watching him, though he couldn't see anyone else in the area. When he was halfway to the building, Kal saw a light flash in the bushes to his left, something directing a sliver of sunlight at him.

He changed direction, weaving around the piles of waste, toward the source of light. As he strode through the bushes, the thin leaves brushed against his chest and face and obscured his vision. The plants rustled against his clothes, overwhelming everything else and making it impossible for Kal to hear anything but the whisk of the thin leaves against his clothes.

He stopped and looked around. Kal could see small pieces of the landscape over the tops of the bushes as they rose and sank with the wind. There was nothing there, though—perhaps he'd been mistaken. As he was about to turn around and walk back into the lot, Kal felt something press against the back of his head.

"Move and you're dead," whispered a voice into his ear. "I'm gonna step back. You turn around, you move, you do *anything* but what I tell you, and you're dead. Put your hands out so I know they're empty, and nod if you understand me."

Kal felt the pressure leave his scalp. He slowly raised his arms out from his sides and nodded his head. A moment later, he felt the almost imperceptible pinch of a hypo-syringe on his neck. The drugs worked almost instantly—Kal saw the ground rushing up to meet him and then was out.

❖

Kal's eyes didn't seem to work. He could hear a voice talking to him but couldn't understand what it was saying. There was a thumping, rhythmic and deep, that he could feel throughout his body. He continued to struggle to lift his eyelids. He could smell something, a mixture of ozone and grease, almost metallic. Finally, he opened his eyes and saw a patterned metal floor, inches from his face. A fine layer of dust covered it. Kal tried to turn his body but found it still unresponsive.

"Colonel, can you hear me?" asked the voice. It took a moment for Kal to place it—Li Wei.

"General now," Kal croaked back. He tried harder to turn his body and face his friend, but it still wouldn't respond.

"It may take a bit for the drugs to wear off," Li Wei advised him. "I'll try to move you."

Kal felt arms underneath his shoulders, pulling him up into a sitting a position. Li Wei turned Kal's upright body so his back was resting on the wall and he was facing into a small metal lined room. A thick coat of mineral dust covered everything and floated in the air, creating a miasma of sepia light that crept upward from strips between the walls and floor. Li Wei crouched in front of him, his previously short hair now stubble, his dark eyes studying Kal intently.

"General?" The eyes softened, but the rest of Li Wei's face remained a solemn mask. "Congratulations on getting promoted. What better time to rejoin the EDF, eh?" The mask broke slightly as he gave a wry smile.

"Ugh, there's no EDF anymore. The Nasi destroyed

them." Kal rested his head on the wall behind him.

"Damn." Li Wei sat back, defeated for a moment. When Kal had last seen him, the young man was recovering from addiction. Despite his ordeal, he had emerged from it with a sense of hope. That hopefulness seemed gone, destroyed by the Nasi—events had taken their toll on him. "So, what is there? What are you a general in?"

"Samsara Fleet—we're all that remains. Just a few ships and a bunch of pissed-off soldiers. Ekon's with us." Li Wei's smile widened when Kal mentioned his friend. "We're not much, but we destroyed one of their ships at least. We're not giving up."

"Really?" Li Wei's asked. "Maybe all of this will be worth it then."

"It is," Kal replied, wincing as he felt sensation returning in his legs, needles digging into his skin.

Li Wei noticed the grimace on Kal's face. "Sorry," he apologized, "all visitors go through the same process. We disabled your neural implant as well."

Kal touched the side of his head and felt a small disc embedded in the skin. Implant disruptors were able to interfere with the interface between the implant and a person's brain. Out of habit, Kal tried to pull up his interface with no success. For a moment, he felt alone. His implant was as much a part of him as his legs or eyes.

Finally, he dropped his hand down and reluctantly nodded—he understood the need for safety. "So, where are we?"

"I'll help you up. You have to meet Chief," the rebel

responded. He grabbed Kal's arm and pulled it over his shoulder, using it to lift Kal to his feet. Kal felt his legs buckle, but Li Wei was solid, and didn't stagger from Kal's unsteady weight. "Also, there's someone else here that you'll probably want to see."

With Li Wei supporting Kal, they walked to the large riveted door. "Open," Li Wei shouted.

The door opened with a piercing creak, and they stepped through into a large rectangular chamber, at least fifty by one hundred meters. It had the same decrepit industrial feel and fine coating of dust as the room they had left. Lights dangled from the ceiling, clearly added on by the current inhabitants, using string, wire, and whatever other materials were available. They had organized the room by pushing tables together and adding makeshift partitions. The chaotic energy reminded Kal of the operations center of a station.

Li Wei slowly escorted him through the room, weaving around the tables and groups of people. Everyone was immersed in their work, not bothering to look at them as they walked past. Kal tried to see at what they were working on, but wasn't able to get an unobstructed view of any of the screens.

Three chairs sat in a triangle at the far end of the room. In one of them sat a young woman, maybe in her early thirties, with both sides of her head shaved and long brown hair cascading from the middle. Her unnaturally blue eyes seemed to shine in the dark light of the room as she stared at Kal intently, the side of her mouth turned up slightly.

Li Wei gently sat Kal down on one of the chairs, then sat in the remaining one. "General," he said, "meet Rafaela Pham, chief of the Tiradentes Liberation Front."

Chapter Six

Nicole sat with her back against the wall, bored out of her mind. No one had said a word since Kal and Kondari had left, and she didn't dare use her neural implant to check the local net, in case they could use it to pinpoint her location.

"This must be rough for you." Private Pudari turned to look at Nicole. "You know, being used to the good life in an embassy and all."

"Actually, this is pretty familiar to me—I grew up in a commune on Earth," Nicole replied. "I've been through much worse than this."

Pudari was quiet for a moment, processing Nicole's response, before responding. "I'm from Earth too. I lost everything. The Ukh—the Nasi never gave 'em a chance. They'd been planning it for a while, using traitors to help them."

Nicole said nothing. Pudari seemed like a different person. When Nicole had seen her on the *Oruc*, she had been the picture of pleasant professionalism. Now, she had removed her mask, her normally pleasant expression replaced with a hostile stare. Nicole returned the look evenly—she hated herself so much that she no longer cared what others thought of her. She was focused on the things that could go wrong for Kal and Private Kondari.

"I've heard some stories about you," Pudari continued. "Heard you helped out the Nasi before this all started. Bet you feel real *stupid* now."

Nicole kept her mouth shut. There wasn't anything she

could say. Pudari's eyes remained on her, waiting for a response, but Nicole knew there was nothing to say, no defense that would be acceptable. Over time, Pudari would realize that it wasn't Nicole who was responsible for what had happened to her family.

"They're coming into the communes." The whisper from Sergeant Jones cut through Nicole's thoughts. She quickly crawled next to him.

"Where from, what sides?" she whispered back.

"Can't tell," he replied. He sat still, listening to the communication intercept through his neural implant. "The patrollers are grumbling over the net, complaining about having to be in here. Typical grunts. We just need to stay quiet and they'll leave."

Nicole wished she could share his confidence. She knew that communes like this one were mazes. Finding anything or anyone was impossible, but she also knew it could happen. She remembered sitting in their family's room as a child and having the local police burst in, guns pointed at them. It happened at least once a year. They'd throw a few things around for appearances and then leave as quickly as they had entered, trying to make a show of force to let the locals know that their rights were nonexistent. The brutes always claimed they were looking for someone or something, but they had never really cared; they just needed to pretend like they were looking.

Nicole felt Humanity wasn't much different between planets, and these Domespat patrollers would go through, make a few arrests so things looked good, and then move on, just like on Earth. Like Jones had said, there was nothing to do but wait.

She stayed close to the sergeant, not wanting to rejoin Pudari and her overt hostility. She wished that they had more communication intercepts, but there hadn't been time to fabricate them before they headed for New America. The large bulk fabricators could build simple things, but for delicate electronics, it took much longer. The experimental intercepts had to be built by hand, which was very slow.

Nicole thought about Kal and Kondari, wondering if they had contacted the rebels. Hopefully Kal was paying attention to the Nasi net; it would be disastrous if he ran into the Domespat on the way back. Her mind turned to Pudari. She clearly knew about Nicole's past and resented her for it. The private occasionally shot looks toward Nicole when the rest weren't looking. Nicole wondered what had made her decide to make her hostility known after keeping it quiet on the ship.

"Dammit," Jones swore. Nicole's jerked her head up—she must have drifted off for a moment.

"What?" she asked in a whisper.

"Sounds like they just saw Private Kondari coming back in. He's pretty hard to miss."

"Is Kal with him?" she whispered back.

"No, doesn't sound like the general is with him. They didn't mention anyone else at least."

"Did they take him in to custody?" It felt like her worries of a moment ago were coming true.

"Not yet, but they're tracking him," Jones responded, showing annoyance at Nicole's barrage of questions. He kicked Ekon's feet and motioned to Sakata and Pudari.

"Get up," he hissed. "The Domespat are tracking Kondari on his way back in. We may have to get out of here quick."

Ekon jumped up and unfastened the latches on the ceiling air vent, then dropped into a kneeling position, weapon trained on the door. Pudari and Sakata were already in position, their pistols at the ready.

Nicole felt the adrenaline pulsing through her veins as they waited for an update from the squad leader. She kept eying the door, expecting Kondari to burst through at any moment. The whine of a kinetic weapon followed by the wailing of plasma fire caused Nicole to jump. With the twists and turns of the commune, it was impossible to say exactly where the sound had come from, but she could tell it was close.

"Kondari's down," Jones swore. "We have to get out, now. Kimathi, get up in the vent. Sakata and Bergeron, you're next, then Pudari. I'll be last, to cover our exit."

Ekon was in the vent before Jones had finished his instructions. He pulled Private Sakata up and then extended a hand for Nicole. Nicole grabbed the outstretched arm and Ekon pulled her into the vent with ease. She pulled out her handgun, hoping she wouldn't have to use it, and trained it down the shaft, waiting for Jones and Pudari to join them.

"Okay, Pudari will take lead," Jones said, his voice barely audible. "Keep quiet and let's get the hell out of here."

"What about Kondari?" Pudari asked. "We can't just leave him."

"We can't get him now—we don't know where he is or if

he's even alive," Jones responded. "Let's get out of here, then we'll regroup and figure out our next move."

Pudari said nothing, but knocked Nicole into the side of the vent as she crawled past and away.

❖

The vent made a soft creaking sound as the group quietly padded down its length. Nicole had given up on holding on to her kinetic pistol while crawling and had re-holstered it, hoping she would have the time to take it out if needed.

Ahead of her, Pudari's slim figure continued to advance methodically, occasionally pausing at a fork or intersection as she oriented herself. To Nicole's surprise, the soldier seemed to know where she was going. Even for her, someone who grew up in a commune, the vents were impossible to navigate.

Nicole heard a sharp grunt come from the room beneath them. "Trahl, you see anything?" The women's thin, nasally voice was so loud in her ear, it could have come from within the vent.

Everyone stopped and froze in place. Nicole strained to hear the response of whoever the Domespat patroller was questioning, but wasn't able to make out a sound.

She heard the dull thump of someone being kicked, followed by another grunt. "Talk, now," the woman's voice rang out. "Last chance."

Nicole could picture what was going on beneath them. A citizen lying on the ground—dirty, malnourished, confused by the questions of the patroller standing above them. The person tried to sit up, to take a moment and understand what was being asked of them, but the questions were confusing and seemed to come too fast for them to respond. Nicole knew what would happen next. She felt her muscles tightening as she waited for the report of the kinetic round and the sound of it tearing through the innocent civilian, followed by the thump of their body hitting the floor.

Instead, she heard a raspy, quiet, almost indistinct voice. "Over there."

There wasn't a response. Instead, the group heard a final grunt and then footsteps, three or four Domespat moving further through the commune. Once the footsteps had died down, the group started moving again, traveling farther down the vent.

As she rounded a corner, Nicole saw a glimmer of light in the tunnel in front of them. Pudari stopped, and Sergeant Jones noiselessly slid between Nicole and Pudari to see what was going on. After a quick back and forth, Jones turned back to her.

"Get your weapon ready," he instructed.

Obediently, she pulled her weapon out of its concealed holster. She checked her ammunition and silently went through the instructions that Jones had given her during their training sessions on the *Oruc*. Nicole continued crawling, bracing herself with one hand while holding her pistol in front of her with the other. The light continued to grow as they moved down the vent. She realized that whatever it was, it wasn't daylight—it was yellow and dim.

Abruptly, the floor gave out from under her with a shriek of metal tearing itself apart. The collapsing vent pitched her forward, into Jones, who had braced himself against its sides with his arms and legs. Her momentum knocked him loose and caused them both to collide with Pudari. The trio slid down the vent and slammed onto the dirt-covered floor of the commune. Nicole rolled on the ground, trying to breathe— the fall had knocked the air from her lungs. She heard a melee above her, the sound of metal hitting flesh, fighting, yelling. Jones's head dropped on the ground in front of her, making a small, sickening bounce before his eyes rolled up in the back of his head. She had recovered enough to look around and saw that Pudari was also down, a blood stain blossoming on her right arm. Around them were three Domespat patrollers, weapons drawn. On the ground was a fourth, clutching his abdomen where blood was trickling out.

"Stand up," said one of them, a female officer. She was dark-skinned, maybe in her twenties, with a puckered scar on her cheek. She reminded Nicole of a younger, less friendly version of Chief Kanumba.

Nicole staggered to her feet, still feeling the effect of the impact. Raising her arms, she looked down to check on Jones and Pudari. She wasn't a doctor. Their injuries looked bad, but not fatal. Two of the soldiers patted her down, taking everything out of her pockets. One of them, a kid, maybe eighteen years old, spent a little too long checking for contraband in her groin. She could hear his heavy breathing in her ear. She shot her elbow back into where she thought his face was and was gratified to hear a muffled yell and feel something give.

"Serves you right, Ferdinand," said the officer with a cruel smile.

"I'll see you later, bitch," whispered the patroller into Nicole's ear.

"Well miss, you and your friends are coming with us," the woman smiled.

❖

It took a half hour for the Domespat patrollers to find their way out of the commune. They pushed Nicole stumbling in front of them, her arms restrained behind her, as they ran into one dead end after another. Pudari, who hunched over from her wound, and Jones, who could only walk a few meters before having to retch, hampered their progress.

Nicole staggered out of the dark corridors and onto a street. The overcast sky looked iridescent compared to the darkness of the commune, despite the sun settling on the horizon. A Domespat transport, flanked by two patrollers, was waiting for them on the street. The patrollers threw Nicole and the two soldiers into the back of the vehicle unceremoniously. Nicole winced when Jones's head ricocheted off a bench as they pushed him in. As soon as the three prisoners were inside, the door closed behind them and the windows went opaque, preventing Nicole from seeing anything outside the vehicle.

"You okay?" she asked, turning to Pudari and Jones.

Jones didn't respond, his face screwed up in a grimace of

pain. "Fine," Pudari grunted, not bothering to look up. Her wound continued to bleed, but there was little she or Nicole could do to staunch the flow with their hands restrained behind their backs.

"Do you think that—" Nicole asked.

Jones coughed loudly, interrupting her. "Shut up. It's bugged," he said between gritted teeth.

Nicole realized he was right. The vehicle almost certainly had microphones listening in on their conversations. She closed her mouth abruptly and tried to maneuver herself from the floor onto a bench.

After several minutes, the vehicle rose and then sped forward. They'd only been traveling for about five minutes when she felt it descending—they had arrived.

The door opened with a hiss, and two patrollers picked Pudari and Jones off the floor. Nicole winced as the two soldiers were pulled up by their arms and dragged out of the transport backward. Pudari gave an involuntary gasp as they hauled her out of the vehicle, her legs trailing behind her. Jones started swearing almost incoherently as the guards shoved him out of the vehicle headfirst onto the ground.

The officer who had found them grabbed Nicole by the shoulder, her grip painfully tight. Stumbling out of the transport, she found herself in a small, well-lit garage. Several Domespat transports, identical to the ones she had been in, stood in neat rows. A pair of patrollers shoved Jones and Pudari in front of them, following an illuminated strip along the floor toward a large double utility door in the back of the room. There were a handful of other people not in uniform, walking around the bay repairing and maintaining the vehicles, oblivious to patrollers who had just arrived.

"Come on, sweetie," said the woman holding onto Nicole with a sneer. "Let's get you comfortable."

The Domespat officer shoved Nicole through the large bay door into what must have been a converted police station. She could see a faint line where they had replaced the Tiradentes Police crest with their own. The Domestic State Patrol crest was a shield with an open eye in the center, a wreath of laurels surrounded the shield, and the initials DSP directly beneath the wreath. It gave her the intimidating feeling of being watched—probably the designer's intention.

The station was humming with activity. Domespat officers and patrollers roamed the hallways, laughing and joking with one another. If they caught Nicole looking at them, they returned her gaze with a glare—one patroller even spat in her face. Nicole was hauled through several guarded security gates and into the prison area, a hallway with doors on either end.

The woman shoved Nicole into one of the cells, the door hissing shut behind her. The room was a brilliant white color, about five meters on a side. A small toilet sat in one corner and a bed, without sheets, was attached to the wall on the other. Nicole turned around to look back at the door.

The entire side of the door was a viewscreen, allowing Nicole to see the hallway on the other side. "I'll be back," the woman told Nicole. "Think about where your loyalties lie, and be ready to tell the truth."

The image on the viewscreen cut out, leaving only the

same featureless white as the walls. Nicole sat down on the bed and stretched her shoulders and arms to relieve the creeping stiffness and soreness from the restraints. The movement seemed to aggravate the pain she already was feeling, so she stopped.

She tried to fight against the despair that she had been holding in check since their capture. To come as far as she had only to find herself in prison, again, was almost too much to bear. After the EDF had treated the wounds she had sustained from her assassination attempt, they had placed her inside one of their prisons. Left to rot—or so she thought—because of her unforgivable crimes. If Kal hadn't realized that she could still be of use against the Nasi, she would have died in that prison cell on Caracas Station. She had worked so hard to atone for what she had done, to regain others' trust. Now she was once again in a prison, with her jailors spitting on her.

She wondered what had happened to Kal. Hopefully he had contacted the resistance and would bring whatever intel he learned back to Samsara Fleet. She could live with her capture and eventual torture if she also knew it had been for something. In the corner of her mind, there was the thought of rescue. Kal, Ekon, and Sakata were still out there—they might try to rescue them. Nicole wondered if she would be worth it.

It was jarring to sit in this station, captured by the very Humans who had been allies only a few months ago. She remembered a conversation that she and Kal had had with a Qudoru named Yitari. The slug-like creature had asked if there were any recent sins in Humanity's history. Kal had said there were none, and she hadn't corrected him. But she knew that there were many, and they still occurred. Sins like how they allowed their poor and sick to suffer in the communes. Or how they allowed Earth, a planet that most colonists never saw, to exploit its colonies. The Qudoru believed that bad things happened to individuals and civilizations because of sins they had committed.

Nicole was skeptical. She had never met a person or civilization without sin—it was an aspect of living. *Perhaps that's the point,* she thought to herself. *It's their way of rationalizing why bad things always happen.*

Many of the patrollers in the Domespat had probably been normal citizens until the Nasi had taken over the planet. After only a few months, they had transformed. The Nasi had exploited the greed and lust for power that was inherent in Humans. It made her wonder what would happen if they were to free New America from the Nasi. Now that the UEG was gone, what was stopping Choi or some other politician from creating a Human-controlled fascist state?

She felt the exhaustion of the past day overtaking her thoughts. The pain in her shoulders remained, but seemed to dull as she felt her eyes closing. Her body slid down the wall and slumped onto the bed as unconsciousness overtook her.

Chapter Seven

Rafaela Pham smiled thinly and stuck out her hand. "Pleased to meet you, general." The strength of her grip surprised Kal. "Don't listen to Li Wei," she continued, "I'm not the chief of the TLF, just this cell. We're all dedicated to sending the Nasi back to whatever hell they came from."

"Glad to hear it," Kal replied. "We're going to need every person we can get."

"Ain't that the truth," muttered Li Wei darkly.

"When I heard from Li Wei that you'd contacted his mother, I talked to the other cell leaders. You're our first chance to talk with someone from off planet. We've gone through hell, and one of the worst parts is not knowing what is happening in the rest of the galaxy. I imagine that you have a lot of questions. But I'm going to need for you to fill me in first. We've been operating blind since the Nasi came and need to know what resources we can get from the UEG and EDF."

Kal hated to be the one to tell them, to tell them that the EDF no longer existed, that the war had been over almost before it began—but they needed to know.

"The EDF and UEG don't exist anymore," Kal replied grimly. Rafaela froze, and her eyes widened in shock. "The Nasi destroyed them and captured all of our colonies."

"It's all over," Rafaela muttered.

Kal held up his hands in a placating gesture. "It's not all over yet. The Nasi destroyed the EDF, but they didn't get every ship and soldier. There were many of us that escaped or were in transit when they attacked. We've built a new force, Samsara Fleet, to continue the fight. Our fleet already destroyed one of their battleships and almost got another. We've been learning, adapting, and figuring out how to beat them."

"So, what have you learned? How do we defeat them?" asked Li Wei. "Every time we run a mission we lose more people—" He halted.

Rafaela stiffened. Li Wei probably hadn't intended it, but his comments were a direct criticism of her as their leader. "Maybe it'd be best if you started at the beginning," she said. "Li Wei already told me about your escape from Kirkira Station, but I need to know what happened after. What the rest of the galaxy is like now."

Kal spent the next hour detailing all the events that had occurred since he had last seen Li Wei. Li Wei or Rafaela often would interrupt to ask a question. Many of them were ones that Kal couldn't answer. How many Nasi were there? What was their goal? How many systems had they taken? Where were they from? It was maddening for him to admit the amount of ignorance they still had.

After Kal finished by describing the reason for their mission on New America, he stopped and leaned back in his chair. The two rebels looked defeated—the promise of his presence replaced with the cold reality of exactly how much Humanity had lost.

"So how haven't we lost again?" Li Wie asked.

"Because we're still here, we're still fighting. We can't lose if we're still able to fight them," Kal replied.

Rafaela nodded. "Speaking of fighting," she said, "do you have any of the devices you built from the Nasi salvage? If we had those, perhaps we would stand a chance against the Nasi and Domespat."

"I can share the schematics," replied Kal. He had copies of the plans to both devices on his neural implant. "I need to have my implant reactivated though."

"Of course, of course." Rafaela whistled and motioned to a man watching them who walked over. "Liu, reactive the general's implant."

Liu grabbed a small handheld device from a table. The boxy device barely fit in his hand and had small wires crisscrossing the outside of its housing. Liu pressed it against the side of Kal's head. He felt a strange, tingling heat, then heard something clatter against the floor. The fighter picked up a small metal disc that he had dislodged from Kal's scalp. Seeing Kal's curious gaze, he held it out for him to inspect. "Small EMP disc, creates a field around the implant and disables it without harming anything else. Had to make this one myself since they're a prohibited item." The man looked down at the disc with pride.

Kal's implant went through its initial boot-up sequence, projecting small dots on his vision and small tones in his ears to calibrate itself. Finally, it was fully functioning again, and Kal was able to connect it to the communication intercept in his pocket.

We have one officer down! someone screamed across the channel. *Hit with a kinetic pistol. Assailant was a big guy, maybe two meters tall with brown hair and light skin.*

I see 'em. The responding voice was female. *Takin' a shot . . . target is down.*

Confirmed. Target's dead.

Kondari, Kal thought to himself.

"What's going on?" Rafaela saw the dark look on his face.

"I'm listening to the Domespat net now," Kal said. "One of my soldiers was just shot by a patroller. Sounds like they killed him."

"Shit," Li Wei said, running his hands through his hair. "Where are they?"

"Not sure," replied Kal. "The soldier they shot was the private who was supposed to come with me. After I had the run-in with the Domespat checkpoint, I'm guessing he headed back to the commune."

Kal continued to listen, his head down so he could focus on the chatter over the net. Kondari had returned to the commune after they split up at the checkpoint. Somehow, he had come across a Domespat patrol and fired on them. Kal shook his head—if the kids had just run away, he probably would still be alive. Now the patrollers had doubled their search party, intent on rooting out any other "terrorists".

"They're in the commune. Is there anything we can do to help them?" he asked Rafaela.

"No, nothing," she replied flatly. "I can't send my people in there with Domespat crawling through the place. Your friends will need to get out on their own. After that, we can figure out a way to find them and help them."

Kal continued to listen to the Domespat chatter on the net. Many of the calls were from patrollers getting turned around and lost in the corridors. It would have been funny if almost everyone he cared about wasn't in danger. In his mind, he could picture the Samsara Fleet soldiers hiding out in the tiny room, listening to their intercept and wondering if they were going to be caught.

DSP Base, this is Echo team—we have apprehended three terrorists trying to escape. They put up a fight, we have one patroller down. Two of the terrorists were injured. We're bringing 'em in.

Kal cursed under his breath.

"What—" Li Wei stopped talking as Kal made a motion to be quiet, the Domespat were still talking.

DSP Echo, do any of the prisoners match the description of the person of interest?

Negative, came the reply.

Okay, bring the prisoners to Mosaic Station. DSP Bravo, continue your search for the POI.

Kal monitored the net for several more minutes, waiting to hear if they captured the other two members of Samsara Fleet. From the descriptions of the prisoners, it sounded like they had Nicole, Jones, and Pudari—which meant Ekon and Sakata were still out there.

"You have someone who can listen to their net?" Kal asked Rafaela. "I can't talk to you and listen at the same time."

She nodded and motioned for Liu to come back over. "Liu, the general's got a device called a communication intercept. It breaks through encryption so we can hear enemy transmissions." Liu beamed. "Until we find someone else, your job is to listen in and record everything that they are saying over the net. If there's something that is time sensitive, let me know immediately."

Liu grabbed the device from Kal and then listened impatiently as Kal explained how to connect it to a neural implant. While they were talking, Kal also transferred the schematics via implant. As Kal spoke, the rebel studied the device, rotating it in his hand like a child with a new toy.

"I'll need that back," Kal said as Liu took the device back to the table where he had been working.

"General, now that I have the design specs, this one is already obsolete," Liu responded confidently.

"So, three of my soldiers are now being held at the Mosaic Domespat Station." Kal sat back down and turned to Rafaela and Li Wei. "How do we get them out?"

The two looked at each other, apprehension behind their eyes. "We've never done that before," Li Wei responded. "Always considered it too risky."

"Doesn't matter anyway," Rafaela said. "They won't hold 'em there long. They're going to figure out pretty quickly that your friends are from off-world. When that happens, I guarantee they'll move them into the Nest."

"The Nest?" Kal asked.

"It's what we call the compound that the Nasi are building within Tiradentes," Li Wei explained. "A nest of vermin. To Chief's point, the Nasi stay pretty hands off, just killing anyone that gets their notice. But anything that may relate to the larger war effort, anything that is interplanetary, they'll want to be personally involved."

Rafaela bit her lip. "We can't breach the Nest. Their security is too much. Even with the intercept and the cloak, we wouldn't stand a chance."

Rafaela brought up a holo outlining what they knew of the Nest. The complex was still under construction, but the Nasi were already inhabiting the main tower, and their jail cell was somewhere near the top of the building. The good news was that the perimeter security was not fully complete; the bad news was that the Nasi had air support and rings of security to prevent anyone from even getting near the tower.

"Don't you have operatives?" Kal asked. "People that can help with this kind of thing."

Rafaela's eyes flashed. "I don't think you understand what we have here. We're in an abandoned industrial facility outside of the city with a handful of people. We don't have enough weapons to go around—the Domespat lock up any citizen they find with one. It's not so simple to mount a sudden assault on the most secure facility in the city."

"It's worth the risk," Kal responded. He couldn't believe that Rafaela and Li Wei were so quick to give up. "We've already lost everything. What more can they take?"

"They'll take our families," Li Wei answered softly, a tear streaking down his face. Kal realized why the young man had been so distant. His mother.

Kal closed his mouth. He didn't know what to say as Li Wei stood up and walked away.

"Like I said," Rafaela continued, "it's not as simple as you're making it. We can help you and provide information on the Nest and about the Nasi, but we're not ready to singlehandedly storm their base. My guess is they'll take them to the tower. We've got no way to get in the facility, much less climb hundreds of meters."

She rested her arms on her knees. "We want to help your soldiers, but not at the cost of the liberation front or your mission. This would be suicide. If we want to win, we need to use our heads, not our hearts. We need you to get back to your fleet and let them know of our situation. We'll need any help Samsara Fleet can give us—weapons, intelligence, anything. The Nasi are ruthless, and if we move too soon, the TLF will be over before it even starts."

Kal knew she was right. They had reached a rebel cell on New America, and he shouldn't jeopardize that for the chance of getting back his people—the stakes were too high. But he knew there had to be a way to even the odds, to give them a chance. Right now though, he was only one person and the rest of his team was split into three groups scattered across Tiradentes—he stopped himself. *Four* groups. The crew of the *Oruc* was still hiding in the agricultural zone outside of the city.

"Chief, you're right," he admitted, "but we still have our ship to even the fight. Never using your heart, that's how machines think. Hell, that's how the Nasi fight. I'm never going to abandon my soldiers. With the *Oruc*, we can break in there and get them out—a classic smash and grab. I only need a few volunteers from your group."

"I'm listening," she replied skeptically.

Kal outlined his plan, reminding her they still had the ship along with seven battle suits hidden in the culvert outside

Tiradentes. Kal, along with six resistance fighters, would travel back to the *Oruc* in the battle suits. They would blast a hole in the building's side, near where they thought the jail cells were, and conduct an aerial insertion into the Nest using the firepower of the ship for cover. Once inside, they simply needed to grab the soldiers and get out. Kal knew that the Nasi did not have tactical fighters for support, which meant that the *Oruc* wouldn't face heavy resistance if it stayed close to the ground on its way toward the Nest. Even if the mission was a success, they wouldn't be able to stay on the planet any longer, but it would be worth it. While Kal was talking, Liu and several other TLF rebels had walked over to listen, waved over by their chief.

"I don't like it," Rafaela said when Kal had finished. "It's a risk." She bit her lip again. "But it's a calculated one, at least." Chief looked around at the ring of fighters surrounding them. Kal could feel their energy, their desire to take it to the Nasi. Finally, Rafaela sighed. "Screw it. I'm sure you'll find the volunteers you need, and we can also fly you back to where the battle suits are. We have some informants among the Humans who work at the Nest, and I can give you all the information we have. It should be enough to help you locate the general area where your soldiers are being held."

"Chief, one thing. If we can distract their security, it'll take some heat off them," said a rebel.

Kal looked around the room. It reminded him of his time on Kapustin Station—these fighters were eager to make a difference, to fight the Nasi. They were tired of running and hiding; they wanted to act. He looked at the fighter who has just spoken, and a familiar face stared back at him. Her blue eyes looked tired, but the optimism that he had first seen months ago was still there. Her long brown hair, which she had kept in a bun, was now shoulder length, framing her angular face. Sandra Chedjou saw him looking at her and gave a small curtsy, smiling as she did.

"Good point, Chedjou," said Rafaela. "Get a squad of people together. I think there may be some looting in the Mosaic District tonight." She winked.

"Will do, Chief," responded Sandra, "but I'd like to go with the general for the mission. We have history together."

Rafaela raised her eyebrows and nodded her head in assent.

"How long until they move the prisoners to the Nest?" Kal asked.

Rafaela shrugged. "Hard to say. Probably an hour or two, based on what we know of the Domespat. Not long enough to mount an offensive on Mosaic Station. Frankly, once they get to the Nest, I don't know how long until they'll be tortured and killed, so we have to move."

Kal thought of everything they would have to do in order to make his plan work. He just hoped that they'd have the time.

❖

"Li Wei . . ." Kal began. He stopped, searching for the words. "I'm sorry."

The rebel shrugged and kept his eyes locked ahead,

scanning for Domespat patrols, as they sped over an access road, the transport flying three meters off the ground. The TLF base was in an abandoned factory in the industrial zone outside of Tiradentes. In order to reach the battle suits, they had to circle around the city's perimeter. Kal and Li Wei sat in the front, with the other TLF fighters on the back benches of the vehicle.

"Your mother must have been a brave woman," Kal continued. "It must not have been easy for you these past months, knowing she was vulnerable like that."

"She knew what she was doing," Li Wei responded, refusing to look at Kal.

"True. But it still doesn't help ease the pain." Kal looked out the side of the transport. The sun had set, covering the landscape in inky black darkness. On one side of the vehicle, small lights dotted the horizon, evidence of the large factories that made up the industrial zone. The facilities they passed were likely automated, relying on bots to bring the raw materials, run the production, and ship it out when complete. There wasn't any sign of people or activity; the only movement was the occasional light of a cargo drone moving materials to or from a factory. The buildings themselves were flat and featureless, usually surrounded by large yards containing the materials and end product, waiting to either be processed or sent away.

"How's your life been since the Nasi came?" Kal asked, changing the subject.

"Well, honestly, I didn't know what to expect," Li Wei replied, seeming grateful for the change of subject. "At first, I was just happy to be alive. The Nasi only seem to want our resources for their new base. It's Choi and her Domespat that have made life miserable."

"So you decided that you had to do something about it," Kal concluded.

"Damn right," Li Wei agreed. "I watched as her thugs rounded up anyone they thought might be a threat and made them disappear. They took bribes and looked the other way when it suited them, or just took what they wanted. Only a few weeks after the NAE took control, everything had changed. People grew callous and mean."

Kal kept silent, waiting for Li Wei to continue.

"One day, I was walking home. A kid didn't get out of the way of a patroller, so they got sent to the hospital, with a broken rib. I couldn't believe it—these Nasi had taken over our planet and here we were beating each other. When I got home, I told my mother I wanted to join the resistance. She didn't argue with me, all she asked was how could she help." He wiped his face against his shoulder. "I told her she couldn't, it would be too dangerous. But she wouldn't leave it. I gave her the location of the rendezvous point and told her that if any of my friends ever came looking for me to give them the coordinates and contact me."

Li Wei pulled in a shuddering breath. "I knew it was a risk, but I didn't think of the cost. I should have known"—he slammed his fist on the transport's viewscreen—"but I didn't want to think about it."

Kal gave him a moment before replying. "Sounds like she wanted to fight back as well, in whatever way she could."

"She hated them as much as I do, maybe more." Li Wei smiled.

"We're going to make her sacrifice worth it," Kal vowed.

"Yes, we will," Li Wei vowed. "I can't wait to see every single Domespat gutted and hanging by their neck around Tiradentes."

The image caused Kal to pause—he wondered if Li Wei recognized the way the war was changing him. He let the conversation die and turned to look out the window of the vehicle. Hatred could be corrosive, and he believed that Li Wei was not a vindictive man at heart.

The industrial zone had given way to the agricultural, and lights now illuminated the path they were skimming. It made Kal feel like he was traveling through a tunnel or through space at an impossibly high speed. Overhead, the moons of New America—Santiago and Quito—shined. Together, the moons and the lights overshadowed the stars in the sky, making them almost impossible to pick out unless Kal pressed his face against the transport's window.

Li Wei pulled into a small clearing by the side of the road and gently set the vehicle down on its landing skids. Wordlessly, Kal and Li Wei stepped out of the vehicle and walked to the back, where Sandra and six other TLF rebels were already climbing out. They formed a loose semicircle near the vehicle.

"Remember, no communication if you can help it," Kal reminded the group. "I'll be in the lead."

They all nodded their heads, shuffling slightly on their feet. He could tell that despite their prior EDF experience, this was the first mission for some of them. The excitement of a new operation had given way to the realization that not everyone may return.

"Li Wei"—Kal turned to look at his friend—"thank you for your help. I don't know when we'll see each other again."

"I'm sure we'll see each other again, General." Li Wei smiled. "Just get out of here and bring us the help we need to free New America." He gave Kal a friendly pat and got back in the transport. The vehicle silently lifted off and sped down the road toward Tiradentes.

"Let's go," Kal instructed the group.

They crept single file through the sparse brush. The moons gave off enough light that they didn't need to use their headlamps. After crawling down a ravine and into the irrigation ditch, Kal led them to the culvert where they had stored their battle suits. He walked several meters into the tunnel and switched on his headlamp, the light casting a blue halo in front of him.

Kal approached the battle suits and realized that someone had taken two of them—there were only five remaining. Activating his implant, he confirmed that the two missing suits belonged to Ekon and Private Sakata. Kal smiled. They had made it out of the commune—finally, some good news. They must have headed back to the *Oruc* to get help to rescue their comrades. He needed to get back to the ship before they left.

Two of the TLF fighters agreed to follow the tunnels back into Tiradentes on foot. With two suits gone, they wouldn't be able to travel to the *Oruc*. Kal and the remaining insurgents stepped into the gray suits, the backs stitching themselves up and sealing them in. He gestured to the fighters to confirm they were ready, then loped back the way they had come, with the four rebels spaced behind him at regular intervals. He had to reach the *Oruc* before it left without him.

Their trip back to the ship was uneventful. As they cruised over the fields, the suit's night vision, combined with the two moons overhead, made it appear as if it was midday. Kal prayed to himself that they would arrive before the ship left— if they weren't able to make contact before the *Oruc* departed, he wasn't sure what his next course of action would be.

As they got closer, Kal caught himself looking at the sky periodically, half expecting to see the ship fly past them. When they finally got to the location, he felt a warm sense of relief as he stepped through the illusion created by the holographic projectors and found the *Oruc* in the same spot, engines spinning up.

Ekon and Major Garcia ran down the cargo ramp of the ship as Kal took off his helmet.

"Sir, am I glad to see you." The relief was clear on Ekon's face. His smile vanished as he saw the rebels behind Kal, who were taking off their helmets.

"Major Garcia, Sergeant Kimathi, meet the fighters of the Tiradentes Liberation Front," Kal announced with a halfhearted wave of his hand.

Garcia grinned and walked toward the rebels, slapping the backs of their battle suits and greeting each of them. Ekon remained where he was and studied each of their faces, looking for Li Wei, then gave a start when he saw Sandra. The two of them rushed toward each other and embraced, Ekon's arms not fully closing around Sandra's suit.

As the rest of the team entered the *Oruc*, Ekon and Sandra stayed where they were, talking quietly to each other. Kal walked up the ramp, letting the two friends have a moment with each other—he knew that they may not get another chance.

After stowing their suits in the cargo bay, the team made their way to the *Oruc's* galley. Ekon recounted what had happened in the commune after Kal had left. After the others had been captured, Ekon and Private Sakata had made their way back to the suits using the irrigation tunnels and then returned to the *Oruc*, hoping that they would figure out a plan to locate and free the prisoners once they got to the ship.

After Ekon had finished speaking, Kal described his abduction to the TLF base and meeting with their leader, and outlined their plan to recover the rest of their team inside the Nest. The uncertainty and immaturity that Kal had seen in the young sergeant at his house was gone. He listened to the plan with rapt attention and made several suggestions. The difference between the Ekon of several hours ago and this one was like night and day, his Tac-I training having taken over. He was grateful that they had regained contact with Ekon and Sakata, if for no other reason than their fighting prowess. The TLF fighters had motivation but could not match the expertise of the two battle-hardened Tac-I soldiers.

Kal projected the TLF's diagram of the Nest onto the galley's viewscreen. The three-dimensional wireframe outlined the entire base's structure and highlighted key areas and defensive positions. Unfortunately, much of the base was unknown—maddingly blank on the diagram. The entire compound was about fifty square kilometers in area with an enormous wall surrounding its perimeter. A large tower, rising about six hundred meters, dominated the center of the compound. Three more towers and an enormous circular building, all still under construction, were immediately adjacent. Concentric rings of buildings in various stages of construction circled out from the center, becoming progressively shorter the farther out they were. The TLF believed the prison was near the top of the central tower, though its exact location was unknown. An area hatched with lines showed the jail's estimated location.

Kal finished his brief and then turned from the viewscreen to face the room. "We're short on time. Based on what the TLF have told us, the Nasi have almost certainly already moved our people to the Nest. Our plan is simple—we leave here and fly directly there. We'll split into two teams and conduct breached entries at the top and bottom of the suspected prison area." As Kal talked, he used his implant to highlight key areas on the diagram. "The *Oruc* will stay airborne and provide cover and supporting fire as needed. We don't know what sort of firepower the Nasi will bring to bear, so we need to get in and get out as fast as possible."

"What if they're not there?" asked one of the TLF fighters.

"If we can't find them or we confirm they're not there, we leave," Kal responded. "For this operation, we'll be using our suits' communications. The Nasi may hack into the system, but there are too many moving parts to remain radio silent." He looked across the room to make sure he had their attention. "If Sergeant Ekon, Major Garcia, or I say to get out, then stop whatever you're doing and get out."

Kal sat back down and Ekon took his place, leading the group through the plan a few more times. He quickly outlined several of the specifics: determining their search patterns, team composition, and other details that would be critical to their success. Kal wished they could take several days to get more intel and prepare for the mission, but time was a resource they just didn't have.

"Okay, we're prepared as we're gonna be," Kal concluded after Ekon had finished. "Suits should be charged and ready to go by now. I want everyone back in 'em and we're out in five."

He just hoped that they would make it to their friends in time.

Chapter Eight

Nicole couldn't be sure how long she had been in the Domespat cell. They had disabled her implant, and there was nothing in the featureless room to track the passage of time. She spent the hours sitting on the bed, leaning against the wall, reflecting on what might happen to her.

She was under no illusion that they would treat her humanely—the Nasi and the Domespat had proved they would do whatever it took to get what they needed. Nicole knew herself, and though she was good at many things and tougher than most, she was honest enough to know that she wouldn't be able to resist them for long.

She contemplated taking her own life—perhaps she could bludgeon herself on the toilet bowl or try to get herself shot by resisting. But as she thought about it, she knew she wouldn't be able to go through with it. The one thing Nicole took comfort in was that only Kal and Garcia knew the location of Samsara Fleet.

After her realization, Nicole felt a sense of calm wash over her. There was nothing she could do except wait. If she was lucky, there may be some way for her to redeem herself before dying. She promised herself that she wouldn't cower or beg, she would hold her head up high and face the Domespat or the Nasi with whatever dignity she could muster.

The door swished open, and the Domespat officer who had brought her into the cell walked through, her weapon raised.

"Come with me," the woman instructed, weapon pointed

directly at Nicole's eyes.

Nicole pulled herself off the bed, her legs screaming. Once she was standing, the woman grabbed her roughly by the shoulder, pushing her through the station into what was clearly an interrogation room. The room was sparse: a desk stood in the center with two chairs on either side, facing each other. The walls were the same featureless white material as her cell. The Domespat officer shoved Nicole in a chair and sat facing her, placing her weapon on the table.

"You're a long way from Earth or Gorash, Ms. Bergeron," the women said.

Nicole didn't speak; she tried to fix the officer with the most defiant stare she could muster. She wasn't surprised that they had identified her. Nicole was a former attaché, and she was sure all of her information was public since she was a former UEG employee.

"Let me be clear so we don't waste time with lies. I'm Lieutenant Rok, the officer in charge of the DSP Echo team. You're Nicole Bergeron, former UEG attaché to the Kurz government. We know that you're a terrorist, here to subvert the lawful New American Empire. One of my patrollers was shot and killed trying to apprehend you and your associates— Changying Pudari and Asif Jones, both EDF soldiers." Rok leaned back in her chair and looked Nicole over before continuing.

"So before you tell me some bullshit story, realize that we know who you are and we know why you're here."

Nicole remained silent.

"Since you're an enemy operative from off-world, the Nasi

will be coming shortly to question you. If you talk now, perhaps we can spare your life, maybe even let you free." Rok gave a sickly-sweet smile. "The Nasi are not so lenient."

Nicole felt the heat rise in her face. "You're a traitor! How can help the Nasi after everything they did?"

"After what, they destroyed Earth?" Rok tilted her head. "So what? I don't know anyone there. I've never been there. Earth did nothing for me or this planet. With the Nasi here, things are changing for the better. Law and order are back. People like me, people who give a damn about making sure our people are safe—"

"Safe?" Nicole was incredulous.

"Yeah, at least Choi and the Nasi actually make citizens accountable for their actions. They let people like me, people who care about security, keep the peace." Rok chuckled. "But I guess you think you can stop us?"

"I'm here to *help* New America," Nicole responded.

"We don't need your help." Rok retorted. She paused for a moment, realizing that the questioning was going off topic. "But tell me, Ms. Bergeron, how many of you are there? We've already located several more of your comrades and are bringing them in now. If you let us know where the rest are, we may not bring in their corpses."

Nicole could tell that the woman was bluffing, trying to draw Nicole out. They knew there had to be others, but Nicole refused to believe that the Domespat had found Kal and the other soldiers.

"You found us all, it's just—" A fist smashing into her face, directly beneath her eye, interrupted her words. Nicole's vision exploded in a cascade of rainbow hued light, and she felt sharp tendrils of pain creep across her head.

Rok's had a smile on her face—she was enjoying this. "You lie. But no matter, we'll find them. What about your ship? We know it's in the agricultural zone."

Again, a bluff; they had no idea where the *Oruc* was. The agricultural zone was the obvious place for someone to hide a vessel, but it was enormous and it would take weeks or months for the Domespat to find it. Despite the pain, Nicole felt heartened by the questions. Rok was grasping at straws, trying to trick her into revealing information.

"The ship left," Nicole replied.

Nicole expected the next blow and turned her face to expose her jaw rather than her eye. "Lies again. Keep this up—I'm enjoying myself. You'll tell us where the ship is, eventually." Rok interwove her fingers and cracked her knuckles directly in front of Nicole's face.

Nicole remembered her oath to herself. She wouldn't cooperate. Lieutenant Rok clearly couldn't control her temper—perhaps she could use that. "I'm surprised your Nasi masters don't already know all of this. Seems like they're not as all powerful as you think." Nicole forced herself to lean forward, pushing her face as far across the table as she could. "Wouldn't it be a shame if they can't stop the people from throwing you into this jail where you belong?"

Rok rewarded Nicole's jab by reaching over the desk and slamming her head into the Plasteel table. She felt her nose give and the warm flow of blood streaming down her face, the metallic taste in her mouth.

"Keep talking like that and there won't be much left of you for the Nasi. They defeated the EDF and overthrew the UEG in weeks. They have nothing to fear from you or the rebels."

"They're using you. Once they're done with your little empire, then what? They'll treat you no differently than the rest of us."

"You don't seem to understand. The Nasi aren't going anywhere," Rok talked as if she were speaking to an obtuse toddler. "There is no choice here except whether to help the Nasi or to hide. They've already won, and the people who are smart accept that and work with them. It's too late for you—"

The door to the room slid open and two Domespat patrollers, weapons ready, walked through. They barely glanced at Nicole's bruised and bloodied face.

"Ma'am, they're here," one reported.

"Ah, well. Guess we won't have more time to talk." Lieutenant Rok stood up from her chair and turned to the patroller. "Tell the Nasi that the prisoner was uncooperative. They may need to use enhanced interrogation techniques."

The Domespat guard fastened a gag over Nicole's mouth and led her through the station to the same bay she had arrived in earlier. The sun had set, and the lights of Tiradentes spread out beneath them like a blanket, ending abruptly where the agricultural and industrial zones began.

The guard shoved Nicole into the back of a transport,

closing the door before she had hit the floor. Jones and Pudari already sat on the back bench, gags over their mouths as well. They both looked exhausted, and the wounds they had sustained earlier were still untreated, their bodies covered by a crust of dried blood. Nicole nodded to them, trying to instill her happiness at seeing them into the simple gesture. They both nodded back, and Jones even gave a small wink.

The trip from the Domespat station only lasted a few minutes, but Nicole completely lost any sense of where they were—the tinted windows preventing her from seeing anything outside of the vehicle. She could tell that the transport had increased in altitude. The gentle pressure of their ascent was unmistakable.

After a few minutes, they touched down, and the back door opened. Four-fingered hands reached into the vehicle and dragged each of the prisoners out. Nicole felt the powerful arms lift her easily and set her standing on the ground outside.

Nicole looked around the landing bay. She felt like she was standing in a large, alien forest. Irregular columns, which branched and spread as they rose to the high ceiling, stood at irregular intervals throughout the room. The walls glowed with an otherworldly iridescence and stretched between the columns like a cloth stretched across a frame. The membranes' surface was rough, with small nooks and dimples lining the walls and ceiling of the room.

Nicole focused on the Nasi who had pulled her out of the vehicle. Its blue eyes, almost identical to hers, met her gaze without emotion. The creature was slightly taller than her but was much thinner than any Human Nicole had seen. Its hair was short and looked like the buzz cut she had seen EDF recruits sporting. Its purple skin had intricate black swirls and patterns that seemed to adorn its entire body. The guard wore a uniform, loose-fitting gray shirt and pants, along with a pair of black utility boots.

"Welcome to New Tiradentes," the creature said formally in a feminine voice. Her Human Standard had a thick accent, making it difficult for Nicole to understand initially. "We will place you in holding rooms until we question you. Any attempt to escape will be met with overwhelming force and will only bring severe pain."

The Nasi spoke the words matter-of-factly, her face betraying no malice. She made a gesture with one of her spindly arms, and other guards stepped forward to remove their muzzles.

"We're not going to tell you anything," Private Sakata growled as soon as her gag was removed.

"Yes, you will," the Nasi replied flatly. "The question is whether you will do so willingly."

She turned and walked away. Another Nasi grabbed Nicole by the shoulder and firmly guided her through an arched doorway. The inside of the Nasi building was a series of undulating tunnels made of the same membrane that she had seen in the large bay. Nicole felt like a fly caught in a spider's web as they led her through the corridors. After multiple turns and changes in levels, they placed her in a small prison cell. Without a word, the guard turned around and walked out of the room, the door closing behind them.

The room was about the same size as the Domespat cell she had come from, though it lacked the bed and toilet. Nicole walked to one wall and examined the material. It looked like a piece of cloth, with thousands of tiny strands woven together. She wondered how they had made this building—she'd seen nothing like it before. Some strands let off a faint light, which created the luminescent effect she had seen from a distance. Nicole pushed her shoulder against the wall, expecting it to give, but to her surprise it held firm, feeling just as solid as the ones in the Domespat station despite its delicate appearance.

Nicole lay down on the floor, turning on her side so that her hands did not dig into her back. There was nothing left for her to do but wait for the Nasi to come and get her.

Nicole jerked awake as something tapped against her foot. She looked into the brown eyes of a Nasi guard standing over her, weapon pointed in her face.

"It is time to get up, Ms. Bergeron," he instructed. At least she thought it was a male based on the deep baritone.

Nicole pulled herself up with some difficulty, because of her bound hands, and followed the guard through the building. He didn't seem concerned that she would escape, barely turning his head to look back. *He's right, where would I go?* she thought helplessly.

After several minutes, they arrive at a large door, which

dilated open as they approached. Nicole followed the guard into what looked to be an office. The room was sparsely furnished, with only a desk and a small seating area. The Nasi seated behind the desk stood up as she entered and motioned to the chairs near the door. His long, dark hair was tied in a braid, and the markings on his body were even more intricate than on the other Nasi Nicole had seen. The tight black patterns were edged with silver, causing them to glisten and sparkle in the light cast off by the ceiling and walls.

The guard placed a small device on her restraints, and they unclasped, falling to the ground. She wanted to moan in relief as she worked her arms and shoulders, trying to relieve the soreness.

The Nasi behind the desk stood up and walked firmly toward Nicole. "Would you like something to eat or drink?" he asked. "We are learning to appreciate the food of our ancestors. My personal favorite is coffee, the bitterness is freeing on the palette."

Nicole tried to ignore her parched mouth—she wasn't about to accept anything. She shook her head and watched cautiously as the Nasi sat down across from her, crossing his legs and leaning back casually.

"Why did you bring me here?" she asked.

"Ah, good question, Ms. Bergeron. Before we get into that, I should introduce myself. I am Provincial Governor Kile Fermott." He took a small bow in his chair. "As provincial governor, I am responsible for the Nasi Collective's settlement activities in Tiradentes and across the planet."

"What do you mean *settlement*?" she asked.

Governor Fermott smiled. "Well, we have spent centuries planning our reunification with Humanity, and we have no desire to go back again. So, we are making certain adjustments to the Human planets, creating our own areas where our people may live. We sincerely hope that we can help our Human cousins through our example."

"Is that why you destroyed Earth?" Nicole replied venomously.

"That was a tragedy—unavoidable, but a tragedy nonetheless," the Nasi frowned. "As we planned our return, we knew that Humanity would not eagerly accept our help, so we had to make a choice." He paused. "Earth, or our goal of a better life for all Humanity. We felt that, in the end, the only proper choice was the latter. The decision was not made in haste—we actually did it for the benefit of your species."

"Of course you had a choice!" Nicole shouted at the Nasi. His expression remained placid, unchanged by her sudden outburst.

"When we returned to Earth, we found that Humanity had spread beyond their homeworld. However, you had achieved very little else. Your species had stagnated over the centuries and was now at the whim of its neighbors. We Nasi have advanced well beyond our forbearers and want to share this knowledge. But knowledge without wisdom is like placing a gun in a child's hands."

"How can you be so smug and self—" Nicole began.

Governor Fermott continued to speak, ignoring her interruption. "So we decided that we would need to lead our Human cousins to enlightenment. However, we knew that you would not willingly accept this leadership. We decided that a quick and decisive strike would be much more humane that a protracted campaign against the people we hope to save."

"What about the other planets and systems you wiped out—the homeworlds of the Kurz, Qudoru, Tounous, and X'Ado?" she asked. It didn't make sense to Nicole. The Nasi destroyed the very planets and resources that they would need to settle this part of the galaxy.

"We sought to subjugate your neighbors so you may flourish. When you are ready, you will have the industrial output of all their colonies and fertile soil to grow your empire." Governor Fermott let out a sigh. "I understand that this may seem almost incomprehensible or cruel when you do not have a full understanding of our plan, but trust me when I say that it is all for Humanity's own good."

Nicole could feel every muscle in her body grow taut, as she pictured herself jumping across the small table and driving her fist right into his mouth.

"I know that your family was on Earth. I am sure you had a very close bond with them." The Nasi leaned forward, his face looking almost sympathetic.

"Yes, they were my family, and you killed them."

"I understand your anger. Although we Nasi have grown beyond the concept of family, I imagine that nothing I say can take away that anger." Fermott took a long drink from the glass he held. "But I believe that their deaths can serve a purpose. Perhaps we can work together to create a legacy that will honor their memory."

Nicole felt her anger competing with curiosity as she

listened to the governor speak. What had happened to the Nasi that had transformed them so thoroughly? She felt less kinship to them, offspring of Humanity, than to the Kurz or X'Ado.

"I know that you were an agent of ours before we returned," Fermott said. "I know you provided information to us on Gorash. Perhaps we can work together again. To help build a better future."

She couldn't believe what she was hearing. The Nasi had destroyed her home, killed her family, and attempted to kill her as well. It was almost laughable that Fermott thought there was a chance she would work for them. Nicole attempted to get out of her chair, but before she was even halfway up, Fermott had fluidly leaned forward and pushed her back with one hand, slashing his nails across her cheek with the other. Nicole fell back, stunned, feeling a single droplet of blood trickle down her face.

"We dislike violence. But we are not afraid to use it." The governor's voice remained patient and calm, as if they were two associates discussing a business deal. "I am very slow to anger, but I will warn you, if you get out of that chair again, I will make you feel pain."

Nicole felt chilled by the matter-of-fact manner in which he made the threat. She knew he would do exactly what he had promised without thinking twice about it.

"Now, as I was saying." The Nasi paused for a moment, then gave her a nauseating smile. "Ah, yes. We found your work to be helpful and think you still can aid us. You have shown yourself to be resourceful, not only in the information you provided but in your ability to survive through so much."

"So you want me to betray my friends and help you subjugate Humanity?" Nicole asked.

"Ah, I thought that might be your initial reaction. As opposed to some of my colleagues, I have been around you Humans for years and have been able to learn a bit about how you think." His smile became self-satisfied. "As I stated, we are here to help Humanity. You are a middling power in the galaxy, caught between larger, more advanced species. With our help, you can achieve a greatness that would be impossible without us. Imagine, Human ships with our technology and oversight spreading across the galaxy. Spreading civilization and knowledge that will last forever—a civilization without hunger or poverty. These are the things we offer."

"Under your rule," retorted Nicole.

"Perhaps at first, but would that be so bad? Look at this planet—we have let your own elected officials rule, and look what they have done: created a police state and enriched their own wealth at the expense of the people. I know that you have experienced this firsthand."

"But you put Choi and her 'New American Empire' in power," Nicole retorted. "You're responsible for them."

"We put your planetary governor in control, actually," corrected Fermott. "When he refused to work with us, we had to resort to others." The Nasi gave a shrug. "We respected your chain of command, your government's structure, until we found someone willing to work with us. It was Choi—a Human your people elected, I might add—who set up the new government the way it is. We respect your people's wishes and only interfere when we see opportunities or see threats to our overall plan."

Nicole's heart sank a little as she realized that he wasn't completely wrong. The New American Empire and the Domespat were purely Human creations, designed by Choi to keep herself in power. They relied on the backstop of Nasi power, but Humans had created a dictatorship.

"You have seen us only at the beginning of our vision." Fermott pressed his advantage. "Over the next several years, we will create a new order based on Human rule, with us Nasi to guide you. We still need allies to help us achieve this. You can help make this conflict between us and the remains of your Earth Defense Force relatively bloodless. Your help would prevent conflict and excise the last vestiges of cancerous tissue."

Nicole touched her starfish pendant, feeling the rough edges and the sharp prick of the arms. The Nasi were evil. They were zealots. But she hated how there was a small grain of truth in what the governor was saying. She had seen the inequality and suffering that existed within the UEG and other civilizations. Were the Nasi that much worse than Choi or the former EDF? Nicole could imagine the Domespat wiping out millions of people if they had the power and motivation to do so. However, the Nasi hadn't even given Humanity a chance—they had killed billions with no warning.

"I can see your uncertainty," Fermott said. "That is understandable. Perhaps you doubt our resolve?" The governor stood up and walked to his desk. A hologram of a small city appeared next to him. In it, a tall central tower was surrounded by a geodesic dome and multiple shorter towers. Beyond that were several rings of gradually shortening buildings. "We call this the Foothold. You are in the large central tower of the one here in Tiradentes right now. We are building one of these on each of Humanity's colonies to ensure that we will thrive here."

Nicole studied the holo, trying to estimate the amount of Nasi that could live in one of these compounds—she guessed it to be in the millions.

"You see that our Foothold is more than just a place for us to live," the governor continued. "It will provide us the resources to defend ourselves and travel between our universe and your own with much greater efficiency—ushering in a new age of prosperity between our peoples."

"Your universe?" Nicole asked.

"Yes." Fermott nodded. "Our universe. You Humans tested out early fold drives using our ancestors, making them the unwilling test subjects for a technology that you didn't understand. Who knows how many people died or lost in space forever . . ." He shook his head. "Our ancestors ended up stranded in another universe—a twisted mirror universe, that is both the same as yours and completely different."

Nicole sat still. This explained so much. How in only a few hundred years, the Nasi could change so dramatically from their Human ancestors. Why they had never found the Nasi. She only hoped that she would have the opportunity to share it with others.

"After decades of work, we developed a drive that would

allow us to travel back. The only problem is that to travel between the universes is extremely difficult, to put it mildly. Once our Foothold is complete, we will be able to travel freely between them, allowing people and resources to come and go at will."

Fermott stopped, facing the heavens with an almost religious fervor. She could see a flicker of pride or joy run across his face as he thought about the future he had described.

"As you can see," he said after a moment, "we are not going anywhere, and there is no point in resisting us. I only hope to avoid more unnecessary bloodshed." Governor Fermott breathed in deeply. "Take a moment to think it over. Ask yourself whether you want the blood of innocents to be on your hands."

The governor tapped on a small, wrist-mounted screen. A few seconds later, a Nasi guard walked into the room and waited for the governor's instruction. "Take Ms. Bergeron back to her cell—she needs some time to think."

He turned to face Nicole. "Ms. Bergeron, it has been a pleasure talking to you. I hope we may still come to some sort of agreement."

Nicole opened her mouth to reply, but before she could speak, she felt a force lifting her up and the world went dark.

Chapter Nine

The enormous tower at the center of the Nasi base stood out against the skyline. Not only was it taller than anything nearby, but its shape was unnatural, sinuous with a small bulb at the top—like a plant sprouting from the ground.

Kal stood on the back ramp of the *Oruc,* watching the tower as they approached. Looking down, he could see the rooftops of the city fly by below them, only meters from the bottom of the ship. They were flying nap-of-the-earth, the ship hugging the terrain so the Nasi sensors wouldn't be able to track them. Based on what they had heard over the intercept, it seemed to be working—their low altitude, combined with the cloak, had tricked the Nasi into thinking the *Oruc* was simply an atmospheric disturbance, a bug in their sensors.

Ready sir? Major Garcia asked over their private net.

Ready, Kal responded.

Multiple missiles streaked from the *Oruc* toward the upper floors of the tower. They intended most of them to hit at their intended breach area, but had also targeted other areas of the compound to maximize confusion and prevent the Nasi from massing their reinforcements in any one location. The *Oruc* flew right behind the missiles and came to an abrupt stop next to the tower as the last one detonated. Kal could hear the cries of alarm and confusion over the Nasi internal net through the ship's intercept.

Alpha team, follow me, Kal called out as he engaged his thrusters and jumped off the ship's cargo ramp.

The missiles had their intended effect. Two gaping holes, separated by a few floors, marred the tower's facade. They had divided the assault force into two teams, Alpha and Bravo. Alpha team, led by Kal, would enter the tower above the suspected detention zone and work their way down. Bravo team, led by Ekon, would enter below and work their way up. Kal flew into the gaping hole the *Oruc* had created, followed by three TLF fighters—Sandra, Wang, and Autry. Ekon was with Sakata and the other TLF fighter—Calderone.

Alpha team has landed in the building, Kal reported over the net. *No resistance so far, beginning our sweep.*

Acknowledged, Alpha team, Garcia responded. *The Nasi are regrouping. There are assault teams converging on your location. You've got minutes at most.*

Roger, Kal replied, and cut off the net.

He scanned the room using his suit's sensors. There were three heat signatures in the darkness and smoke of the destroyed room. It was impossible for Kal or the targeting AI in his suit to discern between Humans and Nasi using only the infrared cameras. He needed to get closer.

Wang and Sandra hastily swept the room while Kal and Autry covered them, kinetic rifles held at the ready.

We've got a Human, Wang announced over the net. *Short female with blond hair. I think it's one of our targets.*

Kal couldn't believe their luck. They had found Nicole. *Agreed, that's one of ours. Take her back to the* Oruc.

The other two are hostiles, both unconscious, reported Autry.

Restrain them and then let's keep moving, Kal replied.

126

As he was assisting Autry in restraining one of the Nasi, Kal noticed a small computer, about ten centimeters square, on his wrist. He unfastened the device and placed it inside his suit's storage compartment. Perhaps Chief Kanumba could get some intel out of it.

After they'd restrained the two unconscious Nasi, the team entered the hallway outside the room. Turning left, they moved through the corridor, clearing rooms as they passed. The hallway traveled in every direction but straight, limiting their field of vision to only a few meters. As they worked through the hallway, they found only empty offices, smaller but otherwise identical to the one where they had found Nicole. Kal grew frustrated. They needed to find something soon—their time was running out.

Alpha leader, this is Bravo leader. We have located the prisoners, but the enemy have us pinned down and we need assistance. Kal could hear the strain and fear in Ekon's voice.

Roger, on our way.

Kal turned around and sprinted back the way they had come, with the rest of Alpha team on his heels. As they were nearing their infiltration point, a hail of plasma fire forced them to a halt. The four soldiers dove into the nearest doorway as the plasma bolts landed around them, a few striking their suit's energy shields.

We've got at least three Nasi between us and the exit, reported Wang as he leaned into the hallway.

We need a better angle to see the enemy. Autry, Chedjou, get into the room across from us. Wang and I will provide cover fire. Kal ordered.

Kal and Wang fired their kinetic rifles toward the Nasi positions on full auto, forcing the Nasi to stop shooting and take cover. Kal nodded toward Autry and Sandra, and they dove into the office across the corridor.

They're advancing, reported Sandra. *We've got at least five hostiles converging on our position.*

I see six of them, Autry called out over the net. *They're—*

Kal swore as Autry's icon on his tactical map turned red.

Autry's been hit and there's another group coming from the opposite direction, Sandra called out on the net. Kal realized that there was no way they were going to make it past the Nasi guards—their only choice was to go around them.

Get ready to jump back in this room, Kal ordered Sandra. *Wang, provide cover fire when I give the word, and Sandra, get back in here.*

Kal ran to the outside wall of the room and attached an explosive charge. The walls looked flimsy, and the explosives that Kal carried on his battle suit should make short work of them.

Get in the room, now! Kal ordered as he dove away from the primed charge. An explosion ripped through the room, throwing the furniture across the space and instantly filling it with smoke. Kal felt the jolt of the concussive blast through his armor. When the smoke cleared, the outside wall was undamaged; the fabric-like material didn't even have a scratch.

Oruc, this is Alpha Leader, Kal called out over the net.

Go ahead, Alpha Leader, Garcia responded.

Fire a missile on our location, Kal said.

Say again. You want us to fire on your location? Garcia asked. Kal could understand his confusion.

Yes, we're pinned down and need out, now. Fire at will! Kal yelled over the net.

Roger sir. Domespat atmospheric craft have engaged us. You'll need to hold tight for a few seconds until we can get into range, Garcia responded.

Kal turned to the TLF fighters. *Listen up,* he ordered. *We need to defend the room at all costs until the* Oruc *makes us a new exit. Get into position.* Sandra crouched down against the inside wall with her rifle aimed at the door leading to the hallway. Wang ran to the ruined desk and crouched behind it—he must have figured it would at least provide some cover. Seeing nothing close by, Kal knelt and trained his rifle on the doorway.

After what must have been only a few seconds, but felt like an eternity, several grenades flew into the room, landing near Wang's position. The fighter reacted quickly and threw two of them into the hallway, then dove on the third as it exploded. The blast ricocheted his body off the ceiling and slammed him into the wall. The blast had blown the front of his suit open, the jagged metal bent inward—Kal didn't need to look at the red icon on his tactical map to know the man was dead.

Two Nasi in armored exoskeletons rushed through the door single file, crossing as they entered the threshold. Sandra fired on them, but her shots went wide, hitting the wall or punching out into the hallway.

Kal remembered the decades he had trained as an EDF marksman and breathed out slowly, evenly, and fired. He aimed at the joints in the aliens' armor, firing quick bursts—inhale, aim, exhale, squeeze; inhale, aim, exhale, squeeze. He felt muscle memory take over and watched with detachment as the kinetic rounds ripped through armor. When the second Nasi went down, a third ran into the room and pointed their rifle at Kal. He dropped into the prone position while aiming his weapon at the incoming Nasi. His round glanced off the guard's face shield, momentarily stopping him in his tracks. As Kal felt his suit hit the ground, several rounds pierced the helmet and exited out the other side, along with a fine mist of bio matter.

Good shot, he congratulated Sandra. She wordlessly nodded back at him.

Kal pulled out a grenade of his own. *Get ready*, he called out. Without waiting for her response, he threw the grenade through the door and into the hallway, hoping to slow the remaining Nasi soldiers. He watched the open door, waiting for the explosion.

When it came, it was much larger than Kal had expected. A blast threw him forward, tumbling head over heels, and tossed him against the inside wall of the office. The *Oruc* had finally been able to fire a missile on their location. The blast shoved him across the room, and his head now rested against the interior wall he had just been facing. The exterior wall had disappeared, the *Oruc's* missile destroying the strange, fibrous material.

Kal, we got to go. Get up! Kal shook his head, trying to

clear the cobwebs.

Right, right, he responded. As Kal unsteadily rose, he saw one of the Nasi lying on the floor. This was not the same one he had seen earlier—it didn't have the odd silver highlights in its black skin markings.

Sandra, grab hold. Kal pointed to the unconscious body. They both stowed their rifles in their suits' thigh holsters, the rifles automatically compressing to fit. Sandra grabbed a foot, Kal grabbed a hand, and they dragged the unconscious form toward the exit created by the *Oruc.*

Get in the ship—we have three more Domespat ships incoming, Garcia shouted over the net.

Kal and Sandra picked up the pace, moving as fast as they could toward the jagged hole in the wall. *Engage thrusters on three,* Kal instructed Sandra. *One . . . Two . . . Three.*

They fired their thrusters and launched themselves out of the building, toward the ship. Rounds spat from the side machine gun on the *Oruc,* past Kal and Sandra and into the room behind them. They landed jarringly on the cargo bay floor of the *Oruc,* their momentum carrying them off their feet and causing them to slide several meters before stopping.

We're in, Kal called out. The ship was already retreating from the building before he had finished speaking.

Kal used his implant to check the ship's sensors. Three Domespat fighters were converging on the *Oruc's* location. Normally they would be no match for the upgraded corvette, but the *Oruc* had fired much of its ammunition, and its energy shields were weakened from the dogfight while they had been searching the tower.

Get this prisoner into Bergeron's stateroom, he instructed Kanumba, who was manning the kinetic machine gun. She nodded and dragged the Nasi by its shoulders up the ladder to the second deck. Nicole's stateroom doubled as a brig when needed.

Alpha squad, Ekon's called out over the net. *We need you here now.*

We're on the ship, Kal responded. *Three Domespat fighters are attacking. Once Garcia can stabilize his flight, we'll be on the way.*

We need help now, Ekon said.

Kal inspected his suit's status—all systems were still in the green. The *Oruc* was twisting wildly through the air, almost touching the rooftops of the buildings below them as it evaded the Domespat fighters on their tail.

Garcia, can you keep a constant heading for three seconds as you fly by the tower? Kal asked over his private connection with the cockpit. *We're going to have to do a full-velocity jump.*

Normally, a soldier would only leave a ship in their battle suit if the ship was hovering or traveling in a straight line at a low rate of speed. Otherwise, they could lose control as soon as they left the ship and fly into a building, the ground, or the ship itself. A full-velocity jump was an emergency procedure where the soldiers left the ship while it was traveling at full or near-full speed. It was possible, but the ship had to fly in a straight line and the soldier had to be extremely good at handling the suit, or lucky, or both.

Roger, I'll let you know when to jump, Garcia answered.

Kal called Sandra to the back ramp of the cargo bay, and they both leaned out and grabbed the handholds at the top of the door. Looking out the bay door, Kal could see the rapid staccato flashes of the Domespat fighters firing at the *Oruc*.

Okay, go! Garcia shouted. Kal and Sandra dropped out the bay door and the wind slammed into them like a brick wall. As soon as they were free of the ship, they engaged their thrusters, trying to keep themselves from spinning out of control or being driven into the rooftops. The suits' thrusters took hold, and they leveled off, hovering mere centimeters over the buildings directly outside the Nasi compound's wall.

As Kal and Sandra rocketed up toward the top of the tower, he checked the tactical map. One of the three icons in Bravo team was now yellow, meaning the soldier was injured but still alive. *Bravo team, heading to your location*, Kal advised. *Get ready.*

As he neared the gaping hole in the building's side, Kal activated his suit's rocket array, the rectangular launcher that normally lay along the back of the suit. When primed, the square launcher rotated itself to sit on the suit's shoulder and directed its compliment of five rockets, each about twenty-five centimeters long, frontward.

Kal landed and looked around the decimated room. It appeared to be a detention area, with small cells lining a nondescript hallway. The blast from the *Oruc* had damaged the interior walls, creating several openings through the cells and between the cells and the hallway. Kal followed his tactical map, heading down the twisting hallway toward Bravo team.

Fire! Kal yelled over the open net as he and Sandra turned the corner.

At least six armor-clad Nasi had pinned down Bravo team in a room at the end of a hallway. Kal and Sandra fired their full complement of rockets at them, using their suit's AI to target them as the Nasi soldiers staggered along the hallway. The small rockets flew down the hallway, and detonated near the Nasi position, shredding them form behind.

Before the smoke had settled, Kal and Nicole ran forward, firing their rifles at any moving shapes they could see amid the debris. Singe marks from Nasi plasma fire surrounded the doorway at the end of the hallway. Kal and Nicole rushed through it to find the rest of their team scattered throughout the small room. Ekon lay writhing on the ground, the cause of his injury unclear. Calderone leaned against the wall, a jagged opening in the side of his face shield—a mortal wound. Sergeant Jones and Private Pudari sat slumped in the corner nearest the door. Kal couldn't tell if they were alive or not. Only Private Sakata remaining unhurt, crouched beside the door.

Calderone is KIA, Sakata reported. *Sergeant Kimathi got hit with some shrapnel from a Nasi grenade right before you arrived, not sure how bad the damage is. Pudari and Jones are injured but should be able to walk.*

Grab Kimathi, he instructed Sandra. *Sakata, follow me, we'll take up a position to cover them.* Garcia came on the net, warning them that there were more Nasi fighters inbound. Kal wanted to take Calderone's body with them, but there was no way to recover him and still make it to the ship.

As the others were helping the wounded, Private Sakata and Kal ran down the hallway until they reached the intersection that led toward the prison. He knew they had to protect it at all costs, otherwise the Nasi would have them trapped in the hallway again, without a way out. Kal knelt, his shoulder pressing against the strange wall, rifle at the ready. Sakata took up a position across from him.

Streaks of plasma fire erupted from a hallway, splashing against the wall next to Kal's head. *We'll stay here to cover your exit*, Kal said. *Let me know when you're clear of the building.*

Roger, said Sandra as she ran past, dragging Ekon down through the hallway in his battle suit.

Jones and Pudari hobbled behind her, moving as fast as their injuries would let them. As the group reached him and Sakata, they took a right toward the prison and the *Oruc*. The Nasi fire continued to hit near them, with a few rounds glancing off their suits' energy shields.

Kal checked his suit's status—he was getting low on kinetic rounds and energy, and he could see that Sakata was low as well. They fired sporadically toward the Nasi, trying to conserve their rounds while keeping the guards from advancing. A rocket streaked past their position, exploding in the room where Bravo team had taken cover.

We're out! Sandra yelled.

Kal stood up and flung his last two grenades blindly down the hall. Sakata also stood up but had no time to react when a Nasi grenade landed at her feet. The explosion shredded her suit and flung her into the middle of the intersection. Kal screamed in frustration as he saw several plasma rounds tear through her now-disabled suit.

He stopped momentarily, wishing there was something he could do but knowing that he would only get himself killed—Sakata was already dead. A plasma round hit his suit's shield, spurring him to continue running toward the *Oruc*. When Kal reached the prison, he turned into a destroyed cell and activated his suit's thrusters, launching himself out of the building.

The *Oruc* was several kilometers away, conducting evasive maneuvers to evade the growing fleet of Domespat fighters that were congregating on the building.

I'm out, Kal called over the net.

Roger, Garcia acknowledged. *Sending you extraction coordinates. We've got too much company to stop though.*

Kay maintained his altitude and flew around the perimeter of the tower toward the extraction coordinates. The *Oruc* was gradually making its way back, enemy fighters converging on it from all sides. Kal used his suit's AI to calculate his approach vector and velocity for the extraction. The *Oruc* would slow as it passed Kal so that he could fly into the cargo bay as it passed.

As the *Oruc* approached his position he let the suit's AI take control. The suit matched the ship's direction as the *Oruc* went by him. As soon as the ship was past, his suit accelerated directly into the cargo bay. The moment Kal's feet were on the bay floor, the ship's door lifted shut behind him.

Get us off planet, Kal instructed Garcia. He could hear the ship's engines strain as Garcia slammed the throttle to max.

The change in momentum was too much for the ship's inertial dampeners and almost threw Kal against the bay door.

He stood still for a moment, his hands shaking in the suit's gauntlets. He wanted to sit down and cry, but knew that there wasn't time. They had recovered the prisoners, but they were far from safe.

Kal trudged to the side of the bay and locked his battle suit back into its charging cradle, lined against the bulkhead. He felt sore, like a Kurz fighter had kicked every inch of his body, but was grateful to realize that he had escaped without injury. The rear of the suit opened and Kal stepped back, away from the bulkhead, feeling an immediate chill as the air hit his sweat-drenched body.

He almost leaped up the ladder to the second deck and collapsed into the mission commander's chair in the cockpit. The flight crew were staring at the screens in front of them, and Kal didn't say a word, not wanting to distract them.

The *Oruc* was flying nap-of-the-earth over the seemingly endless rooftops of Tiradentes. Kal could see the sun rising on the port side of the ship, casting faint feathers of light across the city. The sight was beautiful, the peaks and valleys of the city casting long shadows across the landscape. He wondered what the people beneath them were doing at that moment. Did they know what had just happened?

Ten Domespat Pugione fighters followed closely on their tail. The old atmospheric craft were no match for the speed and agility of the cutting-edge corvette. The Pugione were at least twenty years old. The rapid advances in weaponry during the Torgham war had forced them into obsolescence. Kal guessed the EDF had sold the fighters to the New American government to use in police work and counter-smuggling operations.

The two Nasi capital ships that were orbiting the planet were converging on the space over Tiradentes. The *Oruc* could not leave the atmosphere until it was clear of the plasma weapons range of the ships.

As they continued to speed over rooftops, Kanumba listened to the intercept, calling out any pertinent information. The Pugione fighters gradually fell farther behind, losing visual contact with the *Oruc*. Their cloak was working—the Nasi capital ships reported they could not follow the *Oruc* with their sensors.

The city rooftops gave way to tree-covered hills. As they traced along the hilly landscape, Park announced they had lost the Domespat fighters. Garcia pulled the nose of the *Oruc* up, sending them hurtling through the atmosphere. The ship's inertial dampeners again had a hard time adjusting to the sudden maneuver, and Kal could feel himself pushed back in his chair.

"They can tell we're leaving the atmosphere," announced Kanumba, still listening to the intercept. "They're going to saturate the area with plasma fire."

Immediately after Kanumba finished speaking, bolts shot from the planet's surface. They fired the shots in a spread formation, hoping to get lucky. Streams of plasma fire filled the vicinity of the *Oruc's* flight path, occasionally coming close, but none hitting the ship's shields.

"How long until we're clear to fold?" Kal asked.

"About two minutes, sir," Park responded after he examined his monitor.

A fold drive required the exact right gravitational conditions to work correctly. Planets, ships, asteroids, or other debris could affect the drive and cause the ship to implode instantly when engaged. In order to minimize the risk, ships had complex sensors to detect the gravity waves in an area. The ship's sophisticated AI could calculate their changes of successfully folding and calculate the best locations to fold from. Thankfully, the gravitational constraints of the drive were only critical at the point of departure.

As they hurtled through the space around New America, the planet growing smaller behind them, Kal could feel the rush of adrenaline subside. His hands started shaking softly as it left his body. Images of the violence and bodies he had just witnessed flashed through his head. He pictured Private Sakata's ruined battle suit and felt a stabbing pain in his side.

"Okay, we're at three nines," Park announced. Three nines meant that the ship's computer gave them a 99.9 percent chance of surviving if they folded from their current location. Although the commercial standard was eight nines, the extenuating circumstances meant they had to cut some corners.

Garcia pressed the button on his monitor, and the *Oruc* instantly moved a fraction of a light-year away from New America and into deep space—safe for now.

Chapter Ten

Nicole ran her fingers through her hair, rubbing her scalp. Despite the pain medications, her head still throbbed. A large, coarse bandage lay to her temple, covering a deep gash.

Nicole did not remember getting hurt or her rescue. Taisha told her what had happened when she regained consciousness aboard the *Oruc*. When the ship had launched several missiles at the Foothold, blasting a hole in the tower's side, the explosion had thrown her against the far wall of the room and knocked her out. Kal had recovered her and captured the Nasi guard and brought them both on board the ship. She hoped to talk to the guard soon, but right now her injuries kept her bedridden.

Normally, the ship's medical bot could heal her injuries in hours using its suite of advanced nanobots. However, Jones and Pudari had been given priority. The bandage on her head was layered with a cocktail of advanced medicines that not only reduced the pain but would also speed the healing process.

Nicole had been unconscious for almost twelve hours— long enough for the ship to begin its voyage back to the rest of Samsara Fleet. Nicole knew Kal would want to speak with her as soon as she was ready. She wondered what the general would make of everything that Governor Fermott had told her. Nicole was also eager to talk to General Samaha, the commander of Samsara Fleet. The information she had would completely change their perception of the Nasi and their invasion.

Nicole had another reason to be eager to return to the fleet. At her suggestion, they had sent scout teams to the two species near Human space that were still unoccupied by the Nasi: the Torgham and the Goro. A fleet as large as Samsara Fleet needed resources and support to remain operational. Without help from either of these two civilizations, Nicole didn't know how long they could keep fighting. Unfortunately, both had their issues with Humanity—the Torgham had fought a bloody war against the UEG only decades before, and the Goro saw them as savages.

She thought about the words of the Nasi governor. He was right—Humanity hadn't reached its potential, it had stagnated over the past century or two. However, the Nasi method of coldly cutting anything and anyone that stood in their path revolted her. As a diplomatic student, she had had to study countless alien species and cultures. Never had she heard of one as coolly ruthless as the Nasi. And she wasn't sure whether she really believed they were trying to help Humanity.

"Ah, you're awake." Taisha walked into the room. She had on the classic loose shirt and breeches of a free spacer. More and more of the crew wore them, copying the style from their leader, Kal.

"Yeah, I'm up," she responded as she swung her legs over the side of the bunk she had been laying in.

"You ready for some food?" Taisha asked.

"That would be nice." As soon as Nicole thought about food, she felt pangs of hunger hit her. She couldn't remember how long it had been since she last ate.

They plodded the few meters to the galley, Taisha diligently watching her like a new mother. The room was vacant, except for Private Changying Pudari, who sat at the table. The private was hunched over, staring at the tabletop; her face was blank and her mind was clearly elsewhere.

Taisha had told Nicole that they had lost two Tac-I solders on the mission—Kondari and Sakata. Nicole remembered that Pudari and Kondari had been close, spending much of the voyage to New America talking to one another.

"I'm sorry about Hasin. I know you were close." Nicole placed her hand lightly on Pudari's shoulder.

Pudari shrugged her shoulders, throwing Nicole's hand off.

"Let's grab something," Taisha said. Nicole walked toward the food fabricator on the wall, leaving Pudari to her thoughts.

Food fabricators were an unfortunate necessity of shipboard life. The machines took raw materials and created facsimiles of normal dishes. They were quite versatile, able to create anything from soups to roasted chicken. However, the fabricated food was only a poor imitation of the real thing, the flavors and textures always off. There were some people who actually preferred fabricated food, but Nicole found it barely edible. It was growing on her though.

Nicole ordered a bowl of soup and took a seat at the end of the table, trying to give Pudari her own space. The soup was nearly boiling. After burning the roof of her mouth, Nicole pushed the bowl away to let it cool.

"How are Ekon and Jones?" she asked after giving Taisha

time to take a few bites.

"The medbot is still treating them in the bay, but they'll be fine," the chief responded. "Sergeant Jones is worse off—besides the concussion, he had several broken bones and internal bleeding. Seems the Domespat didn't exactly treat him with kid gloves. Ekon only has the concussion and a few superficial lacerations. I would imagine they'll both be up in the next few hours."

"We went on that mission with seven people and only five returned—not to mention the two TLF fighters who died as well. We can't go on like this."

"We'll get better. We're getting better." Taisha spoke between mouthfuls. "We just have to make sure it's worth it."

"We learned a lot," Nicole said. She outlined what had happened during the trip, detailing her capture and the conversation with the Nasi governor.

"Another universe," Taisha said disbelievingly. "It's like something out of a holo."

Nicole nodded.

"This completely changes our understanding of fold drives," Taisha continued. "Whole academic holos—hell, entire courses—will have to be rewritten."

"I wonder what the other universe is like," Nicole said, "to have changed the Nasi so much. Not only biologically, but morally and socially. They really aren't Human anymore, and the change happened so quickly, over only a few hundred years."

"Yup, they're bastards." Taisha smiled.

"Well, there's more to it than that. They must have gone

143

through an enormous amount of trauma—"

"You changin' sides again?" Pudari asked, leaning toward the two women. The private glared at Nicole, her dark eyes rimmed with red.

Nicole wanted to reply but felt a pang of guilt from her actions on Gorash and kept her mouth shut.

"Cause we have one of them on the ship now," continued Pudari. "I'm a little worried that maybe you'll decide to free 'em."

Taisha came to Nicole's rescue. "Private Pudari, don't you have someplace better to be? Maybe I should check with Sergeant Jones."

Pudari slowly stood up, wincing as she rose, her eyes remaining fixed on Nicole. "Kondari always said not to trust you. After all you've done, I don't believe a word of what you say."

"Get the hell out," Taisha ordered.

"Yes, ma'am." Pudari's gaze flickered to Taisha and then back to Nicole. "I'm watching you. Not gonna let anyone else die at the hands of those bastards." She turned and walked to the recycling bin, dropping her uneaten food and plate into the receptacle. The two women watched as she shuffled out of the room without looking back.

"I know she's been through a lot, but . . ." Taisha rolled her eyes.

"She's still grieving. She lost a friend."

"I can talk to Sergeant Jones, if you want," Taisha offered.

"No," Nicole replied, "that'll only make things worse. She'll cool off."

The chief raised an eyebrow. Nicole hoped she was right.

❖

Kal lay in his bunk, staring at the featureless ceiling. He could sense the malevolent presence of their Nasi prisoner in the stateroom turned brig across the hall from him.

After they'd folded out of the New America system, Kal had ran down to the cargo bay to help treat the wounded— Jones and Ekon both had traumatic brain injuries, Pudari had multiple lacerations and a broken rib, and Nicole had a laceration on her head. They had four wounded and two killed in action after only one day on the planet. After assisting Kanumba in moving their casualties, treating the wounds, and calibrating the medbot, Kal had retreated to his stateroom— he was emotionally and physically exhausted.

He thought back to the Torgham War twenty years ago— the last time he had been faced with the terrors of combat. Kal had been a mid-level officer when the war broke out. Over years, the EDF and Torgham had killed millions as they fought. He remembered the decompression drills and rushing to find his portable breathing apparatus. He remembered the first time he saw an EDF ship destroyed and realized the tiny specs that were floating in space were the frozen corpses of the crew.

The horrors of the Torgham War paled compared to what he was going through now. The scale of death was so much greater, and Kal wasn't sitting on the bridge of ship or station, watching from a distance. The death and killing was right before his eyes. His mind drifted back to Sakata's ruined suit, lying on the floor of the Nasi tower. The events on New America weighed on him, brought back emotions he thought had left.

A chime at the door interrupted his thoughts—it was Major Garcia. The major strode into the room after Kal opened the door.

"Sir, you got a moment?" Garcia asked.

"Sure, what do you need?"

"I wanted to talk to you about our prisoner." Garcia looked toward the hallway. "What are we going to do with it? We've got five more days until we reach the fleet. I don't like that thing on the ship."

"I know, but we have to bring it back," Kal replied.

"We don't even know what those things can do." Garcia stopped his pacing and stared at the flickering stars through the viewscreen.

"We have to take that risk," Kal said. "Otherwise, we lost two soldiers for nothing."

"I know." Garcia sat down in a chair and sighed. "But I've seen enough of them to know not to underestimate them."

"What's it been doing so far?" Kal asked. The brig had a suite of optical, temperature, chemical, and auditory sensors. He had ordered an armed guard posted outside the room at all times, monitoring all the sensor feeds. They had also thoroughly searched the prisoner while it was still unconscious, checking for anything that could help it escape or be used as a weapon.

"Nothing." Garcia rubbed his temple. "Thing just sits

there looking at the viewscreen."

"We're going to have to talk to it," Kal said.

Garcia gave a bleak smile. "I had a feeling you'd say that, sir. Are you sure? We don't know what those things can do."

Kal nodded. "Yeah, I'm sure. We need to talk to Bergeron first though."

"She's still recovering from her wounds," Garcia said.

Kal remembered the painful knot his stomach when he had seen her bloodied face on the cargo bay of the *Oruc*. He worried they'd killed her. He couldn't remember being more relieved than when he saw her chest slowly rise and fall as Chief Kanumba evaluated her.

"Let her rest," Kal said. "She's earned a day off."

"I think we all have," Garcia agreed.

The door chime rang, causing Kal to look up from the novel he was reading. He opened the door, allowing Sandra into the room.

She had changed and was wearing the merchant outfit that many people on this ship seemed to favor, including Kal. After they had stabilized the patients and started toward the fleet, the young rebel had grabbed one of the unused bunks in the crew quarters.

"Seems like an upgrade over your last ship," Sandra said as she walked around the stateroom. She was referring to Kal's old civilian ship, the *Queen Anne's Revenge*. When they had first met, Kal had been drifting through the galaxy aboard

Annie. It had been a pile of junk, barely space-worthy and a complete mess inside. Kal idly wondered if the ship was still around—the EDF had confiscated it on Caracas Station.

"It's not too shabby," Kal agreed. The *Oruc* was definitely an enormous step up from *Annie*.

"I don't suppose there's any chance that you'll take me back to Tiradentes?" Sandra asked.

"No," Kal replied, "not for now at least. I'm sure they'll be more recon missions to New America though."

Sandra sat down. "I wonder what the Domespat and Nasi will do after our little assault."

"Not much they can do—almost everyone involved is dead or gone."

Sandra shook her head. "You don't know the Domespat. That won't stop them. They'll round people up, anyone they think might be involved, or anyone they have an issue with. They don't need a reason to jail or kill people, just an excuse."

"Do you think the TLF is in any danger?" Kal asked.

"Yes. No. Maybe." She shook her head. "We take pretty careful precautions before we go on missions. But who knows?"

"When did you join?" Kal asked.

Sandra told Kal about what had happened to her since they had separated on Caracas Station. As soon as she had left the landing bay, Sandra had headed straight to the EDF recruiting station and signed up. The Nasi attacked before she could leave the station. After the battle, the remains of the local government shuttled Sandra back to Tiradentes, where she reunited with her family.

For the next several months, Sandra idly stayed with her parents, waiting for something to happen. She watched as the Nasi installed the Domespat and Choi tightened her control over the planet. Either the Nasi or Domespat had disabled the local net, so there was little for her to do except wait.

Everything changed when a Domespat patroller killed Klarissa—one of her friends who had travelled with Kal—in her own home. He had been harassing Klarissa's father, and when she stood up to the man, he shot her point blank.

After her friend's murder, Sandra looked for some way to fight back. When Li Wei told her about the TLF, she was all in. She packed her bags and left her home, saying nothing to her parents.

"Did you ever talk with them or send them a note or anything to let them know you were okay?" Kal asked.

"I asked some friends to check in on them from time to time," she replied. "They knew what I had done, and they were okay. At least, last time I checked."

Kal wondered if she knew about Li Wei's family yet. He thought about saying something, but it wasn't his place; Sandra and Li Wei had known each other since childhood. "I'm sorry we took you away from New America. We'll get you back there, eventually."

Sandra shrugged. "I'm not worried about leaving. I figure I can do more fighting the Nasi with you than I could back home. Besides, it'll give me a chance to see the stars."

Kal smiled—even the Nasi and the Domespat couldn't shake her core optimism.

Sandra shifted in her seat. "What about you, Kal?" she asked. "How did you end up here?"

Kal told her the story of everything that had happened to him and Ekon since they parted ways. He detailed their escape under fire from Caracas Station and arriving at a secret EDF base in deep space, Kapustin Station. Kal tried to keep things light as he described how they had traveled to multiple systems attempting to defeat the Nasi, before finally defeating one ship at the ruins of Kapustin Station.

"You've been through more than me," she said after he had finished. "So, what'll happen when we get to Samsara Fleet?"

"Not sure. They'll be a lot to tell them about. We'll debrief, get resupplied, and get back out there. Our team's mission is to get information and establish alliances, whatever the cost. You can't do that sitting with the fleet."

"What'll happen to me?" Sandra asked.

"Well, I think that the fleet will want to help the TLF. There will be more missions going back to New America; you could join them. But I'm guessing that's not what you want."

Sandra shook her head.

"There's always room for more people in the fleet," Kal assured her. "I am sure you—"

"Kal, do you have time now?" Nicole's voice on the intercom interrupted him. "I need to tell you about what happened on the mission."

"Glad to hear your voice," Kal responded. "Sure, let's meet in the galley in five. We'll need everyone there."

"Okay." Nicole cut the line.

Kal turned back to Sandra. He stopped beating around the bush. "Sandra, we've got our work cut out for us. If you want to stay with this crew, you can."

Sandra broke into a smile. "I was hoping you'd say that, sir."

Chapter Eleven

Nicole stopped and took a moment to sip her water—she'd been speaking almost as fast as she could. After arriving at the galley, Nicole had related her conversation with Governor Fermott to Kal, Karl, and Sergeant Jones. Her head was still pounding, but she felt it couldn't wait. They needed to know what the Nasi leader had said.

They listened quietly, letting her give the details of the conversation interspersed with her impressions and analysis and hypotheses. She hadn't had time to think about the encounter so much of it came out in a jumble.

Sergeant Jones broke the silence as Nicole drained her water. "So they see us as their little brother, it sounds like." The taciturn noncommissioned officer looked no worse for wear despite his ordeal—the medbot had done an excellent job. The only sign that he'd been injured was a bandage wrapped around his head.

"They're the big brother from hell," Karl quipped.

"Could they really believe they're helping us?" Kal asked. "The governor may have just been buttering you up."

"Maybe," admitted Nicole, "but I think he was being sincere. We can't apply our own logic or morals to an alien culture. We at least know they intend to stay here either way."

Jones shifted in his seat. "I don't like those Footholds. These overlords come and rule us while sitting in their walled palaces."

"Do we really believe they came from another universe?" Karl asked, eyebrow raised.

"It would explain a lot," Kal admitted. "I know it sounds far-fetched, but it is possible."

"It is," Karl admitted. "It would completely change our understanding on how fold drives work, though."

"You don't know how they work?" Jones turned to look at the pilot.

"Me personally? No. Our fleet's scientists? A little, but basically no." Karl gestured. "We know they do work, which has been good enough."

"It explains their rapid evolution," Kal said. "Another universe would have completely different laws of physics. Radiation, gravity, electricity, biology—all of them could work differently."

Nicole refilled her glass. "It also would explain their behavior. Isolated in another universe like that would completely change the fabric of society."

"We need to talk to the prisoner," Kal said. "We need to fill in some of the blanks."

Garcia shook his head—clearly he'd been expecting this and didn't like it.

"I think we should leave it to the fleet," Jones said, surprising Nicole. She would have thought he would be eager to question the prisoner. "That thing gets loose on this ship and we're all dead." For the first time, Nicole thought she detected an edge of fear in the NCOs voice. She couldn't blame him—she remembered the ease with which the Nasi guard had pulled her out of the transport.

"I know it's a risk," Kal said as he fixed Karl and Jones with his gaze. "But it's a risk we need to take. The Nasi have plans, and time is of the essence. We're not going to win this war by strength or numbers—it'll take speed and cunning."

"We could try to remove the oxygen in the room until it passes out," Karl said. "Then we put every restraint we have on it."

"There's the chance of severe brain hypoxia," Nicole warned. "We'll be taking a risk that we kill it or do permanent damage."

The four of them went back and forth, trying to figure out if there was any other way that didn't risk killing the prisoner or turning it into a vegetable. Unfortunately, they couldn't come up with anything better.

"Let's do it," Kal said. "Sergeant Jones, can you prep a few of your soldiers for security?"

"Yessir."

"Okay, let's meet outside the brig in an hour," Kal said. "Let's see if we can get some answers."

Nicole stood next to Kal in the corridor opposite her old stateroom. Sergeant Jones, Ekon, and Sandra knelt in a semi-circle, kinetic pistols armed and pointed at the door. Garcia carefully lowered the oxygen in the room while watching the prisoner's vitals. After fifteen minutes, he announced it was unconscious.

"Okay, open it," Jones said after another five minutes had passed.

The door opened with a hiss as the air between the room

and the rest of the ship regulated. Nicole watched on the viewscreen next to the door as the three Tac-I soldiers cautiously entered and spread out. The door closed behind them and Jones cautiously crept forward until he was kneeling next to the unconscious Nasi. He quickly applied restraints to bind its legs together and secure its arms against its torso. Once Jones had finished, Ekon joined him and helped carry the prisoner so it was sitting on the bunk, slumped back against the wall.

"Okay, ready," Jones called from the room as the door opened.

Nicole and Kal strode in, moving two chairs so they faced the Nasi prisoner. Nicole studied the creature's face as she sat quietly, waiting for it to wake up. He looked to be a male in his mid-twenties. His face was smooth and angular, with sunken cheeks that gave him a malnourished air. Nicole realized that the purple hue to his skin was uneven, lightening around the eyes and mouth. The black patterns that swirled around his body were even more intricate than she had first realized, the swirls and loops circling in on themselves.

"Seems the tables have turned. Eh, Ms. Bergeron?"

Nicole almost fell backward. She thought she caught a trace of a smirk on the Nasi's face, but if it had been there, no evidence remained a second later. She was grateful that Kal also had jumped backward at the alien's voice.

"You are looking at my Sishen, are you not?" the Nasi asked, cocking his head and using his legs to readjust himself.

"Is that what you call the tattoos?" Kal asked.

The Nasi nodded. "They are more than tattoos—they are

155

me. The story of my life and people, written for all to see."

"What's your name?" Nicole asked.

"I am Soldier Salah Badu." He inclined his head. "You've come here because you don't believe the governor or you want to know more." He let the last word hang. "I think it is both, actually."

"We need answers," Kal responded.

"Of course you do. But, the governor already gave you all the answers."

"That's not enough," Kal said as he stood up. "Where did you come from? What are you doing here?"

"Like I said, the governor already told these to your friend." Salah indicated with his head.

"Well, tell me then," Kal said. "I want to know."

Salah gave a broad smile, revealing his toothless gums. Nicole found the effect unsettling. "Of course. In order for you to understand everything, I fear I may have to start at the true beginning."

"We've got all the time in the world," replied Nicole.

Salah described how Humans had overcrowded the Earth and leaders were desperate to find a way to escape the solar system and settle others. Famine, wars, and unrest caused the very future of their species to teeter on the brink. They had created a primitive fold drive but could only reliably move ships a mere million kilometers in a fold, not nearly far enough.

Initially, scientists had attempted to use automated probes to test the drives. The AI systems could not handle the fold process and would immediately crash or go haywire—

humans had to be controlling the ships. The governments of the world conscripted debtors and criminals by promising a better life for their children. They gave basic training to these unwilling explorers and then sent them to their almost-certain doom.

The Nasi came from the twelve Humans aboard *UNSA-8123*. When they activated their fold drive, they found they had not moved an inch. Instead, the surrounding universe had changed. They discovered that the very laws of physics had shifted. They were trapped in this new universe and barely made it onto the nearby planet, their universe's version of Earth.

Over the next few years, these first Human settlers, who the Nasi now called the Ancients, fought to survive on the planet. Those times were tough and unforgiving; half the crew died. They gave up on being rescued, realizing that they were the forgotten dregs of Humanity, and instead focused on the future.

The Ancients had to rediscover all the technology they had taken for granted back on Earth, adapting it to the universe they found themselves in. As they procreated, they found their universe had changed their very genetics. Their offspring were not Human anymore; or at least not Human as they saw it. They looked to be almost a completely different species. Over time these first Humans realized that their aging process had transformed, and ultimately ceased. Their offspring grew to adulthood and then just stopped at around thirty years of age.

Over the next several hundred years, the Nasi surpassed

the technical achievements of Humanity. Hostile species surrounded them, and it required every bit of their cunning and ingenuity to survive. This made the Nasi stronger and made them develop faster than even they thought possible.

Despite their achievements, many never stopped wanting to return to Earth. They worked tirelessly on creating a fold drive that could travel between their new universe and the one they had left. Finally, they developed a drive capable of returning.

Several years ago, the first Nasi ship returned. They realized that the drive only worked in one direction because of the differing physics in each universe. Moving between the two universes burned the drive out, making it impossible for regular travel between them.

They also discovered that Humanity had grown stagnant and complacent. Humans had realized only a portion of their potential and were subject to the whims of their neighbors. The children had found their parents, only to discover that their parents had grown feeble and doddering. At first, the Nasi didn't know what to do. Was Humanity able to be saved? Were they worth saving? The Nasi leaders decided they would take the wisdom and technology that they had learned and guide Humanity to a position of dominance. They would help them to regain the hunger to advance and to expand that they'd had hundreds of years earlier.

Over several years, they studied Humanity and its neighbors, learning their cultures, technologies, and—most importantly—their weaknesses. The Nasi developed a plan that would allow them to return to their universe and, at the same time, raise Humanity to its rightful place. However, it required a tremendous sacrifice: losing Earth.

"So, what's next? What are your plans?" Kal asked once Salah finished.

"I think I've told you enough," the Nasi sighed.

Both Kal and Nicole tried to get Salah to answer more questions, but the creature refused. He met their questions with a steady gaze and a single raised eyebrow.

Finally admitting defeat, they stood up to exit the room.

"General Norman. Ms Bergeron."

Kal and Nicole turned around.

"In time, you'll realize that we are helping you. We're guiding you to a better future."

❖

Kal idly stirred his tea, waiting for it to cool. He could adjust the settings on the fabricator to decrease the temperature, but preferred watching the steam and heat slowly dissipate from the cup in front of him.

He didn't know what to make of Salah's story. On one hand, he found it fascinating. He could only imagine what this other universe was like and what the Nasi had been forced to endure. On the other, the fanatical edge to Salah's tale had him worried. The prisoner was a genuine believer—he felt they were doing the right thing. Kal hoped that not all the Nasi felt the same way. He had a hard time believing much of the Nasi's purported motivation in coming back to this universe. They seemed on a campaign of conquest much more than one to help Humanity. He knew, though, that different species, or even factions of the same species, could have wildly different ways of thinking.

"Sir," a voice called from behind him.

Kal turned to see Private Pudari walking through the galley door. She activated the fabricator with her implant and pulled a steaming bowl of soup out of the machine.

"Pudari, how are you feeling?" Kal asked. Although she hadn't been as bad off as Ekon or Sergeant Jones, Pudari had gotten more than her fair share of injuries—both physical and emotional—on New America.

"The medbot did a good job, sir," she replied. "Good as new."

Kal wanted to broach the subject of Kondari—he had seen them talking and wasn't sure how close the two had been. But he didn't want to pick at any wounds that were still fresh. After a few minutes of light small talk, their conversation faded into an awkward silence.

"Sir," Pudari said, shattering the quiet, "can I speak freely?"

"Of course," Kal replied. He wondered if anyone had ever answered in the negative to that question.

Pudari nervously traced her spoon along the rim of her bowl, producing a light scraping noise. "I'm concerned about Ms. Bergeron", she said.

"I understand—"

"I know that you and she are friends." She cut off Kal, the words coming out in a rush now that she had started. "But I've watched her—she's planning something. I don't think it was a coincidence that the Nasi governor called for her."

Kal tried to stifle a sigh. So, this was why Pudari had come into the galley.

"We're all in danger as long as she has free rein on the ship. I wouldn't be surprised if she releases the prisoner."

"You have any proof?" Kal asked.

Pudari paused. "No," she admitted, "but look at what happened on New America. She's got a history."

"What do you want me to do?"

"Restrict her movement, sir. We can lock her in Chief Kanumba's cabin until we get to the fleet. Then let them sort it out."

"I'm not doing that," Kal replied, holding up his hand to forestall any interruptions. "She's done nothing wrong. Would you like me to treat you like that? Treat you like a criminal on a hunch?"

"Sir, she collaborated with the Nasi," Pudari said, slamming down her spoon. "We went to New America with seven soldiers. Two died, and four were injured."

"Including her!"

Pudari picked up her bowl. "Sir, she's a collaborator. Don't let your personal feelings get in the way of your duty!"

Kal felt his face flush. "Stop there. I'm doing my duty, same as you, same as Nicole. Get past this, now."

Pudari stood up with her barely touched bowl of soup. "Fine, I'll drop it." She dumped the bowl and its contents into the recycler. "Remember—I warned you, sir."

Kal didn't have time to respond before the young private had walked out of the galley.

161

Kal was leading his daily staff meeting in the galley, the final one before they rendezvoused with the fleet in twelve hours. His leadership team had almost completely recovered from the injuries they'd sustained on New America but there was still a sense of foreboding that seemed centered on the Nasi prisoner in Nicole's stateroom.

"How's the prisoner?" asked Kal.

"Same as always," replied Nicole. "He just sits there. I haven't been able to get any more information that the fleet would find useful. I doubt he knows anything he hasn't told us already."

"He's not exactly their top brass," said Sergeant Jones. "I doubt they tell him anything more than where to be and when."

"Any luck on the device?" Kal asked Kanumba. The chief was working on cracking the device that Kal had found on the Nasi governor's wrist.

"Close, sir," she replied. "So close. Their encryption is pretty weak. If I don't get it, the fleet engineers will. I just don't want to hear them talk trash if they do."

Kal was eager to learn what was on the small device. Only through pure luck had they stumbled upon the personal computer of the most powerful Nasi on New America. If they could get even a fraction of the information off it, the mission would be considered a success.

"Sir, what do you think will happen with the TLF?" asked

Jones. "Do you think that Samsara Fleet will provide aid?"

Kal nodded. "I think so, yeah. The question will be, how do we get through the blockade? I think we caught the Nasi off guard this time. I don't think it will work a second time."

Jones pursed his lips, seeming to think it over. "The Nasi might destroy the system too," he said. Kal was surprised to detect a hint of fear in the senior noncommissioned officer's tone—he had thought nothing could rattle him.

"If what we've been told is true, I doubt it," Nicole said. "They'll lose their Footholds on the planet, and they seem to be genuine in their zealous belief that they are Humanity's saviors."

"Ultimately, I think it's a risk we must take. We can't allow the Nasi to hold us hostage with those ships." Kal hated the thought of wagering an entire system on that assumption. At least he wasn't the person who had to make the final decision. That lay with General Samaha, the fleet commander.

"We'll have to see how the negotiations with the Torgham and Goro are going," Nicole added. "If we aren't able to get them to provide assistance, then the fleet won't be able to help itself."

"I'm not holding my breath," said Jones. "I fought against the Torgham, and the Goro have never seemed interested in helping anyone but themselves."

"They might see things differently," Kal said. "Especially when they hear about what the Nasi have planned."

At least Kal hoped so. Nicole was right—without help, Samsara Fleet was finished. There were no ports or planets that they could resupply from, and there was no way that they were ready to take on the Nasi directly. Without help, they were dead in space.

❖

"What do you think?" Nicole asked, absentmindedly touching the red shawl laced with gold embroidery that was draped across her shoulders. She was in Kal's stateroom, sitting across from him in the small seating area by the door. They had just come back from Kondari and Sakata's funeral in the ship's cargo bay.

Military funerals were a way for them to remember and celebrate the soldiers that they had lost. The ceremony was simple. They placed a pair of boots for each soldier—or the remains, if they had them—in the center of the cargo bay. Whoever knew the soldier best would stand in front and tell a story about them. The stories were often funny, always personal, and touched Kal much more than the prepared speeches he had heard at civilian funerals.

To Kal, it was the honesty that made military funerals so powerful. They didn't gloss over faults or try to make the person appear a saint—the speaker simply told the truth. As the commander, he felt somewhat responsible for the deaths of Kondari and Sakata. Although he hadn't pulled the trigger, he had devised the plan and given the orders that led to their deaths.

"Fifty-fifty," Kal made a balancing motion with his hands. "It depends on whether they believe the Nasi will actually attack them. They'd have to be fools not to, but sometimes wishful thinking overtakes logic." They were continuing their conversation on whether the Torgham or Goro would help the fleet.

"If the Nasi think that they're helping us, then they'll attack," Nicole said.

Kal nodded. "The Nasi are going to attack either way, though. We both know it."

He felt a sense of déjà vu. He'd had the same discussion with almost everyone on board—what would happen when they got back to the fleet? Kal was tired of trying to guess at this point.

"I miss the good old days," he said. "Just flying between ports and drinking my troubles away. Not a care in the world."

Nicole gave a wry smile. "I doubt that. I doubt you were ever happy in all those years."

"Perhaps, but at least I didn't have to face my misery. Now it seems like all we do is grieve."

Kal regretted the words as soon as he said them. They were a bridge to a place that neither of them wanted to go. For Kal, it was the wife and children he had lost. For Nicole, it was the grief and regret over her mistakes and losing her family.

Silence hung over the room.

"It's been forever since I have done anything fun," Nicole declared.

Kal was happy to engage the new avenue of discussion. Time to lighten things up. "I know. I used to love watching holos of Earth shows. The ones from Mariga are way too dark."

They discussed their favorite holos, discovering that they had remarkably similar tastes. Both enjoyed comedies, the more detached from reality the better. Kal idly wondered if programs were being made anymore. He couldn't imagine that they were, but even in the darkest times, people needed a relief and outlet from their troubles. Onboard the *Oruc*, Kal mainly read biographies and history books on ancient Earth civilizations. He had a nostalgia for the simpler times, when Humanity wasn't aware that there was anything in the universe but themselves.

They discussed the books that they had read. Nicole enjoyed reading history as well, though she preferred the early interstellar period, when the UEG and EDF were first established.

Nicole yawned and stretched in her chair. She grabbed the empty glass next to her and dropped it in the room's recycler, which would break it down into its component elements.

"Something I should mention before you leave," Kal said. "I've had a soldier express some concerns about you. I'm not naming names, but you can probably guess who."

Nicole's face soured. "Pudari, I bet. She's said some things to me as well."

"I thought you should know. She's young and has seen a lot in the past few months. People want control, so they blame what's near them. It's hard for her to blame the Nasi, who she can't touch."

Nicole nodded. "I've had to deal with this before. In the end, the only thing I can do is stop the Nasi. She'll see that

I'm not the enemy."

"I hope you're right," Kal said, unconvinced.

"Me too," Nicole said as she walked out the door.

Chapter Twelve

Samsara Fleet had grown significantly since Kal had left weeks ago. There were now at least ten capital ships in the fleet, a tremendous increase from the handful they had before—and not all of them Human. Kal had seen a couple of Kurz dreadnoughts, a Qudoru battleship, and even a Tounous carrier.

"Samsara Fleet, this is Brigadier General Kal Norman aboard the *Oruc*," Kal hailed the fleet. "We request landing instructions, and I need to speak with General Samaha as soon as possible as well."

After a slight delay, a reply came back. "General Norman, General Samaha has moved her flag to the Tounous Carrier *Gedorhan's Return*. I am sending instructions to your pilot now."

Garcia nodded at Kal, acknowledging that they had received the docking instructions, and hit the button to allow the automated procedures to take over. The *Oruc* glided through the fleet, the huge capital ships appearing only as small dots to the naked eye because of the enormous distances. Looking at his tactical map, Kal was impressed by the size and firepower of the fleet. The Nasi had struck fast, but the fleet proved they hadn't won yet. He doubted Samsara Fleet could stand against the full might of the Nasi, but they stood a chance if they were smart.

The Tounous carrier grew in the viewscreen as they approached. The dull metallic carrier was a long cylinder with bays dotting the outside at regular intervals. Four weapons arrays, one at each end of the ship and two in the middle, had clusters of torpedo and missile launchers and plasma and kinetic cannons.

The interior landing bay of the carrier was a hive of activity. Tounous, Human, and Kurz fighters dotted the inside of the bay while maintenance bots and crews scurried around, performing maintenance on the ships. The Humans and Tounous walked through the bay, efficient and deliberate, radiating a sense of purpose.

As the crew went through their post-flight checks, Kal connected his implant to the shipwide net. There were instructions to head to General Samaha's office already waiting for him.

"I have orders to meet with General Samaha," Kal said to the flight crew. "I'll find you when I am done."

Garcia nodded and Kal walked through the ship toward the rear cargo bay. Nicole was already waiting for him in the ship's bay, eager, he was sure, to tell the general all they had learned. The two of them stepped off and made their way through the foreign corridors of the enormous carrier. Despite having spent most of the past decade away from the rest of Humanity, Kal felt himself uneasy with the mass of Tounous scurrying around them.

Tounous were a hive species and grew up in large, densely populated underground complexes. Their ships had that same congested, subterranean feel, with cramped circular hallways and dim lighting. The three-legged aliens scurried about, almost crawling over each other as they hurtled down the corridors of the ship.

Kal and Nicole dodged as many of the Tounous as they could while following the directions to Samaha's office on their neural implant. After walking for a few minutes, they arrived at a multi-directional lift and entered, using their implants to tell it where they needed to go. The lifts were cylinders that carried their passengers through shafts in the ship and operated in multiple directions, allowing them to not only change decks but rapidly move lengthwise down the carrier.

They finally arrived at a large oval room. Built-in benches lined the walls, and a viewscreen stretched above. A holo of Earth mountains played on the screen, giving them the impression that the room was perched on the top of a peak. Lieutenant General Aamina Samaha sat on the bench at the far end of the room, reading from a handheld tablet. As Kal and Nicole walked in, she laid the tablet down and stood up, stretching her back.

"Ma'am," Kal said as he shook her hand.

Samaha smiled and gestured for them to sit down. Kal and Nicole took seats to either side of her.

"General Norman, welcome back," Samaha said. "As you probably noticed, a lot has changed since you left. But before we get into that, tell me what happened on New America." Kal appreciated her getting straight to the point.

Kal nodded. "Of course. Also, I have already filed a written brief and submitted it to the fleet's intel team." Since Kal had joined Samsara Fleet, he had restarted his habit of preparing a written debrief after each mission.

For the next two hours, Kal and Nicole described

everything they had discovered on New America. The conversation started with chronological events, but soon dove into specific avenues around diplomacy and trade as the general asked questions. Samaha, clearly surprised at the amount of information they had gained, chased down each lead as they talked, asked piercing and increasingly precise questions to make sure she had every ounce of information. They concluded their debrief with Nicole describing her conversation with the Nasi governor, Fermott.

"So, they're just here to help, huh?" she asked rhetorically.

"It's impossible to say for sure—but they seem to think so," answered Nicole. "My impression is that they're fanatics. The trauma of being stranded and the harsh environment has twisted them. I think there is more that we don't know yet though."

"Such as?" Samaha raised an eyebrow.

"Nothing I can put my finger on, yet," Nicole said. "Just unanswered questions. There seems to be no dissent or disagreement among the Nasi. That seems strange."

"Well, we'll have plenty of time to get the truth." Samaha smiled grimly. "I know you weren't able to crack that Nasi computer yet. Our engineering team is already working on it. Hopefully, it will shed some light on this."

Kal and Nicole nodded. Each answer brought more questions.

"I'll want you at my next staff meeting." Samaha nodded to herself, seeming to have made some sort of decision. "Since you left, ships from the Tounous, Kurz, and Qudoru all found us and have joined our fleet. We've formed a sort of coalition."

The video screens around the room abruptly flickered to a diagram of the fleet. It was a complete status report, with the numbers and readiness of their assets, from the capital ships to the soldiers. The fleet had more than doubled in size since the *Oruc* had left and now stood at eleven capital ships and almost nine hundred fighters. Four out of the eleven ships were Human, with three Tounous, two Kurz, and two Qudoru making up the rest.

"We've entered an uneasy alliance with our neighbors. Although I remain the head of the fleet, I need to include the other species in our decision making."

"Enemy of my enemy..." said Kal.

"Exactly," Samaha replied. "We've also been negotiating with the Torgham so that the fleet can get resupplied. The Goro refused to even talk to us." Kal couldn't blame them. "The Torgham have allowed us to port at Keerloa, one of their colonies, to resupply."

Kal raised his eyebrows. That was surprising news. The Torgham and Humans had been in a bitter war only two decades ago. It showed exactly how desperate both species were that they were willing to work together like this.

"It has taken a while for our new coalition to learn to work together. We have spent much of the time just figuring out how we work as a group and what our goals are," Samaha admitted.

"What did you decide?" Nicole asked.

"Our fleet will remain together until we've removed the

Nasi from all colonies and we eradicate them from our portion of the galaxy," Samaha responded. "Until that happens, the fleet will remain independent and not beholden to any government. After we defeat them"—she shrugged—"well, we'll get to that when we get to it."

"We're better off than we were before, at least," Kal said.

"Yes," Samaha said, "but there's a lot of friction. Fear of the Nasi is a great motivator, but it will only get us so far." The general stood up. "For now, take a break, get some rest. I'll be calling for you both to brief the staff."

Kal and Nicole both stood up, recognizing the tone of dismissal in her voice.

"Kal, Nicole," Samaha said, "good job. Your work has given us a chance. Now we just need to take advantage of it."

"General Norman," the voice said, waking Kal up from his sleep, "report to General Samaha's briefing room ASAP."

Kal quickly threw on his Samsara Fleet uniform. It felt stiff and formal to him after having worn his civilian clothes for so long. He grabbed a quick drink of water and a nutrient pill, no time for food, and then took one of the automated shuttles from the *Ofira* to the *Gedorhan's Return*.

General Samaha sat in the same spot he and Nicole had left her only hours before. A group of a dozen officers, evenly split among Humans, Tounous, Kurz, and Qudoru, sat or stood around her.

"Excellent, General Norman's here," Samaha said, patting

the seat next to her. "Let's begin, Colonel Coats."

Kal took the proffered seat as the colonel stood up and walked to the center of the room. He was short and middle-aged, with wings of white spreading from his temples. "Thank you, ma'am," the man said. "We've been able to decrypt a computer that General Norman's recon team recovered on New America."

Kal could feel himself fading off as the officer described the specifics of how they had finally decrypted the device in excruciating detail. He glanced over at Samaha and the other officers and noticed they were having much the same reaction as him.

"Can you cut to the point?" one of the Kurz interrupted.

Colonel Coats stuttered for a moment, his face reddening. "Uh, yes. So, it seems like this device is the Nasi equivalent of our neural implants. There are battle plans on here for a Nasi offensive on the Torgham worlds. The information is incomplete, but I would expect them to launch this offensive soon."

"Like how soon?" asked Samaha.

"In the next week, ma'am," he responded. The viewscreens around the room displayed a tactical map, showing lines radiating from several Human-controlled colonies toward Torgham space.

"As you can see, they are heading toward the Torgham," Coats continued. "However, we don't know what colonies they are planning to strike or when."

One of the Tounous let out a faint chirp, a sign of annoyance. "We'll be sitting ducks," she said.

The group reviewed the incomplete Nasi plans, discussing where they thought the aliens would strike and what their next move should be. They agreed that the Nasi's most likely target was Geerlok, the Torgham homeworld. However, they couldn't decide what to do next. The Qudoru wanted to remain where they were and avoid open conflict with the Nasi, while the Kurz and Tounous proposed continuing with their resupply. Kal knew that a fleet undergoing resupply was a sitting duck. If the Nasi attacked, they would destroy Samsara Fleet without losing a ship.

"If I may," interrupted Coats, "there is more."

The voices, chirps, and grunts died down. "The brunt of the attack is being launched from Patagonia," he said. "Their detailed battle plans for the assault are probably on that planet."

"We can't just assault another planet," Kal said. "My team barely made it out of the Nasi Foothold on New America. It would be suicide to find them."

"Sir, I think there may be another option," Coats said. "The Nasi have already established a research lab on the planet. They seem to be developing some new type of weapon there. The lab is small and isolated; it should be much easier to infiltrate than one of their Footholds."

"Why would they have their plans in a research lab?" asked one of the Tounous.

"We're not totally sure." Coats cracked his knuckled nervously. "But all indications are that they are there. My best guess is that whatever they're researching there, it's somehow related to the assault."

"We're not going to solve this now," Samaha announced. "Either way, we need to leave this position. We've been here too long. Set course for the Torgham; we'll figure out what we do next en route."

The assorted officers filed out of the room. As Kal watched them leave, he pictured the Nasi fleet traveling toward Torgham as well. The enemy continued to cement their control over the galaxy, and they were running out of time to stop them.

The day after the *Oruc* had returned to the fleet, Samaha had summoned Nicole and Kal back to the *Gedorhan's Return* to debrief her staff in person. It had been a grueling ordeal. Nicole and Kal had sat at one end of an oval room—an oversized version of General Samaha's briefing room—and been grilled by around fifty senior officers from four different species.

Nicole had tried to remain as clinical and impartial as she could during the questioning, but she couldn't shake the feeling of being doubted and questioned as she and Kal went through every decision they had made during the mission multiple times. There wasn't enough space in the room for everyone who wanted to hear the debrief—the faces of officers on other ships filled the viewscreens lining the wall. During the eight-hour session, they went through multiple rounds of grilling, with each species demanding that they retell the story from the beginning.

Kal and Nicole finally finished and could drag themselves back to their rooms on the *Ofira*. Nicole did some light calisthenics in the ship's gym, grabbed a small meal, and dragged herself onto the bed in her cabin and fell asleep, her dreams once again tortured by images from her past.

Still, she felt rested when she woke the next day. She took her time getting ready, enjoying the feeling of not having to rush somewhere for the first time in a while. Nicole sat under the showerhead, feeling the warm water rush down her frame, washing away the fear and exhaustion from their mission. It was a welcome change from the *Oruc*, where the showers emphasized water conservation over comfort.

She had agreed to meet Kal later in the ship's lounge for lunch in a few hours. For the first time in months, her time was her own. She didn't have a meeting or mission that she needed to be at. She knew that this sensation was temporary, and that she'd better enjoy it; Samaha and her staff undoubtedly had another mission for them as soon as the fleet completed their fold.

She contacted Taisha over the ship's net. The chief giggled when she heard Nicole's voice. She didn't have time to talk; she was with Jae-Ho. Nicole smiled to herself, happy for her friends.

Nicole went through the ship's library on her tablet and lay in her bunk reading. It was an old science fiction novel from Earth, before they had become interstellar and met other species. These types of books were her guilty pleasure; they provided insight into the hopes and dreams of those ancient humans. So much of these books were wrong, but occasionally the accuracy of the predictions rang true, sometimes shockingly so. For Nicole, they were a way to understand the time when they were written. They painted a picture of the zeitgeist of their era.

A small tone rang in her ear. Time to meet Kal in the lounge. It was supposed to be a celebration of their survival—not of the mission, but of the debrief.

Most large ships like the *Ofira* had a lounge. The pleasantly appointed room had small tables scattered throughout and video screens displaying calming nature scenes lining the walls. Groups of two or three sat at the tables, murmuring to each other while service bots brought food and drinks. The food came from the same industrial fabricator as they used in the galley, but it somehow tasted richer and more satisfying in the lounge's calm.

Kal gave a wave and smiled slightly as he saw her walk in. He was already sitting at a table near the fall wall.

As Nicole sat down, one of the service bots rolled to their table. She ordered Eggs Benedict and champagne, a small celebration for still being alive after their trip to New America.

"So," Kal exhaled loudly, "are you fully recovered yet?"

Nicole nodded.

"I must've slept for at least ten hours." Kal grinned. "Haven't slept that soundly in years."

"Me too," Nicole agreed. "There's something about being a prisoner of war that makes you tired. I had a wonderful morning, relaxing in my room and reading from the library."

Nicole described the book she had been reading to Kal. It

was about a boy genius training to command Humanity's forces against an alien invasion fleet. To her surprise, Kal had read it as well. Though he refused to mention what happened at the end.

He recommended several other books for Nicole, displaying a deep knowledge of ancient science fiction. It surprised her. Based on the way he talked about his past, she'd have thought he spent his entire life working or drinking. Nicole reminded herself that for most of his life, Kal had been a devoted father and husband, working as an EDF officer and spending nights with his family at home. It was a large part of who he was, but one he never talked about.

Kal took a sip of his water after the server refilled the glass. "It's nice to talk about this kind of stuff," he said. "I haven't in a while."

"Sounds like you're doing a lot of things that you haven't done for a long time," Nicole answered. She knew that even this slight allusion to how he had changed was risky—he almost never talked about himself.

"Yeah," Kal replied slowly. "For whatever reason, this entire war has restarted my life. I'm still coming to grips with it all."

Nicole gave a dry chuckle. "Funny, because it destroyed mine."

"I wouldn't say that," Kal said, smiling. "I mean, you're here in this gorgeous lounge, eating with a handsome officer." He theatrically puffed out his chest.

Nicole rolled her eyes. "You know what I mean. I had a life and a purpose." She paused. "Even if I didn't exactly enjoy it."

"I'd say you have more of a purpose now than ever," Kal replied.

Nicole stopped and thought about it. She had to admit he was probably right. "I guess the alternatives are worse," she said, resigned. "I could have been on Gorash when it was destroyed. At least I'm alive."

"I think that's the best we can hope for, for now," Kal said.

After a pause, they continued talking, comparing their favorite holos from Earth. The conversation remained light, and both of them consciously stayed away from any subjects that could lead them to talking about the Nasi or their pasts. Unfortunately, those were the two biggest things for them to talk about, two rocks that threatened to crush not just them, but everyone in the fleet.

Kal suddenly stiffened as he received a message via his neural implant. Nicole waited patiently while he responded, idly playing with her empty champagne flute.

"Sorry, that's General Samaha," Kal said. "She has requested my presence at her staff meeting."

Nicole's sense of disappointment surprised her—she enjoyed just being around him. Now that Kal had to leave, she thought about the things she wanted to say but was too afraid to utter.

"I understand," she replied, the formality of her words conflicting with the emotion she felt. "It was nice to talk about something other than the"—she made quotes with her hands—"mission. We should do this again."

Kal nodded. "I enjoyed it too. Maybe next time I'll have

the guts to talk about more than just books and holos."

"Me too," Nicole whispered quietly as he walked away.

❖

Kal's ears burned as he walked through the ship's corridors. His parting words to Nicole rang harshly in his own ears. He had meant them as a promise. Kal enjoyed sitting across from her, talking about nothing, but he wanted to tell her more. He had been afraid—of what, he wasn't sure, but he wanted to let her know he was almost ready to share.

She probably thought he was a jerk.

Kal took one of the transport shuttles to the *Gedorhan's Return* and made his way to the fleet command conference room. They had already started.

"—so we will have a multi-pronged approach," said the Kurz standing in the center of the room. A map on the viewscreens displayed Human space with small icons showing the estimated positions of the Nasi fleet.

"Based on our intel, we believe the Nasi will have no compunction in destroying any non-Human system. They seem to view them as simple assets, available for their own benefit. Any meaningful direct action against the Nasi in any Torgham system has a high risk of ending catastrophically."

Kal couldn't help but agree with the Kurz's assessment.

"We strongly believe that the Nasi are planning on sending a large force somewhere into Torgham space. We believe they intend to finish their conquest of this region. Luckily for us, surprise is no longer on their side. The Torgham may not be at war with the Nasi, but they have instituted comprehensive security protocols in their systems."

"What chance would the Torgham have against the Nasi?" asked a Qudoru admiral.

"Based on our estimates, they could stand against them for some time. However, the Nasi battle plans show that a system-destroying ship, which we are calling a dreadnaught, is in their invasion fleet."

"So their plan is to capture the Torgham systems, and if that doesn't work, to destroy them?" asked Samaha.

The Kurz waved its antennae, indicating agreement. "Yes, but this also provides an opportunity. If we can confirm the Nasi attack plans, we can intercept them and wipe out the fleet. It would be a decisive victory against them."

The map zoomed out and showed a detailed view of the Nasi fleet's estimated displacement. Their fleet was relatively small for controlling as many systems as they did—only twenty ships or so. The Nasi had been successful because of the surprise and overwhelming force they had brought to bear on their adversaries. Now, surprise was no longer on their side, and it was the perfect opportunity to strike back.

"If their fleet is so stretched, why are they doing this?" Kal asked. The invasion of Torgham space seemed almost foolishly aggressive.

"We don't know why," admitted the Kurz. "But this is a perfect opportunity. If we ignore it, we may not have another opportunity."

Samaha glanced over at Kal, her face pointed in thought. "I agree with you, General Norman—it seems like a grave misstep on the Nasi's part. But we have to take advantage of it."

"Exactly, General," said the Kurz. "But we still do not know exactly where the Nasi intend to strike and what the full composition of their force will be."

"So without it, we may folding into a ambush?" asked Samaha.

"Yes, ma'am," the officer replied. "But with it, we may surprise the Nasi and destroy most of their fleet."

At that moment, a Qudoru officer crawled forward to the center to the room. "To that motion, we recommend we send a recon team to Patagonia to recover the complete battle plans. The rest of the fleet will continue folding to Torgham space to resupply the fleet." Kal had a good idea which recon team they would send. "The team will recover the battle plans and provide equipment to the local resistance group on the planet. Then they will rendezvous with the fleet at Keerloa."

The officers in the room chattered among themselves—the various chips and whines of their native speech reminded Kal of a zoo he had visited with his family once. He sat quietly, grateful that he did not have General Samaha's job; it was more politics than anything else, and he did not have the skill or temperament for it.

Samaha took control of the meeting and blessed the plan her staff had created. As Kal had expected, the *Oruc* would be the recon team traveling to Patagonia. The staff also recommended sending other small teams to the other Human colonies to gain intel and provide supplies.

After finalizing the plan, the room cleared, the large Kurz

and Qudoru shuffling out of the door with the Humans and Tounous scuttled between them.

Kal stood up and stretched his legs as he noticed General Samaha approached him.

"Rough, huh?" Samaha asked, an eyebrow arched. Kal wasn't sure if she was talking about the mission or the meeting. Either way, he agreed, and nodded.

"A note of warning, Kal. I know you lost several soldiers on New America." Samaha's eyes bored into Kal's. "We sent a recon team to Patagonia earlier—they barely made it out alive. The Nasi there have seen our new technology, and they are prepared. This mission will be even worse."

Chapter Thirteen

The crew of the *Oruc* had one more day for rest and recovery prior to leaving for Patagonia. The fleet engineers needed to complete upgrades to the ship's systems and load the equipment and supplies that they had to deliver to the rebels on Patagonia.

The crew agreed to have lunch together in the ship's lounge. Everyone seemed to be in a good mood, the few days' rest doing wonders. When Kal brought up their destination, Major Garcia, the only one present who was from Patagonia, let out a small groan.

As they talked during the lunch, Kal realized that there was still so much he didn't know about his team. He knew almost nothing about where they came from and what their lives had been like before the Nasi. Everyone lived only in the moment, almost never talking about their pasts. Garcia was especially closemouthed about his life. Whenever the conversation veered too close, the pilot would make an outrageous joke and change the subject. Kal wasn't even sure if he had a family.

After lunch, Kal retired to his cabin and read through the intelligence reports on Patagonia. After Samaha had sent the *Oruc* to New America, she had sent out three other recon teams—one to each of the other Human colonies. Only the *Oruc* and the team assigned to Patagonia had returned—the others were presumed dead or captured.

After the collapse of the UEG, Patagonia had descended into chaos. Multiple factions vied for control of the planet. All of them had sworn allegiance to the Nasi, except for one—the Patagonia Front. The largest faction was the Planetary People's Council, which controlled most of the space around the planet's capital, Kasongo. They had instituted repressive tactics in their area of control, similar to the Domespat. The worst part was that the PPC wasn't even the most repressive of the warring factions, Foyleton was worse. They routinely executed citizens who they felt *could* one day be a threat. The Nasi let the violence continue, leaving the Human factions alone except for the Patagonia Front, which they ruthlessly hunted. Kal doubted the Nasi cared which Human government ran the planet as long as they were subservient.

As he read through the material, his mind wandered to Nicole. Perhaps he should invite her out for a drink? Kal's mind warred back and forth before he finally put down the tablet he was reading and walked toward the ship's galley alone. He couldn't work up the courage to continue their conversation.

As he looked around the galley, Kal noticed the fleet had changed. There were now Qudoru and Tounous sitting and joking alongside their Human allies. All of them now wore the blue uniform of Samsara Fleet, braids on the shoulders showing rank and position. The Nasi invasion had thrown this group of soldiers together, and Kal wasn't sure what would happen when the war ended.

Ten hours later, after a drink and some sleep, Kal walked up the cargo bay ramp of the *Oruc*. The engines were spinning up, a soft hum permeating the air. He walked into the crew quarters to find Sergeant Jones and the rest of Tac-I squad settling in. Sandra now wore the gray Tac-I fatigues with Private First Class rank on her shoulder.

"So, you're officially on the team?" Kal pointed to the rank.

"Yessir," she responded with a sheepish smile. "Guess I finally got my dream to travel the stars."

When Kal had first met Sandra on a small Kurz mining station, before the Nasi had come, she'd told him she was going to enlist in the EDF and train to become a Tac-I soldier. Despite everything that had happened since, she'd made that dream a reality. *Perhaps some things are just destined,* Kal thought. He wasn't sure if the thought was reassuring or terrifying.

"Meet the new soldier, sir," Sergeant Jones said as he noticed Kal in the doorway. The sergeant kicked the bunk next to him, and a young man in his early twenties sprang from the bed, his uniform unzipped in the front. He looked around, his eyes landing on Kal, and stood at attention.

"Introduce yourself, Private," Jones instructed.

"Private Frederick Kinawadi . . . sir." Kinawadi clearly didn't know who Kal was. Since they were about to depart on a mission, the general was wearing his merchant uniform.

"Kal Norman." Kal stuck out his hand, and the young soldier shook it.

"Brigadier General Norman is the officer leading this mission," Jones said. The young soldier's eyes widened, and his body stiffened. "He has led the missions to destroy the Nasi capital ship at Kapustin Station, led reconnaissance missions on New America, and was one of the first Humans to survive an encounter with the bastards. You're lucky, Kinawadi. You will serve under the most experienced officer in the entire fleet. Don't forget it." Kal saw the ghost of a smile cross the NCO's face as Private Kinawadi's eyes darted between Jones and Kal.

"Yes, Sergeant. Happy to be aboard, sir."

"Glad to have you aboard," Kal smiled. "Sergeant Jones, let the cockpit know when your team is ready."

Jones nodded and turned back to the squad. "You heard 'em. Get your gear stowed."

Kal stepped into his stateroom and looked around. Despite having been gone for only a couple of days, it felt foreign to him—as if it had been months instead. A few minutes later, Garcia announced they were ready to disembark. The *Ofira* had paused folding to allow the *Oruc* to leave the fleet, while the other ships continued folding to Keerloa.

An hour after they had departed the *Ofira* and begun folding, the leaders met in the galley to discuss the upcoming mission. Kal kicked it off by reiterating their goals during the mission: infiltrate the Nasi research facility to gain intel and provide supplies to the Patagonia Front. After he had finished, Kanumba described what improvements had been made to the *Oruc* while they were docked on the *Ofira*. The fleet engineers continued to sift through the debris and parts they had found from destroyed Nasi ships—quickly developing modifications to the fleet. Humanity's military technology had probably advanced more in the past six months than it had in the previous decade, by Kal's estimation.

Kanumba then described the supplies that they were bringing to Patagonia Front. They had personal cloaking devices, improved communications intercepts, and a new type of round specifically designed to pierce the Nasi battle armor. They also had detailed schematics, which she would share with each of them, for the devices, so that the rebels could make more on their own.

"Nice." Jones smiled as he leaned back. He quickly went over the new personnel that they had for the mission.

"We've been at war with the Nasi for months," Kal concluded. "We have to be ready for them to change our plans. I'm proud of our team; we've done more than anyone would have thought possible. But remember, the enemy is always adapting, and this time, they'll be prepared for us."

The others looked across the table at each other. They all knew that they had been lucky to make it this far.

"We have three days until we reach Patagonia," Kal continued. "I'd like everyone to get back to basics. I'm not going to tell you how to train your soldiers, but we need to be prepared if it all goes to crap. The Nasi are unrelenting, and we all know by now that nothing ever goes to plan."

"Same as New America," Park said, scanning the tactical map. "We've got two Nasi ships in geosynchronous orbits on opposite poles of the planet. I can't tell if Mandela Station is still operational from this distance or not."

The *Oruc* was conducting a staged approach into Patagonia—making small folds toward the planet and conducting long-range scans between each fold. Since nothing could travel faster than light, the information that they were getting was not only from far away, it was also a week old, meaning things could change as they came closer to the planet.

"Something folded!" Garcia called out.

"Can you tell what it was?" Kal asked.

"Probe of some sort," the pilot responded. "My guess is that it's an early warning device, letting them know we're on the way."

"Shit, that's bad luck," Park swore. In the vastness of space, the chances of them folding within the sensor range of a probe were small. Kal wasn't sure how many of them the Nasi had distributed around the planet, but he was sure there had to be more.

"Quick, fold away," Kal ordered. "We could have a Nasi ship here any second." Kal knew they had to infiltrate the planet—there was no going back.

Park quickly ran the calculations for their new fold trajectory and checked to ensure they were safe to engage. The stars blinked abruptly as he folded the ship away from the planet.

"Can we fold around the planet, come in on another trajectory?" Kal asked as he sat back and dropped his hands in his lap. The three crew members turned around in their chairs so they were facing him. If they could maneuver to a different approach vector, they may avoid any Nasi defense that was expecting them.

"We can," Garcia responded, "but they may have more of those probes, and they'll be on alert either way."

Kal cracked his knuckles absentmindedly as he thought about what to do next. It came down to whether to barge straight ahead or circumnavigate the planet. If they chose the latter, they risked running into more Nasi probes, defeating the entire purpose. Also, folding such short distances was not without risk—the planet's gravity could always interfere with their jump drive.

"I don't think that there is anything we can do except try to fold in from a different angle than what we were at," Kal said.

"We have a few drones," Garcia said. "We could use them ahead of our ship to see if they trigger any of their early warning probes."

"Let's skip the staged approach," Park said. "What more do we need to know? If we just fold directly to the planet, we don't have to worry about any early warning triggers. Any delay gives them more time to be on guard, whatever angle we enter at."

"I agree, sir," Kanumba said. "Let's stopping dancing around and just do it."

"Okay," Kal said, letting his breath out. "Let's just do this. Let everyone know to get ready."

Garcia made the announcement over the ship's intercom as Park validated their coordinates for the fold drive. They would fold as close to the planet as possible. Because the drive was imprecise, he needed to make sure they didn't risk folding inside the planet.

"We've got the coordinates locked in and settings are good," Park said to Garcia.

"General, you ready?" the pilot asked.

"Go ahead," Kal responded. He could feel the noose tightening around his neck.

Patagonia sprang to life in the cockpit's main viewscreen. The planet was a large ball of blue ocean with a spray of green islands. On the other side was Pangea, the sole continent. It was where almost all the population lived—the islands were uninhabited except for resorts, fishing ports, and mineral extraction facilities. Much of the mining and drilling on the planet was undersea, and the islands served as the supply stations for the large rigs.

The two Nasi capital ships remained at the poles. Kal couldn't see any indications of activity or that they were on alert.

"We're clear. So far, no activity on the Nasi net," Kanumba reported, listening through the communications intercept.

"I'm heading straight into the atmosphere, and then we can skim along the planet's surface to Pangea," Garcia said.

The *Oruc* continued to accelerate toward Patagonia, and the planet grew in the main viewscreen. Kal watched the numbers showing their distance from the planet tick down, hoping that they could reach the relative safety of the atmosphere before being discovered.

"They've spotted us," Kanumba said. "The Nasi ships are engaging."

Damn, Kal thought to himself, *the cloak isn't working.* It would make it extremely difficult to make it off planet—assuming they survived entry.

Plasma bolts splayed off of the *Oruc's* port energy shields, causing a shudder to go through the ship.

"What was that?" Garcia asked. "Their capital ships haven't moved."

"I don't see anything," Kanumba said. "Trying to trace the origin."

"While you do that, I'm getting out of here," said the major. He pushed the ship's throttle to the max.

Kal watched nervously as plasma bolts flew past the ship. Two more of them hit the energy shields. The ship's shields were in the red—a few more hits and they wouldn't make it to the planet.

"Apparently they've got fighters now," Kanumba said. "I can't see them on the sensors—they've got some sort of cloaking. I am tracking them visually though." Kanumba marked the location of the Nasi fighters on the ship's tactical display. Now that it had identified them, the *Oruc's* computer could use its visual sensors to track them.

Kal was surprised the Nasi had already built fighters so quickly. In their previous battle with the Nasi, Samsara Fleet had used their fighters to gain an advantage against the overwhelming Nasi capital ships. The Nasi had adjusted, quickly constructing fighters of their own. They would neutralize many of the tactical advantages that Samsara Fleet had enjoyed. Kal hoped they could report their findings back to the fleet. Their tacticians needed to adjust their battle plans to react to the new technology.

A pair of plasma rounds impacted the starboard shields. Alarms chimed as the ship's shields failed, rendering the *Oruc* completely vulnerable.

"Damnit," Garcia swore.

The *Oruc* was at the outside edge of the atmosphere of the planet and still traveling at near top speed. The ship's hull was heating rapidly as they entered the atmosphere.

The Nasi fighters peeled off as they reached the exosphere, clearly unable to continue their pursuit. Ships that could operate in the vacuum of space could not necessarily fly within the atmosphere; the *Oruc* was one of the few that could.

"Inbound!" shouted Kanumba. "A fighter just launched a missile."

"I can't maneuver at all," Garcia shouted. "Deploying counter measures . . . and praying."

A few seconds later, an explosion rocked the ship as the missile detonated at their rear. The entire cabin went dark— they had lost power. Emergency lighting blinked on, making the cockpit appear as a rose-colored cave.

"We've got to abandon ship," Kal shouted. "Get to the bay."

The four of them ran to the cargo bay, almost bowling over Nicole on the way. Without a word, she ran in line behind them—the ship was doomed.

The Tac-I squad was already in their battle suits in the cargo bay. Where the bay door had been was now a smoking ruin—the missile's impact had melted the reinforced door.

Two battle suits remained in their docks, and Kal and Nicole quickly jumped into them while the flight crew grabbed the emergency life packs from a compartment in the bulkhead. Each life pack contained enough propellant to allow the user to land safely from high altitude as well as some basic survival gear such as water, a kinetic pistol, and essential materials for shelter and warmth. The crew members quickly put on their packs, attaching the task mask with respirator over the heads.

Altitude at ten thousand meters, said Jones over the net. *We've got to go. Flight crew first. Your life packs don't have the maneuverability of a suit.*

Garcia motioned to the others and jumped out of the back bay door, the rushing wind immediately taking him. Kanumba and Park followed immediately after, the rushing air pulling them away from the ship as it hurtled toward the planet.

Sir, you and Bergeron go next, Jones instructed. Kal obliged, jumping from the back of the hurtling ship. The bright daylight almost blinded him after the dark, lifeless cavern of the ship. As he gained control of his descent, he could hear the rest of the team talking over the net—all soldiers had made it out safely.

Kal began a fast, controlled descent toward the planet's surface. They were still on the far side of the planet from Pangea. Beneath his feet was open ocean sprinkled with a few verdant islands.

Where do we go? Garcia asked. *These packs don't have a lot of fuel.*

Kal quickly scanned the islands beneath them. One of them had some sort of built-up area, a mining facility or logistics hub most likely.

Head here. Kal updated the shared tactical map so that everyone could see where he was talking about. *There's some sort of base or warehouse there.*

A chorus of acknowledgement returned as the ten members of the *Oruc* gently thrusted down to the surface of Patagonia.

❖

Nicole stepped out of her battle suit and lay flat on the sandy ground, her eyes closed, the sticky heat already causing her to break out into a sweat.

She had a hard time believing what had just happened. The last fifteen minutes were a jumble—her stateroom going dark, the terror of trying to step into the battle suit, feeling herself cartwheeled by the wind as she jumped from the ship. Now at least she felt like she was on something solid. She could feel the sand shift under her body and touch it with her hands. She opened her eyes and saw a few broad-leafed trees and shrubs that could have come from Earth.

No one had spoken since they landed on the island. Each team member sat or lay down, occupied with their thoughts. After a few minutes, Nicole heard the soft swish of someone walking toward her in the sand. She turned and was surprised to find Sergeant Jones approaching, his face as impassive as ever.

"How you doin'?" he asked.

"I've been better," Nicole replied, pushing her torso up.

"I imagine," Jones chuckled, looking around the area. "That was rough. I can't say that I ever get used to these kinds of things. Eventually, you just learn to accept it and move on."

Nicole said nothing. Jones remained a mystery to her. He clearly cared for the soldiers in his squad, but rarely let his guard down. After a moment, the noncommissioned officer gave her a nod and continued to *walk*.

Okay, rest time is over, Kal said over the net. *Meet at my location.*

A disorienting head rush greeted Nicole as she stood up. From her new vantage point, she could see the soft swells of the ocean peeking out between two clumps of bushes a hundred meters away. Nicole scanned the clear blue sky, looking for any sign of Nasi craft without success. She had to imagine that they were already combing the area for survivors.

The team huddled in a small makeshift group around Kal. It looked like no one had sustained any major injuries, though Privates Chedjou and Kinawadi's appearance mirrored Nicole's state of mind. Their faces were almost slack, eyes wide, as they stared around the island, still trying to comprehend the past few minutes. The bright light and dense, humid air were a stark contrast from the sterile, cold interior of the *Oruc*.

There was no chatter on the Nasi nets. Either her communication intercept was no longer working, or the Nasi were using a channel they couldn't detect. It was just a matter of time before the Nasi came across their location.

Kal outlined their current situation. He believed they were

on an island that contained one of the planet's many ocean mining facilities. The good news was that there would be transport drones regularly ferrying raw minerals to Pangea for processing. The bad news was that there was most likely a significant security presence that would be on high alert because of their fiery entry onto the planet.

They would stay together and try to get closer to the facility. The close proximately was so they could avoid communicating via the neural implants, which the Nasi might detect. They walked single file across the sparse island, trying as best they could to make use of the sparse vegetation for cover. The three flight crew members walked in the middle of the formation, with the other six people in battle suits acting as a protective shield.

As they got closer to the facility, Nicole could see glimpses of the drab buildings and machinery between the foliage. She tried to look for any signs of activity but wasn't able to spot anything or anyone. Her suit's sensors hadn't picked up anything so far, which she was grateful for.

Kal brought them to a slight depression in the sandy landscape and took a knee. The rest of the team followed suit and took off their helmets. Nicole could now make out a faint humming sound from the mining facility—it was still operating.

"I've heard nothing over the Nasi net," Kal said.

"Me neither, sir," Taisha said. "They may have realized we've intercepted their communications or are using a different tech than what we've seen before."

Nicole groaned inside—another advantage lost.

"I'm guessing that they didn't have a visual on us when the *Oruc* went down," Kal said. "Their search area is going to be pretty wide."

Garcia wiped the sweat from his eyes. "Well, they knew enough about our location to shoot us down. They should have a good point to start from."

"Yes, but we were in the atmosphere when that missile hit," Taisha said. "The *Oruc* traveled several thousand kilometers after that."

"Fine," Kal grunted. "We've got to assume they don't know exactly where we are, but are looking."

"Sir, our only chance is to hijack a transport from the facility over here," Jones said. "I haven't seen much security so far. Probably a full-auto mine."

Kal nodded his head. "Okay, let's recon the site and get a better idea of what we're dealing with."

"Yessir." Jones divvied them up into three teams. The crew members who did not have battle suits would stay behind and keep an eye out for enemy scouts or patrols. The other two groups would recon the mining facility, looking for security bots or personnel and any way to get off the island.

Jones paired Nicole with Kal and Private Pudari. They would scout the north and east side of the mining facility.

They set off, walking around the perimeter of the mine and staying well clear of any sensors. Intermittently, Kal would raise his hand for them to stop. While Pudari and Nicole waited at a safe distance, he would crawl toward the facility to get a better look. Once he was back, they set off again.

As they walked, Nicole could hear herself breathing, the

ragged sound creating a sort of rhythmic beat. Thankfully, the suit kept her cool and made travel easy, despite the increased gravity of the planet and the muggy weather—though even the suit couldn't stop her heart from thumping as she thought about a Nasi drone or patrol spotting them.

They had almost reached the far end of the compound when Kal suddenly dropped to the ground. Nicole instinctively did the same, though she didn't know why. A large transport flew meters above them. It was boxy, with a drab gray exterior. She figured the transport must haul cargo to and from the facility. As the three of them lay flat on the ground, the transport descended into the mining compound, unaware of their presence. "At least we know that there's a way out," Kal said as he stood back up and continued walking.

They arrived at the far end of the facility, and Kal motioned for them to get down. He took off his helmet. Nicole and Pudari followed.

"How you both holding up?" Kal whispered.

"Good," Nicole answered. Pudari simply nodded. She looked extremely uncomfortable, with sweat beading across her forehead and her jaw clenched.

"I'm going to get closer to see what they're doing with the transport. Then we'll do a final recon and head back. Keep a lookout for any drones or patrollers." Kal disappeared over a slight rise in the terrain, slowly crawling on his hands and knees.

As they'd walked around the perimeter, hope had bloomed in Nicole's chest. The mining base seemed to be loosely guarded, and there was at least one transport moving back and forth from the compound. They still hadn't heard or seen any Nasi fighters or drones in the area, which meant the Nasi search team was probably still far away.

Nicole felt her heart skip a beat as she heard something click behind her. She jumped sideways and felt a bolt of pain shoot across the right side of her body. Nicole screamed over the net as she fell on her side.

Pudari's face appeared in Nicole's field of view, her jaw clenched and her dark eyes alive with malice. "This is the last mission you sabotage," the private snarled, placing the muzzle of her plasma rifle directly on Nicole's forehead.

The perimeter security of the mining base was light. The builders must have figured the remote location was all the security they needed. There were a few sensor arrays—with visual and infrared cameras—but no patrol drones or auto-weapons. The transport that had passed over their heads earlier had almost given Kal a heart attack, but it also meant there was a way off the island.

Kal reached a small rise in the sand directly in front of the facility's perimeter wall. He fired an EMP round to disable one of the wall security arrays and gently used his thrusters to reach the top of the wall.

The facility was several hundred meters across, with most of the space taken up by large storage vats and piles of unrefined minerals. At the center was an elevated platform with a transport resting on top. The small worker drones pushed piles of the minerals from the yard to the base of the platform, and a small corkscrew pulled the material up into the waiting transport, slowly filling the interior bed.

A few repair drones flitted across the yard, stopping at one of the other bots or machines to conduct maintenance. There were no Nasi or Humans in sight—the facility must have been fully automated.

Kal heard a scream of pain across the net. The electric sound of a plasma rifle seared into Kal's senses. He used his suit's thrusters to leap back off the wall and shoot toward where he had left Nicole and Pudari. There wasn't time to worry about staying unnoticed.

Kal touched down in the middle of a nightmare. Nicole was on the ground, the right side of her armor seared open by a plasma bolt. The plasma had fused the metal edges of the suit, and he could see her blackened flesh peeking out. Private Pudari stood over her, helmet off, plasma rifle touching Nicole's forehead.

Kal's body moved faster than his mind—which kept asking questions that he had no answers for. *Had Nicole betrayed them? Was Pudari taking matters into her own hands? Was something else going on?* Kal's kinetic pistol sprang forth from his side arm holster and into his hand. His finger touched the trigger and three rounds burst into the back of Pudari's head. The slugs sent a spray of sickening red mist spurting in all directions. Pudari dropped and toppled over—all life gone before she hit the ground.

Kal let go of the pistol, horrified at what he had done. He

tried to look away, but couldn't—one of his soldiers lay on the ground, dead by his hand. Kal could see the blood streaming from the motionless corpse. He fell down, his legs giving out, and then pulled himself over to Nicole's still form. For a moment, Kal thought she was dead too, the blue eyes unmoving, no visible sound or sign of breath.

Finally, her eyes turned to meet his own, and she let out a small sob. Kal took off his helmet, setting it down on the ground next to hers.

"You okay?" he asked.

Nicole tried to say something, but it never made its way past her lips. After a moment, she just nodded. Tears dripped from her eyes, mingling with the small splatters of blood and creating small streams down the sides of her face. It felt like an eternity before Nicole finally spoke.

"She shot me," Nicole stammered.

Kal nodded. He realized she was wounded. Kal used his implant to check her health. Thankfully, the wound was mainly superficial. The suit's armor had partially deflected the round. There were plasma burns, but nothing life threatening.

"We're gonna have to get you out of the suit," Kal said. The plasma round had severed numerous critical systems, rendering it useless.

Kal turned Nicole face down and activated the suit's manual release. The suit popped open along the back, legs, and arms. Kal quickly exited his own battle suit and gently pulled Nicole out of the shell. She groaned as he laid her gently on the hot sand.

Charring and pink blisters covered much of her right side.

A plasma bolt did damage through both the heat of the round and the kinetic force. The suit had spared her from the kinetic force, but the deflection has increased the amount of surface area that was burned.

As gently as he could, Kal placed a bandage over her side. It would provide immediate pain relief and promote healing, but was no substitute for a medbot. Kal realized Nicole would probably be scarred for the rest of her life.

Kal sat back down for a moment, watching Nicole, waiting for her to say something. He caught the ruined battle suit of Private Pudari out of the corner of her eye. The stream of blood had slowed and was draining into the hungry, arid sand. The image triggered thoughts of what he had done.

Kal cried, softly at first, and then with shaking sobs. He felt everything close in on him—his family's death, the destruction of Earth, countless ships and fleets destroyed, the death of so many soldiers in the past months, the death of one of his solders by his own hand. All of it conspired to crush him beneath the weight of their collective sorrow.

Suddenly, he realized that Nicole had sat up and pressed her head against his. Her arms held awkwardly around his side. They sat unmoving for a few minutes before Kal finally had the strength to pull away. He turned his head to find her eyes, just inches away from his own, looking back at him. For a moment, Kal didn't feel alone. He felt the connection borne by a shared trauma.

"She shot me from behind," Nicole whispered between quiet sobs. "I knew she hated me, but I didn't realize . . . just how much."

"You were easy to blame."

Nicole turned and looked at Pudari's corpse. "What do we do now?"

The question brought Kal back into the reality of their situation. They needed to move Pudari's body somewhere else, quickly. Then they needed to get back to rest of the team.

He felt some strength return. "Just stay here—I'm going to find somewhere to put her."

Kal stood up, his legs giving way slightly, and stepped back into his battle suit. He looked for someplace to hide the body. The island's terrain was giving him nothing at first—the trees and shrubs were too sparse to hide anything that large. As he approached the shore, Kal came across a formation of several large rocks. They were large enough to cover the body, and not so large he couldn't lift them while wearing his battle suit.

Kal returned and reverently gathered Pudari, carrying her halfway between the rock formation and the mining compound. He laid her down gently, activated the cleaning procedure on the suit to render it useless, and then began the painstaking process of carrying the boulders from the shore and placing them gently on Pudari, starting with the gaping hole where her head should have been.

After fifteen minutes, Kal had completely covered the body. He said a few silent words over the grave, then walked back to where Nicole lay in the sand.

"We need to get back," he told Nicole.

She nodded and got on her feet. She had been aimlessly

stroking a small star that dangled around her neck. Her fingers had smudged blood across the golden pendant, making it appear almost pink in the tropical light.

Wordlessly, they walked back toward the rendezvous location to meet up with the rest of the *Oruc's* survivors.

Chapter Fourteen

The sun was low in the sky, the giant orb spreading an orangish glow across the horizon. As Nicole walked, she could feel the increased gravity of the planet pulling her down. Now, without a suit, the smell of salt water and sand filled her nostrils as she walked. She tried to focus on putting one foot in front of the other, but her mind couldn't move past the muzzle pointed in her face and the fine mist of blood.

Nicole fingered the new pendant hanging heavily around her neck. When Kal had left, she had seen a small glimmer shimmering from the blood and muck of Pudari's lifeless body. Nicole had tried to look away, but couldn't resist. The pendant was a small, five-pointed star, mirroring her own necklace. Still dazed, she could not stop herself from crawling to the body and pulling the necklace off. It came cleanly away, and she placed it over her neck, a small reminder of what had happened.

Only Jae-Ho was there when Nicole and Kal arrived at the rendezvous point. Nicole could see the thoughts flit across his face as he saw her bandaged and without her armor and realized that Private Pudari was no longer with them. The young captain opened his mouth to speak, and stopped, the looks on Nicole's and Kal's faces a clear sign they weren't ready to discuss it.

"What'd you find?" Kal asked after he removed his helmet.

"We found a spot with some cover near here, sir," Park said. "The rest of the team is waiting for us."

"Okay, let's go," Kal instructed.

Jae-Ho led them to a small depression covered with dead foliage and debris. The rest of their team sat on the ground, murmuring to each other in small groups.

"Glad you made it back, sir," Sergeant Jones said once they had sat down. Nicole could see the unasked question in his eyes as they flitted to her bandage. It was the same question in everyone's eyes, but no one dared ask.

"Thanks," replied Kal. "What did you find out?"

"Seems like a pretty standard mining facility. There's no sign of any Nasi present, and the security is rudimentary. Shouldn't be hard to enter. While we were waiting for you to return, we counted the transports, and it seems like one departs every fifteen minutes."

"We may get off this island," Kal said. He paused, looking at the ground before speaking again. His voice came out as almost a whisper. "We ran into some trouble and . . . Pudari didn't make it."

"Do you think that any sensors were tripped?" Park asked.

"No," Kal responded in a flat voice.

"But—"

"I said no." Kal's voice rose, cutting off the young captain. "We still have the element of surprise, and we need to move."

After a brief discussion, they agreed to infiltrate the facility immediately. The security was weak, and time was not on their side. The team would enter the facility, climb into the transport, and override the navigation system so they could pilot it to the Nasi lab.

A few minutes later, they set out for the compound. After disabling the security array, the five soldiers with battle suits carried the others over the wall. A gray, metallic dust seemed to coat everything inside the compound, Nicole's feet made soft swishing sounds as she crept through the mine, using the piles of minerals as cover. Despite knowing that there were no weapons systems or security arrays directed at the interior of the compound, she felt exposed without her battle suit.

The team reached the elevated platform in the middle and used their thrusters to climb into the partially filled transport. The vehicle was essentially a large bowl, filled halfway with assorted rocks and gravel. Nicole leaned against the side as the machines continue to fill the transports hopper.

After several minutes, the waterfall of small rocks stopped, and the transport rose into the air and floated toward the edge of the compound. As soon as it cleared the perimeter wall, a kinetic shield appeared over their heads, preventing the wind and elements from displacing the cargo.

Taisha shakily crawled over the gravel and began to hack the transport's navigation system. The chief muttered to herself and cursed as she tried to bypass the automated controls.

"Damnit!" Taisha slammed her fist down on the metal side of the hopper. "I can't break into the system."

"What?" Jones asked through his suit's external speaker.

"I can't break in. The security's too tight for me, and I'm not a trained computer hacker," Taisha said, sliding down the side of the transport.

"So what's that mean?" Jones looked at her.

"It means that we're just along for the ride."

❖

Kal lay on top of the crushed rock, staring up at the blue sky above. He was thinking about Pudari.

He remembered her telling him of her concerns about Nicole in the ship's galley. Should he have done more? What could he have done? He had never imagined that the young private would take matters into her own hands. In retrospect, why hadn't he? She had made her thoughts clear.

The trip lasted four hours, the automated transport drone skimming a few hundred meters off the water as it headed toward Pangea. For the first couple of hours, Chief Kanumba had continued to try to override the drone's navigation system. She had finally given up when she almost caused them to plunge into the ocean. They were at the mercy of the onboard navigation system.

"Any idea of where we're headed, ma'am?" Jones asked Chief Kanumba, jolting Kal out of his thoughts.

She shook her head. "No idea. Someplace on Pangea."

"Thanks, ma'am." The sergeant eyed the large landmass on the horizon.

"Most of the mineral-processing plants are outside the main cities," Kal said.

"Maybe, sir, or maybe they've adjusted the transport to fly directly to one of their Footholds," Jones replied.

Kal shuddered at the thought. They wouldn't withstand a second in a Nasi Foothold.

"Sir, we'll need to get off this thing as soon as we can," Jones said.

Jones split them into groups, pairing each soldier without a battle suit with someone who had one. As soon as the transparent shield above them disappeared, they would jump out and find a place to regroup on the ground. Kal just hoped that the shield opened before they landed.

Clearly, the transport was heading to somewhere around the capital, Kasongo. Unlike New America, Patagonia did not have zones. Its infrastructure and layout were much more organic and similar to Earth's. There was no way to determine exactly where in Kasongo they would end up.

As they approached the capital, enormous towers appeared on the skyline. Kal scanned the horizon, looking for the telltale organic buildings of the Nasi Foothold. Finally, he spotted it. From a distance, it appeared as if the sun had melted one of the angular towers that dotted the skyline. The dark tower's sinuous shape stood out from the other buildings, which pointed straight to the heavens.

Kal said a small word of thanks under his breath as the transport slowed and began to descend. They were still several kilometers from the twisted Nasi Foothold.

As they descended, the sounds and smells of the city saturated the hopper. As opposed to New America, Kasongo had a wild chaos about it. The streets angled and turned, hugging the hilly landscape. The buildings were a mishmash of different styles—geodesic domes, ancient columned buildings, rectangular slabs.

The shield above their heads disappeared without a

sound, and they jumped from the transport. Kal grabbed Nicole around the waist and used his suit's thrusters to clear the lip of the hopper and descend onto a nearby rooftop.

Jones called over the net to ensure that each group had made it out of the transport. The team could use their neural implants since they were in the city. They had already lost the element of surprise, and the Nasi wouldn't be able to pinpoint their locations among the mass of people.

Kal landed on the trash-strewn ground at their identified rendezvous point. The alley was a narrow gorge surrounded by towers and coated with years of neglect. At the end of the alley was a trash heap, boxes and refuse reaching almost to the second floor of the surrounding buildings.

They quickly stowed the battle suits in the mound of trash, covering them as best they could. The suits' built-in security would prevent tampering from anyone who discovered them.

The scout team that had reconned the planet before them had established a communications protocol to link up with the Patagonia Front. It was a series of encrypted signals set over specific frequencies at specific times. It let the Front know that someone from Samsara Fleet was on the planet and wanted to meet. The Front would then respond with a set of encoded coordinates for the meeting point.

Kal sent out the encrypted signals to let the Front know they wanted to meet and set his implant to listen for the Front's response. Now they just had to wait. The team leaned against the walls of the buildings, trying to stay out of sight.

Ten minutes later, the response came. The coordinates were to a wooded area outside of the town. It was too far for them to walk, and they had no way to hire a transport to get them to the location—at least not without potentially notifying the Nasi of their presence.

"Major Garcia," Kal called.

"Sir?" the major asked.

"You know any way for us to get transportation?" Kal asked. "The rendezvous point is outside of the city."

Garcia bit his lip and gave a sigh. "Yeah, sir, I do. I've got some connections around here. I don't know if they'll be able or willing to help. It's been a while."

"What other option do we have?" Ekon asked.

"None," Garcia admitted. "We'll need to walk a bit."

The team left the alley in groups of two and three and followed Garcia out of the alley and onto a large boulevard. People crowded the street, rushing back and forth while street vendors yelled out, hawking their wares. Kal noted the guarded expressions on the faces of the people he passed, many of them with pistols holstered to their bodies. The local city services seemed to have ground to a halt, trash and debris lie scattered on the streets. Remnants of fighting—an abandoned checkpoint, charred and melted walls from plasma fire, small craters from missile fire—were all around them as they proceeded through the city. Fresh graffiti decorated several buildings—logos or expressions of support for one of the factions.

The intelligence reports had not expressed how severe the fighting had become on Patagonia. It was still a war zone. He doubted the Nasi truly cared, as long as they got the materials and resources they needed.

As they walked through the streets, Kal felt his hand hovering over his holstered pistol. He felt the weight of suspicious and hostile glances as they walked down the street.

After thirty minutes of walking, Garcia turned into a three-story pyramid, the sides made of a rainbow-hued glass. Kal noted that the structure looked relatively unharmed—all the windows were still in place, and there wasn't a trace of graffiti.

The door opened into a large, classically styled entryway. The room was gaudy, with fluted golden columns, a red velvet runner, and large golden drapes lining the walls. An enormous gold chandelier hung from the ceiling, bathing the room in an almost painfully bright light.

It immediately reminded Kal of the ornate fronts of the Alliance. The criminal entity was not subtle in flouting its wealth—instead it was a reminder to all who entered.

An attendant bot, also cloaked in gold, rolled into the room. "Master Karl," the synthetic voice said. "Welcome back to Patagonia."

"Thanks," Garcia replied. "Don't let Lukas know I'm here."

"I am sorry, sir. Your brother left strict instructions to inform him if you returned. We have already sent a notice." The bot sounded appropriately contrite.

"Damn," Garcia swore under his breath. "Where is he?"

The bot paused for a moment before responding. "It appears he just entered a supersonic shuttle and is on his way from Foyleton now. We estimate ten minutes until he arrives."

"I would really love to see him, but we gotta go. Can you give me an anonymous credit chit and neural sim? Like right now?" Garcia sounded anything but eager to see his brother.

Kal raised his eyebrows. The UEG had prohibited the sale and manufacture of anonymous credit chits and neural sims. They were almost exclusively used for criminal activities. Garcia was asking for them like he would ask for another roll at dinner.

Since they were not tied to a person, anonymous credit chits allowed someone to buy and sell anonymously. A neural sim was a small handheld device that allowed the user to access the local net anonymously as well. Both were highly illegal and were only found in the hands of criminal enterprises like the Alliance.

The bot rolled away to retrieve the chit and sim. As soon as it was out of the room, Captain Park turned to Garcia.

"What's all this, sir?" Park asked.

"Family business," Garcia replied. He pointed at the walls and then at his eyes and ears. They were being watched.

Garcia's reluctance to talk about his past and his reluctance to return to Patagonia were now clear. Kal couldn't imagine what it would be like for a commissioned officer in the EDF to have come from a syndicate.

Although the Alliance was the premier criminal organization in the galaxy, each planet also had their own local syndicates. The syndicates were independent organizations that ran the local undergrounds on each planet. The Alliance allowed them to survive as long as the syndicates didn't directly challenge their authority or expand beyond their home planet.

The attendant bot returned with the chit and sim, handing them to Garcia. He quickly stowed them in one of his cargo

215

pockets.

"Master Karl, your brother is calling via holo. Putting him through now."

A middle-aged man replaced the bot's holographic face. Kal could see the family resemblance to Garcia almost immediately—prominent nose, dark features, with an olive-colored complexion. However, his face displayed none of the warmth of Garcia's. Instead, an almost-predatory gleam shone from his eyes.

"Ah, the prodigal son returns," the man said, his mouth fixed in a small frown. "And it looks like you brought friends."

"Lukas," the major replied. "I'll be out of your hair immediately."

"Oh, like hell you will. What's it been? Ten years? Wait there. I'll be there shortly. With everything going on, I can't fly directly in."

"I'm not staying." Garcia wiped the false smile from his face, and his mouth hardened into a line. "I told you when I left, I wasn't coming back. As far as you're concerned, I was never here."

Lukas's face turned red, his eyes widening in anger. "Listen up, little brother, you're gonna wait there for me and we're gonna have a—"

"End call," Garcia said to the bot. Lukas's eyes grew even wider as the bot shut down the link.

"He's not gonna be happy about that," Garcia said. "We need to get outta here. As you saw, my brother and I don't have the warmest relationship."

Garcia led them out of the building, where a large

transport was already waiting for them. "Get in," he said. "It'll take us close to the rendezvous point."

"Let's go," Jones instructed, waving everyone into the vehicle. They all climbed in and it immediately lifted off.

Chapter Fifteen

The transport weaved between the looming buildings of Kasongo, flying meters over the crowds on the streets below. Nicole continued to be distracted as she watched the mishmash of buildings fly by their transport. She felt the cold muzzle of the rifle against her forehead and the warm mist of Pudari's blood on her face. Kal wasn't speaking either—they were together in their feeling of complete isolation from the group.

After a few minutes, Jae-Ho turned to face his co-pilot. "Okay, so I gotta ask, sir. What's with your family?"

The other passengers tried to feign indifference, but Nicole could sense that everyone's attention was on the major.

Karl sighed. "My mother led the syndicate here," he replied. "She and my father died because of it."

He let out a groan. "They had what was coming to them. My family got rich from drugs, murder, and slavery. I left a decade ago, before my mother died. Told them I was never coming back."

"Sorry," Park breathed. "That's rough."

Karl nodded. "Yeah. I never wanted to come back. This planet has a lot of bad memories."

The rest of the trip passed in silence, each person lost in their thoughts. As the city slowly gave way to urban farms and warehouses, signs of fighting grew—craters, burned-out vehicles, and a few wrecked atmospheric fighters littered the landscape. It was saddening to think that this death and destruction had come at the hands of fellow Humans, and not the Nasi.

The transport slowly touched down a kilometer from the coordinates for the rendezvous point. The group started walking along the narrow country road, staying far enough away that the dense undergrowth provided cover from anyone speeding by. As opposed to the island they crashed on, dense foliage covered Pangea. The tropical woods vibrated with the sounds of small animals and insects.

They arrived at a dilapidated storage facility. Rectangular metal buildings, covered in a white, peeling paint, were arranged in a perfectly square grid. A rust-covered wire fence, with multiple breaches, surrounded the buildings. The team crouched in the thick bushes near the fence line while Jones and Ekon performed a hasty recon of the area. The Nasi intercept still was silent—they hadn't heard anything since they landed on the planet.

After getting the all clear, the rest of the group joined the two Tac-I soldiers in the center of the facility. Rotting fruit lay in piles in the corners of the storage buildings. Ruined equipment and shell casings suggested that the facility had either been a temporary base or the site of a firefight—or both. In the middle of the facility, two people in mismatched fatigues stood waiting. Next to them was a heavily modified transport, with armor plates fixed to the sides and several missile launchers bolted to its underside.

The two fighters warily watched as the survivors of the *Oruc* walked toward them. They both looked tired, their eyes ringed with shadows.

"Welcome to Patagonia, a paradise turned to hell," said the female. She looked to be older, with light brown skin and long, braided hair dyed a radiant blue. The man standing next to her stood quietly, beads of sweat forming in the stubble on his shaved head.

"Let's get somewhere safe," the woman said, gesturing toward the transport.

They piled into the vehicle, and it slowly lifted over the compound and sped up. They coasted over the country roads, traveling a path that seemed to skirt the city's edge. Nicole noticed columns of dense smoke appearing in the distance and could hear the faint rumbling of explosions and plasma fire.

"I'm Koula, and this is Mohammed," the woman said, pointing at her companion. She looked out the window at the columns of smoke. "Place has gone to shit. Foyleton is making their move. They're tryin' to take the area around the capital from the PPC. It could spell trouble for the Front if they're successful."

The transport abruptly veered off the road, soaring over the countryside and weaving around hills and obstacles. Farms and orchards turned into leafy clumps of trees and wide, sweeping hills. As the forest thickened, they rose and began flying over the canopy, the treetops practically touching the base of the vehicle. When they slowed and dropped with a sickening swiftness, there was nothing around them but an undulating sea of green. Nicole felt her stomach rise to her throat, and Jones looked at her and gave a small smile of commiseration.

The transport rested in a small clearing. Nicole could spot hardened bunkers, partially overgrown by the undergrowth among the surrounding trees. Vehicles, crates of supplies, and small tents were scattered throughout the area. Nicole climbed out of the vehicle, her feet sinking slightly into the mossy forest floor.

Without a word, the two PF guides walked toward a bunker, trailed by the crew of the *Oruc*. Nicole stumbled as she walked into the dark bunker, unable to see. The musty, earthy smell of mold and mildew filled the air, and there were miniscule, softly glowing fungi grew on the walls and ceiling.

The group walked through a maze of dark corridors, their footsteps dull thuds on the dirt-coated metal floor, until they reached a small conference room. Viewscreens were bolted to the walls on either side of the room. Opposite the door was a logo had been scrawled on the wall. Blue letters *P* and *F* intertwined over a silver background. A small elderly man sat in front of the logo, the conference table in front of him seeming to overpower his slight frame.

"Sit," the man instructed.

Nicole obeyed and watched quietly as the man stood up and slowly shuffled to a cabinet in the room's corner, pulling out a stack of glasses. He carried them and walked around the table, stopping at each person and setting a glass in front of them. The man then returned to the cabinet and retrieved a pitcher, repeating the same measured pace around the table as he filled each glass.

He returned the pitcher to the cabinet and then sat back down in his seat and raised the glass in front of him. "On

Patagonia," he said, breaking the silence hanging over the room, "we have a tradition of welcoming guests with a glass of Kidora juice. The first Humans who settled on this planet wrote that the juice of the Kidora was the greatest thing that they had ever tasted, that it made the hardships and privations that they went through as they settled this planet worthwhile."

Nicole was intrigued—she had heard stories, legends almost, of the Patagonian drink. She raised the glass to her lips and took a small taste. The flavor saturated her mouth, and a sensation of warmth spread to every part of her body. It was like nothing she had ever tasted before—she wasn't tasting it, but rather experiencing it, feeling the effects flow through her. Nicole understood why the early settlers would have said that the drink made their sacrifices worthwhile. It was a transcendent, almost religious, experience.

"My name is Commander Bohai Kinkaid," the man said, taking the glass from his lips. "Welcome to Patagonia and to the Patagonia Front. We are honored to have you here."

"Thank you," Kal responded. Nicole could see her own emotions mirrored in his breathless words.

Kinkaid nodded with a small smile. "I enjoy seeing people try Kidora for the first time—it's not something you forget."

"Indeed," Nicole said.

"I believe it reminds us to savor the good in our lives. Despite the darkness that is around us." The commander finished his drink with a small gulp and set the empty glass back on the table.

Nicole finished her glass as well and gently placed it in

front of her.

"Weeks ago, another officer from Samsara Fleet came," Kinkaid said after everyone had finished. "She told us about the Nasi march across the galaxy. Has anything changed? Are there shoots of green from the dung heap?" He smiled wryly.

"We're still fighting," Kal answered. "We've made progress. Every day we learn more about the Nasi and find more allies, like you, in our fight."

"Good," the commander said. "There is still light in the darkness."

Nicole nodded. "Yes, there is. That's why we've come."

Kincaid stroked his mustache slowly and leaned back. "Really? What light have you spotted here, on Patagonia?"

"There's a Nasi research lab on Patagonia," Kal said. "They've got information there that can help us."

"It's not just a lab," Kinkaid said, "The Nasi are producing new ships and fighters there. We've seen them testing them in the skies above. They're faster than anything I've ever seen before." He leaned forward. "We'll help you. Tell Mohammed what you need, and he'll get it for you."

"Thank you." Kal looked relieved.

"Now, let me ask if you have anything for us?" the commander asked. "We were told that you could help us with weapons and technology."

Kal explained what had happened to the *Oruc,* and their journey to reach the Front. Nicole felt a stab of pain in her side as he talked about scouting the mining facility. Pudari's face floated in front of her for a moment.

"That is disappointing," Kinkaid said, his demeanor

unchanged.

"We have the plans at least," Kal said. "If you have the proper fabricators, you can build them yourselves."

"Before the Nasi came, I was a professor of philosophy." Kinkaid smiled. "I rely on my studies more than you would expect in this role. We appreciate whatever you can provide."

Kal returned the smile. "I can understand that commander." He shifted in his seat for a moment. "How is the Front doing? It seems like the fighting has gotten worse since the previous team from Samsara Fleet was here."

Commander Kinkaid nodded in agreement. "Indeed, the fighting has gotten worse. Not because of the Nasi, mind you, but due to ourselves."

He explained how each of the four major factions that controlled Patagonia held at least one of the major cities, except for the Patagonia Front. Because they refused to swear allegiance to the Nasi, they were forced to the countryside. The other factions battled for control of the cities, with Kasongo the major prize. Kinkaid described how Foyleton had started a major offensive on Kasongo, trying to drive out the PPC. The People's Movement had joined in, trying to take advantage of the chaos and to gather whatever scraps they could. The fighting was brutal, with a desperate PPC fighting a battle on two fronts.

The slaughter had helped the Front. They had taken advantage of the chaos to capture supplies and equipment. Their isolation made it easy for them to raid the other factions and protected them from attack.

As she listened to Commander Kinkaid, Nicole thought

about the advanced schematics they had brought. They were intended to help fight against the Nasi. But she realized they would almost certainly be used against other Humans as well. When the Nasi had first started this war, Samsara Fleet's actions had been black and white—good versus evil. Now, it was bleeding together. The idea of what was right wasn't so clear. Was it worth it to sacrifice Human life to defeat the aliens?

"There's one other thing," Kal said.

"You need a way off planet." Commander Kinkaid said.

"Yes," Kal replied.

"That may be more difficult, but I think we can find you something. We have some fast ships that can fold—we just need to figure out a way to get past the Nasi ships in orbit."

"Two steps forward and one step back," Kal said.

"Indeed." Kinkaid smiled, but the emotion never reached his eyes.

After their meeting with Commander Kinkaid, Koula gave the survivors of the *Oruc* a tour of the base camp. The Patagonia Front had established it in a long-forgotten space defense facility. It was their primary operations center, but they had several more spread throughout the countryside. Abandoned bases, such as this one, were ideal—they were no longer on official maps, were isolated, and contained bunkers and infrastructure.

Koula led them to an underground landing bay filled with

around fifty atmospheric fighter craft. They were a mishmash of types, from cutting-edge EDF fighters to ones that would have been more at home in a museum. As they walked through the cavernous bay, she described how the Front used the transport and close air support from the fighters. They used them against the other Human factions much more than the Nasi.

"Foyleton's the worst," Koula said, as she idly traced her hand along a wing tip. "Their leader, Lukas, is a sadist. They've destroyed the land between Foyleton and Kasongo." She stopped for a moment and stared into the distance. "I've never seen anything like it, just bodies everywhere. The Nasi let them fight, though." She sniffed. "As long as nothing interrupts them getting resources, they don't care."

"Lukas?" Garcia stopped mid-stride and looked at the Front fighter. "What's his last name?"

"I don't know," Koula replied. "He used to be a syndicate head. When the Nasi came, he decided it was time to think bigger. The man's a bastard. At least the other factions don't kill for pleasure."

Garcia shook his head. Kal could only imagine what was going through the officer's head.

Koula led them out of the hangar and through the maze of tents and supplies. The Front had laid out the base in an organized fashion, taking advantage of the cover and bunkers. All of the fighters seemed to have a purpose and moved with competent efficiency. Koula explained that they ran constant missions to gather supplies and exploit advantages against the other Human factions. Occasionally, they would take direct action against the Nasi and ambush a patrol or infiltrate a small outpost to gain some sort of intel. Those missions often ended poorly.

Koula stopped at a set of tents arranged in a small clearing. They appeared identical to the other clusters of tents that Kal had seen as they had been walking.

"You can rest in these for now," Koula said.

Kal peeked inside one of them. It was clean and spartan— four empty cots sat in each corner with a trunk at the foot of each. The cool air inside the tent was a welcome respite from the stifling heat and humidity. He quickly lay claim to a cot and left with Sergeant Jones and Koula to find Mohammed while the rest of the team got settled.

"I hate this heat," Jones grunted as they weaved through a row of supplies.

"I grew up on Mariga," Kal replied. "If it hit zero, we felt like it was summer. This is hell."

"Me too," Jones replied. "I never left the tunnels 'til I was eighteen." Kal had never heard Jones talk about his past. The thought of the grizzled soldier as a child was unfathomable.

"This is our ops cell," Koula announced as they walked down a sloped ramp into one of the identical bunkers. The inside of the bunker was a maze—the hallway twisted and turned, and small rooms split off at odd intervals. Koula led them to one of the rooms, where Mohammed was waiting for them.

"General," greeted Mohammed with a nod. "Sergeant."

Kal nodded back, and Sergeant Jones gave a quick grunt of acknowledgement. Mohammed seemed to be a man of few words, which he respected.

"Mo doesn't talk too much, but he's one of the few people in this camp with military experience. He's prior Tac-I, served in the Torgham war," Koula explained.

She turned to Mohammed. "Commander says you're to help 'em."

"What'd you need?" the fighter asked as Koula walked out the door.

"We need support to infiltrate the Nasi lab here on Pangea," Kal said. "We've got to get in there and get any intelligence we can."

Mohammed nodded. "Okay, you'll need a transport and supporting fire. You've got any equipment?"

"We've got our suits. Anything extra would be helpful," Jones said. "More weapons, ammo, and fuel for the thrusters. Suits'd be great if ya got 'em, but"—he looked around the room—"doesn't look like you got any to spare."

Mohammed cracked his knuckles. "No, we don't. But maybe I can help with some of the other stuff. I'll need an hour. You takin' your entire team with you?"

Kal thought about it for a moment. Normally, the flight crew and Nicole wouldn't be on an operation like this one— they weren't trained for it. However, they had all come too far to split up—they were in it together. He nodded.

"Okay, be back here in an hour, general." Mohammed looked back down at the tablet in his hand and began tapping the screen, seeming to have forgotten that Kal and Jones were there.

The two soldiers stood up and began retracing their steps

out of the bunker. "I like that guy," said Jones. "We'll see if he can deliver."

❖

"How ya doin'?" Taisha asked as she walked through the door of the tent she and Nicole were sharing.

"Fine," Nicole replied.

Taisha sat down on her cot, the frame flexing slightly under her weight. "No pressure, but if you want to talk about it, I'm here."

Nicole shook her head. "It's fine."

"Remember, we can't change people."

"I didn't realize how *much* she hated me."

Taisha reached out and grabbed Nicole's hand, saying nothing. Nicole studied their interlocked fingers, the pale white and dark brown contrasting. She noticed the glint of a ring on Taisha's finger—silver, with a gold inlay.

"Taisha?" Nicole's voice came out slowly and rose. "Where'd you get that ring? It looks a lot like—" The smile told Nicole all she needed to know. "When?"

"Back when we were with the fleet." Taisha laughed. "I didn't know when to tell you. Jae-Ho doesn't want to make a big deal about it."

"I didn't think you were into the old traditions," Nicole said.

"I didn't either. But Jae-Ho was determined. And then I thought maybe a little tradition is just what we need."

Nicole couldn't argue with that. She leaned over and

grasped her friend around the shoulders, pulling her close. "Congratulations," she whispered in Taisha's ear.

They pulled apart as they heard the soft whisper of the tent's door opening. "Man, I do not miss this heat," said Karl Garcia as he walked in.

He saw the two women disengaging from their embrace. "What'd I miss?"

"Did you notice anything different about Taisha?" Nicole asked in a singsong, the joy of the moment temporarily displacing the depression and regret from only minutes before.

"You mean the ring? Yeah, Park told me." Garcia sat down on his bunk. "Chief, I know things are grim right now, but no need to throw it all away."

Taisha gave Karl a playful punch on the shoulder.

"Nah, seriously, congrats," Karl said. "I almost got married myself once. He was the son of one of my parent's 'business associates.'"

"What happened?" Nicole asked.

"I left. He wasn't as hot as he thought he was, and I wanted to get out of there." Karl sucked in his breath and put his arms on his hips. "Besides, I figured I could find better. Everyone knows guys can't resist a man in uniform." He gave a playful wink.

Taisha and Nicole laughed. Karl and Taisha talked about their EDF flight training to Nicole and about some missions they had done prior to her coming aboard. They had been ferrying dignitaries around various UEG worlds when the Nasi had attacked.

"Gonna miss that ship," Karl sighed.

Taisha nodded her head. "She was a great ship—top of the line, even before we made the modifications to her."

Jones peeked his head in the tent door. "Get ready. We're getting a briefing in five minutes."

"Ah, duty calls," Karl said as he stood up. "It was fun reminiscing, but time to get back to reality."

"Congratulations Taisha," Nicole said.

"Thanks. Now I just hope we live long enough to enjoy it." Taisha replied, her face falling momentarily.

Sergeant Jones and Kal led the group to a small briefing room inside the command bunker. The room was simple, with a viewscreen hung on one wall and a small circular table that looked like someone had grabbed it from the trash in the middle.

Mohammed stood patiently by the viewscreen as the Samsara Fleet soldiers filtered in. Kal, Jones, and Nicole grabbed chairs at the table while the rest of the team leaned against the bare walls facing the viewscreen.

"So here's the plan," Mohammed said once they were all set. "You're going to need to get infiltrate the research lab, get what you need, and get off planet."

"So we're just launching into it, huh?" Ekon asked.

"Yes. I'm not one to bullshit. You can talk about your feelings after you leave." The Front fighter fixed Ekon with a stare.

Ekon held up his hands in a mea culpa.

Mohammed waited a moment and then continued speaking. "In order to make this work, we'll need a distraction. Our best bet is to launch a feint on the Nasi foothold in Kasongo to pull away some of their security."

As the Front officer spoke, the viewscreen popped on, displaying overhead maps of the fighter lab and Kasongo Foothold. "We've had agents working with the Nasi. We know that the Nasi have a shared security team responsible for both the Foothold and the fighter lab. I'll lead a Front assault team to assault the Foothold, which should pull the security team to our location. Immediately after, your team will infiltrate the lab. You'll need to move quick. We won't be able to stand long against the Nasi and will withdraw as soon as we see their reinforcements arrive."

"I won't tell you how to do your jobs. All the information that I've got is being sent to your implants. We've already got a team in Kasongo retrieving your battle suits, and we can provide a light atmospheric craft to take you to the lab. Once you carry out the mission, you'll need to lie low, very low, until we can get you off planet. I've sent the coordinates for a safe hideout as well. Only me and the commander know them. When the mission is complete, you head there—we'll contact you when we've got a way to get you off the planet."

"How long will that be?" asked Sandra.

"Hell if I know. Hopefully not long." Mohammed shrugged.

"What's the trigger to start the assault?" asked Jones.

"It'll be time based," Mohammed answered. "You'll start

your assault about fifteen minutes after we do. That should give enough time for the Nasi to call for reinforcements. Any more questions?"

The group was silent for a few moments, and then the Front officer clapped his hands. "Okay, be ready in two hours. Your suits should be here in one. Our techs will refuel and rearm them as best they can."

Mohammed walked to the makeshift desk area he had set up in the corner of the room, ignoring them. People slowly began to drain out of the room as they realized that he had nothing else for them.

"Sir," Jones whispered to Kal, "why don't you head back? I've got a few things I want to check out with Mohammed before we go back."

"Sure," said Kal, rising from his chair. "See you back at the tents."

As Kal walked back to the tents with the rest of the team, he felt a nervous tension rising in his body. It had become a familiar sensation in the past year. Only hours earlier, the Nasi had shot them out of the sky and they were already planning another assault. How much longer could he do this?

Chapter Sixteen

When Sergeant Jones returned to the tents fifteen minutes after the rest of the team, he called them together to go over the mission. Nicole admired Kal, and how he had the confidence to stand back and let Sergeant Jones take charge. He knew his strengths, and the strengths of his soldiers, and realized that they had a better chance of success with Jones executing the plan. She remembered several supervisors in the diplomatic corps who could have learned a thing or two from Kal.

They gathered in Jones's tent. He laid a tablet on the floor for the group to crowd around as he went over the plan. A three-dimensional wireframe map of the production facility rose from the device, and he zoomed in and out as he talked. The lab facility consisted of three dome-shaped buildings surrounded by a ten-meter-high wall, topped with security cameras and anti-personnel and anti-vehicular weapon systems. An energy shield covered the entire facility to prevent aerial attacks. The security was an enormous step up from the mining facility they'd infiltrated earlier.

The personnel in battle suits would conduct a high-trajectory insertion, meaning they would use their suits to climb high into the atmosphere over the base. Then they would descend, using their suits' weapons to take out the weapons systems and shield as they flew down into the facility. Everyone else would have a helo pack, essentially a reusable version of the life packs they had used to escape the *Oruc*. It would allow them to fly over the perimeter wall, once the shield was down, and back out again after they had accomplished the mission.

It wasn't clear which of the buildings had the information they needed, so they would split into three teams: Alpha, Bravo, and Charlie. Each team would go through a building, grab what they could, and return to the center of the facility. Once all personnel were accounted for, they would fly out to the waiting transport, which would then take them to a hiding place, and they would wait there until the Patagonia Front extricated them off planet.

Jones went through the plan twice, quizzing them on next steps and what to do if something went wrong. Nicole thought back to the shows she had watched on the holos, where tough-as-nails Tac-I soldiers wore disguises and subtly infiltrated top-secret facilities. She had learned that surprise and preparation were much more important than the heroics that she had seen in the holos.

"Any questions?" Jones looked them each in the eye. "Okay, you've got an hour to check equipment and do anything else you need to. Meet in the center of the tents."

Their battle suits were in one of the bunkers, no worse for wear from being at the bottom of a refuse pile. Ekon helped Nicole inspect her suit to make sure that all systems were fully functional. She was pleased to find that after her months with the Tac-I squad, she could go through the entire pre-mission checklist without prompting from the young soldier.

With a half hour left, Nicole wasn't sure where to go. She headed back to her tent to wait. She walked through the door to find Jae-Ho and Taisha lying together on a cot. Nicole quickly turned her head and felt the heat rise in her face. She stumbled backwards and tripped over a pair of pants lying the floor.

"Uh, sorry, I'll just get out," she stammered.

Jae-Ho laughed as he pulled a thin sheet over himself. "Nicole, don't worry, it's your tent."

"I'll leave and give you two some time." Nicole opened the door, not daring to turn around.

"We're just finishing," Taisha said. "We'll put something on if it makes you more comfortable."

Nicole heard the rustle of clothing being put on, wishing that she was anywhere else. She debated whether she should walk out, despite their protests.

"Okay, we're dressed," Jae-Ho said. Nicole turned around to find the two of them in their clothes, sitting on the cot, holding each other. Her embarrassment faded, and she only felt happiness at seeing two of her friends, together and in love.

"Sorry, Nicole." Jae-Ho smiled. "We're just a little more open with these types of things on Wudexingqiu."

Nicole hadn't realized that Park was from Wudexingqiu. That may be why he got along with Taisha so well.

"No, no, it's perfectly natural." Nicole could still feel herself blushing. "I'm just happy that you two, uh . . . found some time together."

"Me too," Taisha laughed, giving Jae-Ho a small punch on the arm. He pulled her in tightly and planted a soft kiss on her forehead. "We've got to take these small moments whenever we can."

"I'm so happy for you both," Nicole said. "To find someone you care about is wonderful. I'm glad you're able to find these moments despite everything else going on."

Taisha whispered something into Jae-Ho's ear. He gave a small snort. "You're always welcome to join us," Jae-Ho said to Nicole. The pilot raised his eyebrows suggestively.

Nicole couldn't tell if they were serious or teasing her. Either way, her Earthen sensibilities would never let her find out. "Uh, thanks for the offer, but I'll pass."

The two laughed. Jae-Ho asked, "Waiting for the general?"

Nicole's face felt like it was on fire. She hadn't even tried to understand what she thought of Kal. But Jae-Ho's words made her realize her feelings were obvious to others—she just hoped Kal didn't realize.

Taisha playfully shoved Jae-Ho. "Stop it or you'll make her head burst." She looked at Nicole. "He *is* interested, though. My advice, take a chance while you can."

Nicole said nothing, not trusting herself to speak.

"Let's go, we've got a mission." Jae-Ho pulled Taisha in for a last kiss and sprang off the cot.

As Taisha and Jae-Ho finished getting dressed, they told Nicole about places they wanted to see on Wudexingqiu when it was liberated from the Nasi. Unsaid were their worries about what the planet had turned into under Nasi control. New America and Patagonia painted bleak pictures of life under Nasi rule, and Nicole doubted either wanted to think about what it might look like on their home planet.

The three of them stepped out into the small, cleared area

between the tents to find the rest of the team already waiting. They still had fifteen minutes, but everyone was ready to go.

"Okay, Sergeant Jones, looks like we're ready to head out." Nicole couldn't help but hear Taisha's words when Kal spoke. She pushed her feelings aside—there would be time for that later, if they survived.

❖

"General"—Commander Kinkaid held out his hand—"I came to see you off."

The commander and a group of Patagonia Front fighters stood among the aircraft in the Front's hangar in a loose formation. Mohammed stood off to one side, deep in conversation with another soldier.

"Thank you, Commander," Kal replied. "We appreciate your help. If we're able to find out where the Nasi are planning to strike, we can stop them in their tracks."

Kinkaid shook his head ruefully. "I hope you're right, General. As far as I'm concerned, your trip has already been successful. My tech staff has been through the schematics you provided us. These devices will help us turn the tide."

"Glad to hear it."

"Sir, we're ready to go." Sergeant Jones stood next to a decommissioned EDF atmospheric transport. Kal remembered flying in one like it almost thirty years ago. The sensor reflective paint was chipped, and there were streaks and discoloration across the fuselage, but he could tell by the patchwork of new parts that they had taken care of it.

They climbed into the back cargo bay. It was small, roughly an eighth the size of the *Oruc's*, with benches lining either side. The interior looked well used. Paint was worn away on the handholds, and the safety notices and decals that lined the interior were torn or peeling.

After checking to see if the passengers were ready, the Front pilot taxied out of the bunker hangar and lifted off. The transport rose until it was a few meters above the treetops, then the bay door closed and they quickly jetted away.

You ready, sir? Sergeant Jones asked over the net. The question was uncharacteristic of the NCO—he seemed to be treating Kal differently since the island.

Yeah, I'm good.

The interior of the cargo bay didn't have any viewscreens to let Kal see outside the ship. He could trace their course via his neural link with the ship's navigation system. Their destination was near the coast, several hundred meters away from Kasongo or any of the cities on Pangea. As he sat in the back of the aircraft, Kal felt the familiar gnawing at the pit of his stomach growing—it was a strange mix of fear, excitement, and nervousness. Looking around the bay at the clenched jaws and darting eyes, he could tell he wasn't the only one feeling it.

One minute until touchdown, the pilot called over the net.

With a gentle bump, the aircraft touched down, and the cargo bay dropped. Sandra and Ekon jumped down the ramp, weapons at the ready, to establish a security perimeter. The rest of the team fanned out behind them. After all nine members of the team were out of the ship and prone on the

239

ground, it lifted off. The wash from the thrusters sent a blast of hot air, bowing the trees and shrubs as it shot away.

Jones and Ekon quickly checked the team's battle suits and helo packs a final time, confirming that there were no technical issues. Wordlessly, they split into three assault teams—Kal was with Private Kinawadi and Major Garcia. The teams split up and maneuvered around the facility's perimeter. They would launch their assault from the three locations. Kal checked his suit's display—ten minutes.

He led Garcia and Kinawadi as they trudged through the thick tropical bushes and vines. The foliage prevented him from going forward without using his bayonet to slice through the underbrush. When they reached the assault point, the three soldiers knelt, weapons pointed outward, waiting for the timer to reach zero. They didn't say a word, each lost in their own thoughts as they watched the timer tick down on their neural implants.

It finally reached ten seconds. Kal stood up and switched on his suit's thrusters to allow them to warm up. When the timer hit zero, he launched straight into the air at maximum acceleration, the pressure almost causing him to black out. Kinawadi had launched upward simultaneously, while Garcia waited back in the assault position for the signal to use his helo pack.

At fifteen thousand meters, Kal activated his suit's targeting system and cut the thrusters. His momentum continued his upward trajectory while Kal pivoted himself face downward so his suit's main weapons systems pointed at the facility. Once in position, he reactivated the thrusters and hurtled downward, the sudden change in momentum causing him to see black for a few seconds.

The irregular circular shape of the lab stuck out from the green forest around it. Kal's suit picked up the signatures of the pre-identified targets of interest—energy shield generators, weapons systems, and sensors. His heads-up display highlighted them in red, yellow, or green based on the certainty that it was a legitimate target and probability of hitting it. Kal let loose with everything he had—sending missiles, grenades, and kinetic rounds streaming toward the base.

A few seconds later, explosions ripped through the perimeter of the base from the combined assault of five battle-suit-clad soldiers. The energy shield protecting the top of the base blinked out, and his suit began targeting sensors and systems that the energy shield had covered. Targets changed to black as their onslaught had its desired effect and destroyed the Nasi sensors and weapons. By the time he was only a few hundred meters above the base, they had destroyed all identified targets.

The jolt of his sudden landing inside the perimeter sent Kal sprawling back. He quickly jumped up and surveyed the facility. Fire streamed from several places around him, billowing smoke into the sky. Reviewing his heads-up display, he was grateful to see that they had all made it without injury.

Phase two, go! Jones called out over the internal comms—surprise was no longer a factor.

Less than a minute later, the rest of the team flew over the walls, landing in the center of the compound. Jones called out over the net, *Teams, start your sweeps. We don't have a lot of time.*

Kinawadi, Garcia, let's go! Kal said as he walked toward the oblong structure they were going to sweep. As they got closer, he could see the same hallmarks of Nasi construction as he had seen in the Foothold on New America, the taut skin of the building appearing strung over an organic frame. A large awning surrounded the front door, providing cover from the sides and above.

Kal led his team through the enormous front door. The building appeared to be one large cavernous room, filled with computer terminals, loose parts, and partially constructed assemblies. Kal looked for any life forms via the suit's sensors, but the space appeared to be empty. They formed a line and walked the length of the room, looking for any material or information.

Arc-shaped tables with equipment piled on them were arranged in circles and divided the bay into discrete work areas. The equipment in the room seemed both strange and familiar at the same time. Large machines that appeared to have been grown had Human Standard writing across them. Kal bent over to inspect one of them—the display was also in Human Standard.

Sir, I think I got something, Kinawadi said.

Kal walked over to find the soldier standing over a terminal. A large engine, covered in blinking lights, sat on a small platform next to it. Kal could see that there was a Nasi storage drive jutting out of the terminal.

Grab the drive out of the machine, Kal instructed. *It looks like they locked it. Maybe the fleet can crack it when we get back.*

How do I know what the storage drive looks like? the private asked.

Use Chief's guide. Chief Kanumba had provided a digital identification guide prior to the mission. The database contained images and descriptions of various pieced of Nasi equipment to help them make sense of what they saw in the lab. There was still so much they didn't know about the Nasi that it was a guessing game, but at least it could help them a little.

There were several loose parts and tools scattered on the desk next to the terminal. It looked like someone had been working there recently and left in a hurry. Research and production labs like this one were heavily automated, but they still needed scientists and production managers. It appeared they had interrupted someone's work when they assaulted the facility.

Keep on your guard, Kal advised over the net. *Just because we don't see them doesn't mean there aren't any Nasi here.*

As he walked through the lab space, it became clear to Kal that the building was an aeronautics research lab. There were engines, maneuvering thrusters, and other pieces of avionics equipment strewn throughout the room. He knew there must be valuable technology here; the problem was figuring out which things where the important ones. He grabbed anything that looked like it could be a storage device or computer and stuffed it in his suit's cargo pocket.

243

The fleet's scientists would have to sort it out.

We've got contact! Ekon called from one of the other buildings. *At least two of them, unarmored. My guess is they're civilian techs.*

You need backup? Kal asked.

Negative, we've got them cornered. Ekon responded. Kal was glad to hear it—any backup they provided meant less chance of finding the magical piece of intel that would tell them what the Nasi plans were.

We're having trouble entering our building, Jones said. *The exterior doors are all sealed shut, and this material is a helluva lot tougher than it looks.*

We've found some sort of research lab, Kal said. *Picking up whatever we can fit in our suits.*

At least one of us is getting somewhere, said Ekon hurriedly.

Keep movin', we've got another five minutes, tops, Sergeant Jones said.

Bravo Team had made it two-thirds of the way through the bay, and Kal felt like they had little to show for it. Most of the equipment was heavy machinery and large computing systems they couldn't transport. At least their neural implants were recording everything they saw, so the fleet's engineers could review it later.

After passing by another enormous engine, Kal saw a workbench with a half-eaten plate of food. Next to it was a strange Y-shaped device and several tools. Someone must have been working on the device when they started their assault. Kal picked the object up—it could be something useful, and at least it was small enough to carry. As he lifted it, Kal could see an intricate pattern of circuits covering the device. It looked like it was supposed to be plugged into something else—there was a circular port at each end.

We've got Nasi security incoming, Jones's voice shot over the neural net. *All teams meet at the rally point, now!* Despite the synthetic voice from his implant Kal could sense the urgency in the sergeant's words.

Kal ran back toward the bay entrance. Garcia and Kinawadi had both stopped what they were doing and were running in the same direction. The three of them almost collided as they got to the building's entrance.

Ready? Kal asked.

Both soldiers nodded, their kinetic rifles out and at the ready. Kal cautiously made his way out of the entrance and into the middle of a firefight.

Chapter Seventeen

After the three groups had split up, Charlie Team had entered their assigned building. The front door opened to a long, curving hallway that stretched the length of the oblong building. Doorways sprinkled the walls at irregular intervals. Because of time, they cleared each room individually rather than staying together.

As Nicole approached her first door, it dilated open, revealing what looked to be living quarters. A bunk sat in the far corner of the room. A crescent-shaped table, with a chair in front and a viewscreen rising from its back, sat opposite the bunk. All the furniture in the room looked to be part of the building itself, seamlessly integrated with the walls and floor. She walked into the room, knelt down, and ran her hand over the bunk. The shiny material covering it was soft to her touch, despite its hard and almost-metallic appearance. She turned around to look at the desk. The viewscreen affixed to it was off, and she didn't see any way to turn it on.

Nothing in here, Nicole called out over the net. *Moving on to the next.*

The next room she entered looked identical to the first—a living area of some sort that appeared to be unused. The team made their way down the hallway, leapfrogging each other as they cleared rooms. They were all the same, spartan and with no personal items or sign that anyone had ever been in them. It appeared the Nasi hadn't fully occupied the facility yet.

As Nicole stepped out of a room, she felt the heat of a

plasma blast sizzle past her face. Instinctively, she dropped to the ground and pushed herself backward into the room.

Contact! she shouted over the team net. She didn't know how many Nasi there were or where the blast had come from.

Roger, stay in the room, replied Ekon. *Chedjou, cover me. I'm going to try and figure out where the hell the Nasi are.*

Ekon called over the team net and let them know they had contact. She hoped he was right to decline Jones's offer of backup.

Sandra and Ekon worked their way down the hallway past Nicole's position. She waited in the room, listening to them talk over the team net as they made their way toward the source of the plasma fire. She felt useless, hearing the two soldiers slowly progress down the hallway under fire, while she sat back and waited for further instructions.

As she struggled with her sense of uselessness, Nicole resolved to join the Tac-I squad in their training from now on. She'd had enough of sitting and waiting for them to rescue or protect her. Everyone had to pull their weight, and Nicole realized she wasn't pulling hers.

Got one, Sandra called out.

Stay back, there may be more. Ekon replied.

Nicole waited, still crouched next to the door, cursing herself for her uselessness. Finally, Ekon told her to join them. She stood up and scurried down the hallway, past the open doors of the cleared living quarters, until she arrived in a large room. The room was some sort of recreational facility or dining hall, with several groups of benches making a maze in the center.

Ekon crouched over a body that lay behind a bench. *Looks like this is a scientist of some sort,* Ekon said as he motioned for Nicole to come over. *They sure as hell weren't a crack shot.*

Nicole bent down and examined the body. It—no, she—wore a loose-fitting lab coat that looked to reach to her knees. Underneath was a white button-down shirt and black pants that came to her calves. The Nasi's black hair splayed out on the floor, her face fixed in an expression of shock, highlighted by her vivid green eyes. Nicole studied the pattern of tattoos that stretched around the scientist's body. They were relatively ornate—not to the level of Governor Fermott's, but more complex than their prisoner's had been.

I'd guess she was a high-level scientist based on her tattoos, Nicole said as she stood up.

There must be more, Ekon said, *looking around the room. Question is where.*

It's an interesting room, Sandra said as she walked around it.

Nicole stood up and walked along the wall, idly tracing her hand along its surface. The material felt like a textured steel, unyielding and rough. As she walked, she tried to superimpose the interior of the building against its outline—she thought there was a lot of space missing.

Why is there only the one scientist here? Nicole asked, voicing her internal monologue over the team net.

There are probably others in the locked building that Sergeant Jones is trying to enter, Sandra replied. *Maybe we caught this one while it was eating lunch.*

248

Maybe. Nicole let the word hang, her mind already working beyond it. Something felt off about the room—there had to be another entrance, a hideaway that they hadn't discovered.

Nicole tapped her knuckles against the wall—it was solid. There wasn't any sound or give. She continued until she felt something different—she couldn't identify what had changed, but something was distinctive about this section.

Nicole waved at Ekon and pointed at the wall. The young soldier motioned for Sandra to cover him and then ran his armored hand along its surface. After a minute, he pointed for Nicole to stand back, then raised his kinetic rifle and fired three rounds into the wall. The slugs slashed through the material, leaving small holes in their wake.

A moment passed. The wall suddenly disappeared, and two Nasi bounded out, sweeping the room with plasma fire. Nicole dove to the ground, letting out a groan as her injured side slammed against the ground.

We've got Nasi security incoming! Jones called. *All teams meet at the rally point, now.*

Nicole wanted to answer but found herself unable to do anything except suck in her breath, as pain coursed through her body from her wound. Two Nasi soldiers stood in the doorway, wearing fatigues, with weapons drawn.

Ekon and Sandra also dove for cover, their battle suits absorbing any force from the impact. The Nasi trained their weapons on the two soldiers, their bullets narrowly missing. Ekon and Sandra returned fire almost immediately, the whine of their kinetic rifles adding to the din and confusion.

Nicole closed her eyes as she saw one of the Nasi pitch forward, their head seeming to disintegrate from a round impacting it. A second later she heard the thud of another falling onto the floor.

"Step out with your hands up!" Ekon shouted through his suit's external speaker.

Nicole opened her eyes. A Nasi scientist, clothed in a white lab coat, stepped out into the open. He had a pistol clutched in his hand, pointed toward the ceiling. The Nasi was a deep violet hue, same as the others, but Nicole saw that he didn't have the black tattoos around his face or hands.

"Do not fire. I am placing my weapon down," the Nasi said as he bent over, setting the pistol on the floor in front of him.

"Kick it here," Ekon instructed.

The Nasi obligingly kicked the weapon across the floor. It came to rest against the bench next to Ekon.

"I am being held here against my will and will help you if you can assist me in getting transit to my people."

"What do you mean—" Ekon's question was cut off by Jones's frantic call over the net.

Charlie team, get your asses out here!

Kal pressed against the inner wall of the building and peeked his head out to see more of what was going on. Nasi fighters had taken the walls surrounding the facility and were firing down at the Samsara Fleet team. Several of them had a third arm extending from the back of their battle suits, giving them the ability to fire three weapons at once.

Jones and Alpha Team hadn't been able to get into their building in time. The Nasi security team had caught them by surprise, and the three soldiers had taken cover in the small alcove that surrounded the entrance. They kept their backs to the alcove wall and sporadically fired at the Nasi, trying to buy some time.

Equipment and small utility structures in the center of the compound blocked the Nasi's line of sight to the Alpha team members—the only thing keeping them alive. Although Kal had been a logistics officer, he had also been one of the best shots in the EDF. He channeled his training and experience, taking calming breaths as he studied the compound and the Nasi's location. Nodding to himself, Kal stepped out from behind the safety of the alcove he was in and took deliberate aim at the Nasi fighters—taking two of them out before they noticed he was there.

Sir, we need to get to your position, Jones called out on the net.

Kal normally would have considered the distance between Alpha Team and his location to be nothing. But with the constant barrage of plasma fire from the Nasi, it seemed like kilometers right then.

Roger Alpha Team, I'll cover you, Kal said.

Kanumba, get ready to move on my command. Park and I will cover you, Jones instructed.

Jones gave the word, and she ran the ten meters between the buildings, crashing into the side of the alcove.

Chief's secure, Kal said, *send—*

Wait! Nicole's voice broke through the command net. *We've got another idea. We have a Nasi prisoner that we're sending to you, Sergeant Jones.*

What? Keep 'em with you. Confusion and incredulity soaked Jones words.

He's our only way out of here—he can open your building, Nicole explained. *There's still a way out.*

Four Nasi fighters jumped from the top of the perimeter wall and landed behind the building that Charlie Team had just cleared. When they rounded the building, they would have a clear line of sight on their position.

You'd better hurry, Kal said. *Four Nasi just dropped behind you and are moving on your location.*

Sending the prisoner over now, Ekon said.

The Nasi prisoner ran across the open area between the building, crossing directly in front of Kal. His coat flapped behind him as he sprinted across the space, faster than a Human would be able to without the aid of a battle suit.

Four more Nasi jumped down from the perimeter wall behind Alpha team's building. They were closing the trap on the Humans. Kal realized that the Nasi that remained on the wall were firing simply to pin them down so their comrades could finish the job. Time was running out.

Door's open, Sergeant Jones called out.

They're encircling us—we all need to move now. Kal motioned to Kinawadi, Garcia, and Kanumba to join Jones, then stepped away from the safety of the building's alcove. He started firing with everything he had at the remaining Nasi on the walls. He would have given anything for a rocket or grenade, but they had all been expended during the initial assault.

Sandra and Nicole sprinted across the courtyard in front of Kal, plasma bolts streaking through the air in front of them. The soldiers next to him also sprinted toward Sergeant Jones's position. Kal continued to fire from an open position, shocked the Nasi hadn't hit him yet.

He felt a cool stinging sensation on his face as a grenade exploded in front of him, shattering the clear visor of his battle suit. The explosion hurled Kal backward into the building. Fortunately, his suit's armor absorbed the impact without losing power. Kal blinked, his eyes stinging from the blood and sweat running into them, and looked around. The grenade had kicked up a cloud of dust, obscuring everything around him. He shakily pushed himself up, the blood dripping from his face. As he started toward Alpha team's position, he saw Chief Kanumba lying prone on the ground, her left foot severed from the rest of her body.

Captain Park rushed toward her and knelt by her body, placing his arms underneath her armpits to drag her away. The young officer pulled her upper body off the ground and began dragging her back, away from danger. Kal looked directly in his eyes and could see the terror and determination coursing through the young officer's body—there was nothing he wouldn't do for her.

Park's eyes widened as a plasma bolt struck him in the small of his back. The shot seared a hole through his body and exited the front of his suit. Dead, he fell on his side, dropping Kanumba and exposing the Nasi who had fired the shots to Kal.

Kal felt something break. He felt a righteous anger, an anger born of realizing that he had just witnessed the end of something beautiful. He looked at the bodies on the ground, the wreckage of a happy future, and thought of his own loss. Rational thought left him.

He hurdled the bodies of the fallen Samsara soldiers and tackled the Nasi. The alien fighter was unprepared for the assault and fell backward. Kal smashed his right fist—aided by his anger and the augmentation of his cybernetic arm and exoskeleton—directly through the helmet of the helpless Nasi. The fight was already over before it started. After a few small jolts, the Nasi lay still.

Kal sat on top of the body for a moment, his arm and body covered in gore. Plasma fire sizzled across the courtyard, and the smoke and debris from the Nasi grenade dissipated. Kal realized he was still in danger. He looked back and could not tell if Kanumba was alive or dead. He grabbed one of her outstretched arms and dragged her with him as he ran toward the door of the last building.

The door to the Nasi building was already open by the time Kal reached it. Nicole stood inside the doorway, frozen by what had just happened. As he brushed by her, she jumped back as if he had shocked her.

"Close it!" Jones cried out as Kal staggered into the

building.

"I am locking the door." The Nasi prisoner touched the pad attached to his wrist, and the door constricted shut.

The building was a small-scale production facility. Equipment and parts leaned against the exterior walls. Large fabrication machines stood in rows along the walls, still noisily printing out parts and materials. A ship sat at the far end of the room, roughly half the size of the *Oruc*. It differed from the Nasi ships Kal had seen—this one was sleek and symmetrical. Mechanical smoothness and efficiency of design had replaced the almost-haphazard organic nature that he had seen in their other vessels.

"Follow me," the Nasi instructed as he ran toward the low-slung Nasi vessel, tapping on his wrist pad.

Kal picked up Kanumba's unconscious form, cradling her in his arms, and followed the Nasi into the ship's cargo bay. The interior of the ship differed from the other Nasi structures he had been in—straight lines and right angles. The cargo bay was a simple rectangular box. It was completely empty, with none of the equipment or machines Kal would have seen in a Human ship. Handholds lined the walls, floor, and ceiling.

Kal followed the Nasi prisoner through the door on the far end of the cargo bay and to the cockpit at the front of the ship. He motioned for Garcia to follow him.

The prisoner sat down in one of the backless chairs and manipulated the small dials and controls on the otherwise-featureless bulkhead in front of them. Kal could hear a low-pitched hum reverberate around through the ship, and the wall suddenly blinked to life, showing the landing bay outside the ship.

"How long will this take?" Kal asked.

"This is an experimental vessel," the Nasi responded. "It doesn't have our normal quick-start feature. So I think at least a couple of minutes."

Kal and Garcia waited impatiently while the Nasi went through starting up the ship, touching and sliding his fingers across the dials and buttons that made up the console. Kal wondered how long it would take for the Nasi security to breach the building.

"I would advise you all to hold on." The Nasi turned around in his stool to look at the Humans. "This ship has no shields and no artificial gravity."

"Let everyone in back know," Kal told Garcia. The major obligingly slipped out of the cockpit and rushed to the back cargo bay.

The Nasi prisoner tapped on his wrist computer, and the building's ceiling dilated open. Kal grabbed a handhold affixed to the bulkhead as the ship lifted off the ground.

The pilot slid his hand down a control, and Kal felt the momentum try to push him to the floor. Without his suit, the force would have knocked him to the ground. With his suit, he could barely stand upright. The ship shot out of the opening in the roof, turned in the air, and rocketed through the atmosphere. Kal's grip on the handhold prevented him from slamming into the back wall of the cockpit or into the bay behind them. After a minute, the star-speckled blackness of space had replaced the blue sky. Kal felt the pull of gravity lessen until it was absent altogether; only the force from the ship's acceleration remained.

A three-dimensional tactical map lay between the controls and viewscreen. The gray sphere of Patagonia dominated the center of the map, and he assumed that the four green dots were Nasi capital ships.

"Are they firing at us?" Kal asked.

"Yes," the Nasi responded, "but we do not have any sensors beyond the navigational. There is no way to know what is being fired at us. I can see some plasma cannons firing, and I think I saw some missiles being launched." The Nasi's tone was clinical and detached, as if the situation were the most normal in the world.

They continued to speed away from the planet, with no ability to see if the next second would be their last. The Nasi pressed a large blue button on the console, and the stars on their viewscreen shifted as the fold drive engaged.

"We made it," Kal gasped.

"Yes, we did." The Nasi seemed surprised.

Chapter Eighteen

"How is she?" Kal asked as he floated back into the cargo bay with the Nasi prisoner in front of him.

"Alive," Ekon responded, "but our takeoff didn't help her any." Ekon had used a restraint to tie Kanumba's unconscious form to the floor of the cargo bay.

Nicole rubbed the back of her head absentmindedly. The momentum from the ship's sudden departure had launched her against the back bay door.

"We've bandaged her ankle. Also, looks like she got some shrapnel wounds on her side," Jones said. He looked at the Nasi. "Do you have any medbots on this ship?"

"No, this ship is experimental only," the Nasi responded. "We have emergency rations, basic life support, and navigational functions, but nothing more."

"So what's your name?" Nicole asked.

"I am Scientist Bowen Nguyen." He touched his chest with his fist.

"Thank you for saving us," Nicole said.

"You are welcome."

"Bowen, we're gonna need to talk with you privately," Kal said, pointing with the pistol in his hand. Nicole could see that he was still in shock, his eyes wide, breath coming quickly.

Bowen's mouth twisted for a moment, and then he pulled himself out of the bay and toward the front of the ship, where the cabins and cockpit were.

"Anyone else injured?" Kal asked.

"Everyone feels like they got the crap kicked out of them,

but otherwise—no," Ekon responded.

"Okay. Jones and Nicole, with me. We're going to talk to our new friend and find out what the hell is going on." Kal still had his pistol at the ready.

Nicole glided through the cargo bay, using the handholds to course correct and propel herself into the corridor. Two rooms branched out from the small hallway between the cargo bay and the cockpit. Nicole peeked in one to find a small crate bolted to the floor of the room—the emergency supplies, she was guessing. The other room, where Bowen floated, waiting for them, was completely bare.

"We've got questions," Kal said as he maneuvered himself along the bulkhead.

"As do I," replied the Nasi.

Nicole took the lead in their questioning. The drying mask of blood on Kal's face was a reminder that he may not be in the best frame of mind. "Bowen, we appreciate everything you did back there. You understand that you're the first Nasi that we have met who's not trying to kill us, right?"

"This is because I am not Nasi," he replied matter-of-factly.

"What do you mean?" asked Jones.

"The Nasi are a sect of the Jadid," said Bowen. "Fanatics obsessed with returning and bettering Humanity."

"So, Nasi isn't their race . . . it's their sect, or their religion," said Nicole. "What about the rest of you?"

"We are content in our universe. It is where we were born; it is all that we know." The Jadid looked around the cramped cabin. "Your universe is strange and foreign to us."

259

"But the Nasi?" Nicole asked.

"When Humanity cast off the Jadid hundreds of years ago," Bowen said, "our ancestors were desperate to return. But as we grew and prospered in our new home, we came to love it. A small faction, led by the ancient named Esma, never lost their desire to return. As time passed, it became a religion of sorts, a belief that our destiny was to return and better Humanity."

"Why didn't any of the Nasi tell us about this?" asked Jones.

"Why would they?" Bowen shrugged. "They want you to accept them as your saviors. As our technology grew, and we mastered our universe, the Nasi saw the Jadid as superior to our Human ancestors. The natural leaders for a species that they believed had lost its way. The revelation that not all the Nasi believe as they do is not something they would want you to know."

"So what about you? You think you're our savior?" Kal asked, eyebrow raised.

"No. I was the same as most Jadid," Bowen answered evenly. "Thinking of your universe as strange and unsettling. I had no desire to be here any more than you wanted me here."

"Why didn't these other Jadid stop them?" Jones asked.

"The Nasi are zealots, but they are still Jadid. Our role is not to protect Humanity. You are the species that cast us out."

"Even when they take other Jadid prisoner?" Kal asked.

Bowen frowned. "I am not sure if the other Jadid know the

Nasi have taken prisoners. I am the only prisoner that I know of."

"Why you?" asked Jones.

"My expertise in fold drives and inter-universal transport," replied the scientists. "I am one of the foremost experts in my universe—and yours, for that matter."

"So, what to do with you," Kal said.

"I am the only person who can fly this ship. I don't think you have much choice."

"He's right, we need him," Jones said. Kal could see his hand tight on the grip of his pistol. He wasn't pointing it at the Jadid anymore, but he wanted to. "But we gotta be careful. I'll put two guards on him at all times. I'd like him to be in restraints."

"I'm not wearing restraints." Bowen's voice was flat. "I have already proven myself to be your ally."

"He saved us back there," Nicole admitted. The Jadid scientist could be an invaluable resource. Not only for his scientific knowledge, but to help them understand the Nasi. How did they think, what was their culture like? If they antagonized him, they may lose an asset.

Kal stared past the Jadid. Nicole wondered what he was looking at—it wasn't them. Finally, he let out a deep breath. "Fine. Monitor him, but no restraints. He's right, he's earned some trust."

Bowen gave a slight bow with his head. "Thank you."

"Can you decrypt the drives we found in your lab?" Kal asked. "We know the Nasi are planning an offensive, but not where."

"You cannot read those drives with the equipment on this ship," Bowen said. "However, I still may be able to help."

"My lab was a research station for small fighters. My Nasi captors would sometimes talk with me while I was working and let something slip. When you are isolated on a strange world, you can get lonely." He gave a small smile. "They are planning to strike Geerlok, the Torgham homeworld. Many of the fighters we fabricated will be part of that fleet."

"I thought so," Kal said. "Do you know when they are planning to strike?"

"They have already departed," Bowen said, shaking his head. "You are too late."

After Bowen had entered their fold path into the ship's computer and they were underway, Ekon and Jones moved Taisha to a cabin next to the cockpit. According to Jones, she was stable and would recover from her wounds, but was still suffering from shock. Some infection had set in the wound, despite the anti-bacteria agents built into the bandage.

Nicole dreaded having to tell her friend about what had happened to Jae-Ho. That was the actual wound that would never heal for her.

The small ship was bare, absent anything except the small crate of emergency supplies and a bio evacuation system in the same room. They tied the battle suits together using the few restraining straps they had and attached them to a handhold so they wouldn't rattle around the ship's interior.

For the first few hours of the voyage, Nicole floated quietly, mulling over the events of the past day. She dreaded the rest of their journey—days with nothing to do but think about the dead. She remembered the rage and bitterness in Pudari's face as she stood over her; Jae-Ho's cry when he saw Taisha fall to the ground. They were images frozen in her mind, and she had nothing to do but look over them, again and again.

"Chief Kanumba is still recovering." Sergeant Jones glided next to her, grabbing onto bulkhead. "When she wakes up, I think she should have a friend. Would you be up for it?"

"Yes." Nicole was struck by the recent changes in Jones. He had become more empathetic, more considerate than when she had first met him. "I remember when Ekon . . . Sergeant Kimathi, lost his legs. You acted like it was a good thing."

Jones paused a moment before replying. "Losing a leg and losing your husband are two different things." He looked down for a moment. "I've been in the EDF since I was eighteen. We drive our soldiers so that they know how to deal with the tough times. Times have never been tougher than they are now; I don't need to drive them."

"What do we need to do?" Nicole couldn't believe she was asking this.

"We need to realize that we've all lost something," Jones said. "I lost my husband too. You've lost your family. The only thing we haven't lost is hope."

"The only thing we can't lose," Nicole said.

Jones nodded. "This team has already been through more and lost more than any unit I've served with. We lose people on every mission we run. If we don't have hope that it means something, then we might as well stay home." He paused for a moment and then pushed off the wall and back toward the cockpit.

❖

"It's like a reunion," Ekon joked. "The crew of *Annie* back together on another screwed-up voyage." He raised the canteen in his hand in a small toast. Kal remembered the first time they met—it was at a bar in a Kurz mining station. Ekon and Sandra were kids, celebrating graduation, and Kal was wandering the universe, waiting to die. Things had changed.

Sandra smiled weakly and took a small drink from her canteen. "I'd take *Annie* over this ship any day." She looked at Kal. "You miss her, sir?"

Kal glanced up, dazed, the image of Pudari's face disappearing as he focused back on the present. "Uh, not really. I don't really get attached to ships like some pilots do. She had a job to do, and she did it."

"At least she had artificial gravity and an entertainment library," Ekon said.

Kal nodded absentmindedly. He heard the crunch as his fist split the Nasi's face shield and crushed their skull. He saw the life leave Lieutenant Park's eyes as the plasma round tore through him.

"We gotta figure out something to do," Sandra said.

"Otherwise we won't make it back to the fleet."

Kal pushed away from the conversation and floated back toward the cabin where Chief Kanumba lay unconscious. Peeling back the bandages, he could see the redness around her midsection where infection had set in. A drab gray tactical bandage covered the stump of her left ankle. He wondered when he would see her smile again. Probably not soon.

Kal drifted to the cockpit, Garcia was sitting next to Bowen, listening to the scientist explain how to pilot the ship. Kal floated quietly behind them as the Jadid explained the inner workings of the ship and the science behind them.

As the lead scientist on the development team, Bowen had been instrumental in the development of the new Nasi fighters. Not only was he an expert in fold drive technology, Bowen also was one of the few Jadid experts in how physics worked in this universe. Kal understood why the Nasi had kidnapped the middle-aged scientist.

When the fleet had faced off against the Nasi at the battle of Kapustin Station, the aliens didn't have any fighters supporting their large destroyers. Because of the physics and style of warfare in their own universe, their military technology emphasized large capital ships, brimming with weapons and shields over carriers and fighters. In the Jadid's universe, the fluctuations and chaos of their gravity made fleets of smaller ships extremely dangerous. The Jadid had quickly found that they were just as likely to destroy each other as they were to destroy the enemy.

Samsara Fleet had capitalized on this gap, using their attack fighters to devastating results. Bowen informed them that the Nasi had quickly realized that they would need to change their style of combat after their defeat and had immediately begun developing their own fighter program—kidnapping Bowen to jump-start their efforts.

The ship truly was like nothing Kal had ever flown in before. As a commercial pilot himself, Kal could appreciate its precision and speed. "The fleet that the Nasi are sending, do they have these types of ships?" Kal asked.

"Yes, and no." Bowen rotated in his chair, straps keeping him affixed to the seat. "They have ships like this one—atmospheric and space capable, agile, and heavily armed, I might add. They intended this one for something else. It is a skip ship."

"I'll bite. What's that?" Garcia asked.

"With my help"—Bowen looked chagrined—"the Nasi have almost completed developing a new type of fold drive. One that allows small ships to fold between this universe and the other multiple times. Combined with their Footholds, it will ensure the Nasi are secure in their control of your galaxy."

"If these ships are new, how did any of you get to our universe then?" Kal asked.

"The fold drives the fleet used to come here are single use," answered Bowen. "The fold between the universes destroys them."

"How'd they get you then?" Garcia asked as he continued studying the ship's controls.

"They brought a second drive with them to use in case they needed to return," Bowen said. "But with the drive that is on this ship, one can fold back and forth between universes an almost endless number of times."

"So, we can travel to your universe?" Kal asked.

"Unfortunately, no. When you raided the lab, I was making modifications to the fold drive. Without the piece I was working on, this ship is no different from any other."

Kal abruptly glided back to his battle suit and opened the compartment with the Y-shaped piece he had found in the lab. He grabbed it and brought it back to the cockpit.

"Is this the part?" He held the device up.

Bowen's eyes widened. "Yes, that is the diveculum. You grabbed it from the lab."

Kal held the part out of reach. "It was on a table and looked important—so I grabbed it."

"That was a smart move." Bowen regarded him carefully. "That device is my ticket home."

Kal felt exposed for a moment. Was he the only thing between the Nasi and his home? He quickly tucked the part into a cargo pocket, vowing to ensure the security protocols were active on his suit when he put it back.

"If we could repair the drive and make this ship operational, it would be huge." Garcia said. "We could build more, and strike at the Nasi where they live."

"Could you do that?" Kal asked.

"Most likely I could," Bowen answered evenly. "But I won't be a part of any Human fleet attacking Altterra."

"You have my promise," said Kal, looking the Jadid scientist in the eyes. "We would never attack the Jadid. Also, if you can help us, I will personally ensure that you are returned safely to your home."

Bowen looked him over, his piercing violet eyes locking onto Kal's. "Perhaps," he replied, "perhaps."

❖

"Hi." Taisha smiled faintly as Nicole glided into the room. Her eyes darted around the small space.

"Hi." Nicole paused. "How are you feeling?"

"I've been better." Taisha frowned. "Where's Jae-Ho?"

Nicole felt her words fail her—she didn't know how to tell her friend what had happened. Taisha's face collapsed. Small saline droplets bubbled from her eyes, floating around her face.

"No no no," Taisha repeated as her glistening tears cascading across the room.

"Taisha, I am so sorry." Nicole could feel the inadequacy of her words as she said them. How could words do justice to her friend's loss?

Taisha closed her eyes, her soft sobs filling the room, as Nicole waited patiently beside her. Nicole pulled herself close and held her while Taisha absorbed the enormity of her loss.

"How did it happen?" Taisha asked. "I just remember running to that damned building and then nothing."

Nicole wondered if she should spare her friend. Did Taisha need to know that Jae-Ho died saving her? Did she need that burden? Finally, she decided that Jae-Ho had earned that.

Nicole described how the grenade had gone off in front of Taisha and how Jae-Ho had run amid fire and grabbed her before being struck down from behind. As her friend wordlessly watched her, Nicole kept going. She described their escape and their plan to return to the fleet to warn of the attack.

When she had finished, silence greeted Nicole. Taisha's sobs had subsided, and now she floated in the cabin, restrained, with her eyes closed.

Finally, they opened. "Better to have left me. He was so much better than me." The dam broke, and Taisha sobbed and shrieked. Loud, body-shaking noises filled not only the cabin but the entire ship.

Nicole tried to hug her friend, but Taisha pushed her away. Nicole turned and used the handholds to propel herself back to the cargo bay. The sobs of her friend followed her the whole way.

❖

The voyage to Keerloa passed incredibly slowly. Many of them had demons they were wrestling with, and none of them wanted to talk to each other. The Tac-I squad stayed together—Ekon and Sandra spent much of their time talking to each other about their home. Sergeant Jones tried to buoy spirits and support his comrades, tactfully checking in on everyone and listening to any issues they had.

Kal also tried to circulate among his soldiers, to check in on them and reassure them. But he stopped after a couple of days, realizing his state of mind was just making things worse.

When he could sleep, nightmares tormented him. Visions of his family, Pudari, or Jae-Ho haunted him. He always had the same dream at least once every time he went to sleep. It took place in a house where he had lived with his family decades ago. Kal walked down an impossibly long hallway, peering through doorways, looking for his wife and children. He had the uneasy feeling that something was wrong—the rooms were all empty. All of them were the same—open window with sunlight streaming in, a faint breeze brushing the curtains wide. Kal opened a door to find a Nasi in a battle suit, their weapon pointed directly at his head. Kal turned and ran back down the hallway, his children's voices calling for help. The hallway seemed to move, extending itself to prevent Kal from reaching the end. Finally, he reached the far end and opened the door. Pudari stood in front of him, her face disfigured and bloody, a look of pure hate etched in her features. She leaned forward, tongue slithering from between ruined lips, and kissed him, the gore and blood still warm on his lips.

When awake, Kal tried to think about how to occupy his time and be useful. He spent hours war gaming what Samsara Fleet should do. He worried they would be too late, that the Nasi would capture or destroy Geerlok and they would lose everything. They were in a race, and he didn't know where the other runner was. Fortunately, Keerloa was on the way, which meant they wouldn't lose much time stopping to warn Samsara Fleet. Depending on how long the Nasi spent scouting the planet, they may still catch up before they attacked.

As a senior officer, Kal had attended the EDF Advanced Studies University, a two-year-long school dedicated to strategic studies. The university taught senior officers strategic planning through in-depth and rigorous studies of war and the principles behind it. One concept taught was the phases of war—one could describe every war as going through three broad phases. The first was the shaping phase, where the adversaries prepared for their assault or defense. Next was the domination phase, where the adversaries fought to gain a decisive advantage over each other. Finally, there was the consolidation phase, where the presumptive winner solidified their victory and removed all remaining resistance.

The Nasi had successfully won against Humanity in the shaping and domination phases. They had been meticulous in their planning and struck without warning, giving Humanity no chance. Now, the war was in the consolidation phase; the Nasi had the advantage and just needed to make sure they didn't lose it.

This was Humanity's chance to strike back against the Nasi. Their supply lines were long, and they were still setting up infrastructure in this universe. Their soldiers may have been fanatics, but they were most likely tired and homesick as well. If Humanity could win, and win big, they could demoralize the Nasi and change the outcome of the war still.

On the other hand, if the Nasi captured Geerlok and removed the Torgham from the equation, the war would be over. Their mission, and the information they carried, were critical.

❖

"How good are the communications on this ship?" asked Garcia.

"We can only transmit in the clear, no encryption, but should be able to hail your fleet," responded Bowen.

Kal floated behind the two pilots as they approached Keerloa. They had folded to a location far away from the planet and Samsara Fleet, so they would not be surprised. A Nasi ship suddenly folding next to the fleet could cause immediate panic. With the rudimentary sensors on the ship, they wouldn't even know if Samsara Fleet launched missiles at them until they were destroyed.

Garcia transmitted a hailing call over all open frequencies, hoping that someone would hear before a trigger-happy pilot took a shot.

"Samsara Fleet, this is SFS *Park,* commanded by General Norman. Please provide docking instructions." Garcia continued to repeat the message for a minute until a response came.

"*Park,* this is the *Ofira,* can you provide visual confirmation that General Norman is on board?"

Garcia glanced at Bowen, who shook his head.

"This is General Norman." Kal leaned in close to where he thought the microphone was. "I'm here. Run an analysis of my voice to see if it matches your files."

Kal could only imagine what was happening on the *Ofira.* He pictured a junior officer frantically trying to find someone who could tell them what they should do.

"General Norman, this is Colonel Petrov—you're clear to land. We'll send instructions to your ship's navigational computer." Colonel Irina Petrov was the commander of the *Ofira*. She had been with Kal during the battle of Kapustin Station as the acting commander of the ship. After their victory, General Samaha had promoted her to colonel. She was a strong tactician and officer.

"Yeah, that's not gonna be possible," Kal said. "This is an experimental Nasi ship, and we have only rudimentary systems. Can you send us coordinates and illuminate the shuttle bay? We have to land manually."

"Yes, sir. We can do that, stand by."

After a few seconds, Garcia gave a thumbs-up, confirming they had received the coordinates, and Bowen adjusted their course toward the *Ofira*. The viridescent orb of Keerloa grew in their main viewscreen as they approached. Temperate forest completely covered the face of the planet. Aquifers underneath the surface provided the water needed to sustain life. Kal was used to having a host of sensors available to him during maneuvers. He felt helpless as he hovered in the cockpit, waiting for them to land inside the carrier.

As the Park came through the bay doors of the *Ofira*, Kal could feel the ship's artificial gravity pushing down on him. After days of being weightless, it felt like someone had attached weights to every part of his body. The Park finally came to a gentle rest inside the landing bay of the *Ofira*.

The Park's flight crew made their way to the cargo bay, where the rest of the team was waiting. Per Kal's orders, no one had left the ship. He wanted to talk to the *Ofira's* landing crew before they disembarked. Seeing what they thought was a Nasi walking down the ramp without proper warning could cause a widespread panic.

"Okay, you can drop the door," Kal said to Bowen. The bay door smoothly dropped, revealing a small crowd of soldiers and civilians grouped around the alien vessel.

"Kal, glad to see you back." General Samaha smiled. For her, the greeting was like a bear hug.

"Thank you," Kal responded. "The Nasi are adjusting to our new devices and tactics, so our entry to the planet wasn't easy. I should warn you we have a Jadid on board." Kal quickly summarized what had happened on Patagonia, and Bowen's role in saving the team. He relayed the information about the schism between the Nasi and the Jadid, and Bowen's capture.

"Seems like there is, once again, a lot to talk about," Samaha said. "But at least we have confirmation of the Nasi's target."

"Yes," Kal agreed. "My advice is you keep an escort with the Jadid at all times"—he stressed the alien's species—"but otherwise treat him as an honored guest. I trust him; he could be the difference in fighting the Nasi."

Samaha puckered her mouth as she thought. Finally, she spoke. "I agree. He's too valuable an asset to waste or antagonize. Let him know he's a guest on our ship. But we'll have an escort with him, and we will restrict him from certain areas. These measures are for our safety, and his." She turned to one of her aides and asked for an escort detail to report immediately.

"Yes, ma'am," Kal said. He turned and walked back up the ramp of the *Park* to let his soldiers know they could leave. A moment later they all unsteadily shuffled down the ramp, feeling the weight of the ship's gravity.

Someone had dispersed the crowd that had been hovering around the ship. Only General Samaha, Colonel Petrov, their aides, and Bowen's guard detail remained. They all stiffened as their eyes lit on the angular form of the Jadid walking down the ramp. Kal knew what they were feeling—to see their enemy walk down that ramp and to greet him as a friend and guest was difficult. Bowen was oblivious, or attempting to appear nonchalant. He scanned the bay, unconcerned with the small party there to greet him.

"Scientist Bowen Nguyen, on behalf of the *Ofira* and Samsara Fleet, we welcome you. General Norman has told us about how you helped his team on Patagonia. I look forward to working together." Samaha had a broad smile plastered on her face.

"Thank you, General, though I did not have any other choice." If Samaha was shocked by his frankness, it didn't show. "I look forward to working together as well."

"There is much for you and our engineers to discuss. We would love to learn more about this new fold drive you've developed."

"Indeed." The Nasi scientist nodded. "I will need your help to get back to my universe."

"You must be tired from your ordeal," the fleet's commander said. "We've detailed a soldier to escort you to your quarters on the ship. If you need anything, they'll assist you. I'll give you some time to settle in and then would love to talk more."

"I'll begin work now. Please direct me to your lab and ensure you have your engineers there for us to begin."

Samaha spluttered for a moment, caught off guard. "Of course." She gave a small nod of assent to Bowen's escort, who walked away, the Jadid in tow.

"Let's find someplace to talk," the general said to Kal. "I need you and Ms. Bergeron to give us a full debrief, now."

The general led them to the ship's briefing room. It was sumptuous—wood and platinum highlights adorned the room, and viewscreens displaying a real-time feed of Keerloa covered three of the walls.

The four of them sat down around the table, and Kal provided a play-by-play description of everything that had occurred on their mission to Patagonia. Nicole added her insights from her conversations with Bowen during their voyage back to the fleet. Once they finished, General Samaha and Colonel Petrov sat silently for several seconds.

"Sorry for your losses." Petrov reached out a hand to Kal. "It's always tough, even in times like now."

"Indeed," Samaha said, "you've lost more than most. Though I hope you realize how valuable you and your team have been. It was not in vain."

Kal thought of Pudari. He hadn't gone into specifics about the nature of her death, simply saying she had been shot while trying to infiltrate the mining facility. He wondered what purpose her death served.

"So, we now have confirmation that they are heading to Geerlok," Samaha said.

Kal nodded. "Yes, they are en route as we speak. I think

we may still surprise them. A fleet that large will stop and regroup before launching their attack."

"If we do this, it could be decisive," Petrov said. "We win, and we've crippled the Nasi fleet. We lose, this war is over."

"How large is their fleet?" Samaha asked.

"We don't have their exact strength," Kal replied. "We know they've pulled ships from several systems. It has to be at least ten capital ships. One of them is a dreadnaught—their star-killer ship."

General Samaha shook her head. "Then we'd better get moving. I want us heading to Geerlok in the next thirty minutes. Have the flight crews prep for combat. What's the estimated time to get there?"

The general's aide paused for a moment as she used her implant to calculate the travel time. "Eighty-seven hours, ma'am," she replied.

"Okay, we have eighty-seven hours to come up with a strategy and be ready to execute. I want every commander on the net as soon as we are underway." Samaha stood up from the table.

"Yes ma'am," the aide replied.

"This is an opportunity to crush the Nasi fleet," Samaha said. "Let's make sure we're prepared."

Chapter Nineteen

Nicole sat across from Taisha in the *Ofira's* lounge. They had been aboard the ship for almost a day, and Nicole hoped that the change of scenery would help her friend. The fact that Taisha had agreed to see her was a positive sign.

"Jae-Ho would've been happy we named the ship after him." Taisha smiled wistfully.

The woman's face looked gray and drained, and she had bags under her eyes. The ship's medical team had seen her— using nanobots to heal the wound in her side and fitting her with a prosthetic foot. They had treated Nicole's wound as well, though her abdomen still had a puckered scar to remind her of what had happened. The light in the chief's eyes was still dimmed, and she regularly stared off in the distance as she talked with Nicole.

"He acted like he didn't want attention, but you could tell he liked it." Taisha grinned. "After we'd gotten married, I noticed he was using his left hand a lot more when we were flying."

"He was a special person," Nicole agreed. She thought back to Jae-Ho's sly smiles and his dry sense of humor. Sometimes he would come up with the most ridiculous things out of nowhere.

"Yeah, strange to think I've only known him a year." Taisha paused. "I guess I should say, I *knew* him a year."

"You went through a lot together," Nicole said. She grabbed her friend's hand. "You fought with each other."

Taisha nodded. "Yeah, we went through some stuff

together."

"Does he have any family?" Nicole asked. "Anyone we should notify?"

Taisha shook her head. "Both his parents were in the EDF. They were stationed on Earth when the Nasi attacked."

"Whole family's gone now," Nicole said.

"Yeah," Taisha agreed. "One of millions of families."

Nicole sat quietly while her friend recounted how she had met Jae-Ho. She wanted to be there for Taisha, to let her say as much, or as little, as she wanted. She knew that the grief would take a long time to process. It was frustrating to see her friend in so much pain and know there was nothing she could do to change it.

"So, where do we go from here?" asked Taisha, almost rhetorically.

Nicole let the words hang in the air for a moment. "Forward?" she asked.

"Guess so." Taisha sighed. "Unfortunately, the galaxy doesn't seem to care about us, or Jae-Ho."

"Well, we care," Nicole responded weakly.

"We've got a mission. Nothing we can do but to kill those bastards," Taisha said.

"You gonna be ready when we get to Geerlok?" Nicole asked.

"Yeah, I'll be ready." Taisha's mouth tightened. "Whatever it takes."

279

Kal attended Samsara Fleet staff meetings for almost two days straight, with minor breaks. They continued to develop their battle plan—anticipating enemy tactics, defining courses of action, and war-gaming the entire battle. The conversations were long, detailed, and often filled with awkward pauses. Having four species plan a complex military attack resulted in no shortage of misunderstandings.

Nicole attended a few of the meetings—she was the foremost expert on Nasi and Jadid culture in the entire fleet. Otherwise, Kal represented his small team as much as possible. His soldiers and friends deserved as much rest and relaxation as they could get after all they'd been through.

The staff drew up several courses of action, each based on what they might encounter when they folded into Geerlok's system. If the Nasi had already arrived, they would have to retreat immediately; they couldn't hope to defeat the full force of the enemy fleet.

If they could arrive at the planet before the Nasi, they would wait light hours away. When their scout ships reported the enemy had arrived, the fleet would immediately fold as close as possible and assault them from behind as they were engaged with the Torgham home fleet.

Samsara Fleet had defeated the Jadid at Kapustin Station by using their fighters as missiles against their capital ships. The new Jadid fighters would make things much more difficult—intercepting Samsara Fleet's fighters before they got close to the capital ships. Bowen had provided the fleet's engineers with as much information as he could remember on the Jadid's fighter's specifications and technology. They were faster and more maneuverable than anything Samsara Fleet had.

The Jadid was working with the fleet's engineers and scientists to add weapons, sensors, and auxiliary systems to the *Park*. The ship was the most advanced one in their arsenal, and they needed to make sure it was ready for combat.

"Sorry you're back yet, sir?" Colonel Zhou whispered to Kal as they patiently listened to a Kurz general argue for a suicidal frontal attack.

The EDF commander on Kapustin Station had assigned Colonel Zhou to the *Oruc* to assist Kal. Despite the rocky start to their relationship, Kal had learned to appreciate the officer, now commander of the *Merrimack*. Zhou was inflexible in his beliefs but a brilliant tactician. Not someone Kal would want to share drinks with, but an outstanding officer to work with.

Kal looked sideways and grunted. The colonel had made the remark in jest, but he also hadn't been off the bridge of a fleet ship since the war began.

Taking the hint, Zhou cleared his throat and shifted his attention back to the Kurz presenter, who was gesticulating wildly to emphasize his point. Did the officers in the room appreciate what the crew of the *Oruc* was going through? Or was his team just icons on a map to them?

After several more hours of back and forth, the group adjourned with most of the details decided. It had been exhausting—even the Kurz were showing signs of fatigue. Kal was pretty sure most of the Tounous had long since fallen asleep, though it was hard to tell since the insect-like species looked the same whether conscious or not.

"Looks like we have a plan," Kal said to General Samaha.

"Aye." She looked exhausted. "I want you to know that we only have this plan because of your team. Words aren't much, but they're all I have—thank you."

Kal inclined his head to acknowledge her statement.

"We've already been able to smuggle several loads of weapons and tech to the rebels on New America. With the information you have collected both from there and Patagonia, we'll be able to increase our efforts in multiple systems."

Here it comes. Samaha's praise did not come without requests following closely behind.

"I've also been thinking about that ship of yours, the *Park*. I think we need to take advantage of it," Samaha said.

"How so?"

"There's no way that the Jadid fleet would know that the ship isn't theirs. They left after you had captured it—we have the perfect trojan horse."

She was predictable, if nothing else. "Sounds like we're going to be infiltrating a Nasi ship. What makes you think they won't be suspicious? Kinda strange for one of their experimental ships to show up during a battle."

"That's what we need to find out from Bowen," Samaha replied. "I want you to talk with him and come up with a cover story. We'll load your ship's cargo bay with a time-detonated quark bomb. You gain entry to the ship, drop the bomb, and leave. Easy." The general gave a broad smile.

Kal grunted. He wasn't superstitious, but he could feel his skin crawl when she called the mission easy. "I'll talk to Bowen and see what he can come up with," Kal said.

"Good," she replied.

Samaha walked toward the door and then spun around, finger raised. "Oh, and have you thought about giving your little crew a name? Seems small, but it makes a difference."

"I hadn't thought of it." Kal shrugged. "We've had bigger fish to fry."

"Well, figure something out," she said with a grin. "They'll need to call you something in the history texts."

Kal gave an uneasy smile in return and added another item on his checklist.

❖

"Well, this beats the *Oruc's* galley," Jones said as they sat in the *Ofira's* expansive lounge.

Kal, Nicole, Jones, and Garcia sat around a table, discussing the mission. Kal had finished debriefed them on the fleet's strategy for the ambush of the Nasi. They had taken their role in the plan with their normal air of dejected resignation—another scrap piled upon the heap of things they were already dealing with.

"You think Bowen will help us?" Kal asked Nicole.

She thought for a moment, reflecting on her conversations with the Jadid scientist. He obviously was desperate to get to his own universe and planet, but didn't strike her as someone who would unnecessarily put himself in danger. He wasn't cowardly, but he *was* pragmatic.

Finally she replied, "I think we need to make it worth his

while."

Kal nodded. "That's my take, too. He wants to get back to his home. If we can promise him that, he'll do it."

"If he goes, then what?" Jones asked, a flicker of annoyance crossing his face. "We'd be losing a critical asset."

"Not completely," Nicole said. "We've interviewed him countless times already, and he's already provided a ton of technical information from what I understand."

Jones grunted.

"Not to mention," Kal added, "that how we treat him could affect any relationship with the Jadid. We need to get as much out of him as possible and then let him go back."

"I'd like to get more time in the simulations with him," Garcia said. "We've been working on getting the flight characteristics of the *Park* into the simulator. Since they're retrofitting it, that's the only training I can get."

"Do it," Kal said.

"He's already helping our engineers understand a lot of the Nasi weapon and drive technology," Nicole said.

"Let's get what we can out of him before the *Park* is fully operational," Kal advised. He paused for a moment to take a bite of the fabricated sandwich in front of him. Not bad.

"Also, Samaha seems to think our little group needs a name." Kal wiped the crumbs from his mouth. "Any suggestions?"

"The suckers," Garcia replied, straight-faced.

"The morons," Jones added, lips twitching.

Kal made a show of thinking through their suggestions. "Both strong candidates. I was thinking of the expendables.

Nicole, any thoughts?"

Nicole had to hide her smile behind her cup of tea. "All strong candidates, General. I can't decide." She made a show of tapping the side of her glass, brows furrowed as if in deep thought. "I'll add one more candidate. How about Norman's Numbskulls?"

Kal snorted. "Very good—it really rolls off the tongue. But I don't want my name associated with this group of misfits."

"Numbskulls it is, then." Jones thumped the table with his hands.

Kal felt the joke going sideways on him. "I'm not sure the fleet will let us choose that one."

"Sir"—Garcia clasped his hands together and pouted his lips—"the fleet asks so much of us. You are a brigadier general and a hero. This is our only request."

"Fine," Kal chuckled. "The Numbskulls it is. But we are *not* Norman's Numbskulls."

"Excellent, sir." Jones stood up and grabbed the remains of his meal. "Now if you'll excuse me, I have something I want to see about." The NCO dropped his trash into the recycler and walked out.

❖

Nicole scrolled through her notes from her interviews with Bowen. Since boarding the *Ofira* the Jadid scientist had been busy, helping the fleet's scientists in understanding Nasi technology, advising on Nasi military strategy, and talking with her about Jadid culture. Whenever he had a chance, the scientist had also been advising on the retrofits to the Park, spending whatever time he could with the mechanics. Nicole thought he must be exhausted, even if he didn't show it.

One thing was clear—the alien was eager to return to his own universe. He clearly saw his help as being provided in exchange for his return home when the conflict was over. Nicole assured him that this was the case as far as she knew.

A chime sounded; Kal was at her cabin door.

"Hey"—he raised his arm sheepishly—"hope I'm not bothering you."

Nicole put down the tablet she was reviewing. "Not at all, come on in. I'm reviewing my notes from my talks with Bowen."

Kal sat down on a chair in the corner of the tiny room and Nicole turned so that she was facing him. Even on a ship as large as the *Ofira*, cabins were cramped. She could have easily reached out and touched him.

He looked tired. She wondered how much everything that had happened on Patagonia still weighed on him. As she studied his dark, angular face, she felt a sudden wave of emotion roll over her.

"I never said thank you," Nicole said.

"For what?" Kal looked perplexed.

"For saving me. Actually, saving me several times."

Kal looked away. "I was just doing my job," he said, unconvincingly. "You have meant so much for Samsara Fleet—for our little team, too. We wouldn't be alive without you."

"The Numbskulls you mean?" Nicole asked with a smile.

"Yeah." Kal rolled his eyes.

"Well, you mean so much to me." Nicole was horrified as she heard the words fall out of her mouth. "I mean, all of you."

"Nicole." Kal breathed in, seemingly to delay what he was about to say next. "I've told you about my family, about my wife. I haven't really cared for someone since they died. I care about you, though." He stared at the viewscreen on her wall, set to display the stars outside the ship.

Nicole leaned forward and kissed him. He hesitated for a moment and then wrapped his arms around her, pulling her closer. As they held each other, Nicole's mind fixated on the feel of his lips and hands as they were together—the past, their mission, and everything else faded away as she felt the bliss of being with him.

❖

"General!"

Kal turned to look back at the young tech, Sergeant Abrams, who had been briefing him. He realized Garcia and the tech both were looking at him expectantly.

"Sorry, go ahead." Kal wiped the smile from his face and focused on the device in front of him. He felt like he was a teenager again, mooning over a girl in his class.

"Like I was saying, sir, this bomb can still detonate even if not armed."

"Meaning, if we get hit, we send a bunch of people with us, whether this thing is armed or not," Garcia said.

"Exactly, sir. The *Park* could take out one of our own capital ships if close. You sustain too much damage, and this thing will go off." The tech patted the rectangular explosive.

"Good to know," Kal replied. He had figured as much. "What about the modifications to the ship?"

"That's the good news. We've been working with the Nasi—"

"Jadid," Kal corrected.

"*Jadid* scientist," Abrams continued, "and we've been able to add a significant amount of firepower and shielding. Honestly, the power plant on this girl is almost to the level of a small cruiser."

"What about sensors and communications?" Garcia asked.

"Added those too, sir," the tech replied. "We even included the cloak and communications intercept, even though they weren't too effective on your last mission. This thing is about as top of the line as we could make it in three days."

"You think you can fly this thing without Bowen if needed?" Kal asked Major Garcia as he started to walk around to the front of the ship.

"Yessir, I think so. I've been going through all the training scenarios in the simulator. Not the same as the real thing, but pretty damn close in my experience."

Kal stopped in his tracks near the nose of the craft. Painted on the side, in bright red letters, was *NOT NORMAN'S NUMBSKULLS*. Above the words, someone had painted a grinning skull, wreathed in flame. Beneath it, they had painted *SFS Park* in a more dignified white lettering.

Garcia saw Kal's face and abruptly had a bout of coughing. The tech also seemed to have a medical issue that required him to turn away. Once he had recovered, Garcia turned back to Kal, his eyes wide. "What do you think, sir? I think we should probably call ourselves the triple nickel for short."

"When I find Sergeant First Class Jones, I'm going to . . ." Kal trailed off. He could only imagine the glee with which the NCO had updated the ship. Kal also doubted he had been alone.

"So, what's our cover anyway?" Garcia asked, trying to change the subject.

Kal and Nicole had spent a long time talking with Bowen to come up with a plausible reason that the experimental ship would go to the Nasi fleet. Finally, they had settled on the story that they were there to report the status of the battle back to Esma. Bowen had expressed reservations it would work, but it was the best that they could come up with. They just needed to be permitted to land inside one of the Nasi ships.

When Kal told him, Garcia seemed skeptical as well, but held any reservations he might have to himself, which Kal appreciated. They were too close to change the plan now.

The tech had one of the ship's bots load the large explosive into the cargo bay of the *Park*. It took up over three quarters of the bay, leaving a small corridor next to the bulkhead for the flight crew to get through.

The tech had told them that the Jadid had been invaluable in their work. They had needed to figure out how to make the Human-based systems work with the Nasi ship and Bowen had been invaluable in helping them to bridge that divide. The fleet engineers had been awestruck with the technical improvements that Bowen could make in the system. Not only had he improved the *Park*, but he had also given them guidance on how to improve the other ships in the fleet. They hadn't had time to integrate his advice into their current fleet of fighters, but now had the knowhow to do so in the future.

Kal took one last look at the ship's logo, trying to suppress a grin, and checked his implant. They would arrive at their destination in the deep space near Geerlok in less than thirty seconds.

"Let's get inside," Kal suggested. He motioned to Garcia and Bowen, who was pacing outside the ship, looking it over. The three of them walked up the bay doors, past the large explosive, and into the cockpit. Bowen's escort, a young private, trailed behind them.

"You can leave," Kal told the escort. "We've got it from here." She gave a smart salute and walked through the cargo bay and off the ship.

The interior of the cockpit looked the same as Kal remembered, except for a new viewscreen affixed to the lower center portion of the front bulkhead and a chair for a third person. The screen was a digital instrument cluster, containing all the controls for the systems they had added to the ship.

Garcia and Bowen took the two pilot's chairs while Kal sat down on a third seat, which the mechanics had added. Garcia activated the ship's internal speakers, which piped the chatter between the fleet through the cockpit. As they were settling in, the fleet arrived outside the Geerlok system, close enough to make one fold to the planet but far enough away that they wouldn't be detected for days. A squadron of five scout ships immediately departed for Geerlok, using conventional thrusters to get away from the fleet and then engaging their fold drives. The ships would wait for the Nasi fleet to arrive. As soon as they did, the scouts would immediately fold back to the fleet.

The five icons blinked from the tactical map. Kal idly paged through the system diagnostics on the *Park*, familiarizing himself with the new interface and the ship's capabilities. There had not been time for him to get anything but a cursory understanding of the work that Bowen and the fleet's techs had done.

Only minutes later, the five recon ships blinked back onto the tactical map. "Samsara command, the Nasi are already engaged with the Torgham home fleet." The report was quick and breathless.

The net went silent. Kal could imagine the furious conversation that was occurring on *Gedorhan's Return*, Samaha's flagship.

"All ships, fold immediately to Geerlok," General Samaha commanded over the net. "We will not get another chance. We execute as planned. Good luck, all."

Before she had finished speaking, the *Ofira* had folded. The Park's tacmap flashed—and then there was a swath of crimson, the Nasi fleet, on the display.

Chapter Twenty

"Let's go," Kal said as soon as the *Ofira's* landing bay doors opened.

They were first on the launch list, and the small Nasi ship shot into the starry void almost instantly. The ship's acceleration made the fleet's fighters appear as if they were standing still. The inertial dampeners and gravitational system that the engineers had added were top of the line, but Kal could still feel pushed against the back of his seat.

He surveyed the tactical map, trying to make sense of what was unfolding around Geerlok. They had to find the Nasi dreadnaught and get aboard. Absent that, they would go to the largest capital ship in their fleet.

Their first order of business was to adjust their flight path, so they approached the Nasi from a completely different direction than Samsara Fleet. Bowen and Garcia maneuvered the ship ninety degrees and pushed their thrust to maximum—the less time they were near the fleet, the better. Garcia hit a switch on the control screen, disabling most of their electronics—they didn't want the Nasi to notice them until they were far away from Samsara Fleet.

The Nasi were clearly prevailing against the four ships of the Torgham home fleet. Kal could see small decompressions along the massive ships as the Nasi fighters strafed their sides with plasma rounds. Their orbital station appeared to be fully functional—though its shields flickered, a sign they were near failure. Samsara Fleet had been providing the Torgham technical data that they had recovered from the Nasi. He would have bet his paycheck, if he had one anymore, that was the primary reason the Nasi hadn't destroyed their fleet. Also, the element of surprise could only work a few times—the Torgham must have had their fleet on alert.

As the *Park* traveled perpendicular to the path of the Samsara Fleet, fighters continue to pour from the sides of the carriers. The battleships were already in range to launch missiles, and Kal could see a wave of green dots on his tactical map heading toward the twelve Nasi capital ships.

Several Nasi ships began turning to face their new attackers, while the rest continued to press the Torgham fleet, trying to disable or destroy them before Samsara Fleet was in full weapons range.

The *Park* was the fastest ship on either side and passed Samsara Fleet's anti-ship missiles, despite having gone several thousand kilometers out of their way. Garcia turned their electrical systems back on. Already, Kal suspected the Nasi would be highly suspicious of them. He held on to the hope that Bowen was right, and the Nasi would not destroy the *Park*—that the technology on board was too valuable.

Their viewscreen dimmed as the power plant on one of the Torgham battleships overloaded, causing the ship to erupt in a blinding flash and creating an immense cloud of debris. The Torgham's three remaining ships, two carriers and a battleship, continued to show signs of stress—flickering shields, uneven rates of fire, and minor explosions on their hull where Nasi fighters had successfully breached their armor.

"They just need to hold out a few more minutes. Come

on," Kal could hear Garcia whispering under his breath.

Samsara Fleet hurtled towards the Nasi at full speed. Their initial wave of missiles had reached their intended targets, with most of them doing little to no damage. As the distance dwindled, the fleet launched another salvo of missiles at the Nasi.

Six of the Nasi capital ships had turned around and directed their primary weapons systems at Samsara Fleet. Even with the element of surprise, they may not be able to defeat the Nasi.

Kal studied the viewscreen in front of him, looking for any hint of which ship was the Nasi dreadnaught. The intercept no longer worked; the Nasi must have figured out that the fleet had compromised their communications. They were relying on Bowen to spot the dreadnaught with the limited sensor data that the *Park* could provide.

Kal noticed that a ship engaged with the Torgham was behind the others. As he manipulated the three-dimensional tactical map, he realized that they'd positioned the other five ships around it.

"I think this is it," Kal said as he highlighted the ship on the map. "Bowen, can you confirm?"

The Jadid brought up a visual on the ship Kal had identified. He looked at it for several seconds before replying. "It could be, but it's hard to tell. Each ship is slightly different."

Bowen adjusted the image to its maximum magnification and scanned the side of the Nasi ship. He let out a small shout and zoomed in on a small array of irregular rods that lined the side of the ship. "See this? It's part of the fusion disruption cannon. It is the dreadnaught."

"Can you open a direct line to them?" Kal asked.

"I will try." The lanky scientist adjusted the controls on the ship's communication cluster, sending a high-beam communication directly at the Nasi dreadnaught.

"This is experimental skip ship alpha requesting emergency landing," Bowen said.

He continued to repeat the message multiple times. The small hiss of space radiation on the channel was the only response. Kal felt himself tense as they waited for any sort of response.

"Alpha"—the sudden sound caused Kal to jump in his seat—"this is the *Divine Retribution*. State your reason for being in this system."

"Governor Boujettif of the Patagonia system has ordered us to rendezvous with your fleet," Bowen replied in his typical monotone. "We are to provide an update as to the success of the operation on Geerlok to Grand Ancient Esma."

"We will need you to fold out of the system until hostilities have ceased."

"We cannot fold," Bowen replied. "We have received damage to our drive from enemy activity."

"Wait." The line went dead for several seconds. Only the hiss of deep-space radiation could be heard.

Bowen angled his head toward Kal and Garcia. "They are most likely scanning us now to determine if we are telling the truth. Either they will let us dock or we're about to have multiple Nasi fighters engaging us."

Garcia gave a crooked smile and shrugged. "Well, exciting either way."

"Permission to land granted," the *Divine Retribution* responded. "Head to the transmitted coordinates."

Garcia input the coordinates into the ship's navigational computer. As they began to move toward the dreadnaught, he adjusted their path to avoid the heavy areas of fighting. The two clouds of fighters had made contact with each other, and several dogfights were occurring between the squadrons.

Kal held his breath as they weaved through squadrons of Nasi, Torgham, Human, Kurz, and Tounous fighters. They couldn't engage their shields; it would be a sure-fire tip off to the Nasi since their shield signatures were not Nasi. They had to rely on their speed and agility to get them through the maelstrom.

The Nasi and Samsara fleets were close enough that Kal could see bright flashes of plasma bolts hitting their energy shields with his naked eye. Samsara Fleet was holding their own so far—a far cry from several months ago, when the Nasi had decimated the unsuspecting home fleets of the species that made up the fleet. Their attack had also relieved pressure on the Torgham. The energy readings from their shields were now at a constant power, and they were maneuvering to buy Samsara Fleet time.

The high whine of proximity alerts diverted Kal's attention from studying the battle picture.

"We've got kinetic rounds incoming," Garcia reported, adjusting their flight path. "Damnit, they're from a squadron of Kurz fighters. The morons don't realize we're on their side."

"Cut hard left," Bowen instructed, "we should be able to weave between them here." The Jadid pointed to a spot on the tactical map where there was a gap between the fighters of the Kurz squadron.

The *Park* sailed through the small gap, kinetic fire from the Kurz trailing behind them. The *Park* was so fast that the Kurz targeting computers were having a hard time anticipating their speed.

As they passed the fighters, the *Divine Retribution* loomed ahead of them. Looking at a magnification of the ship, Kal realized that its hull was not a uniform black. Striations furrowed the surface, and there were streaks of gray, silver, and gold along the small ridges. Small nodules seemed to have grown haphazardly along the ship's bulkhead, their purpose completely unclear. The irregular rods that Bowen had pointed out were visible, and Kal could see a faint aura of plasma and electricity glistening along the length of each.

As they approached, a small portal opened in the ship's side. The door dilated open, a stream of light shining from the dark ship's surface like a beacon. The *Park* rapidly decelerated, pushing Kal against his restraints, and slowly entered the ship.

The Nasi landing bay was almost completely empty, except for a handful of assault ships. Each landing pad had a small terminal with tubes and wires running from it, most likely use to refuel and resupply the fighters. The cavernous room was dark, the only light coming from a phosphorescent glow emanating from the walls. Support columns grew from the floors to the ceiling, their branches spreading as they neared the top. Kal could see the small violet and gray dots of Nasi technicians moving with a feline grace through the bay. What Kal guessed were maintenance bots scurried behind their Nasi masters, their squat frames loaded with parts and materials.

"Alpha, this is control. Land in bay three Zulu, lower your ramp, and await further instructions." The bay door behind them constricted shut.

Bowen glided the *Park* to the correct landing pad, gently touching down on the skids that had extended from the ship's underside.

As soon as they had entered the bay, Kal's nervousness had disappeared and a sense of calm had come over him. There was nothing to worry about—they had no choice. No way out, except one. "Well, it's now or never," Garcia said, glancing at his comrades.

"As soon as the bomb is off the ship, we have a minute," Kal said. "Let's do this and get the hell out of here."

Bowen pressed a button on the controls to lower the *Park*'s cargo ramp and activate the unloading sequence for the bomb. Kal watched it slowly glide down the ramp through the cargo bay's internal camera. As soon as the built-in thrusters had transferred it off the ship, the bay door raised shut. Garcia quickly pressed the controls to raise their energy shields and bring their weapon systems online. The time for subterfuge was over.

"Alpha, explain yourself. What are you doing?" The normal drone held a trace of annoyance. "Answer now or we will be forced to—"

Garcia slapped the viewscreen and closed the connection. "I'm done listening to that." He activated the ship's kinetic and plasma cannons, saturating the fibrous bulkhead of the Nasi dreadnaught. The rounds splashed against the side of the ship, causing the dark, variegated pigment of the walls to fade. Several Nasi soldiers sprayed the Park's bulkhead with plasma fire, but the ship's energy shields were more than enough to diffuse the rounds.

"Your weapons are breaking through the hull," Bowen observed. "Though, I am not sure if we will be clear before we are vaporized."

"Damnit," Kal said. "Anything we can do to speed this up?" He noticed Nasi running into several of the ships on the landing pads.

"That's the main structural bulkhead. Only missiles or large-scale cannons would pierce through," Bowen replied.

Three of the assault craft clearly had their engines warming up. It wasn't clear how long it would take before their systems went on line. "They're warming the ships up to fire at us," Kal said.

"If it makes you feel any better," Bowen said arching an eyebrow, "I think we are much more likely to die from the bomb than those assault craft. I've seen enough of this ship to know it will take a minute of sustained firing from them to breach the shields."

Garcia's snorted and doubled over coughing before gasping out, "Thank you Bowen, love that can-do spirit."

The alien looked confused.

"What about the missiles?" Kal asked.

Garcia shook his head. "Won't work. They'd probably blow a hole right through the side. But would also set off the device."

Kal watched the bulkhead continue to lighten under their barrage. The Park's internal control board was flashing red—they were using every single ounce of power the engines could produce.

"What about us?" Kal asked. "Can we just blow through the side?"

Bowen thoughtfully rubbed his slim nose. "Perhaps. Perhaps. I would give us a fifty percent chance of survival."

The *Park* started to rock as the Nasi assault ships peppered their side with plasma fire. Cannons on assault ships were used to clear the landing zone while troops were dismounting. They were not built for ship-to-ship combat. However, they were much more effective than the small rifles the Nasi had been using before. Kal checked the viewscreen—fifteen seconds until the quark bomb detonated.

Kal muttered a curse. "Punch it, Garcia," he said. It was time to try their luck.

"Punching it." Garcia shifted power to their front shields and maxed out the thrusters. Before Kal had a chance to react, a screech of metal reverberated through the hull as they broke through the dreadnaught's side and were back in the darkness of open space.

"Sir, I really wish that we would stop driving into and out of enemy capital ships," Garcia said as he checked the damage to the *Park*.

Before Kal could respond, alarms rang through the

cockpit. Several Nasi fighters had noticed their departure and were targeting their ship.

Bowen began to furiously input parameters into the fold drive, his fingers flying across the bulkhead console at a superhuman speed. The timer at the corner of the cockpit's viewscreen ticked down to five. Kal looked at the drive's readout. They had a fifty percent chance of a successful fold.

"Ready," Bowen called out. The timer was down to two seconds.

Garcia slammed his hand down and activated the drive. The viewscreen changed to a field of iridescent sparkling stars that blinked in and out of existence with an orangish glow.

The supplementary viewscreen that the fleet's techs had added went dark. Garcia gave a curse and hit it softly, muttering under his breath. Kal felt an uneasy sensation in his stomach as he stared out at the twinkling orange lights. He realized the ship's artificial gravity had stopped. Instead, he felt the sensation of multiple gravities, not pulling him in one direction but pulling and pushing in a chaotic, overlapping manner. He looked at the Jadid scientist.

"Bowen, where are we?"

"We have folded into my universe," Bowen said. "It is time for me to go home."

With an oath, Kal grabbed his pistol from his holster and pointed it at the Jadid's head.

Colonel Petrov had granted Nicole's request to watch the

battle from the bridge of the *Ofira*, saying she should be there as "an official liaison officer of the Numbskulls." Nicole sat in a chair on the back wall of the room. Restraints kept her in place in case the gravity went out. A large viewscreen dominated the front of the room. The display had the tactical map of the battle in the center, with smaller displays showing ships' status and a live feed from outside the ship. Officers sat at clusters of consoles, with Colonel Petrov's command console in the center. Despite the activity, the room was relatively quiet. Most of the communication was through neural implants rather than out in the open.

Nicole had her implant connected to the ship's systems, allowing her to hear the chatter of conversation on the bridge and the communications between the *Ofira* and the rest of Samsara Fleet.

The *Ofira* was engaged with one of the Nasi capital ships, trading missile and cannon fire as they slowly circled around one another. Swarms of Samsara and Nasi fighters looped and swooped around each other, creating an incomprehensible mess on the tactical map. She could tell that their fleet's advantage in numbers was slowly dwindling as the superior Nasi fighters destroyed three Human fighters for each one of their own lost. Thankfully, the *Ofira's* upgraded energy shields and point defense systems were holding up against the Nasi onslaught.

Colonel Petrov sat in the center of the bridge, clearly in control. She continually inspected the situation on her personal tablet, calling over officers as the battle progressed. Nicole could see a small sheen of sweat on the woman's neck as she bent down to look at her tablet. Other than that, she seemed as cool as ice, firmly and decisively giving orders to her crew.

Nicole had tried to find the *Park* in the mess of icons on the tactical map. It was impossible. She had no way of knowing what was happening to her friends; the *Park* was under complete radio silence. She hated the thought that they could die and she wouldn't know when it happened. In the clinical and distant atmosphere of these large fleet engagements, it was easy to feel detached from the death and destruction.

Nicole grabbed onto her chest strap as the *Ofira* suddenly heaved to the side. The impact threw several soldiers to the floor. A number of the ship's systems flashed yellow on the main viewscreen. Nicole could hear frantic conversation over the net as the *Ofira's* staff tried to understand the full scale of the damage.

General, someone called out over the fleet's net, *we're taking heavy fire. We need to do something soon or the fleet will be destroyed.*

Agreed. Nicole couldn't tell who was speaking. It wasn't one of the Human commanders though. *We're also taking significant damage. We cannot win if we get into a battle of attrition.*

Keep doing what you're doing. Samaha's voice held an edge of frustration. *The Frygr and Lokryz have almost destroyed one of their ships. We need to hold on until then.*

Nicole glanced at the tactical map. She could see that the two Kurz ships had bracketed one of the Nasi battleships, peppering it from either side. The computer's AI estimated that the Nasi's shields would fail in the next few minutes.

Holy sh—static cut the speaker off and a brilliant explosion obliterated one of the Nasi ships. *Kal*, thought Nicole to herself. She zoomed in to the area around the debris field from the Nasi ship. Was there anything still moving?

Seconds later, the Nasi ship that had been taking fire from the Kurz ruptured into two as a missile evaded its point defense system and buried itself inside the hull.

Battle team Kurz. Head toward Geerlok at top speed and assist the Torgham, Samaha ordered.

The three remaining Torgham ships were miraculously still holding their own against the Nasi. They had positioned themselves on the opposite side of one of the planet's moons, using it to block the Nasi plasma cannons. The Nasi ships spread around the planet, trying to corner the damaged Torgham. Fortunately, they still hadn't been able to pin them down. Nicole knew it was a matter of time until the Nasi grew tired of the little game. Eventually, they would decide to turn their attention to the planet—firing on population centers to subdue the people.

There were ten Nasi ships remaining. Five were engaged with the remaining Torgham home fleet and five were trying to block Samsara Fleet, which was still several minutes out from Geerlok. The *Frygr* and the *Lokryz* were barreling toward the planet, halfway between the two groups of Nasi ships. The battle hinged on whether the Nasi or Torgham would break first. If the Nasi could bring the full weight of their fleet to bear on Samsara Fleet, they wouldn't have much of a chance.

One of the Torgham home fleet ships burst into a bright nova of light, its engines or power plant overloaded. The viewscreen dimmed to adjust for the flash, and Nicole could hear Petrov shout. The officer slammed her hand on her armrest and sprang up from her chair.

Fighter wing Alpha, concentrate all fire on target Delta; fighter wing Bravo, focus on defending us from enemy attack. Engineering, push all power to our fore shields and set heading directly at the target. Colonel Petrov was sending them straight at the nearest Nasi ship. She was going to end the battle one way or another.

Ofira, what are you doing? Samaha's question overrode all the chatter on the net.

We're ending this, ma'am. We'll destroy target Delta, Petrov responded.

This is the Merrimack—*we'll attack their flank,* Colonel Zhou said.

The *Merrimack* was the closest ship but was already engaged in a firefight with one of the smaller Nasi vessels. It was a tremendous gamble for them to turn away from the enemy to support the *Ofira*.

The *Ofira* continued to speed toward the Nasi ship, which was traveling perpendicular to them. A squadron of Nasi fighters swarmed toward them but the ship's fighter escort flew to meet the enemy, causing the previously pitch-black space to flicker with plasma and missile fire. The *Ofira's* upgraded point defense system blocked or intercepted most of the Nasi fighters' attacks, but several shots still got through. On the viewscreen, Nicole could see the icons for their fighter escort blinking from green to red as the Nasi fighters destroyed them.

We're in range, Commander, one of the fire support officers reported.

Fire all weapons, Petrov instructed. *I want everything we've got on that ship.*

Plasma bolts and kinetic rounds streamed from the *Ofira* toward the Nasi ship. A wave of missiles sped right behind, their white exhaust glimmering against the darkness of space. The Nasi ship's point defense system fired small interceptor rounds to destroy the incoming missiles. The plasma bolts and kinetic rounds struck the ship's energy shields and hull, which absorbed the blasts without wavering.

The Nasi ship returned fire, sending plasma and missiles at the *Ofira*. Their broadside volley struck the *Ofira's* front energy shields, which barely held. Nicole watched their shield's power reading dip into the red on the viewscreen. They could only take a few more hits.

Another blast rocked through the ship and slammed her sideways in her seat. The internal net exploded as officers tried to understand what had happened. One of the Nasi missiles had gotten through their point defense and hit the bow. The blast had created a deep crater, rupturing one of the front cargo holds. But fortunately, the wound was not fatal.

Proximity alarms blared before Colonel Petrov ordered them silenced. They were dangerously close to the Nasi battleship. Nicole realized that Colonel Petrov had no intention of turning—she would destroy the Nasi ship. If it meant the destruction of the *Ofira*, then it was clearly a price she was willing to pay. As she looked at the determined faces around her, Nicole realized that she was willing to pay that price as well. There was too much at stake for anything else.

A few seconds before impact, the front viewscreen blacked out. Groans and creaks echoed through the ship's superstructure, and Nicole was slammed forward against her restraints. At first, she thought they had hit the Nasi ship, but quickly realized something else had happened. As the viewscreen flickered back to life, she saw pieces of the Nasi ship floating in front of them. It had been destroyed. The *Merrimack* had been able to hit the ship's engines only seconds before impact. The blast had shredded their hull and defenses. But they were still alive.

Amazingly, the *Merrimack* had already turned and was engaging the Nasi ship that had been pursuing it.

Nicole felt the sensation return to her hands as she gradually released the sides of her chair. They had done it.

❖

Nicole sat in the main conference room of the *Gedorhan's Return* as the commanders reviewed the battle. They took turns, stepping to the center of the room and detailing exactly what they had seen and done. The fleet's staff recorded everything and would produce a detailed report, highlighting the success and failures of the mission so that the fleet could improve.

After the *Ofira* and *Merrimack's* victory against the Nasi battleship, the tide had swung heavily in favor of Samsara Fleet. By the time the last two Nasi ships had folded out of the system, Samsara Fleet had lost four ships. Besides the Torgham ship lost, the *Yamen*, *Khukri*, and *M'Kora's Decision* had been destroyed. The *M'Kora's Decision* was an especially tough loss since it was one of the largest carriers in the fleet, behind the *Gedorhan's Return*. In addition to the four capital ships, they had lost 143 fighters during the battle.

Despite the heavy casualties, a sense of hope and victory permeated the air. For many of the soldiers, it was the first time they had seen a Nasi ship damaged, much less destroyed. The question that no one could answer was how significant their victory was. They did not know the exact size of the Nasi fleet. The intelligence section estimated they had destroyed a quarter to a third of it, but it might be much less.

Nicole wished she also felt the sense of hope the others did. Losing the *Park*, and Kal specifically, weighed heavily on her. She refused to mourn, though—she had seen her friends escape more dire situations than this. Nicole held out hope that they had somehow made it out alive.

After the battle, the fleet had conducted a thorough sweep, looking for any survivors and objects of interest. Debris lay about the system, and science and engineering teams were almost salivating to get their hands on it. Nicole couldn't blame them; they had only survived this long because of the reverse-engineered technology they had picked up from Nasi wreckage. Unfortunately, the sweep had found no evidence of the *Park*.

After the last commander was finished, General Samaha stood up and moved to the center of the room. Her lips were turned up in a thin smile, but the emotion did not reach her eyes. Although the battle had been a success, she had railed against Colonels Zhou and Petrov for disobeying her orders and committing to a frontal attack on a Nasi battleship. Unfortunately, she couldn't argue with success, and it may have been the most successful battle in the history of Humanity.

"We've won a great victory today," Samaha said to a chorus of cheers, thumps, and whistles. "But for it to truly mean something, we have to capitalize on the advantage we gained. We can't give the Nasi time to build any more of those fighters."

"Ma'am, just right. We believe the remaining seat of the Nasi strength is in the Human colonies," a Kurz admiral said. "Our best course of action is to strike there now. We have the element of surprise on our side and will have the numbers as well."

The comment launched a flurry of discussion. The staff outlined the pros and cons of immediately launching an attack on the Nasi fleet orbiting the Human worlds. It was a risky move. They had little intel about how the remaining enemy ships were positioned.

"Ma'am, are you sure you want to risk everything? Again?" Nicole's question came out more forcefully than she expected. "We won this battle, but it could have gone the other way. If we lose the fleet, we lose everything."

Colonel Petrov shook her head. "That's the same

mentality we had at the beginning of this war. We sat and hid away from the fighting, scared to risk anything. It was only when General Norman went against orders that we actually did something. If it wasn't for that decision, we'd all be dead."

"I know, but is that always the answer? Eventually, we'll lose. Do we want to risk everything again?" Nicole's question hung in the air for several seconds.

The low rumble of a Kurz broke the silence. Her nostrils flared arrhythmically, a sign of unease or nervousness. "I agree with the civilian. When the Nasi attacked Gorash, our home fleet was on maneuvers. We had to address their insult, so we sent our entire fleet to find them." She blinked several times. "We attacked the Nasi without hesitation, sending ship after ship against them. In the end, they destroyed every ship except the few that are in this fleet now."

The admission shocked Nicole. Kurz rarely expressed feelings and mistakes so openly. Also, she was their most junior officer present, and her words sounded dangerously close to criticism. Criticizing superiors in public was a serious insult and could be grounds for capital punishment. She could tell by the darkening colors of the other Kurz that they were taken aback as well.

The room devolved into a buzz of overlapping conversations. Nicole's implant could not decipher the back-and-forth in Kurz, Torgham, and Tounous going on around her.

After several minutes of the chaos, General Samaha raised her hand in the air. "Enough! We *will* attack. You make a good point, Ms Bergeron, but we cannot risk passing up this opportunity. The fleet will depart tomorrow for Human space. Emissary T'Kalu, can we resupply and refuel on Geerlok before leaving?"

The Torgham emissary touched two of his tentacles across his face, a sign of gratitude and respect. "General, we're grateful for what your fleet has done today. We'll provide what we can to assist you."

"Thank you." Samaha touched her heart, then turned her attention to the staff arrayed around the room. "We leave in five hours—get ready."

Chapter Twenty-One

"Your weapon won't work here, Kal." Bowen gently nudged the muzzle of Kal's pistol away from his head. "And I think you know by now that you and Karl are not a match for me without your battle suits."

Kal swore and holstered his pistol—he knew Bowen was right.

"You piece of shit," Garcia snarled.

Bowen shook his head. "I kept my end of the bargain. I doubt your commanders would have kept theirs."

"So you lied," Kal said.

"I helped you destroy the *Divine Retribution*. I gave your people invaluable information that may save your species. I gave you an understanding of who the Nasi are and what they want." Bowen clenched his jaw in an uncharacteristic show of emotion. "Now I am done being a prisoner."

Kal's mouth clamped shut. Could he blame the scientist?

"Once we get to Altterra, I will reconfigure this ship so you can return home." Bowen's face relaxed. He saw Garcia's questioning look. "The fold drive is experimental. It can only travel in one direction and then must be reconfigured. This can only be done on Altterra."

Kal felt like hitting something. His mind reeled at the hopelessness of their situation. His soldiers and friends were fighting for their lives, and he was a universe away, floating in space.

"I need to adjust the drive so we can fold in this universe," Bowen said. "It should take an hour, and then we can begin our voyage to Altterra."

Kal and Garcia remained strapped in their cockpit chairs while the Jadid worked on reconfiguring the ship to operate in his universe. After a quick, whispered conversation, they agreed they had no option other than to hope Bowen was telling them the truth. Neither of them knew how the fold drive worked and there was no way they could physically overpower him. But they refused to help the Jadid as he reconfigured the fold drive.

The momentary silence gave Kal time to inspect his surroundings. The differences between this universe and his own were simple, yet profound. Everything seemed to operate completely differently. Colors had changed—Bowen now looked much more green than violet, while Garcia and Kal were shades of orange. Their implants no longer worked; Kal couldn't even pull up a status screen. He thought about how terrifying it must have been for those first Humans, the Ancients, who had found themselves in this universe—alone.

After an hour, Bowen floated back into the cockpit, the micro-variations in gravity causing his trajectory to fluctuate slightly as he came through the door. "The drive is ready—we should be on Altterra in a day."

The two Humans watched as the Jadid scientist plotted their heading into the ship's computer and engaged the drive. The pinpoint lights of the surrounding stars streaked across the viewscreen into lines as they folded. It made Kal feel as if they were speeding through a tunnel of light, rather than traveling through the darkness of space.

Bowen saw Garcia's looks of astonishment. "Yes, even

folding is different here, Karl. The fundamental laws of physics are different."

"Is that why it will only take a day to reach Altterra?" Garcia asked. In their universe, the trip from Geerlok to Earth was over a week.

"Yes—we can travel much greater distances in each fold," Bowen responded. "The gravitational effects on the drive are much less. It was frustrating to learn how slowly one must travel in your universe."

"I imagine," Kal muttered absently as his mind drifted to Samsara Fleet and Nicole.

The first several hours of their voyage were quiet. Kal had no desire to speak to Bowen after he had hijacked the *Park* and brought them there. He guessed Garcia felt the same, since the normally talkative pilot sat in his chair without saying a word. Bowen normally never spoke unless spoken to, anyway.

The Jadid made clear that he would remain in the cockpit. To make sure that they touched nothing, Kal assumed. After a few hours, the two Humans unstrapped themselves and made their way to the cargo hold.

Once they were alone, Kal and Garcia began speculating about the outcome of the battle. The uncertainty ate at both of them. The unexpected manner in which they'd disappeared made it worse. The rest of the fleet, if they survived, must have thought them dead.

Their whispered conversation then turned to Altterra and the Jadid. What would they find on this planet? What would the Jadid do when they landed? Would they be able to make it back to their own universe?

After several hours, both soldiers fell silent, consumed with their own thoughts. Kal couldn't help but think about Nicole. Had she survived the battle? She probably thought they were dead, destroyed with the *Divine Retribution*. He realized he felt a sense of absence, knowing how far away he was from her. It was something he hadn't felt in decades.

"Karl. Kal. We have arrived in the Altsol system and are beginning our approach to Altterra." Bowen's voice came from the cockpit.

"Real original names," smirked Garcia as the two pulled themselves toward the cockpit.

Altterra was both strange and familiar. It had the same landmasses and oceans that Kal remembered from his time stationed in the Sol system. The land was not the same green he remembered, but a strange interwoven patchwork of multiple colors. The oceans surrounding the land were white, almost the color of milk, with striations of blue running for thousands of miles. Kal looked for any evidence of Jadid settlements but couldn't see anything that marred the natural surface of the planet.

"Get strapped in," Bowen said without looking back. "We are on our final approach."

The *Park* descended smoothly through Altterra's atmosphere over what would have been the North American landmass. They crossed the Atlantic Ocean and ended up over what would have been Northern Africa. Kal could see more detail in the land below them. The patchwork had given way to a mix of yellow and red vegetation. It was a mix of shrubs and bushes, rather than the forest he had expected. The planet's gravity weighed more and more on them, compressing Kal into his seat and making it harder for him to breathe. He estimated that the gravity was at least a quarter more than the Earth equivalent he was used to.

"Tazirbu control, this is scientist Bowen Nguyen. I request special landing access. I have urgent information and two Humans on board, as well."

There was no response. Finally, the control tower responded, providing a series of coordinates for them to land and strict instructions to remain on the ship.

"They are sending us to one of the private landing pads," Bowen said off-handedly.

The city of Tazirbu grew in the viewscreen. Kal could understand why it hadn't been obvious from orbit; its colors blended in almost exactly with the surrounding landscape. Muted shades of almost every color merged into a chaotic red and yellow metropolis. The city shared the organic quality that Kal had seen on the Nasi ships, making it look like something that had sprouted from the ground. Only the immense scale and size of the buildings truly marked it as something that was not natural.

The *Park* slowed to a hover directly over a large, irregular, domed building. An aperture on top opened, allowing them to descend into its center. At the edges of their landing pad, Kal could see a large contingent of Jadid waiting a safe distance as the ship landed. They all appeared to be armed, carrying what looked like large sticks pointed at the ship. He couldn't help but wonder if they truly were Jadid, or if they were about to be captured by the Nasi.

Bowen deactivated the ship's power and slowly stood up, as if moving through water. Kal and Karl followed suit, unbuckling their restraints and staggering toward the back of the ship. The additional weight of the planet's gravity felt like a yoke on Kal's neck. Though, there was an uneven quality to it—again, almost as if gravity was pulling him in multiple directions at once.

Bowen looked back, anticipating Kal's question. "It will feel strange at first. In my universe, gravity is not a constant."

The cargo bay door was already open, and Kal could see the dust-covered floor of the landing pad beneath them. A team of four Jadid, in battle suits, ran into the bay, their stick-weapons pointed at Kal and Karl.

"Hands up, feet apart," a soldier instructed. Kal and Karl both obliged.

The Jadid quickly scanned them with a handheld device and then instructed them to stand next to Bowen. While two soldiers covered them, the other two quickly inspected the ship. After they finished, the four Jadid stood, weapons trained on Kal and Karl, waiting for something or someone.

A tall woman glided up the cargo ramp with an ethereal grace. She came to a stop in front of the two Humans and looked at them with a neutral expression. She had an otherworldly beauty that made it impossible for Kal to take his eyes off her. The woman's luminescent blue eyes stood out from the dark lilac hue of her face. A corner of her thin lips twitched up as she regarded at them, making it seem like she was thinking of a joke she didn't wish to share. Kal remained quiet, waiting for her to break the silence.

Finally, the woman waved the guards away. "You may leave—there is no threat here." The four soldiers tromped down the ramp.

"Scientist Nguyen, you have returned. From Earth, it appears." The last sentence was somewhere between a statement and a question.

Bowen bowed as she regarded him. "Not exactly, ma'am. I come from the Human's universe, but Earth no longer exists."

The woman sucked in her breath, the small grin gone.

"The Nasi have destroyed Earth along with many other worlds in the Human's universe," Bowen said. "It is as we feared."

She shook her head. "We knew of your disappearance, Scientist Nguyen, and suspected the worst. I had hoped that the Nasi were just talk, but it appears not."

The elegant Jadid woman fixed Kal and Garcia with her gaze. "I am truly sorry for your loss. To have lost everything must have been devastating. I am the Governor of Altterra, Madeline Huang," she continued. "We are honored by your presence, whatever the reason."

Karl took a sideways glance at Kal.

"For your own safety, we will have a security detail assigned to you. We have never had Humans visit us here, and once our people know, there may be a"—she hesitated—

"disruption."

"Thank you," Kal said, bowing his head slightly. "We appreciate your hospitality. We need to return to our own universe as fast as possible, though."

The governor nodded sadly. "We had heard the Nasi have begun their return." She frowned. "They are fanatics of the worst sort." She inclined her head toward the open bay door. "Please follow me."

They followed the governor out of the ship's bay. At least twenty soldiers stood in a ring around the ship, their weapons held at the ready. Governor Huang led them out of the cavernous building, where a transport was waiting for them. The vehicle reminded Kal of a potato, bulbous and misshapen, with a brownish hue. An aperture opened in the vehicle's side, allowing them to crawl into an interior lined with seats. The ship's walls were viewscreens, like a spaceship, allowing them to peer out but preventing others from looking in.

As the car lifted off, Madeline began talking again. "The Nasi are fanatics of the worst sort. Their belief in returning to Humanity's universe has consumed them beyond the point of reason. Out of respect for our mutual suffering, we have let them be, allowing them to pursue their dreams of what they call the glorious return." She frowned.

"About a year ago several of our leading scientists"— Madeline gestured at Bowen—"began disappearing. That was when we suspected they were close. Then, months ago, a quarter of their fleet disappeared without warning, and we had confirmation they had started."

319

"Why didn't you do anything?" Karl asked. "If you knew this was going on? If you knew they were kidnapping your people?"

Madeline sighed. "Many reasons. Caution, for one. But mostly because we were grateful. The Nasi are unstable and difficult to deal with. Their leader—"

"Esma?" interrupted Kal.

"Yes. Grand Ancient Esma, as they call her. She is a demagogue. We felt it better if her attentions were occupied elsewhere. We hoped—we still hope—that eventually, they might leave our universe altogether. Yesterday, we received word that they had begun moving their settlers and the rest of their fleet to your universe."

"Settlers?" Kal asked.

"Yes, their gateways are open so they can bring in citizens to establish a permanent presence," Madeline replied. She noticed Kal's inquiring look. "Gateways are portals in their Footholds that allow them to create durable connections between this universe and yours."

"If they have these gateways in their footholds, why do they need their fleet?" asked Kal.

"The gateways allow them to transport small things— people, equipment, supplies—for a limited period. They can't bring their ships through them."

"So, the Nasi just grew four times more powerful?" Garcia asked, leaning forward.

"In your universe, yes. They needed to ensure their gateways were operational before they sent their fleet." Bowen answered. "Now they do not need to resupply them from Altterra. In the past few years, our understanding of inter-universe travel has exploded. The *Park* and the gateways are extensions of the work that I, and other scientists, have done."

"And you didn't stop them?" Kal asked.

"No, we didn't," Madeline answered evenly. "We have an understanding with the Nasi. We share much more in common with them than with you, the species that forgot us."

"Billions died," Kal said as he grabbed the loose fabric of her tunic, "and you don't—"

Kal felt pain shoot from his hand down his arm. Madeline had twisted his hand off her clothing and held it in front of her. The movement was so fast that Kal didn't have time to register it. Her blazing eyes and thin features made her appear like a raptor grasping onto its prey.

After a moment, Madeline's look softened. She released Kal's hand and cast her eyes downward. "We care," she replied, voice firm. "It is regrettable, but ultimately, why would we risk war with our own?"

Kal could feel Garcia's body tensing beside him. The pilot balled his hands into fists, his knuckles white with the pressure. Thankfully, he said nothing.

"Where are we going?" Kal asked, turning to the viewscreen to hide the grimace of pain on his face.

"The Ancients sent for you. We are taking you to their palace."

"What do *they* think about what the Nasi are doing?" Garcia asked. "They're from Earth, right?"

"I do not know," the governor replied. "A century ago

they decided to step back from our internal politics. All of them except Esma, that is."

Kal stared out the viewscreen. The vehicle skimmed through the streets, low to the ground, weaving between the buildings of the city. Groups of Jadid walked along the street covered in swathes of loose robes and tunics fringed with threads of silver and gold. The buildings twisted and turned above Kal's head, casting shadows across the streets below. The varied hues of the city were muted; a patina was layered across it all, dulling the colors and casting everything in a greenish brown hue.

They finally arrived at a large complex of buildings, separated from the rest of the city by an irregular wall, about ten meters high. Awaiting them was a group of ten soldiers, each brandishing one of the odd Jadid weapons and wearing a bright white cloth wrapped around their right arm.

The door to the vehicle opened, and the two Humans followed Madeline out, with Bowen taking the rear. She walked past the formation without stopping, leading them into a wide, low-slung building that was topped by what appeared to be an ornamental spire.

"This is where Scientist Bowen and I leave you," Madeline said. She raised her arm to the door. "The Ancients are waiting for you."

Kal and Garcia walked through the tall ornamental doors and into a large elliptical room. An intricate pattern was etched into the walls with fine silver thread. The patterns looked to be the same style as the tattoos on the Nasi—the chaos belying some deeper meaning. In the center of the room was a large table that seemed to sprout from the floor. Around it sat five people, three men and two women. As Kal and Karl proceeded to the table, they all rose in unison, their faces betraying nothing.

"Damn, I can't believe what I am seeing," said one of the men, glancing at the other people around the table. "Sit down. We need to talk to you."

❖

Garcia relaxed almost immediately, sliding down into one of the empty seats at the table. "Thanks, it's nice to sit." The pilot leaned back in the seat, trying to make himself comfortable. "The gravity on this planet is rough."

The Ancients all smiled, a look of knowing passing between them.

"Yes, it was one thing we had to get used to when we came here," said one of the women. She had light skin and blue eyes that contrasted with the straight dark hair that grew past her shoulders.

For a moment, Kal wished Nicole was there with them. He was never good in situations that required diplomacy. Eventually, he would say something offensive.

"Thank you for having us," Kal said. "I am Brigadier General Kal Norman of the last remaining Human force, Samsara Fleet, and this is Major Karl Garcia."

Kal had to remind himself that the people around the table were centuries old. None of them seemed to be older than forty. Aside from the robes that they wore, they looked no different from any Human Kal knew.

The five Ancients went around the table introducing themselves: Richard Kingsley, Bao Wang, Jian Chen, Girish Khatri, and Salina Musa. Kal could see a bit of hesitation as each stood and said their name. Their mannerisms seemed a strange mix of the foreign and the ancient. The only hint that they were more than they appeared was the confidence and certainty with which they spoke. These were people used to being obeyed.

After the introductions were complete, the Ancients offered them a drink they called tcha. Kal took a small sip from the glass they set in front of him. At first, it tasted very similar to tea. After a few seconds though, he could feel himself sweating from the heat of whatever spices were in the drink.

After they had all finished their drinks, Girish set his glass down with a small clink and turned his full attention to Kal and Garcia. "Now that introductions are out of the way, why don't you tell us why you're here—and start from the beginning."

Kal and Garcia described what had happened, starting with the Nasi attack on their homeward and ending with the battle outside Geerlok. The Ancients peppered them with questions, many of them seeming unrelated to the story he was telling. The questions were illuminating; the Ancients knew nothing about their species anymore. When they had last seen Earth, Humans had not even left the Sol system. Earth had been a dying, overcrowded planet. They had missed the perfection of the fold drive, Humanity's first contact with other species, and the eventual creation of the

United Earth Government and settlement of the colonies. The Ancients would sometimes ask about specific countries, some of which Kal had never heard of.

"So sad to think that the Earth is no more," Bao said when they finished, a wistful look on his face.

"I thought we would never see home again," Richard said, "but it's sad to be certain of it."

Girish shrugged. "I'm not going to lose sleep over it."

Salina nodded in agreement. "Earth was dead to us a long time ago. Only difference is that now it's dead to everyone."

Kal was shocked. "How can you say that?" he asked. "Your home, gone. Your people, gone."

"Our people?" Jian sniffed disdainfully. "Not *our* people. *Your* people. Earth cast us out and never stopped to even think about us. *Our* people are here."

Girish nodded as well. "We were told that they would forgive our debts, that we would get a chance for a new life. All we had to do was volunteer. Then, when it all went wrong, they left us to die."

The others nodded. "There was no way for them to get you," Kal responded.

"Not that they cared." Jian scowled. "We were expendable."

Richard held up his hand. "We understand why you are upset. But for us, Earth was a place that cast us aside. Some of us harbor more or less resentment than others. But the five of us"—he motioned around the table—"decided that part of our past was over."

"Not all of you," Garcia shot back. "Seems like it's very

much still going on for the Nasi."

Kal saw a flicker of uncertainty from the Ancients. They looked at each other quickly, an unspoken conversation. Richard sighed. "True, Esma never could let it go. She came to see the return as a sort of religious mission."

"She's the one who created the Nasi," Kal said.

Girish nodded. "Over time, she let her hate and ambition take over. As our strength grew, she decided she wanted to return, to punish Humanity."

"She tells her followers, the Nasi"—Jian spat out the word—"that they're there to help Humans. To help them regain their place in the galaxy. But we know Esma. She craves power and adoration, not justice."

"What about you?" asked Kal. "You don't want power?" He eyed the enormous room they were in.

Girish chuckled. "Maybe, a bit. But we have enough power and adoration. We have anything we want. As you might have noticed, the anger has receded, but it's still there. We've lived with it so long, I doubt it will ever go away."

"The five of us"—Salina gestured around the table— "don't want anything, anymore." She frowned slightly. "Perhaps it is because we have lived so long. Perhaps *too* long."

The other Ancients regarded her thoughtfully. There was an undercurrent of things not said in the cool glances that they shot one another.

"So, why let Esma and the Nasi do this?" Garcia asked. "You could stop her."

"Perhaps. Perhaps not." Jian gestured with his hands.

"The Nasi are extremely powerful, even compared to the rest of the Jadid. But we left politics a century ago. It was time for our children to rule and for us to step aside."

"But you could change all this if you wanted to," Kal pleaded. The Ancients stared back at him impassively.

"At least you can help us get back home," Garcia almost shouted. "We need to help our people."

Jian nodded. "Yes, I think we can do that. We—"

"Perhaps we can do more than that," Bao interrupted. The other Ancients swiveled their heads to stare at him. "Perhaps, there's the question of what's right. Also, Esma is becoming dangerous."

Girish scoffed. "What's right? Has the past not taught you anything? Right, wrong, doesn't matter when you're trying to survive."

"However, we aren't trying to survive anymore." Richard's dark skin was flushed. "I think we should think about this. Perhaps morality is something to consider."

"You're both insane." Jian stood up from the table, her black hair swirling around her face. "You'd risk war with Esma for them?" She flung her arms out at Kal and Garcia.

"Do we just let her do what she wants?" Richard asked, shooting up from his chair. "She's kidnapped our children. What happens if the Humans are not enough?"

"Enough," Salina said, her lips tightened and eyes narrowed. "This is a conversation for private."

At once, the tension evaporated from the room. Jian and Richard both sat back down in their chairs, adjusting their robes as they did so.

"We will get you back to your people," Salina said. "Governor Huang will arrange your return."

"Thanks for your help," Kal said, trying to keep the edge of sarcasm out of his voice.

Garcia didn't bother. "Yeah, really big of you."

They stood up and walked out of the room. They had to get back as soon as possible. Samsara Fleet was facing an enemy that was even more powerful than they realized.

Chapter Twenty-Two

"It will take at least a day for us to reconfigure the *Park* so you can return," Bowen said. The Jadid told them he had been instructed to take them back to their universe. He hadn't appeared as upset about it as Kal would have expected.

Kal and Major Garcia sat across from Governor Huang and Bowen in one of the dining halls within the Ancients' compound. The room was packed with long, rectangular, gray tables sandwiched close to each other, benches on either side. It was empty, except for the four of them—Madeline had had the room cleared before they arrived.

A humongous spread of food covered the table. It was a bright cornucopia of various local meats and vegetables that stood out against the drab decor of the room. Several pitchers had been placed next to the food, filled with colorful drinks.

"What are we supposed to do until then?" asked Garcia, sipping his glass of tcha.

"You will need to wait," Huang replied, "patiently."

"Not my strong suit." Garcia's lips twitched up in a devilish smirk.

"Can you tell us anything about the Nasi fleet?" Kal asked. "Any information would be helpful. Types of ships, strengths, locations, anything?"

"I know little myself," Huang replied. "But we will provide you with everything that we know. It is not as comprehensive as you might like. The Nasi distanced themselves from the rest of the Jadid, especially as they came closer to their return."

"So, they're basically a cult, huh?" Garcia said.

"Not a cult as much as extremists," Bowen replied diplomatically. "Ancient Esma has twisted them into thinking that it is their birthright to return and guide you Humans."

Garcia grabbed a slice of green meat from one of the serving dishes and plopped it into his mouth. His eyes widened, and he quickly grabbed another piece. "This is pretty good," he said. "Spicy, but good."

"It is from an animal called a ground dog. We consider them quite the delicacy," Governor Huang replied. "I think the chefs wanted to make a good impression. They normally only serve this type of food for the Ancients."

As they continued to eat, Kal and Garcia tried to pry more information out of the reluctant Jadid about the city and the planet. From previous conversations with Bowen, Kal knew that family and friendship was something different for the Jadid. Their society had changed, or maybe evolved, from Humanity's. However, both Jadid were reluctant to discuss anything about their own lives, continually changing the subject.

"We need to go." Huang stood up. "They need to feed the palace staff."

"Sure, sure." Garcia dragged himself up. "We don't want to keep people from their food."

The four of them stood up and walked out of the dining hall and into a corridor. The two Jadid led them through the maze of hallways, toward their quarters for the night.

A shaft of light appeared on the wall in front of Kal and

Garcia. A door had opened, leading to the area outside the palace compound. Kal could see the movement and buildings of the city through the doorway as a Jadid guard walked outside. It looked to be a large marketplace bustling with crowds of Jadid.

Before Kal had time to react, Garcia abruptly turned and walked out the door. Kal chased the pilot outside, curiosity and caution battling in his mind. They stood at top of an enormous set of stairs that led down into a square marketplace. It was bustling with activity. Jadid slowly paced through it, stopping to talk to one another or inspect the wares at one of the temporary stands that dotted the square. In front of them, two guards stood scanning the crowd, their backs completely turned to the Humans.

Suddenly, one of the Jadid in the market shouted and pointed directly at Kal and Garcia. Immediately, all the other Jadid turned and stared at them. A low hum of conversation enveloped the marketplace as the citizens stared and pointed. One of the guards turned and saw the two Humans. She quickly tackled Garcia while the other guard pushed Kal through the door and against the wall of the corridor.

"Get back." Governor Huang pushed Kal down the hallway, away from the door and out of sight. She had a furious expression on her face, blue eyes glistening, her mouth twisted into a scowl. "Make sure he stays there," she instructed the guard as she walked outside.

Kal could hear the rumbling of the crowd growing and Jadid yelling, "Humans" as they converged on the open door. Garcia was not-too-gently tossed through the open door and slumped against the wall next to Kal with a low groan.

"Why did you do that?" Bowen asked, his eyes wide.

"Couldn't help myself," Garcia groaned. He pushed himself into a seated position on the floor, his back resting on the wall.

The door shut behind Governor Huang as she strode to where Garcia was sitting. She grabbed one of his arms and effortlessly pulled him to a standing position.

"You have no idea what you've done," she hissed.

A squad of ten Jadid guards ran down the hallway and surrounded them. "Since you cannot behave like a guest, we will treat you like a prisoner," Huang said, her anger dissipating and her calm demeanor returning. "You will be confined until we are ready for you to depart."

The guards led the Humans to a small cluster of cells that were eerily reminiscent of the Nasi cells in the Foothold on New America. Huang watched from the door as the guards shoved them into the room and the door constricted shut.

"You will be held here until it is time to leave," Huang said via the room's viewscreen. "I will honor my promise and will see what information we can provide to you while you wait."

After the screen went blank, Kal turned to look at Garcia. There was the ghost of a smile on the major's face. He saw Kal's look and shrugged his shoulders. "I just couldn't help it."

After several hours, a guard brought a small cart into their cell. It was loaded with food, drink, and two tablets that looked like slate tiles at first glance. It was only upon closer inspection that Kal was able to realize exactly what the devices were. Although the interface was like the Human tablets he had used all his life, the technology that powered it was completely different. The screen wasn't electronic. The surface of the tablet physically changed, adjusting form and color as he manipulated it. A thin coating of sand seemed to rest on the surface of the tablet, creating the image he saw.

The two soldiers began scanning through the contents. The tablets seemed to have identical information stored on them, detailed diagrams and inventories of the Nasi ships and capabilities.

"There's no way we can defeat this," Garcia gasped, eyes fixated on his tablet.

Kal gritted his teeth. It was exactly like Governor Huang had said. The original Nasi fleet that had entered their universe was only a quarter of their strength. The new ships would almost quadruple their strength. The only good news was that only three of their ships could destroy systems, and all three had been part of the first wave. The *Divine Retribution*, the ship that they had presumably destroyed, was one of them.

With the gateways now open, the Nasi fleet could sustain themselves indefinitely. If they could perfect the technology that was on the *Park*, the Nasi could travel several times faster than Samsara Fleet simply by folding between the universes. As he looked through the information, he felt his heart sink.

"I don't know how to stop them." The words spilled out of his mouth. He no longer cared that one of his soldiers was next to him; the emotion was too raw for him to hide his feelings. With their gateways established and their new fleet, the Nasi enjoyed every strategic advantage. Samsara Fleet's efforts had only delayed the inevitable.

Kal tossed the tablet onto the floor and fell on his back. The information that the Jadid had provided was short and damning. The Nasi outnumbered Samsara fleet almost five to one.

After a few minutes of despair, Kal's mind began racing to think of a strategy that would give them some chance against the Nasi. Any way he looked at it, they didn't have a chance.

"I don't know if we can do this, Karl," Kal whispered, not bothering to turn his head to look at the pilot.

"Sir?"

Garcia's single word struck Kal. There was a sense of longing, a desire for reassurance in it, that struck him to the core. If he couldn't pull himself together, everything would truly be lost. The pilot had placed his faith in Kal, and he couldn't let him down.

"What am I saying, Major Garcia? We defeated them at Kapustin. We created Samsara Fleet. We can do this." Kal put a confidence into his words that he didn't truly believe. He could tell that Major Garcia did, though. He had to.

"Damn right, sir."

The cell door dilated open with an almost imperceptible hiss, causing them both to jump. Bowen walked through the door.

"Kal, Karl." He inclined his heads toward each one. "You need to come with me."

They stood up and followed the Jadid through the door. A squad of guards were waiting outside and surrounded the three of them as they walked out of the detention area.

"You should know—your being here has become a problem," Bowen whispered as they walked.

"How so?" asked Kal.

"When the two of you entered the Ancients' Market, you brought back issues that were long dormant."

"Like what?"

"We've severed our ties with Humanity. Left our origins in the past. This brought all of that back. Having Humans here, and in plain sight, made that history real."

Bowen brought them to a small, squarish room. Benches lined the walls. As they entered, the five Ancients stopped their conversation and regarded them coolly.

"There you are," Girish snorted.

"You wanted to see us?" Kal asked.

"What were you thinking?" Salina asked. "Holos of Humans here on Altterra are dominating the net. Our citizens are confused as to what it means. Your indiscretion will take years or decades for us to recover from." Salina shook her head.

"You very well may have changed the course of Jadid society with one foolish action," Richard added.

"Now, crowds gather outside the palace, asking for more information," Bao continued. "It's exactly what we *didn't* want to happen."

"With all due respect," Garcia responded, "it didn't seem like you cared about our people being slaughtered by the

Nasi."

Kal could see the anger in the five sets of eyes. Several of them tensed, as if holding themselves back. "This coming from the people who want our help to get home," Jian spat.

"And before you go," Richard said, "we'll put you on the net. We will record a live broadcast to all of Altterra. A broadcast where you say nothing."

"So, just look pretty," Garcia said.

"Exactly," Richard replied. "We need our people to trust us and to trust their government. We will let them see you and then explain that you are leaving."

"If it's not clear, your return home is conditional on your compliance" Bao added.

Kal and Garcia looked at one another and the pilot shrugged. "Sounds like we don't have much of a choice," Kal said. "But we expect you to honor your end of this deal."

Girish snorted. "Rich coming from the two of you. We will make the broadcast in an hour. Your escorts will take you to the right location."

Two guards stepped between the two Humans and the ancients, effectively ending the conversation. The guards escorted them out of the room, down the hall, and into a small sitting room. A maze of benches wove through the center of the room. Viewscreens covered two of the walls, and an odd-looking machine took up the other.

"Wait here," said an escort. "Someone will be back to retrieve you. In the meantime, there is food and entertainment for you."

"Entertainment?" Kal raised an eyebrow.

"Yes, the viewscreens in this room connect into our holo network. The computer can help you." The guard hesitated for a second before speaking again in a whisper. "What is it like? In your universe, that is?" His questions rushed out of his mouth in a most un-Jadid-like way, like a child asking a parent.

Before Kal could reply, the other guard shoved his comrade out of the room with a grunt and activated the door. Kal and Garcia stood up and walked around the room, inspecting.

"Huh, interesting," Garcia murmured, as he studied a machine on the wall. It had the same strange screen as the tablets the Jadid had given them earlier. The small granules of the screen moved and changed color as the pilot paged through the menu. As Kal watched Garcia, he realized it was the Jadid equivalent of a food fabricator.

The menu was a strange combination of the familiar and the foreign, much like everything about the Jadid.

Kal picked a dish called "Tooth of the Dragon," and Garcia chose "T'luk." They took their steaming dishes to one of the benches and sat down facing the viewscreen. It had thousands of holos—mostly dramas—for them to choose from. Rather than watch one show, they kept changing, jumping around to get a better understanding of the Jadid.

Some of the shows would not have been out of place within the Human colonies. But there was no mention of Humanity or the universe that the Jadid had left hundreds of years ago. The shows centered on the same clichés and foibles of everyday life that Human ones did. However, the motivations and behavior of the characters seemed odd and unrealistic. To Kal, they were uncomfortably depressing. One show centered on a man who had been starving for a decade and wasn't able to eat because of missing limbs. Another was a comedy about a Jadid who had suddenly started aging. The main character discussed his eventual death with a sense of happiness and expectation.

After an hour, a short female guard opened the door and beckoned them. Obediently, they left the room and followed their two guards until they reached the large room where they had first met the Ancients.

The chairs along the table had been moved so that they faced in the same direction. The Ancients were already seated and murmuring to each other. Kal couldn't hear what they were saying, but from their faces and the way they gesticulated wildly, the subject was contentious.

"Take a seat." Jian motioned to the two empty chairs at the far end of the table.

A small team was across from them, holding what Kal assumed was a holographic camera. The Ancients stopped their conversation and adjusted their clothing. They had changed into red robes complex patterns of gold thread running through the fabric.

"Your excellencies, are you ready?" the cameraman asked.

"Yes, let's go ahead," Richard instructed.

Jian leaned over confidentially to the two Humans. "Remember, not a word unless spoken to."

Kal nodded and tried to look as official as possible,

painfully aware of the sweat stains on his blouse.

"Citizens of the Jadid, an amazing thing has happened to us today." Richard looked directly at the camera. "We have received two emissaries from Humanity."

The camera operator pointed the three-pronged holo sensor at Kal and Garcia. Garcia gave a broad smile and waved, receiving an elbow from Kal and a stern sideways look from Jian.

"You may have seen them earlier today when we invited them to come and view the Ancients' Market," Girish continued.

"Although we cannot disclose the full nature of our talks, we feel safe in saying that they are enamored with and enthralled by the success we have had," Bao said. Kal attempted to make an enthralled look.

"We know that there has been much speculation over their appearance earlier and want to reassure our children that we will always keep you as informed as possible of our discussion." Salina gave a reassuring smile.

"These Humans have come here only with the help of our top scientists, who have been able to pierce the veil between our universe and theirs," Richard said. "We will continue to talk with Humanity about their role in casting us out. We hope they will accept their culpability in our history so that we can grow together." The cameraman pointed the camera directly at the Humans.

Garcia shot up. "If we're still around." The five Ancients swept their heads toward them, daggers in their eyes. "We're being destroyed by the Nasi and are begging for any help

339

you can provide."

The cameraman pointed the camera at the floor and shut it off.

"How dare you?" Girish was on his feet, his hands flat on the table and face red.

"Get them out of here," Jian told the guards. He looked at Kal and Garcia. "You are not going anywhere." The guards grabbed them by the arm, roughly hoisted them out of their chairs, and shoved them out of the room.

"Couldn't resist?" Kal asked Garcia as the Jadid pushed them towards the detention cells.

"We need real help, otherwise we're doomed," Garcia shot back. "The risk is worth it."

Kal couldn't argue with his logic. They *were* desperate, and the Jadid could provide the aid they needed. They might be the only ones who could.

After their cell door constricted shut, Kal began pacing back and forth. He tried to think of some way they could return to their universe. Unfortunately, he couldn't see a way out. He looked up as the door constricted open, revealing Bowen's angular face.

"Come on," the Jadid called, beckoning them. "You've got to go now."

The two Jadid guards lay slumped against the wall, their weapons draped across their bodies. Kal and Garcia ran after the Jadid as he bounded through the hallways. Bowen stopped at a confluence of several of the corridors and peeked around the corner.

"We can't . . . keep . . . up," Kal panted as he reached the scientist. Bowen looked back and sized up Kal. He gave a brief nod and then jogged down one of the hallways at a slightly slower pace.

Finally, they arrived in the same clandestine landing bay that they had arrived in. The *Park* sat idle on the ground with two guards posted by the cargo door. Bo stopped next to the entrance of the room and pressed himself against the wall. He motioned for Kal and Garcia to do the same.

"Run to the *Park* as soon as the guards go down," Bowen instructed before he nonchalantly walked toward the ship.

Kal and Garcia remained hidden in the dark entranceway, occasionally peeking into the bay as they waited for the signal. Bowen said something to the guards and then strode up the ship's ramp. A few seconds later, a small device rolled from the ship and emitted a strange pulse. It appeared like a shockwave, minus the explosion. The guards instantly dropped to the ground.

The two Humans sprinted across the small landing pad and past the unconscious guards. As soon as their feet were on the ramp, it began to rise, and Kal could hear the whine of the engines spinning up.

Bowen was in the cockpit, his hands flying across the controls as he prepped them for takeoff.

"Guess there's no one to see us off," Garcia said. "I hate long goodbyes anyways."

"After what we did, I think it's lucky we're leaving at all," Kal replied. "Thank you, Bowen."

The Jadid nodded his head and continued working.

"How long until we'll be back in our own universe?" Kal

341

asked.

"It will take about a day until we are back at Geerlok," Bowen replied.

"Let's just hope we get there in time," Garcia said as he fastened his restraints. If history was any sign, they were in for a bumpy ride.

Chapter Twenty-Three

As Samsara Fleet folded through the space between Geerlok and Human-controlled space, Nicole had been a silent attendee at the almost-constant meetings of the fleet staff. She spent most of them trying to focus on what was being said while fighting against the haunting thoughts of Kal that tried to drown everything else out. Her mind told her that there was almost no chance that he was still alive—or if he was, little chance that she would see him again. Even so, she couldn't let go of a glimmer of hope.

"So, it's decided. We will strike at Patagonia," General Samaha concluded. She sat in the center bench of the *Gedorhan's Return's* main conference room.

"It makes sense, ma'am," a Tounous admiral said. "It is the site of their shipbuilding facility. We can cut off their production immediately. The resources from the other Human colonies and the other planets they have conquered will be ineffective without it."

"We still don't know what they are doing on Wudexingqiu and Mariga," a Human general said, standing up. "We should send out reconnaissance to scout those planets before committing our forces."

"Then we give up the element of surprise," the Kurz admiral next to Samaha said. "We strike now and crush them."

"We've been through all of this several times." Samaha raised her hands to quiet the room down. "If we are to strike, it must be immediately. The most valuable and decisive target is Patagonia. It's pretty clear."

Nicole observed the tone and body language of the officers as they spoke. She could hear the hope and optimism in their voices. This could be the end of the war. If they took back the Human planets and cut off the Nasi's industrial base, the war could be over almost as fast as it began.

She wondered what would happen to this portion of the galaxy. Would another fleet try to swoop in and take over the scraps that the Nasi left? Perhaps the Nordlok or the Z'Ta?

Their next steps seemed so simple—too simple. There still were so many unknowns that she couldn't help but feel they were missing something. Less than a year ago, the Nasi had seemed invincible. It was hard to believe that they were so close to defeat.

After making the decision to conduct a rapid strike on Patagonia, the meeting transitioned to planning the attack. Several officers came to the center of the room and laid out their plan for the operation. The fleet would fold in as close as possible to the planet to prevent the Nasi from escaping. Since the capital ships were too large to conduct a phased approach—their mass and formation made the operation too risky—this was the second-best option. The planners estimated that based on known strength, and the Numbskulls'—or the Skulls, as the staff had started to refer to them—recent recon there that there would be only four capital ships at the location. It should be a relatively quick battle compared to Geerlok.

❖

An ethereal chime broke through the audio of the holo Nicole was watching via her neural implant. She shut it off and opened her cabin door to let in Sergeant Jones.

"I see you civilians get the best cabins," Jones said, eying the room.

"I think the expression is, rank has its privileges." Nicole raised an eyebrow and smiled.

"Indeed." Jones sat down across from her. "Just don't get soft. We'll be back out there sooner rather than later."

"I don't think we have the luxury of relaxing," Nicole said. There was no room to be soft anymore.

"This war is not nearly as over as what people are saying." Jones put his hands on his knees and leaned forward. "The Numbskulls still have a lot of work ahead of us."

Nicole gave a wistful smile at their team's short-lived name. She raised her eyebrow at the earnest sergeant. The Skulls didn't exist anymore—their leader, and both their pilots, were dead or gone.

"I think someone else will have to do it," Nicole replied.

"Like hell they will." Jones shook his head. "We still have our Tac-I squad, we've got Chief Kanumba"—he paused, finger pointed at her—"and we've got you."

"What about a pilot or a commander?" she asked.

"Major Garcia and Captain Park were terrific soldiers and pilots. Some of the best I've served with." Jones leaned forward. "But the war isn't over. And there will be no shortage of pilots willing to join us." He chuckled to himself. "We'll just need to break them in slowly."

"And a commander? Are you going to lead our little team?"

"Not me. You." Jones finger remained stubbornly directed at her. "You know more about the Nasi than anyone alive. You've stood toe-to-toe with the bastards. There's not a single person in this entire fleet who knows them as well as you."

"I can't be the commander, I'm not even an officer," she protested.

"So what?" He shrugged his shoulders. "You have more combat experience than almost anyone else in the fleet." Jones looked her in the eyes. "Ma'am, do not sell yourself short. You are capable of leading this team in every way. Frankly I don't think we've seen the last of General Norman or Major Garcia. But we *need* to continue to fight, we *need* to be ready for what's coming. We *need* someone with the knowledge and vision to lead."

"Why can't you do it?"

"Oh, I could. I'd probably be damn good at it, too." Jones chuckled. "But I can't be their commander and their squad leader. I'm good with getting my hands dirty, leading soldiers through tough times and getting the mission done. If you want to capture a base, I'll wager there no one in the galaxy better than me. But I'm not the person to tell you which base to capture." He held up a hand as Nicole opened her mouth. "I'm just bein' honest. General Norman, he knew it too. He knew that once we stepped down that ramp, I was in charge. When we got back up, he was the boss."

Nicole shook her head. "I appreciate it, Sergeant Jones.

Really, I do. But again, I'm not an officer."

Jones scoffed. "So what? The EDF's gone. Samsara Fleet doesn't have those rules as far as I know. You're in charge if we say so. General Samaha wouldn't disagree."

Nicole paused for a moment. Was the idea really that farfetched? She'd done more in the past year than she'd done in the rest of her life. But she'd also been the only person in the fleet to betray her species. Should someone like her really be leading soldiers?

"After what I've done—"

"Doesn't mean crap," Jones interrupted. "What's done, is done. I know I'd want to make amends if I were you. This is your chance."

She wanted to say yes. But the doubts remained. It was hard to change her self-image. To go from an overly educated bureaucrat to the leader of a recon team. "Maybe. I have to think about it. But don't count out our friends. I know Kal and Karl will be back. Don't ask me how, but I can tell." The strength of her conviction still surprised her.

Sergeant Jones smiled. "I don't doubt it, ma'am. Either way, I think you should consider it. If nothing else, until they get back to the fleet. General Samaha is a decent officer, and she'll appoint someone good to lead the team. But we need something more, someone better than just good. You're more than just an attaché."

The more Nicole thought about it, the more she realized he may be right. Kal and the Skulls had essentially created the fleet. They were the ones who had been the first to leave Kapustin Station. They were the ones who had found the technology that had given the fleet a chance.

"Thank you, Asif."

"Sergeant Jones, please, ma'am. Not because I don't respect you, but because I do."

"Sergeant Jones then, thank you."

Without another word, the sergeant stood up and walked out of the room, ending their conversation. Nicole felt like a small piece of the puzzle that was Jones had fallen into place.

"Ms. Bergeron, I'm surprised that you wanted to talk with me." General Samaha looked up from the tablet she was holding. The general sat on the long bench that lined the circumference of her ready room on the *Gedorhan's Return*.

"General, thanks for speaking with me." Nicole sat down next to the woman and turned to face her.

"How are things with the Numbskulls?" Samaha smiled as she said the name.

"Frankly, not good. With General Norman and Major Garcia gone, we need a new leader at the helm."

Samaha placed her tablet on the seat next to her. "One day, when the historians comb through the holos and write the narrative of what has happened here, I doubt they will write much about Brigadier General Kal Norman. But the truth of it is that he is the reason that we're alive and not under Nasi control. They say the victors write the history. However, you also must be alive to write the history. What *actually* happened, the real heroes, gets buried, and ultimately even the people who remember the truth pass away."

"What are you saying?" Nicole asked.

"I'm saying that Kal has contributed more than people will ever know. Despite my protests, people think I started Samsara Fleet. We know that isn't true, but people don't care."

"Kal didn't start it either," Nicole said. "It existed when we joined."

Samaha nodded. "True. But officers that left Kapustin Station when Kal went against orders did create it. Kal's decision to take the *Oruc* and stop hiding inspired them to do the same. Then he led your group to get the intel and technology that helped the fleet stand a chance against the Nasi."

Nicole remained silent. Samaha obviously believed Kal gone, and Nicole didn't trust herself to say anything. Besides, it wasn't really Kal that she wanted to talk about.

After a brief silence, Samaha gave a loud breath, clearing the air. "But I'm guessing you wanted to talk about something else."

"With Kal gone, it made me think. I've been part of this fleet from the beginning, sitting on the sidelines in many ways. I want to do more—I want to fight with these soldiers, not just be an observer." Nicole paused, unsure of what to say next.

"I wouldn't say you sat on the sideline." Samaha gave a kind smile. "You want me to commission you?"

Nicole nodded. "Yes, I think so. I *know* so." She spoke rapidly, the speech she had in her mind fading quickly. "As

Sergeant Jones has said, I've been on more combat missions than almost anyone else in the fleet. I've been training with the most elite team this fleet has to offer. I've had countless classes in alien cultures and governments that can be of use during missions."

"I get it." Samaha raised her hand. "I don't doubt your qualifications. If this was the EDF and we weren't at war, there may be a problem. But this is Samsara Fleet, and I get to make the rules as I go along right now. I'd be honored for you to swear the oath."

Nicole felt a sense of pride welling in her chest. She had thought she would have to fight, tooth and nail, to be accepted as an officer. But General Samaha had recognized her value without a second thought.

"I think lieutenant colonel is about as high as we can go," she continued. "Otherwise, there may be rumblings of preferential treatment. Direct commissions are unusual, but not without precedence. Your experience in diplomatic affairs plus your experience in fighting the Nasi make you imminently qualified."

"Thank you." Nicole didn't have any other words.

"Thank you, *ma'am*." Samaha winked. "You know a certain NCO spoke to me about this earlier. I have a feeling that he picked you. If that's the case, you should be honored. Not many people know, but he should have been mandatorily retired years ago. He was only allowed to stay on the EDF's payroll because of his exemplary record of heroism. I'm appointing you as the new commander of the Numbskulls. I have a feeling that they won't argue."

"*Temporary* commander," Nicole corrected. "Ma'am."

Samaha nodded. "Of course, temporary commander. You are the temporary leader Numbskull. Congratulations, Lieutenant Colonel Bergeron. I know your team isn't big on uniforms, but you'll need at least one set for your commissioning ceremony."

❖

"To Lieutenant Colonel Bergeron!" Sandra Chedjou raised her glass into the air.

"Here, here!" Sergeant Jones raised his glass and then swallowed the champagne in a single gulp.

The commissioning ceremony had been short and sweet. The *Ofira's* crew had cleared out the tables in the lounge and moved the chairs into neat rows. Nicole had stood in front of them, wearing the uncomfortable Samsara Fleet uniform, and repeated her oath of office. Samaha told her after the ceremony that she had simply used the old EDF officer's oath, substituting in "Samsara Fleet."

A surprisingly large number of people had shown up. Colonels Zhou and Petrov were both in attendance, along with several of Samaha's staff officers. The crowd comprised every single species in the fleet. Nicole didn't even know who half the people in attendance were, but all of them were wearing their dress gray uniforms and looked ecstatic to be there. Nicole felt like she was in a holo.

"Congratulations, ma'am." Ekon walked over and grabbed her hand, placing his other on her shoulder.

"Thank you." She smiled.

"I know Kal would have been proud. You meant a lot to him." Ekon looked earnestly into her eyes. She studied the young man's face, surprised at the empathy and maturity of his words. The Ekon she first met, the immature kid, was being replaced by someone else.

Taisha reached around Nicole, pulling her close in an embrace. She could hear the choked sound of the chief's breathing and realized that she wasn't able to say anything, too overwhelmed with emotion.

"Ma'am, I think you'll make a fine officer," Jones said as he gulped down another glass of champagne. "You just need to remember what I said. When we set foot off the ramp, I'm in charge."

"I'll remember that, Sergeant Jones." Nicole smiled and took another gulp of her drink.

❖

"Colonel Bergeron, you plugged into the net?" Colonel Petrov asked.

As the senior tactical officer, she would watch their entry into the Patagonia system from the cockpit of the *Keying*. The small ship was already familiar to her. It was the same model as the *Oruc*, minus the advanced tech. Taisha and Lieutenant Hitesh Sampson sat next to her, ready to go in case of an emergency. They had connected their ship's viewscreen to the Ofira, so they were seeing exactly what the soldiers on the bridge saw.

Petrov has picked the Numbskulls to be the emergency assault team for the *Ofira*. They were there if things went sideways, and Petrov needed someone on the ground or someone to infiltrate a ship. The ship's engines were already running and the Tac-I squad was aboard and already in their battle suits. They were able to leave the *Ofira's* landing bay at a moment's notice.

The *Ofira* and the rest of Samsara Fleet were about to enter the Patagonia system. Their fold-in point would be extremely close to the planet, so they could catch their enemies by surprise. Unfortunately, they would enter the system blind. If they sent scouts or drones ahead, they could tip off the Nasi that a fleet was about to fold into the system.

Okay folks, get ready, General Samaha's voice crackled over the net. *After this battle, drinks are on me.*

Nicole could feel the butterflies in her stomach trying to exit via her throat and gripped the armrests of her chair to steady herself. It was her first time that she was an officer during a battle, and she felt an added sense of responsibility on her shoulders. No longer was she just an observer. She felt much more present. Everything was more vivid, more real, than it had been before.

The main viewscreen transformed, and the enormous sphere of Patagonia dominating the main panel. Red icons popped up on the tactical map as the sensors began picking up Nasi vessels. The initial two continued to grow to four, then eight, and finally stopped at seventeen.

Nicole was confused. Was the map showing even the small Nasi fighters and assault ships? Had the Nasi pooled all their ships around Patagonia?

Crap, we've got problems, Colonel Petrov swore as she began signaling for her staff. *We need to come up with alternatives now. There's no way we can win in a fight against this fleet.*

Attention, all vessels, abort the attack, Samaha's voice crackled over the fleet's net. *I want Ofira, Merrimack, and Frygr to provide cover fire. All other ships immediately leave the system. Rendezvous at Rally Point Delta.*

The *Ofira* and the *Frygr*, a Kurz carrier, both disgorged their fighters and pounded the Nasi ship between them with plasma cannons. It was caught off guard. Their shields absorbed several rounds of the plasma fire but flickered as they became overwhelmed. They abruptly dropped, and the plasma bolts tore through the thin hull of the defenseless Nasi ship. Nicole could faintly see the telltale plumes of escaping atmosphere as multiple rounds slashed through it. Finally, the ship's reactor exploded, cleaving it into several chunks that veered off in different directions.

We got one of 'em, Petrov called over the fleet's net.

Great, keep it up. Samaha replied. *But remember, your mission is to distract and stall them while the rest of the fleet escapes. As soon as we do, make sure you're able to haul ass out of there.*

The Nasi ships, which were scattered around the planet, had all recovered and started moving toward Samsara Fleet. They had split into two, with five of their ships moving quickly away from the planet and the other three creating a makeshift picket line, attempting to block the onrush of the superior

Nasi forces. Looking at the map, Nicole wondered how long they could survive.

Petrov instructed the navigation team to plot all the potential fold zones in the area. The *Ofira* would need to have quick avenues of escape calculated in order to evade the oncoming Nasi ships once the rest of the fleet folded out. They continued to progress slowly toward the planet, making the Nasi ships deal with them rather than chasing the retreating Samsara vessels. Luckily, many of the enemy ships were still too far away to engage the fleet.

Missiles streaked from several of the closer Nasi ships toward Samsara Fleet. They directed most of them at the fleeing vessels, and the *Ofira's* point defense system was able to detonate the few directed at them.

Nicole estimated it would be at least another few minutes before the first Samsara vessels could fold out of the system. Now fully recovered from the surprise attack, several of the Nasi ships had their thrusters maxed out and were speeding toward the retreating Human, Tounous, and Kurz ships.

Full rear thrust. Pull back to cover the fleet, Petrov called over the ship's net.

Nicole estimated that the distance between the fleeing Samsara Fleet vessels and their Nasi pursuers was too great. The Nasi could not get within weapon's range before most of Samsara Fleet ships could fold out of system. She gave a silent word of thanks to the ether and began studying the fold points that were highlighted on the map. Perhaps they'd make it out of this alive.

Most of the Nasi ships continued their pursuit, gaining on

the retreating Samsara Fleet. The three picket ships provided cover and did their best to slow them down. They coordinated their fire on the pursuers as they tried to bypass the picket. They had some success, and scored direct hits on two of the Nasi ships, causing a them to alter their path to avoid them. Another ten ships were almost in weapons range of the *Ofira*.

One of the Nasi ships was able to bypass the picket. As the retreating Samsara Fleet ships neared the first available fold point, it let loose a volley of high-speed missiles at the Qudoru battleship *Mahoru*. A missile shot past the ship's point defense system and crashed into the aft engine nacelles. At first, there was no evidence it had done anything. The ship continued forward, unfettered. Then, abruptly, a large piece of the *Mahoru* hurtled off, propelled by a quickly fading gout of plasma, stretching hundreds of meters into space. The ship spun on its axis and veered off course.

Mahoru is down. No response over the command or emergency nets. The message came over the bridge's net from the *Ofira's* operations chief.

Nicole cursed under her breath. The Nasi had destroyed almost half the ships they had sent to Geerlok. Despite their victory at the Torgham planet, they were on the verge of collapse. Her spirits lifted somewhat as she saw the green icons on the tactical map blink out—some of Samsara Fleet had escaped.

Okay, we need to get out ourselves. Have all fighters return to ship immediately, Petrov said over the net. *What is the closest fold point?*

Nicole looked over the tactical map, frowning at the grim picture it painted. The Nasi had surrounded the *Ofira*, *Merrimack*, and *Frygr*. With the rest of the fleet gone, the Nasi ships began moving toward them.

Operations, any thoughts? Petrov asked.

We can use the planet to shield us from the Nasi and slingshot toward Fold Point Two Alpha, the operations chief said.

Nicole jumped on the net. *Ma'am, there are significant planetary defenses on Patagonia. We'd be a sitting duck.*

Nicole remembered what Patagonia's defenses had done to the *Oruc*. She had no doubt that the Nasi had continued to increase their lethality.

There isn't another way, Petrov responded. *The Nasi are too fast for us to speed past. If we use the planet, we can at least give ourselves a chance.*

After Petrov talked with the other commanders, the three ships accelerated at full speed toward Patagonia. The enemy continued to converge on them. Nicole felt a small sliver of hope. The maneuver had forced some of the Nasi ships to reverse direction, and opened space between them and the fleeing vessels. They might actually make it.

Colonel Petrov, a voice broke through the net, *we've got a priority call on an unsecured channel from the planet. It's General Norman.*

Chapter Twenty-Four

The voyage to Geerlok seemed to take an eternity. Kal's mind oscillated between wondering what Bowen had done and the Nasi fleet that was in their universe. The Jadid scientist had been tight-lipped about setting them free. When they asked why he did what he did, the alien didn't seem to know himself. He appeared confused and torn. His time with Samsara Fleet must have affected him more than he had realized. Either way, Bowen made clear that any further questions were unwelcome. Since he had saved their lives, Kal and Garcia weren't about to argue.

Kal thought about the Ancients' reactions to their requests. Although they'd tried to appear as a united front, Kal had the impression there were large fractures just beneath the surface. The five of them, six if he included Esma, had gone through hundreds of years together. He couldn't fathom the closeness and familiarity of their relationship. He had hoped that they may change their minds if Kal and Garcia went along with their plan. But they had surely destroyed any goodwill with their betrayal and escape.

Bowen arrived at the coordinates for Geerlok and reconfigured the fold drive to shift between the universes. When they arrive back in their own universe, Kal almost cried when he saw the glittering stars and felt the *Park's* artificial gravity working again.

There was only a single Torgham ship remaining, and Samsara Fleet was gone. The planet seemed unharmed, though their long-range scanners identified a significant amount of wreckage in orbit—several ships must have been destroyed.

After entering orbit, they tried to establish contact with the Torgham. Normally, they would dock at the local station, but they didn't have the time. It took almost an hour for Kal to work his way up the Torgham military hierarchy and find out what had happened to the fleet. An admiral let him know Samsara Fleet had won the battle and left the previous day, heading to Human space. Their exact destination was unknown.

"They're going to counter-attack," Garcia said. "It's what I would do."

Kal gave a sigh. "Except that they don't know what's waiting for them." He had hoped that they might take a couple of days to regroup, but it seemed like the fleet was going for the jugular.

"Is there any way we can catch up to the fleet?" Kal asked as they stood in the Park's storage room slash galley.

"What about just returning to your universe, folding, and then popping back to ours?" Garcia asked Bowen.

The Jadid shook his head. "It's possible, but we would need to retrofit the fold drive once again. This ship's experimental, and I hadn't completed the design. Moving from my universe to your own is relatively safe, but moving from here to there is fraught with risk." Kal didn't want to know exactly what relative meant to the Jadid.

"I have a thought." The Jadid tapped his finger rhythmically against the side of his forehead. "For fun, I have been examining the fold algorithms that the fleet uses. I think

I've found some inefficiencies that may help us catch up."

"How?" Kal asked.

"I may be able to increase the distance traveled between each fold. There are several gravitational abnormalities that your algorithms do not account for. If my calculations are correct, we would arrive there"—he tapped on his wrist computer—"twenty-three hours earlier."

"So we'd arrive at the same time as the fleet," Garcia concluded.

Bowen nodded.

"What are we waiting for?" Kal asked. "Let's go."

Bowen set to work updating the *Park's* fold computer. Using a small keypad in the ship's cargo bay, he activated an automated shelf, extracting the drive from the bulkhead so that he could work on it. The Jadid typed away on his small wrist computer and made slight adjustments on the drive with a stylus-like device he pulled from his cargo pocket.

After two hours, Bowen sealed the drive back in the ship's hull. "We can begin the fold process. The question is, which planet should we head to?"

"Patagonia," Kal said without hesitation. He'd been thinking about it while the scientist was working. It was the only logical target for the fleet. By re-capturing the planet, Samsara Fleet could stop the production of Nasi fighters. He knew Samaha would not go to Wudexingqiu or Mariga, since they hadn't scouted them. That left New America and Patagonia. Although New America had a larger population and more resources, it was the continued development of fighters that was the biggest threat to the fleet—at least from

General Samaha's perspective.

"Roger," Garcia acknowledged. He motioned to Bowen. "Bo, let's get going."

The Jadid looked confused for a moment. Then he realized Garcia was speaking to him. The trace of a smile appeared on his otherwise stoic face. Bo turned and followed the Human pilot, clearly weighing the nickname in his mind.

❖

During their voyage to Patagonia, Garcia spent most of his time befriending Bo, as he called him. The scientist was reluctant at first, but after several days of work by the gregarious pilot, he had softened. Kal swore he actually heard the taciturn Jadid laugh once—it was an unnerving sound.

"Bo, how much time do we have left?" Kal called out from the cargo bay.

"About three minutes until we're there," Bowen called from the cockpit.

"Sir, any idea what we're going to do when we get there?" Garcia asked.

"Nope. Not a clue. We'll need to see what's going on first," Kal replied.

During the voyage, Kal mainly kept to himself, trying to figure out what they would do when they arrived at Patagonia. Occasionally, Major Garcia would join him, helping him to war-game their options. They had thought about trying to conduct a staged approach to the planet, but determined that there was no real advantage to doing so. Samsara Fleet would try to surprise the Nasi ships orbiting the planet and fold in as close as possible. They would be in for a shock when they saw exactly how many Nasi there were. He estimated it would be anywhere between fifteen and twenty ships. The *Park* should be able to slip around them unharmed because of her speed and Nasi identifiers. But he did not know how they would actually make a difference in the face of so much firepower.

Kal had also taken stock of the material they had on hand. Besides their plasma cannons and missiles, there was a small arms locker that the maintenance team had installed before the battle of Geerlok. Inside was a small collection of rifles, pistols, and some grenades. Since they didn't have battle suits, they were the only weapons available if they had to leave the ship.

Kal walked into the cockpit and sat down behind the pilots' chairs. The stars flickered on their main viewscreen as they made their way to Patagonia. Finally, the stars stopped changing. They had arrived at the last fold before entering the space around the planet, a light-day away. As they had feared, a vast fleet of seventeen Nasi ships surrounded the planet. There was no sign of Samsara Fleet, but the light they were seeing was a day old.

"Will they notice if we fold into the system?" Kal asked.

"Yes," Bo replied. "With that number of ships, they'll certainly be able to see us fold in. However, our ship identifier is as a Nasi experimental craft. They won't attack."

"They'll still be tracking us," Garcia said. "I don't think it buys us a lot of time."

"We don't need a lot of time. We just need to get into the

system and see what's happening," Kal said. "If the fleet's not there, we fold back out."

Bo activated their drive, and the watery planet of Patagonia appeared before them on the main viewscreen. Garcia's fingers flew across the controls as he ran scans of the entire system.

"Confirmed, we've got seventeen Nasi capital ships. Based on their signatures and size, there's at least five carriers in there." Garcia continued talking as he manipulated the sensors. "Looks like we've got further build-up on the planet. The Nasi have vastly increased the size and lethality of their anti-space weapons systems. Anything gets too close to the planet and they're toast."

Kal gritted his teeth. In a few short weeks, the Nasi had turned Patagonia into a fortress.

"We're being hailed," Bo said.

"Answer it," Kal instructed. "Tell them we're conducting tests of our fold drive and need to land on the planet."

"Okay." Bo relayed the message to the Patagonia system control. After a few seconds, they received landing approval and a set of coordinates for a site near Kasongo.

Garcia continued to scan the system and the Nasi fleet. "Looks like they also upgraded the station with—" He zoomed in an area outside the orbital zone of Patagonia. "Wait, we've got multiple folds into the system—it's the fleet."

"I imagine they are not pleased right now," Bo said.

"Yeah, I bet they're crapping their pants," Garcia agreed.

"Don't do anything yet," Kal instructed. "Let's see what

happens."

Samsara Fleet had folded into the system surrounding one of the Nasi battleships. The ship didn't have time to do much as the fleet plastered it with plasma and missile fire, overwhelming its shields. As the *Park* continued to drift toward Patagonia, Samsara Fleet split into two parts, with three ships setting up a hasty defense and the others trying to quickly fold out of the system. They had to get some distance between themselves and the planet and ships before they could safely activate their fold drives without being obliterated. The Nasi had recovered quickly from their surprise and sent their full force at the now-retreating Samsara Fleet. Kal swore as a missile destroyed the *Mahoru's* aft engines.

"Sir," Garcia interrupted Kal's concentration. He looked up at the major. "The Nasi have surrounded the three picket ships. They'll be toast unless they have an avenue of escape. One of them is the *Ofira*." Kal pictured Nicole in his head. She, along with the rest of their team, would be on the ship.

Garcia was right. The three ships were almost surrounded by Nasi. Their only hope lay in moving directly toward the planet. As the remaining ships of Samsara Fleet slowly blinked out, they sped up. They were going to try to slingshot past Patagonia, away from the Nasi fleet. Then they could find a fold point on the other side of the planet. Unfortunately, they did not know about the upgraded planetary defenses that would cut them to shreds.

"The Nasi will destroy them if they get close to Patagonia. We need to disable their space defense site here." Kal highlighted the portion of the map where there was a large anti-space installation. The site was right on the *Ofira's* projected trajectory. If they could disable it, the fleet *might* have a chance to escape.

"Head toward this site, and we'll need to figure out some way to destroy it."

"We'll need to be fast," Garcia said. "There's not too much time before they pass by the planet."

"Now I am soiling *my* pants," Bo said.

Garcia sniggered. "Aren't we all, my friend, aren't we all?"

The *Park* hurtled into Patagonia's atmosphere, the friction causing the external temperature sensors to max out.

"What'll we do when we get to the site?" Bo asked, peering backward to look at Kal.

"There's no way we can infiltrate that site in time," Garcia said. "We may be able to strafe it though."

"Isn't that exactly what it's designed to stop?" Garcia asked.

"Not exactly," Bo said, eyes fixed forward. "This site is designed to destroy battleships and cruisers. Small ships like ours might sneak in, especially since they still think we're a friendly."

"I wouldn't be sure of that," Garcia retorted. "We've got planetary fighters scrambling on an intercept. We're way off our flight path."

Kal didn't have time to worry about the fighters. He was focused on their target. There were at least three missile silos and four batteries of large-caliber plasma cannons. Surrounding it all was a network of high-performance point defense systems and anti-plasma drones. The entire base had also been hardened with barriers and shields to defend against orbital fire. Any ship that came near the site would be toast.

"At least they're still building out their defenses," Garcia observed. "They haven't had time to move the plasma cannons." The storage tanks for plasma cannons were notoriously unstable. If they could destroy one, the rest of them would go up as well.

"Do we have any life packs?" Kal asked. Bo nodded in the affirmative.

"Garcia, how good is the autopilot that we installed on this ship?" Kal asked.

"I'm sorry to say that they never were able to get it fully installed," Garcia responded. "This may be a one-way trip."

Kal blanched; he was afraid that would be the answer. He also knew that they had to disable the site whatever the cost.

"The ship comes with a rudimentary autopilot," Bo said. "We need some automation when conducting tests. It's not really designed for atmospheric flight, though."

"Can you make it work and tie the weapons control to it?" Kal asked. "We need the ship to fly directly into the center of the site with all weapons blazing."

"I think so," Bo replied, getting out of his seat to kneel in front of one of the control panels in the cockpit.

"We've got ninety seconds. Can you do it?" Kal asked.

"Yes," Bo called out. He already had one of the access panels detached and was furiously typing on his wrist computer.

Kal checked the tactical map. The remaining three ships were following the flight path that Kal had expected and were speeding toward Patagonia. He had to let them know of the danger and to ask for extraction.

"*Ofira*, this is General Norman," Kal called out to the fleet on the encrypted Samsara net.

"Kal?" The voice of Colonel Petrov on the other end was incredulous.

"Yes. The Nasi have made big upgrades to their defenses on Patagonia. I know what you're planning, and they'll cut you to pieces if you get too close." Kal sent the coordinates of the anti-space site to the *Ofira*. "We're going to disable this site. Can you send someone to pick the three of us up?"

"Roger, we're sending Colonel Bergeron and the Skulls," Petrov replied. *Colonel Bergeron?*

"Thanks, send them now. If you don't see a light show down here in the next two minutes, be ready for evasive action." Kal severed the connection. The *Park* was now completely in the planet's atmosphere, about three thousand meters above the sparkling gray ocean. The day was cloudless, the sky so bright that it almost hurt to look at it through the viewscreen.

"Thirty seconds until we're over the target," Garcia yelled. "You ready, Bo?"

"Almost finished." The Jadid made a few more adjustments using his stylus device and then jumped up. "It is ready."

They sprinted through the passage to the cargo bay. Garcia had already activated the door release from the cockpit, and the ocean flowed below them. They each grabbed a life pack, pulling it over their shoulders and closing the leg straps. After he finished, Kal ran to Bo and helped him with his pack—the Jadid's long frame and unfamiliarity with the pack were costing valuable seconds.

"Ready?" Garcia already had a foot off the back ramp.

Kal nodded. Garcia stepped off the ramp, his pack's thruster bursting to life almost immediately. Bo followed, and then Kal. As soon as he was free of the ship, Kal felt the sickening sensation of free-fall. His stomach jumped into his throat as he felt his life pack activate, regulating his descent.

As he fell toward the ocean, Kal watched the *Park's* plasma cannons streak toward the base, followed by the contrails of the ship's small array of missiles. As the missiles hit, they sent small shockwaves through the air, followed by plumes of smoke. The *Park* was not far behind. It plunged into the small isle, setting off the stored missiles and plasma. The explosion dwarfed the others that had come before it. The shockwave hurtled Kal backward, almost causing him to drop out of the air, and making him cry out in pain as his eardrums ruptured. He felt a wave of heat wash over him from the blast.

The next feeling he had was the shock of hitting the ocean. The warm water woke him up like a slap to the face. Kal checked his implant, trying to determine where his shipmates were. There was nothing.

Kal, Karl. We're tracking you, hold on. Kal smiled as he heard Nicole's voice. He leaned back, his life pack keeping him afloat as he waited for her.

❖

"Let's go," Nicole yelled.

As soon as the words were out of her mouth, she could feel the ship rising from the bay floor. Taisha and Lieutenant Sampson cleared the *Ofira's* bay doors and launched the *Keying* at the planet's surface.

After Kal's broadcast, Petrov had ordered Nicole to retrieve the downed soldiers and meet up with the fleet at Keerloa. It was a mission that Nicole was all too happy to accept.

"We've got at least five fighters converging on the *Park*," Taisha said. "We'll need to deal with them if we're gonna pick them up."

Sampson grunted in response.

The *Keying* hurtled into Patagonia's exosphere, heading almost perpendicular to the planet's surface. The sudden impact of hitting the atmosphere overloaded the ship's gravitational dampeners and rocked them as they descended.

"Do you see them?" Nicole asked. She saw nothing on her command terminal, but Taisha and Sampson had a lot more experience with these systems than she did.

"Yes," Sampson replied. "Heading toward them."

You ready? Nicole asked Sergeant Jones through her implant.

Yes, ma'am, just give us the word.

A blinding flash appeared on the horizon. "Guess we know where they went," Taisha deadpanned. As they got closer, Nicole could see a dark mushroom cloud forming on a distant island.

"Are you still tracking them?" Nicole asked, fearing the worst.

"Yes, they're still alive," Taisha reported. "I have three life pack beacons, plotting them on the tactical map."

Two of the signatures were next to each other, but the third one was several kilometers away, complicating their rescue mission. The Nasi fighters had spotted them and had adjusted their paths to intercept the *Keying* instead of the *Park*.

Humming softly to himself, Sampson pointed the ship's nose toward the ocean and leveled off a few meters above the water. Nicole was impressed—the waves were practically touching the bottom of their ship. Despite the pressure, the middle-aged pilot moved purposefully and mechanically, never giving a sign of emotion.

"Okay, we're a kilometer out from two of the life packs," Taisha said.

Tac-I squad, you're good to drop, Nicole called over the ship's net.

Roger, dropping now, Jones responded.

"Wait, we've got two fighters locked on to us." Sampson maxed their thrusters, pushing Nicole back into her seat. "We can't wait for the Tac-I squad to return, we'll have to circle back."

"Can we take them?" Nicole asked.

"Probably not," Taisha replied. "The things are fast. This ship just can't keep up with 'em."

"We'll have to circle back through to pick them up and

then get out of here," Sampson added.

They gently banked left, skimming across the surface of the ocean in a wide arc. Plasma bolts landed in front of them, sending gouts of water and steam into the air. Some of the bolts hit their aft shields, which redlined as it absorbed the blasts.

Keying, we've got Norman and Garcia, Jones reported over the net. *We're sitting ducks out here, though. Get back now.*

We're circling back around. No time to stop though, Sampson replied. *We can slow, but you'll need to re-board on the move. We won't be able to retrieve the Jadid.*

"What?" Nicole looked at the pilot.

"Ma'am, we don't have the time." Sampson didn't meet her gaze.

"He's one of us," Nicole said. She looked at the map, trying to figure out how they could reach Bowen without getting blasted out of the sky.

"It's not one of *us*." Sampson turned to look at her. "It's not worth risking all of our lives for it."

Nicole was furious, but there was no time to argue with the pilot. She called out on the net, *Go pick up Bowen. We'll meet you there.* She looked at Sampson pointedly as she said the last sentence. He met her gaze and shook his head, curling his lips inward. She knew she owed her life to the scientist and had a good feeling that Kal and Karl would not still be alive without him as well. *She'd have time later to address Sampson's insubordination.*

Good call, ma'am. Jones cut the line.

She watched the four Tac-I soldiers soar across the water toward the Jadid's position on the map.

The *Keying* continued its wide turn and oriented itself to match the heading of the Tac-I soldiers. As they got closer, the ship would fly directly above them, slowing down only long enough for them to glide into the back cargo bay. From there, their path would be a straight line to Bowen's location so they could retrieve both groups in one pass. While they were at the reduced speed, they were sitting ducks. But they should have to only perform the maneuver once.

Beginning our pass now, decreasing speed by fifty percent, Sampson called out over the net.

Nicole watched nervously as they soared above the three battle-suit-clad soldiers. Two of them held people in their arms, cradling them like a child. After the Keying passed, the three soldiers flew directly into the ship's open cargo bay.

Plasma fire continued to bracket them, the intensity and accuracy increasing as they slowed down.

"We've got less than half our aft shield strength remaining," Taisha reported.

"Ma'am," Sampson said, "we can still abort the second pickup. Sergeant Jones isn't there yet. If we stay on this approach, we won't make it."

"Keep going!"

Nicole ran down to the cargo bay. The Tac-I soldiers were still in their battle suits. Kal and Karl lay on the bay floor, looking like drowned rats in their soaked clothes. Kal gave her a broad smile as he her saw her come in. Despite the adrenaline pumping through her veins, Nicole found herself returning the smile, and a weight lifted off her heart as she saw his face.

She slapped the bulkhead control panel, opening the port-side gunnery door. The ship-mounted machine gun slid down from the ceiling of the bay and extended out of the doorway. Nicole sat down in the gunner's chair and turned off the safety. Air rushed through the gun hatch, blowing her hair back and stinging her eyes.

The kinetic machine gun was intended to be used against personnel when the ship was in a hover mode. It had 180-degree coverage that extended to the front and back of the ship. The gun's small display, which was tied to the *Keying's* main targeting computer, allowing her to see the three Nasi fighters approaching on their tail. It automatically provided her firing solutions based on the speed and trajectory of the aircraft.

Sampson, I'm at the gunner's hatch. On my command, bank hard right. I'm gonna give them a surprise.

Ma'am, that's suicide. You've got no chance of hitting them. Sampson's frustration mirrored her own.

Damnit, can you do it? she asked. Nicole wanted to throttle the obstinate pilot.

We can, Taisha cut in. *It might catch 'em by surprise for a second. We can't bank for long though, as we'll be exposing the broadside of the ship.*

I won't miss. Nicole pre-selected her targets using the weapons menu. *Okay, go.*

Nicole slammed against the machine gun as the *Keying* banked sharply right. The three trailing fighters were lit up on the gun's heads-up display, and she could see the steady stream of plasma pouring from their front cannons.

Nicole depressed the trigger and a solid stream of kinetic rounds poured forth, curving through the air at the three ships. It took a moment for the Nasi to recover from the unexpected maneuver. They started banking as well—trying to get behind the *Keying*. As the four ships turned around each other in a strange, aerial dance, Nicole continued to stream the kinetic rounds at the enemy fighters. A few of the Nasi plasma rounds impacted the ship's starboard shield, causing the air in front of Nicole to ripple as the shields absorbed the blast.

"Damnit." Nicole knew her window to hit the enemy ships was closing. Soon, they'd recover and be right back on their trail. She remembered back to the quick training session Taisha had given her months ago. The ship's targeting computer wasn't able to anticipate the movement and speed of the Nasi fighters. She would need to do it herself. Nicole moved the targeting reticle to lead the approaching fighters, focusing her fire on the lead ship. Her display pulsated with a red tint, a warning that it was about to overheat and shut down.

"Just a little bit more," Nicole muttered to herself. She could see the line of kinetic fire pouring from her weapon toward the lead ship. It faded out of her sight, halfway between the two fighters.

The lead fighter emitted a gout of fire and corkscrewed into the ocean below, clipping the wing of one of the others, which tumbled through the air and fell into the water as well, unable to recover in time. The third remained on course, banking the other direction in order to avoid the deadly machine gun.

Nice shooting, Taisha called over the net. *You bought us a little time.*

Smiling to herself, Nicole closed the hatch. The weapon automatically retracted into the ship's bulkhead as the panels slid shut. She ran back to the cockpit to find Kal already standing behind the two pilots. He looked unsteady on his feet and was using the backs of the pilots' chairs to brace himself. He gave a small nod and a smile when he saw Nicole rush in. She returned the smile and sat back down in her chair, continuing to command the mission.

I've got the third target, Jones reported.

Almost at your location, Taisha replied. *Get ready.*

The remaining Nasi fighter had recovered and was back on their tail. The *Keying*'s aft shields were down to a quarter power—it was a close call whether they could pick up Jones and Bowen. A couple more direct hits, and they'd be done.

The *Keying* soared over the Tac-I sergeant as he hovered with this feet dangling in the undulating ocean waves. As soon as they had passed over Jones, he catapulted himself into the ready bay of the ship, his arms wrapped around the Jadid scientist.

"Get us off planet and to a fold point," Nicole instructed after checking to make sure the back bay had closed.

Sampson increased the ship's throttle to max thrust and pointed their nose directly up. The ship climbed vertically through the atmosphere, the remaining Nasi fighter close on their tail. As they entered the exosphere, the Nasi plasma fire tapered off.

"They're not able to leave the atmosphere," Kal observed.

Nicole checked the tac map. The *Ofira* and the other two Samsara Fleet ships had folded out of the system. Unfortunately, the Nasi were now on the fold point they had used, cutting off the *Keying's* main avenue out of the system. The capital ships and small fighter wings were directly between them and almost every good fold point. Despite the vast spaces, the extended range of the Nasi weapons systems and the speed of their fighters meant limited options. Their only chance was a fold point that would require them to thread themselves between two of the Nasi capital ships. The distance between the ships was wide enough they wouldn't be within their plasma cannon range, but they would still have to contend with their fighters and missiles.

"Activate the cloak," Nicole ordered. She knew it wasn't perfect, but perhaps it would throw them off a little.

"Ma'am, that won't fool the Nasi," Sampson said. "It'll just draw power from other systems."

Nicole grabbed the old lieutenant by his collar, forcing him to look her in the eyes. "Sampson, if you can't follow a simple order, I swear I will make the rest of your pitiful career a living hell."

Sampson's eyes widened in shock for a moment. Then his lips curled and his brows furrowed as his eyes met her own. "Yes, ma'am." The pilot shrugged, pulling his collar loose, and then turned to face the controls.

With the cloak activated, Nicole felt slightly safer. To

Sampson's point, she wasn't sure if it provided any help beyond the psychological. There was nothing for the pilots to do except fly straight toward the fold point at maximum velocity. The Nasi's reaction would determine their next course of action.

"We've got misses launched," Taisha said flatly, as if it were an everyday occurrence. Which, Nicole had to admit to herself, it was becoming.

Two volleys of missiles streamed toward them, one from each of the ships they were weaving through. Their paths were uneven, the missiles making jerky adjustments in their course as they streamed closer to the *Keying*.

"The cloak seems to confuse their missile's guidance system somewhat," Taisha observed, facing her co-pilot as she spoke.

"Let's hope it's enough," Kal replied.

"Get the countermeasures ready," Nicole instructed.

"Commander"—Kal turned to Nicole—"I wouldn't use those unless we have to. They'll give away our position if the Nasi don't already know it. Also, this ship has a very limited supply."

Nicole appreciated his tact and support. "Good point. Just get them ready then."

As they continued toward the fold point, the Nasi missiles were getting perilously close. She could see Sampson fidget in his chair, hoping she would give the command to release the countermeasures. *Let him sweat a little*, Nicole thought to herself.

"Ma'am, we're at eight nines and ready to fold," Taisha

said.

"Do it," Nicole ordered. The stars shifted as they escaped the Patagonia system.

Chapter Twenty-Five

The trip to Keerloa was a revelation for Nicole. Given her studies of anthropology, Kal and Karl's descriptions of their experience on Altterra fascinated her.

When Humanity had first learned of the Nasi, they had not known what they looked like, where they came from, or even their real name. Over the past several months, they had discovered their shocking history and learned that the enemy they were fighting were much more complex than simple killing machines.

Kal and Karl also told her about the extent of the Nasi fleet. With their full strength now brought to bear, the enemy seemed unstoppable. A fraction of their full fleet had laid waste to five civilizations; it was impossible to estimate what their full fleet could do.

Although Bo, as he asked to be called, refused to talk about it, she knew he had sacrificed everything for them. Something about this experience had changed him and continued to change him. Every day he became less like a Jadid and more Human. She had even heard him tell a joke.

By unspoken agreement, Nicole and Kal shared the stateroom during the voyage back. Nicole felt overjoyed to see him and selfishly took advantage of every chance she had to be with him. Despite his higher rank and experience, Kal didn't intrude on her command, attending the daily briefings as an observer. In private, he mentioned how happy he was for her.

Lieutenant Sampson spent most of the trip in his cabin.

Nicole's fury with the pilot had died down after a day of transit. She had resolved that she would request his transfer as soon as they returned to the fleet. If he couldn't obey orders, then he was a liability more than an asset—let some other officer deal with it.

Nicole tried to talk with Taisha. Her friend was still deep in mourning and spent most of her time in her cabin, alone. Every time she spoke to Taisha, Nicole found herself wracked with guilt. Her happiness and Taisha's misery were too close and too raw for them to talk. Only time and space could bring them together.

After a week, the *Keying* folded into the Keerloa system and received instructions to land on the *Gedorhan's Return*.

"Kal!" There was a genuine warmth in General Samaha's voice as Kal and Nicole walked into her office. "I have to admit, I didn't have the same sense of certainty as Colonel Bergeron that you were still alive. I'm glad to be wrong."

Kal and Nicole sat down next to each other on the bench. The general's smile faded as they sat down, revealing recently worn lines across her face. She was aging before their eyes from the stress. Her hair now had several wisps of white at the temples.

The general shook her head. "We're still trying to figure out what happened back there on Patagonia. If you hadn't taken out the emplacement, I don't think we would've made it."

"That's not the half of it," Kal said. "There's a lot that you need to know."

Kal described their narrow escape from the Nasi landing

380

bay and their experience on Altterra. Nicole could see the frustration in his furrowed brow as he tried to get across the alienness of the world and the universe. Samaha was more interested in his description of the Jadid and their society and the rift between them and the Nasi.

"So, that was just a quarter of the Nasi," Samaha asked as Kal finished.

"Yes, I am guessing they split their forces between the planets," Kal replied.

Samaha looked defeated. "I don't know how to stop that. We barely defeated the contingent at Geerlok with our entire fleet. Do you think the Jadid would help us?"

Kal looked thoughtful. "Maybe. But the Ancients want to be away from us, to have nothing to do with us. Perhaps in time they may change their mind."

"Time is something we don't have," Samaha said.

"I've been thinking about it, ma'am." Nicole leaned forward. "Even though the Jadid may not be an option, there are other potential allies out there. The Wata, Nordlok, and Z'Ta will have to face the Nasi, eventually."

"We've got a lot of work to do," Samaha mused to herself. "We have to assume the Nasi are heading here already. They'll come again, and there won't be anything we can do to stop them."

"The Torgham might provide ships for our fleet. At least they'll be more willing to help us resupply," Kal said.

"They probably *won't* be willing to contribute ships," Samaha said. "They'll need them to defend Geerlok—no matter how hopeless it may seem." She smiled. "Not the logical move, but I'd do the same thing."

Nicole would do the same thing as well. Many times, the logical thing to do was not the right thing to do.

"Okay, time for me to get to work." Samaha seemed reinvigorated, despite, or maybe because of, the bad news. "I need to talk with my staff and you need rest. Go back to the *Ofira* and relax while you can."

"What's next, ma'am?" Ekon asked as he took a swig of his beer.

The Numbskulls had pushed several tables together in the lounge of the *Ofira*. The eight Humans and one Jadid sat together, drinks in hand, enjoying the moment.

Nicole shrugged. "We don't know yet. But we'll have to move soon. We have to assume the Nasi are on their way again."

Kal studied Nicole's face. His eyes pored over her—from the blond hair to the sharp features and blue eyes that sometimes made you feel as if she was looking through you. She had grown, had made herself into something more than she had been when he had first met her. Her guilt had made way for something stronger—resolve.

"We'll know soon enough." Jones raised a glass. "But for now, to the Skulls! We've gone through more than I care to think about. But we got the job done."

"And to those we have lost," Taisha added quietly, raising her glass.

Jones looked her in the eyes and nodded. "Heroes, each and every one of them."

They clinked their glasses together, looking at each other, some smiling, some with tears slowly tracing down their cheeks. Kal thought about those that they had lost. Jones was right, they were all heroes, even Pudari. He took another sip of the flavored water in his glass.

"What about you?" Garcia turned to Bo. "What are you going to do?"

The scientist cocked his head. "What do you mean?"

"Well, when we go back out, are you coming with us?" the pilot asked.

"I didn't know I had a choice."

"That's the right attitude." Garcia smiled broadly. "Once you realize that there isn't any other option, you'll be happier."

Kal had been wondering the same thing. If Bo wanted to stay with them, he'd make it happen. He knew he would have to make some deals, though. Samaha's staff was salivating to get their hands on him. The intelligence and scientific knowledge that the Jadid had were invaluable.

"To Bo." Jones raised his glass again.

"So, I think I need to address the elephant in the room," Sandra said after several more toasts, her words melting around the edges. "Which one of you is in charge now?" Sandra eyed Nicole and Kal.

Kal and Nicole laughed and then looked at each other. They hadn't discussed it.

"Well, I think we'll be a command team," Kal said.

"Colonel Bergeron has earned her position."

"Yes sir, she has," Sandra agreed.

Jones smiled at that, and Kal saw a look pass between him and Nicole, causing her alabaster skin to turn pink.

The team sat around the table for a couple more hours, toasting everything from the *Oruc* to General Samaha. After Ekon and Sandra performed their school musical from five years prior, Kal and Nicole excused themselves and walked back to Kal's stateroom, holding hands, and not giving a damn what others thought.

❖

Kal opened his eyes, expecting to see Nicole sleeping peacefully beside him. Instead, there was a wrinkled bedsheet, a faint outline of the spot where she had lain.

He pushed himself up to find Nicole already dressed in the blouse and cargo pants that had become the unofficial uniform of the Skulls. She sat in a chair across the room, staring off into space. He could see her eyes moving back and forth, reading something that was being projected into her field of vision through her implant.

"Hey," Kal called, "whatcha doin'?"

Nicole smiled as her eyes focused on him. "Just reading through your mission notes. They are so detailed. And this is coming from a UEG bureaucrat."

"Former bureaucrat." Kal returned the smile. "Something I learned from many years in the EDF. Good mission notes save a lot of time in answering questions later."

Kal heard a tone through his implant and could see that it was General Samaha trying to reach him. He opened up the line.

Kal, I need you two on the flagship now. I've already asked Bowen to come as well. He could tell Samaha was excited since she was almost stumbling over her words.

What's going on? Kal asked.

We have visitors—a Jadid fleet just folded into system. They want to speak with you.

Nicole looked at Kal. He could see his puzzlement and excitement echoed back at him.

Perhaps they did care after all.

Author's Note

First of all, thank you again to any and all who have taken the time to read this book. As an author, I adore bringing interesting characters and worlds to life. You, the reader, are the reason I do this and knowing that people are enjoying the story make it all worthwhile.

I found this book to be harder to write than the first one, *For the Ones Who Remain*. With the Kal, Nicole, and the rest of the crew introduced, I had to conform to the rules and characterizations that were set out in the original book. It is strange to look back at something you wrote and chide yourself for the artistic decisions that <u>you</u> made.

That said, I am ecstatic with how this novel turned out and am excited for the future adventures of Not Norman's Numbskulls and the rest of the fleet. I hope that you will join me to see what else happens.

Also, please consider subscribing to my newsletter. This helps me to communicate directly with readers who are interested in my writing and let them know when I have new work coming out. I will not be sending out adds, share your information, or do anything evil with your email address. You can find the link to subscribe on my web page: https://www.rileycollins.info.